His Smile Was Gentle,

as was the hand that stroked her cheek. Emily stiffened slightly at his touch, but only for an instant. This was what she wanted, had wanted from the first moment she saw him. Later she could ask why; now she wanted only to satisfy the remorseless hunger he triggered in her.

"Lucas..." she breathed softly. "I'm not sure this is a good idea."

"I want to make love with you, Emily. I could dress it up in a lot of fancy words, but that's what it comes down to." His eyes met hers. "I think you want the same thing."

The look in his eyes told her that he was vulnerable to rejection, but he would accept it. Somehow, knowing that he cared enough to be hurt if she rejected him made the decision easier. Emily took a step toward him, and then another.

Dear Reader,

Welcome to Silhouette! Our goal is to give you hours of unbeatable reading pleasure, and we hope you'll enjoy each month's six new Silhouette Desires. These sensual, provocative love stories are both believable and compelling—sometimes they're poignant, sometimes humorous, but always enjoyable.

Indulge yourself. Experience all the passion and excitement of falling in love along with our heroine as she meets the irresistible man of her dreams and together they overcome all obstacles in the path to a happy ending.

If this is your first Desire, I hope it'll be the first of many. If you're already a Silhouette Desire reader, thanks for your support! Look for some of your favorite authors in the coming months: Stephanie James, Diana Palmer, Dixie Browning, Ann Major and Doreen Owens Malek, to name just a few.

Happy reading!

Isabel Swift
Senior Editor

SDRL-7/85

MAURA SEGER
Treasure Hunt

Silhouette Desire

Published by Silhouette Books New York

America's Publisher of Contemporary Romance

SILHOUETTE BOOKS
300 East 42nd St., New York, N.Y. 10017

Copyright © 1986 by Maura Seger

All rights reserved, including the right to reproduce
this book or portions thereof in any form whatsoever.
For information address Silhouette Books,
300 East 42nd St., New York, N.Y. 10017

ISBN: 0-373-05295-2

First Silhouette Books printing August 1986

America's Publisher of Contemporary Romance

Printed in the U.S.A.

MAURA SEGER

was prompted by a love of books and a vivid imagination to decide, at age twelve, to be a writer. Twenty years later, her first book was published. So much, she says, for overnight success! Each book is still an adventure filled with fascinating people who always surprise her.

One

The path leading up from the dock was steep and studded with small stones that slipped under Emily Nolan's high-heeled shoes and caused her to wince. She was tired, hot and thirsty. Her shoulder-length auburn hair stuck to the back of her neck. Perspiration had gathered beneath the over-sized sunglasses that hid her thickly lashed blue eyes. The tip of her upturned nose was already sunburned, and she had little doubt that the rest of her face would soon follow suit. As if all that weren't enough, her feet were beginning to hurt.

Not the best state to be in as she approached what gave every indication of being a difficult encounter.

What possessed Lucas Hawkins to live on such a remote island? she wondered as she paused briefly to catch her breath. The neatly tailored suit she had put on that morning in New York was fine for a summer day in the city, but after two plane trips and a boat ride it was wilting fast and so was she.

Wiping her forehead with a crumpled tissue, she tried to muster some enthusiasm for the gently waving palm fronds, the golden crescent of the beach lapped by the turquoise waters of the Caribbean, and the picturesque assemblage of small fishing boats riding at anchor in the harbor. Under ordinary circumstances, she would have been delighted to spend a few days in a secluded island paradise. But considering her reasons for being there, she could feel nothing more than apprehension.

Having reached the top of the path at last, she dropped her bag, took off the sunglasses, and nodded to the man slouched behind the counter of a small shack that apparently served as a combination boathouse, general store, and bar.

"Excuse me, I'm looking for Lucas Hawkins. Could you tell me where I might find him?"

The man's smile was brilliantly white against his ebony skin. "He be gone right now, miss."

Emily leaned forward slightly, hoping she had misunderstood him. The lilting West Indian accent was beautiful, but it took a while to adjust to. "How's that again?"

"Gone now, miss. Over by St. Vincent. Back maybe tonight, maybe tomorrow." He spread his hands and shrugged. "Who can say?"

"But...I radioed ahead.... He knew I was coming." Exasperation showed in her voice, though she tried to suppress it.

"Could be, miss. But he be gone still." The man smiled again. "Big rum load come from Barbados. Lots of folks go."

Great. Lucas Hawkins had deserted her for a load of rum. Her mood was going from bad to worse rapidly. For two cents—heck, for nothing at all—she would have turned right around and headed back to New York. Unfortunately, that option was not open to her. "Do you have any idea where I might get a room?" she asked resignedly.

The boatman scratched his head, thought for a moment, then nodded, "Hotel up on Prickly Hill. Not so many folks stay dere dese days. Could be room for you."

Emily thanked him, picked up her bag, and continued on her weary way. Prickly Hill turned out to be aptly named. It was covered with cacti of all sizes and descriptions. They hemmed in the narrow sandy path and made every step treacherous.

"Ouch!" A tiny drop of blood showed through the sheer stockings she had kept meaning to remove during the boat trip. She rubbed the wound ruefully before going on with even greater caution. By the time she reached the top of the hill, she had been stung several more times. The silk blouse she wore beneath her linen suit was sticking to her, and a dull pain had begun to throb directly behind her eyes.

Her first glance at the ramshackle building that sported a faded sign reading Voyager's Rest was less than reassuring. The paint on the one-story wooden structure was cracked and peeling. Enough shingles were missing from the roof to make it look as though it was mottling. Weeds and vines choked several of the windows, all in keeping with the general air of disregard about the place. Still it might offer a bed for the night, perhaps even a cold shower.

Spurred on by thoughts of such luxuries, she climbed the half-dozen creaking steps to the dilapidated entrance, passed the porch swing hanging by one end from a rusted chain, and eased open the torn screen door.

The lobby—to use the term loosely—was empty except for a scattering of dingy rubber plants in chipped pots, a sagging couch spotted with mildew, and a rattan peacock chair minus its seat. A yellow-eyed ginger cat with a bent tail perched on the chair back, blinking at her imperturbably. Only Sidney Greenstreet was needed to complete the picture of a seedy dive in the back of beyond.

Emily grimaced as she approached the sorry excuse for a counter that took up the farthest wall. It was bare of all the usual accoutrements of hotel reception—registration book, officious assistant manager, and so on—but did boast a rusty bell. She brought her hand down on it sharply and was rewarded by a tinny ring, which resounded hollowly in the silence. She waited—one minute, two—when nothing happened, she rang the bell again.

"Belay that, matey," a gruff voice demanded.

She jumped slightly and looked around, unable to see where the voice had come from.

"What's your name, sweetie?"

There was a doorway behind the counter. Emily went toward it.

"Davey Jones'll get you. Watch out! Watch out!"

She pushed aside the tattered length of material covering the door and found herself in a tiny room crammed with books, papers, an ancient rolltop desk and a parrot cage.

Parrot? She took a step forward, peering suspiciously at the disreputable green bird calmly cleaning his claws. He glanced up, blinked his beady eyes, and squawked, *"What's your name, sweetie?"*

"Emily. What's yours?"

"Davey Jones'll get you."

"Of course, how silly of me. Pleased to meet you, Davey. Would you happen to know if I can have a room for the night?"

"He dinna know, lassie, but I might."

At the sound of the low, raspy rumble softened by a Scottish burr, Emily turned swiftly. A man had come into the room. He was of medium height, with a big belly that strained the good nature of his frayed blue shirt and flopped out over the waistband of his khaki shorts. Ending just above his knees, the shorts revealed slightly bowed legs. Bright red hair hung to his shoulders. A thicket of cinnamon-hued whiskers reached fully halfway down his chest. As Emily watched, he belched fragrantly, scratched his belly and said, "Would you be having a reservation?"

"Reservation?" she repeated incredulously. The chances that anyone had purposely planned to stay at the Voyager's Rest anytime in the last century were so remote as to be inconceivable. Only innate good manners prevented her from pointing that out. "Uh...no...I'm afraid not. I had expected to find Mr. Hawkins when I got here, but apparently he isn't on the island at the moment...."

"Went to Barbados for the rum," her unlikely host informed her as he belched again.

Emily backed up a pace. "So I've been told. It seems I'll have to wait for him. I need somewhere to stay." When that failed to elicit the desired response, she asked, "Is this the only hotel on the island?" Perhaps she'd get lucky and discover that there was a glorious resort just around the next corner, where she could bask in luxury while awaiting the return of the tardy Mr. Hawkins.

Redbeard dashed her hopes with a shake of his head. "This is the only one. Always has been, probably always will."

"Well, then...could I have a room?"

He considered that, then shrugged. "Dinna see why not." Small bloodshot eyes narrowed between folds of skin. "If you can pay for it."

"Of course I can," Emily retorted in exasperation. "I have my American Express card, traveler's checks, a letter of credit from Barclay's Bank. Which do you take?"

"Cash."

"Cash...?"

"Carib dollars, British pounds, French francs, Italian lire, American greenbacks. Cash."

"Oh, I see...well, let me check...." She rummaged in her purse for a moment, then nodded. "Yes, I have cash. How much is one night's accommodation?"

"One hundred and fifty dollars American."

"That's preposterous!"

"Take it or leave it."

"I'll leave it! I'll sleep on the beach before I let myself get ripped off like that." Grabbing her bag, she turned sharply and headed for the door.

"Davey Jones'll get you!"

Redbeard wheezed with laughter. "So will the sand flies and the mosquitoes. Not to mention the crabs, worms, slugs, and..."

Emily stopped where she was and glanced back at him over her shoulder. "Twenty-five dollars American for the room and breakfast tomorrow."

"Seventy-five and I'll throw in a free drink at the bar."

That sounded like a decidedly dubious offer. She shook her head. "Fifty, no drink, and I find my own breakfast."

For so disreputable a man, Redbeard could look downright tragic. Morosely, he said, "You drive a hard bargain, gel. How's a poor man like me supposed to make a living?"

"That's my final offer. If you want more than fifty, I'll take my chances with the crabs."

He looked her up and down assessingly before finally nodding. "Aye, you would, wouldn't you? And when Lucas comes back, you'll be telling him how poorly you were treated. Not that he'll care. You won't get any sympathy from him."

"I don't expect any," she said as she handed him the money. He counted the bills carefully before nodding. "Now if I could have my key..." She held out her hand expectantly.

Her host sighed again, loudly enough to make the rafters tremble. He made a great show of searching through piles of dusty papers on the desk before he at last surfaced holding an old-fashioned iron key. "Here's one, though I'll be darned if I can tell you what room it goes to." He handed it to her with a flourish that was somewhat spoiled when he added, "Not that it matters since there aren't any locks."

"No locks..."

"We're a friendly bunch," he told her with an encouraging leer.

"I'll bet." Making a mental note to push a piece of furniture in front of her door before retiring for the night, Emily picked up her case again. It seemed to weigh more each time she did so. "If you'll show me where the rooms are..."

Redbeard pointed her in the right direction, then left her on her own. Down a dimly lit corridor small green lizards roamed unhindered and more than one bird's nest was in evidence. She opened the first door she came to and peered inside.

The room was small and sparsely furnished with a single-width iron bed, a small chest of doubtful vintage and a chair missing half of one leg. Dust and sand were everywhere. The air smelled of mold and other things she didn't care to identify. For a moment she thought of going on, but common sense told her it was not likely there would be any improvement in the other rooms. Resignedly, she stepped inside.

When the windows were opened, the ancient ceiling fan turned on, and her bag unpacked, the room looked a little better. Or perhaps she simply willed herself to think so. The long trip from New York had exhausted her. She could concentrate on nothing except getting out of her sodden clothes and under a cold shower.

After carefully propping the chair against the door, Emily removed her suit. It had always been one of her favorites, but now it was nothing more than a wilted hank of fabric she could not bear to put on again. The same went for her blouse and everything else that she stripped off.

The shower creaked ominously when she first turned it on. Pipes rattled and gurgled, the floor under her feet vibrated, and she had a horrible vision of some primordial boiler about to explode. But at length a thin stream of rusty water trickled from the shower head. She let it run for several minutes, until it was reasonably clear, then got under it and sighed with relief. The water might only be tepid, but it felt blissfully cool on her overheated skin. She soaped herself generously—with her own bar, prudently brought along—then shampooed her shoulder-length hair. By the time she turned off the shower, the pipes had begun to rattle again, sufficient warning not to task the facilities too far.

Wrapped in a robe, she returned to the bedroom and slipped on fresh underwear, shorts and a cool top. All were brand new. She had purchased them that afternoon at the Barbados airport while she was waiting between planes. Instructions to make the trip had come down only that morning. She had barely had time to catch the flight out of New York and there had been no opportunity to pack anything of her own. Not that it mattered very much; she was used to traveling light.

With her feet in sandals and her hair brushed free of tangles, she felt considerably better. There was even a little spurt of excitement as she thought of what had brought her there. This assignment was easily the most important of her career. She did not intend to let anything interfere with it.

Back in the lobby, there was no sign of either Davey or Redbeard but, by dint of following her nose, she found her way to a surprisingly pleasant stone veranda overlooking the path she had climbed a short while before. There were no chairs in evidence, but a stone parapet running the length of the terrace provided seating. The ginger cat was there, crouched sphinxlike while keeping one eye on the lizards and birds. Emily perched nearby and surveyed what she had to admit was a stunning view.

The islands of the Grenadines, of which Devil's Reef was the smallest and most obscure, were rightly renowned for their beauty. Situated some twelve to thirteen degrees north of the equator in the Tobago Basin off the coast of Venezuela, they were the result of an ancient upheaval of underwater volcanoes. No place on earth seemed closer to paradise than these islands, which were caressed by the trade winds and warmed by the sun.

Her earlier bad humor fading, she allowed herself to feel grateful for the position of trust that had resulted in her being sent on so sensitive and vital a journey. In the ten years that she had worked for Sentinal Insurance, she had risen from processing claims for dented cars to investigating the wide range of cases that fell within the company's aptly named Specials division.

In the process, she had been to more places and done more things than she would ever have thought possible. She had also learned a great deal about herself. Her strong points were intelligence and tenacity. Her greatest weakness was a tendency to become impatient with both herself and others when events didn't proceed as she thought they should. That was what she had been doing since arriving on the island, and she regretted it now. If the past years had taught her anything, it was to enjoy each day as it came and not to try to hurry through it.

This particular day had brought her from the air-conditioned sterility of her midtown Manhattan office to the balmy shores of the Caribbean. Not bad, all things considered. If along the way she had to put up with a snide parrot, a chewed-up cat, a piratical hotel keeper, and an absent quarry, so be it.

Not until her stomach rumbled did Emily break off her perusal of the setting sun and go back inside. She found the kitchen by, once again, following her nose. A single, swift glance was enough to tell her she would not want to eat anything prepared there. Remembering the array of groceries in the wooden shack near the dock, she made her way down the path toward the beach.

A string of gaily colored lights outlined the shack from which calypso music floated on the night air. She could make out the shapes of people—perhaps half a dozen were congregating there—and heard their laughter. For a moment she stood uncertainly, not sure she wanted to intrude. A faint residue of the shyness that had plagued her as a child made her hang back. Until a booming voice rang out. "There you be, gel. Looking for grub?"

"I wouldn't say no to something to eat," she admitted.

Redbeard nodded and made room for her at the bar. "Give the little lady one of your specials, Basil," he suggested to the tall black man who had directed Emily to the hotel.

"What's that?" she asked as she perched on a stool and let her toes wiggle in the warm sand.

"Lobster, miss," Basil told her. "Caught dis mornin' on de reef."

What was that old saying about never telling a book by its cover? The best she had been hoping for was a stale hamburger. It seemed as though she was going to do a great deal better.

Basil turned away for a moment to pop a lobster on the glowing grill behind him, then said, "Somethin' to drink, miss? Rum punch?"

"Best in the Carib," Redbeard informed her. "Makes it himself. Famous from Port-au-Prince to São Paulo."

Emily would have loved a Coke but found it impolite to say so. Instead, she accepted a tall dark drink and sipped it gingerly. But only at first. After another sip, she said sincerely, "This is delicious. Is that guava juice I taste?"

Basil grinned broadly, pleased by her acumen. "Dat be right, miss. And a few other dings I keeps to myself."

"Nutmeg," Redbeard muttered in a stage whisper. "He grates fresh nutmeg into it. Won't admit it, but I've seen him do it."

"Now, Cap'tin," Basil chided, "you be givin' away all my secrets."

"Captain?" Emily repeated. "Do you skipper?"

"Used to," her host allowed morosely, "'till the *Aberdeen* ran up on the reef one night. Barnaby Thatcher's the name." Belatedly, he thought to ask, "Who might you be?"

"Emily Nolan." They shook hands gravely.

"Nolan..." Barnaby murmured to himself. "Would you be any relation to Farragut Nolan, out of St. Lucia?"

"Not that I know of. My people were from Chicago."

"A fine city, Chicago. Wouldn't you say so, Basil?"

"No doubt abou' dat, miss. Very fine. Butter with de lobster?"

Glancing down at the delectable plate of shellfish put before her, Emily nodded rather bemusedly. "Yes, please, and I wouldn't mind another of your rum punches. Care to join me, Captain?"

"Why I would at that. You know," he added astutely, "you seem different since you got out of those fancy clothes."

"I was very hot and tired when I arrived," Emily admitted wryly. "But a shower fixed me up."

His bloodshot eyes widened with surprise. "Shower? You mean you got water out of them pipes?"

"Certainly. Wasn't I supposed to?"

Barnaby pulled his earlobe reflectively. "Can't see what harm there is in it, but I wouldn't count on it happening agin if I were you."

Swallowing a butter-dipped morsel of sweet lobster, Emily murmured, "There's...uh...no regular water supply in the hotel?"

"Sure there's that. What kind of establishment do you think I run? Those toilets'll flush nine times out of ten." At Basil's skeptical look, he amended, "Well, five times anyway. 'Course they run on salt water. Anything else..." he shrugged philosophically.

"Cistern be too old," Basil explained succinctly, setting down her fresh drink. "Clogs up. Leaves, sand, dead birds, dings like dat, stop it workin' right."

Struck by a sudden memory of how she had stood open-mouthed under the shower and let the tepid water trickle down her throat, Emily took a quick sip of her drink. "How interesting. I suppose there must be many problems to life in the tropics that people elsewhere never really think about."

That was enough to set Barnaby off and running. For the next several hours, he regaled her with tales of his adventures sailing from the Bahamas to Curaçao. It was well past midnight before Emily at last got back to her room, after complimenting Basil on a superb meal. Thanks to a judicious application of rum punches, she slept soundly through the night, undisturbed by the small lizards that peered at her from the headboard or the brightly plumed birds that made their home in the closet.

It was the birds that woke her shortly after dawn. Some family squabble had broken out, accompanied by much cawing, scolding and irate fluttering of wings. Emily opened her eyes groggily. For a moment she could not remember where she was, then recognition flooded in and she sat up reluctantly. In her opinion, the proper approach to any day was to be slow and cautious. She had never been one of those benighted types who sprang from bed cheerful and energetic. Rather she slid out hesitantly, fumbled for her slippers—after making sure that nothing had moved into them during the night—and plodded into the bathroom.

A short time later, revived by her continued success with the grumpy pipes and fortified by thoughts of coffee, she ventured out. The sky was blissfully clear, the water glinted invitingly, and the air was fragrant with the scents of frangipani and hibiscus. Most of the small craft she had noticed the day before were gone from the harbor, probably off fishing. But Basil was already at his post and greeted her with a smile.

"Mornin', miss. You sleep well?"

She grinned and nodded. "Sure did, thanks to your punch. You wouldn't know where I could get some coffee, would you?"

"You be welcome to join me for a pot. De Cap'tin, he not get up for a while yet."

"Has he lived here very long?" she asked, propping herself up on the same stool she had occupied the night before.

Basil nodded as he poured them both cups of thick, chicory-scented coffee. "Been 'round dese islands some time now."

Emily took a sip and smiled appreciatively before she said, "He looks like a pirate."

The tall black man laughed. "You tell him dat, he like it. Maybe he tell you some of his stories."

"Stories?"

"He knows all 'bout de pirates and such like used to sail dese waters. Has ol' books 'bout dem and maps of where de hid dere treasures. Dat how he lost de *Aberdeen*, searchin' for buried treasure."

"I thought those were only legends, about the pirates burying their loot on deserted islands," she said.

"Who can say? De Caribbean hides many secrets, miss. Very many." He cast her a shrewd glance. "You stay here awhile, you find out."

A slight shiver of apprehension ran down her spine. Emily ignored it. "Unfortunately, I can't stay long. I've only come to find Mr. Hawkins. Do you still think he'll be back today?"

"Hard to say. He maybe go some other island to trade rum, or go fishin', or just sail 'round." White teeth flashed again. "Hawkins not be like men with families and such. He free spirit, like de wind."

Like the wind, Emily thought glumly several hours later as she sat on the ramshackle dock staring out over the water. There was still no sign of Lucas Hawkins. The annoyance that had bubbled just beneath the surface ever since her arrival on the island was back in full force. He had known she was coming to offer him an important job, and he had still chosen to go off on some damn fool errand of his own, after rum no less. Not even the wind was as feckless as that.

Once again, she considered leaving and reluctantly rejected that alternative. Time was of the essence on this job. Hawkins had come highly recommended. To try to replace him at this stage would involve a delay she could not accept. Still, she was beginning to think she might have no other choice when, late in the afternoon, a double-masted schooner at last came into view. The wooden hull of the yacht was unusual enough in this age of fiberglass to catch anyone's eye, but what really interested Emily was the man standing behind the wheel, guiding the boat to its mooring.

He was quite tall, over six feet, and well-built without being bulky. His hair was a tangle of ebony curls long enough to cause him some annoyance as he brushed a strand out of his eyes. He hadn't shaved in several days, and his square jaw was darkened with a thick growth of whiskers. The ragged cutoffs that were his sole garment left his torso and legs bare. His skin had the deep bronze color of long exposure to the sun. He moved with agile grace as the boat was secured and he stepped onto the dock. Basil was there to greet him. The two men spoke for several moments. Hawkins, if that was indeed who the new arrival was, threw back his head and laughed. Then he glanced in Emily's direction.

Something happened to her then; afterward she was never quite sure exactly what it was. A sense of recognition, almost of remembrance. A shock that was actually physical, even, for a fleeting moment, a preternatural glimpse of what was to come. It was similar to, yet much stronger than, the more common experience of déjà vu. Any such vagaries of the mind were not like her; they violated the sense of reality on which she so strongly depended. She clamped down on her imagination with such swiftness that the instant out of time might never have occurred. Resolutely schooling her features to blankness, Emily rose.

Lucas stopped where he was, at the end of the dock, and watched her come toward him. He stood with his bare feet planted apart and his hands on his lean hips. A slight frown furrowed his brow. She was not what he had expected. Over the radio she had sounded cold and crisp. Her voice, even distorted by the static, had conjured up visions of tailored suits and sensible shoes, no-nonsense hair and asexual manners. The slender, lightly tanned woman with long, coltish legs, slim hips and waist, and full breasts was innately feminine. She showed it in the graceful movement of her body, the slight, unconscious sway of her hips, and the way she tilted her head to look at him.

"Mr. Hawkins?" Her voice was low and a little husky, undercut by a faint but unmistakable note of disdain. Ms. Nolan was clearly not pleased with him. Sheer male instinct demanded that he change that—but not by attempting to placate her. He'd never placated a woman and wasn't about to start now.

"That's me," he said coolly, turning away to watch the rum being unloaded. As though as an afterthought, he added, "You're Nolan?"

"Emily Nolan. I arrived yesterday... as planned."

The reminder of his failure to meet her as arranged did not faze Lucas. He merely shrugged and looked unconcerned. "Schedules are very flexible here in the islands. You have to stay loose."

He looked as though he had a great deal of experience doing that, she thought disparagingly. It would be hard to imagine a man more at home in his environment. Everything about him proclaimed the easy, laid-back style of the dropout from society, the eternal Peter Pan determined never to grow up. Once again she wondered at the wisdom of trusting such a man with so difficult and sensitive a mission.

"Perhaps I made a mistake coming here..." she said, almost to herself.

He shrugged disinterestedly. "Could be."

She looked up at him sharply. "If you aren't interested in the job, I'll have to find someone else immediately."

"What makes you think I'm not interested?" he asked as he walked up the path toward the hotel.

Emily had no choice but to follow him. She kept a wary eye on the cacti as she said, "Your delay in getting here, for one thing. This job needs a man who takes his responsibilities seriously; otherwise it can't possibly succeed."

"Has it occurred to you," Lucas said mildly as he continued to climb the hill, "that I have other responsibilities besides waiting around for you?"

"No," she said frankly, struggling to keep up with his long strides, "it hasn't."

That startled him into a laugh. On top of everything else, she was honest, a quality he valued highly, if only for its rarity. On impulse, he offered her a hand as they negotiated the last, steepest part of the road. Equally without thought, Emily accepted. Their fingers touched and there it was again: the fleeting instant of recognition, as though their bodies knew each other in a way their minds could not.

Flustered, Emily had to restrain herself from drawing back. This was something new to her, and she was not one to run from a challenge. But she still had the uneasy feeling that the situation was taking a sudden, unexpected turn, the consequences of which she could not visualize.

Lucas was thinking much the same. At thirty-two, he had known his fair share of desirable women, and then some. He was no stranger to the many faces of passion, but he had never before experienced so immediate and forceful a response to any woman. It shook his presumptions, which he did not appreciate. Irately telling himself he was really reacting to his recent celibacy rather than Emily herself, he took the rest of the path quickly and immediately dropped her hand.

"Where's Barnaby?" he demanded brusquely as they entered the hotel.

Put off by his abrupt change in manner, she responded in kind. "I have no idea." Tartly, she suggested, "Maybe he's 'hanging loose' somewhere."

Lucas's hazel eyes narrowed. His gaze swept over her challengingly in a move intended to put her in her place, even though he wasn't quite sure what that might be. "I don't have much patience with sarcasm," he said quietly.

Emily glared back at him. Without giving an inch, she said, "And I don't have much patience with tardiness. I've already wasted more than enough time in this place. Let's get clear now whether or not you're going to do the job."

Lucas stared at her for a long moment. She looked straight back unflinchingly. Ten years of corporate infighting did not desert her. Nothing could be discerned from her expression except absolute determination. At length, he said, "All right, we'll talk." Before she could relish her victory too much, he went on quickly, "After I find Barnaby and take care of a few other things, I'll meet you at Basil's place in, say, half an hour."

That was the best she was going to get, Emily realized. After grudgingly agreeing, she went back to her room to get the papers she would need, then made her way down to the beach. With the fishermen out in their boats and no visitors in the harbor, it was very quiet. Sandpipers scurried at the water's edge while gulls circled overhead. A yellow-breasted bananaquit fluttered about in search of crumbs.

A half hour passed, then five minutes more. Emily moved impatiently on the stool. She had told him the truth when she said that punctuality counted heavily with her. She did not appreciate people who were late, perhaps because she had once done so much waiting for those who often did not show up at all. Still the absurdity of caring about precise increments of time in her present setting did not elude her. She distracted herself by watching the bananaquit, who had found the sugar bowl set out on the counter, and was perched on the rim helping himself.

"That stuff isn't good for you," she told him softly. The bird paused, cocked its head at her for a moment, then resumed pecking. Presumably, he knew better than she.

Five more minutes passed. Emily gave in to temptation and glanced at the watch strapped to her wrist. She toyed with the idea of going off somewhere and letting Lucas cool his heels waiting for her. Only the suspicion that he wouldn't bother stopped her. Instead she began going through the papers she had brought, studying them once again even though she had them virtually memorized.

A shadow falling over her shoulder caused her to look up. Lucas was standing directly behind her. "Sorry I'm late," he said. "It took longer than I'd expected to roust Barnaby out."

Emily smiled coolly. "Did it? I hadn't noticed. It's so lovely here."

Lucas shot her a swift glance. Was she serious about not having noticed that he had kept her waiting, or was she simply trying to get his goat? If the latter, she was succeeding only too well. Brusquely, he said, "Let's get on with it. All I know so far is that Sentinal Insurance wants me to find something for them."

She glanced around carefully, confirming that there was no one within earshot. Only then did she begin to explain what had brought her to Devil's Reef.

TWO

"Two months ago," Emily began quietly, "The yacht, *Venturer*, went down off Barbados. Three members of the crew were lost. The owner, Winslow Goodway, was not on board at the time. However a rather valuable shipment was."

"What kind of shipment?" Lucas asked.

She hesitated only a moment before saying, "Diamonds. Approximately one thousand carats in all, made up of gemgrade stones of one carat or more. Included in the packet were several stones larger than five carats. Those alone are valued at close to a million dollars. The total value of the shipment is in excess of two million."

"What possessed Goodway to transport so many diamonds at the same time?" Lucas exclaimed. "And why by ship?"

"I don't know," she insisted. "But such a method of transport did not violate the terms of Mr. Goodway's insurance policy with Sentinal. We are liable for the loss. Half a dozen crew members and two independent witnesses have testified that the diamonds were indeed on board. That being the case, we had no choice but to reimburse Mr. Goodway in full. Having done that, the diamonds now technically belong to us. We want to recover them."

Lucas nodded. What she was describing was normal procedure for an insurance company that had taken a major loss. As a salvage diver with a better than average reputation, he'd been involved in such recovery operations before.

"What makes you think the diamonds are still there?" he asked. "The currents are strong in that area. Chances are they've traveled miles by now."

Emily shook her head firmly. "The packet was inside a safe in the captain's stateroom. The safe is made of steel and weighs three hundred pounds. I don't think the current could have moved it."

"No...probably not," he acknowledged. "But there are other considerations. For example, how certain are you of the wreck's location?"

"Reasonably. We know exactly where it was when it went down, and we've done a computer projection to allow for possible drift over the last two months. That puts it about here...." She unfolded a small map and indicated a spot about ten miles southwest of the Barbados Ridge in the Tobago Basin.

"The water there is close to a thousand feet deep," Lucas said. "That makes diving impossible."

"Normally it would, but in this case we believe the yacht is on an underwater island projecting above the ridge to within fifty feet of the surface."

"The chances of that are extremely remote."

"Nonetheless we have confirmation of that fact."

Lucas stared at her steadily. "How? Unless someone has already dived to the wreck."

"No, no one has. We have access to certain... resources." She pulled out a grainy photograph and offered it to him. "This is a high-altitude survey of the area. If you look there—" she indicated the spot "—you'll see the shadow of the wreck."

Lucas looked. Slowly, he said, "This photo was taken by satellite. Sentinal must be calling in some pretty big IOUs."

"We have no choice, given the magnitude of the loss. At any rate, we are now confident that the wreck is intact and accessible, so we can proceed with recovery."

"Which is where I come in?"

"Exactly." Quietly, she added, "We're offering the usual finder's fee of ten percent, or in this case two hundred thousand dollars."

As she spoke, she watched Lucas's face carefully to see what his reaction would be. If the possibility of earning that much money impressed him, he gave no sign of it. Instead he asked, "How long have you worked for Sentinal?"

"Almost ten years." She answered automatically, still working on the fact that he wasn't terribly interested in the money. That worried her. In her experience, greed was the most powerful motivator. She understood it and knew how to cope with it. In its absence, she might be hard-pressed to either anticipate or control his actions.

As Emily considered all this, Lucas was also busy with his own thoughts. She had worked for Sentinal for ten years. That put her age at somewhere around thirty, almost the same as his. A good age for a woman, old enough to have learned to know something about herself, and the world.

"I suppose you understand the difficulties of a job like this," he said. "Speed and secrecy will be absolutely essential."

"Of course. There must be many people who would stoop to just about anything to beat us to the diamonds."

"You're wrong about that," Lucas said cryptically. At her puzzled look, he explained, "Whoever else wants the diamonds will sit back and let us do the dirty work. It's afterward that they'll try to make their move.''

"I hadn't thought of that," she admitted. "But it doesn't really change anything. Security must be ironclad from the beginning. No leaks."

"How many people know you came down here?"

"Only Mr. Goodway and the directors of Sentinal."

"Think again," he said. "Did you book your ticket yourself?"

"No... Our travel department did that."

"So there's another two people, the clerk in your department and the clerk at the airline. You flew into Barbados?" Emily nodded and he went on. "There's the crew of the plane and your fellow passengers, the immigration and customs agents, plus whoever might have seen you passing through the airport. Not to mention the staff of the charter plane you took to Union Island, and the crew of the boat that brought you here. Then there's everybody on this island. Get the idea?"

"Yes," she said stiffly, "but I don't see what it has to do with anything. None of those people could have known why I was coming here."

"That's true, but someone might have been curious enough to try to find out. So the sooner you hotfoot it out of here and let me get to work, the better."

"There's just one little problem with that," Emily said softly.

Lucas eyed her warily. He was already learning that her voice was a barometer of her emotions. It tended to drop slightly whenever she was most determined. "What's that?" he asked.

"I'm coming with you."

"Like hell."

"There's no way I'm turning over a job like this to a stranger without my being on hand to keep an eye on things."

"There's no way I'm saddling myself with a woman on a job like this."

Emily bridled but held on to her temper. She was no stranger to chauvinism, and she had long since decided not to let it get to her. "My being a woman has absolutely nothing to do with my ability to participate in this mission. I am a certified diver and I can take care of myself, both in the water and out." Quietly but with implacable firmness, she added, "My involvement with the mission is nonnegotiable."

Lucas stepped back a pace and regarded her narrowly. Her calm, even serene expression annoyed him. He wanted to pierce her composure and see what lay beneath. "Just how do you propose to inflict yourself on me if I say no?" he inquired with deceptive mildness.

She smiled gently. "Simple. I gave you the wrong map."

A string of blistering curses later, Lucas said, "Where's the real one?"

"There isn't any. I've got the location memorized. The photo I showed you is accurate, the wreck is reachable, but only I—and the directors of Sentinal—know precisely where in the Barbados Ridge it can be found."

"There can't be too many underwater islands poking up there."

"Forty-two," she pointed out matter-of-factly. "By the time you check them all, or even a few of them, I'll have brought in another crew and recovered the diamonds. And thanks to your warning about possible poachers, I'll make sure we're well able to protect ourselves."

"You're just looking for an excuse to hire someone else," he charged.

"Maybe, and if you say I can't go along, you'll have given it to me." She looked at him hopefully, as though waiting for him to do himself in.

Lucas was sorely tempted, but he wasn't about to let her have her own way. If she insisted on being part of the mission, so be it. Once at sea, he'd leave no doubt of who was in charge. Tough she might be, but he'd still come out on top.

An image surfaced in his mind of his own bronzed length stretched out on top of silky thighs and rounded breasts. He blinked it away impatiently and glowered at her. "You'll have to work. This won't be any pleasure cruise."

"Fine," she said composedly. "When will we leave?"

"There are a few things to do first to get *Banshee* ready."

"*Banshee?* What kind of name is that for a boat?"

"It's Gaelic," he said with forced patience. "For a fairy woman."

"It also means a harbinger of death. Isn't that kind of grim?"

"Not to me. I like the name, and as it happens to be my boat, I'd thank you not to make aspersions..."

"Good Lord but you're touchy. I was only curious. *Banshee* it is. How long will you need to get her ready?"

"The rest of today. But we can't get everything we need here. We'll have to make port along the way to pick up food, oxygen tanks and so on."

"They'll have all that in Bridgetown," she pointed out, mentioning the capital city of Barbados near where they would be diving.

He shot her a disgusted look. "I thought you wanted this to be a secure operation. If we stroll into Bridgetown and start buying up a ton of gear, word will get out in no time. The way to do it is to stop at several small harbors on different islands, picking up a bit at each place. It'll take longer but be safer in the long run."

"If you say so," Emily murmured doubtfully. On a few things at least, she would have to defer to him. If only to keep him agreeable.

They spent the remainder of the afternoon loading supplies onto *Banshee*. The beautiful sailing yacht looked deceptively small from shore. Below deck she was fitted out with a stateroom, a comfortable seating area that could sleep two and a kitchen that boasted among its amenities a microwave oven.

After spending a second night in the small hotel room, she was more than ready to leave and was up at dawn to pack her bag. To her surprise, she found Barnaby waiting for her in the lobby. "Darn," she said when he spotted her, "you caught me trying to sneak out."

"I found the money you left on the counter last evening, gel," he said roughly, "but I wanted a word with you before you left."

"Badly enough to get up this early?"

"Who's been to bed? Plenty of time for that later. Join me for a cuppa?"

Remembering the state of the kitchen, she shook her head quickly. "Thanks, but we're leaving early, so I've got to be going."

"Off with Lucas, are you? The lad's a fast worker."

"Maybe we knew each other before," she suggested, seeing no reason to disabuse him of the notion that their departure was for purely personal reasons. "Perhaps I came down here to join him."

Barnaby shook his head firmly. "You aren't his type. He likes 'em warm and willing; you're something a man would have to work at."

Wryly, she said, "I'll take that as a compliment. Now if you'll excuse me, I have to be going."

"Where would that be?"

"Here and there, wherever the mood takes us." She smiled brightly. "Isn't that the whole point of the islands—to hang loose?"

"I suppose," Barnaby muttered doubtfully. He clearly did not believe her, but Emily wasn't about to spend time worrying about that. She smiled again, thanked him for his hospitality and headed for the dock.

Lucas was already up and at work. He was wearing the same ragged cutoffs from the day before, and he still hadn't bothered to shave. When he saw her, he scowled. "Where have you been? I said I wanted to get an early start."

"Good morning to you, too," she said as she stepped onto the deck. "Do you always wake up in such a cheerful mood?"

His finely drawn mouth turned up at one corner. "You could always bunk with me and find out."

"Thanks just the same, but I prefer the couch."

He shrugged broad, bare shoulders as though it didn't matter to him one way or the other. "Suit yourself. Get your gear stowed, then come up on deck. You can make yourself useful helping with the rigging."

The sun was rising above the horizon, and the day was already turning warm as they sailed away from Devil's Reef, their course plotted for Grenada, the nearest large island. "We'll take on fresh vegetables there," Lucas explained, "and ice, then head north to Carriacou for more provisions."

"You're sure this island-hopping is really necessary?" Emily asked as she fought to subdue a recalcitrant mainsail and secure the rigging.

"I am. Hey, watch what you're doing! Get those sheets fastened."

"I'm not exactly an old hand at this," she snapped. "Maybe you should do it yourself." Her arms were aching from the unaccustomed strain of pulling on the heavy sail. She'd had no chance to put on suntan lotion, and she could feel her skin beginning to burn. The wind was whipping her hair around her face so that she could barely see. On top of everything else, she would just about have killed for a cup of coffee.

"I told you this wouldn't be any pleasure cruise," he pointed out a bit smugly.

Having at last secured the sail, she straightened and glared at him. Normally, she had no difficulty controlling her temper, but something about this man brought out the worst in her. Angrily, she snapped, *"That* goes without saying. Anywhere *you* are could hardly be a pleasure. Now if there's nothing else Your Highness requires, I'm going below." Without waiting for his response, she stomped down the gangway to the galley.

"Fix some breakfast while you're down there," Lucas yelled after her. "That is, if you know how to cook."

Tempted to tell him what he could do with breakfast, Emily opted instead for a more prudent approach. She was going to be stuck on this boat with him for several weeks; there was no point making things worse than they already were.

Half an hour later she carried a platter on deck and calmly began to set the small table positioned under a sunscreen. Lucas frowned as he watched her, until the aromas of fresh bacon, hash browns and fried eggs began to waft his way. The rattling of the anchor chain announced his intention to join her.

"Not bad," he said a short time later after he had finished off half a dozen rashers of bacon, three eggs, most of the hash browns and a pile of toast. "You even make good coffee."

"Thanks so much," Emily murmured. "I can't tell you how pleased I am that my humble efforts meet with your approval."

"All right," he allowed grudgingly, "maybe I was being a little hard on you. But you have to admit you had a lot of nerve insisting on coming along."

"It wasn't my idea," she pointed out. "If I'd had my way, I'd be sitting in an air-conditioned office in midtown Manhattan."

"Instead of having to rough it on board a sailing yacht in the Caribbean?" he asked wryly.

"So it isn't all bad. That doesn't mean I'm glad to be here. For one thing, I'm worried about what you said about other people being interested in the diamonds. Did you really mean that?"

Lucas refilled both their cups before answering. When he did, his voice was low and pensive. "In some ways, this part of the world hasn't really changed all that much in the last couple of centuries. Tourists come down here from the States or Europe, they stay at fancy resorts, and they go home thinking they've seen the Caribbean. In fact, all they've seen is a carefully managed stage set. The *real* Caribbean, where real people live, is very different."

"I know there are problems down here," Emily said. "Unemployment, poverty, political unrest, but are you saying there's more to it than that?"

He nodded thoughtfully. "For years this area was the happy hunting ground of some of the most bloodthirsty pirates ever to crawl out from under a rock. They roved the sea lanes with impunity, sinking who-knows-how-many ships. Now what you have to ask yourself is what conditions caused all that to happen. To begin with there were people unhappy about not getting what they thought of as their fair share of the pie and determined to do something about it. Add to that an infusion of wealth, in the form of the ships that came through here, often carrying cargoes of gold and gems. Throw in a maze of islands where to this day a boat can vanish, and you've got the perfect mixture for banditry on the high seas."

"The point being that those circumstances exist today just as they did several centuries ago?" Emily asked.

He smiled, pleased by her swift perception. "That's it. To the tourists, crime in the Caribbean means getting a wallet stolen on a beach or something like that. To the island authorities, it means the usual assortments of burglaries, assaults and so on that happen anywhere. But once you leave the islands and get out on the water, a completely different sort of crime comes into play, much more serious and potentially deadly."

"If you're trying to scare me, you're succeeding."

He doubted that; she didn't strike him as the sort who could be scared by words. "All I'm trying to do," he said softly, "is bring home to you the seriousness of our position. We have to play it very cagey, cover our trail, throw out disinformation, the whole bit, or we won't have a chance of coming through in one piece."

"Let alone with the diamonds?"

He shook his head. "They'll be like blood to sharks, and believe me they'll have pretty much the same effect."

His choice of metaphor made Emily's stomach churn ominously. Normally she was an excellent sailor, but her breakfast was suddenly sitting very heavily. She had undertaken many sensitive missions for Sentinal, but never one in which the danger had been clearer.

"I think you should know," she said with as much steadiness as she could muster, "that I'm a fairly good shot."

A flicker of admiration shone in Lucas's hazel eyes. Stubborn and high-handed she might be, but he couldn't fault her on courage. "That's good," he said noncommittally, "though with luck we won't need to test your ability. I'm hoping we can look enough like a pair of lovers out for a sail to throw people off the track."

"Is *that* what we're supposed to look like?" Emily queried, wondering if he could see the sudden wave of color that washed over her cheeks. She hoped she had gotten tanned enough to hide it.

"It's the safest ploy," he said calmly. "After you insisted on tagging along, it occurred to me that you might actually come in handy as camouflage."

"It's so nice to be useful."

"Now don't get on your high horse again. All I meant was that it's safer for us to look like we've got nothing on our minds except each other." Their eyes met as he added, "Think you can manage that?"

"If I try very hard."

Much as Lucas hated to admit it, her tart tongue was beginning to have an effect. The knowledge that she didn't think much of him was proving unexpectedly hard to take. Generally, he cared little for the opinions of others, not because he was a callous or insensitive man, but because he had chosen long ago to go his own way—free of the ties that usually bind people together, and make them worry about how they are perceived.

His isolation had always suited him. But as he looked across the table at Emily, watching the sun play on her amber hair and taking in the delicate purity of her features, he wondered how it was that being with her made him feel lonely while being by himself did not. Perhaps because she made him yearn for things he did not believe he could ever have.

She cleared up from breakfast while he got the boat underway again. Below deck, after she had finished the dishes, Emily hesitated briefly before getting a swimsuit out of the built-in drawer beneath the couch that would serve as her bed. She had seen something in Lucas's eyes while they were talking that told her Barnaby might be wrong about her not being his type. It was folly to encourage him, and she had no intention of doing so, but that didn't mean she couldn't relax for a while and get a little sun.

He glanced up as she came back on deck, his swift appraisal missing nothing of her figure in the white bikini. She thought he stiffened slightly, though she could have been wrong about that. All he said was, "Be careful you don't get burned. I'm not playing nursemaid."

The mere thought of him having to do so spurred Emily to apply twice her usual amount of sun protection. That done, she stretched out with a book and resolutely ignored him. Or at least she tried to. The novel was one she had been wanting to read for months, but somehow it couldn't hold her attention. She was too vividly aware of the man standing tall behind the wheel, guiding the elegant boat with unerring skill. He was a far cry from the pinstriped executives she tended to date, men who were part of her world and played by its rules.

What rules Lucas obeyed, if any, were a mystery to her. She supposed he was honest, or Sentinal would never have approved him for the mission. After all, what was to stop him from absconding with the diamonds instead of turning them in for the reward? Even stolen, the gems would bring close to a million. Surely enough for him to resettle in a different part of the world far from prying eyes.

For a moment she wondered if that might be what he was planning, but that thought faded almost as quickly as it arose. There was no sense worrying about imponderables; she had more than enough to think about as it was.

Lulled by the smooth flow of the boat and caressed by the gentle trade winds, Emily drifted into sleep. She woke some unknown time later with the sensation of being watched. Lucas stood over her, large and dark against the sun. She blinked and sat up hastily.

"What time is it?"

"Past lunch. I hope you haven't overdone."

"No, I don't think so. If you're hungry, I'll fix something."

His expression was inscrutable as he looked down at her. She wondered if he had been watching her while she slept, and why that possibility made her so uncomfortable. "That breakfast will hold me for a while yet," he said. "Anyway, we're in for some rain. You might want to get under cover."

A glance at the sky showed Emily what he meant. Where there had been pure blue there were now heavy gray clouds and the dim yellow light that meant a heavy squall. She had known before she arrived in the islands that late summer was the beginning of the rainy season, but the last couple of days of blinding sunshine had made her briefly forget. It looked as though she was about to be reminded, forcibly.

"Will we be all right?" she asked as she got up.

He laughed and started back toward the helm. "This is nothing to *Banshee*. She's outridden hurricanes. But you might not take it as well."

Oh, she mightn't, might she? Stung by the suggestion that she was some shrinking violet afraid of a little water, Emily went below deck just long enough to pull on a T-shirt over her bikini, then she joined Lucas at the wheel.

He looked surprised to see her. "It's going to get rough."

"That's fine with me."

Letting it go at that, he turned his attention to the roiling waves slapping against the prow. The wind had picked up, and the sky was now completely obscured by heavy clouds. Emily watched, fascinated, as the squall line approached. The first drops of rain were unexpectedly cold.

What followed was unlike anything she had ever experienced, at once frightening and exhilarating. The wind tore at her hair and plastered the thin T-shirt to her body. Salt spray washed over her. The wild pitching of the boat made her hold onto the handrails tightly; even so it was all she could do to keep her balance. This fierce, unrelenting face of nature was in sharp contrast to the neat, artificial world she knew so well. She had the sense of being of no more consequence than a leaf being tossed about on a raging river. Yet she also felt closer to the ultimate source of all things than she had ever been.

Almost too soon it was over. The haunting song of the wind in the sails died away; the sea grew calm. There were patches of blue in the sky, and off toward the horizon the gold and green rise of an island began to appear. "Grenada," Lucas said as he glanced down at her. "We'll make port in a couple of hours." His expression was unexpectedly gentle as he added, "You came through that very well."

"Thanks," she said a little shakily, "it was quite an experience. Will the weather get much rougher?"

"It shouldn't until fall when hurricane season starts, but Mother Nature has been known to step up her timetable."

"I can see what you meant now by *Banshee* having no trouble. She's magnificent."

Unknowingly, she touched a chord in Lucas. There were few things he cared for more than the sailing yacht he had personally restored, and which had been his only real home for the past eight years. "I'm glad you like her," he said a little gruffly.

They were busy for the rest of the sail, tidying up from the effects of the storm. By the time the red-tiled roofs of Saint George's, capital city of Grenada, came into view, little evidence of the rain remained. As Lucas maneuvered through the forks of the headland that surrounded the anchorage, Emily could see why the town was called the most beautiful in the windward islands.

Built on a hill overlooking the sea and guarded by an old stone fort, it combined the best of French and English influences. She was delighted when he announced that they would be spending the night there.

Three

Dinner was a simple meal served on deck under the moon and stars. Lucas had set steaks out to defrost before the storm hit. He cooked them over a hibachi while Emily prepared a salad and baked potatoes in the microwave. They shared a six-pack of Venezuelan beer.

"Tomorrow," he said when they sat back replete, "we'll go into the market. Saturdays are always fun there. I'd like to be out of here by midmorning and on the way to Carriacou."

"What's there?" Emily asked drowsily. She was curled up in one of Lucas's sweaters he'd lent her when he realized her wardrobe did not stretch to such comforts. The soft wool smelled of sun, salt and an intrinsically masculine scent. She rubbed the sleeve against herself unconsciously as she waited for him to answer.

"A buddy of mine who sells diving equipment. I want to pick up some extra tanks and get the air compressor checked out." He spoke absently, his attention focused on Emily.

She continued to surprise him, being far more helpful and congenial than he had expected.

Relaxed as she was now, she was even more appealing than before. It was all he could do to keep his mind on business. Were she to give him the slightest encouragement, he suspected he would be very tempted to make the ruse of their being lovers a reality.

But she did not. Instead, she excused herself and went down to the galley to straighten up. Lucas stayed on deck to secure *Banshee* for the night, then he stuck his head down the gangway long enough to say, "I'm going on shore for a few hours. You'll be fine on your own. Just don't touch the anchor chain."

"On shore? Why?"

"Just something I need to do." On a lighter note, he added, "Don't wait up."

She most certainly wouldn't, Emily thought irately as she listened to the sounds of oars dipping in the water as he rowed the dinghy away. If he wanted to go off and leave her by herself on a strange boat in the middle of nowhere, that was fine with her. She'd forget he even existed.

That was easier said than done. Lying awake on the sleeper couch in the lounge, she was acutely aware of every whisper of the wind and every creak of the boat. Though she knew they were securely anchored and if worst came to worst, the wharf was within easy swimming distance, she still felt as though she had been left to fend for herself in an alien environment. And all so Lucas could do... what? No stores would be open at this hour, so he couldn't be looking for supplies. Besides, they were going to do that the next day. Perhaps he had friends in town, though remembering what he had said about the need to keep a low profile, she doubted he would be in the mood to go visiting. But then what could have prompted him to go ashore?

She got her answer—or thought she did—shortly after midnight when he returned. The reek of raw whiskey heralded his arrival. Lying rigidly under the sheet, she listened as he bumped into something, cursed under his breath, then opened the door to his cabin. For a few more minutes she could hear him moving around, clumsily, she thought. Then there was silence.

Emily fell asleep eventually, worn out from worrying about what was going to happen to a difficult, dangerous mission that depended on a man who couldn't fight the urge to go out and get drunk. She was still thinking about that when she got up the next morning and wearily pulled on her clothes.

To her surprise, a pot of coffee was already perking on the stove. She poured herself a cup and went on deck, where she found Lucas stretched out on a chaise lounge, one long leg crossed over the other and a mug like her own balanced on his stomach. He opened an eye as she approached and nodded. "Morning, sleep well?"

"Tolerably," she said as she gazed down at him frostily. In the back of her mind she noted that he had shaved. With his square jaw and firm chin no longer hidden, he was more attractive than ever, a fact that she obscurely resented. Tartly, she asked, "How about yourself?"

"Not too bad. I got back around midnight and hit the sack a little while later."

"And your trip to town? Did you enjoy that?"

He raised an eyebrow at her sarcastic tone and hoisted himself into a sitting position. "Okay, let's have it. What's eating you?"

"Nothing, unless you count the fact that we've got enough problems without your going on a bender."

"Bender? What the hell—"

"You heard me. You went on shore last night and got drunk. So much for keeping a low profile. If the smell was anything to go by, the whole island knew you were around."

A dull flush crept over his cheeks as he listened to her scathing words. For a moment he was tempted to let her believe that he was capable of such behavior; what did he care, anyway? But then he admitted that he did care, whether he liked it or not, and he couldn't let her go on thinking the worst of him.

"We'd better get something straight right now," he said quietly. "Either we're in this together or we aren't. If we're partners, then we've got to give each other the benefit of the doubt."

"How can I when you—"

"Let me finish. I went into town last night for one reason only: to find out if anyone was asking questions about us or the wreck of *Venturer*. The only place to learn that was in the dock-front bars, so that's where I went. Sure I had a couple of drinks; I also had half a bottle of not very good whiskey spilled on me by a sailor who was in his cups. But I did not get drunk. Nor do I have any intention of doing so. Is that clear?"

Emily had grown increasingly pale as he spoke. Besides the wrong she had done by jumping to unwarranted conclusions, she was also struck by how unlike herself she was behaving. It wasn't in her nature to think the worst of people, yet with Lucas she had done exactly that.

"I'm sorry," she murmured, "I really had no right to think what I did. Everything you've said makes sense. I just wish I had known ahead of time."

"I didn't tell you because I figured you'd worry," he said shortly.

"Yes...I would have." She hesitated a moment, then sat down beside him. "Did you find out anything?"

He hadn't really wanted to tell her what he had learned, but now he couldn't avoid it. Quietly he said, "Someone's been asking around. I got a description, but I don't recognize whoever it is. I put the word out that we're on a pleasure cruise, but frankly I'm not sure it will be believed."

"Why not?"

"Let's just say that you aren't the only one who tends to credit me with the worst possible motives."

"I really am sorry. . . ."

"It's okay. I'm not blaming you. Looking back, I can see how you would have jumped to the wrong conclusion. Anyway, what we have to be concerned about is the fact that somebody is at least curious about our movements."

"Is there anything we can do?" Emily asked.

"Just try to look like what we're supposed to be, starting with our trip to the market." He smiled at her reassuringly. "Ready to get going?"

"I guess so . . . sure. Let's go."

He nodded approvingly, which for some strange reason sent a warm glow all the way through Emily. She was grateful for the distraction offered by the colorful marketplace that was a pleasant ten-minute walk from the inner harbor. Baskets of fruits, vegetables and spices filled the outdoor displays, and the cheerful voices of vendors praising their merchandise mingled with the rhythmic beat of a steel-drum band entertaining the shoppers.

With her hand clasped securely in Lucas's and his longer stride moderated to match her own, it was all too easy to fall into the fantasy that they really had nothing to be concerned with except each other. For a brief time she tried to imagine what it would be like if they really were on a pleasure cruise. How would it be to wake in his arms in the morning, share the day with him in easy companionship, and retire at night to the same bed?

She turned away from him suddenly, pretending to be attracted by a display of saffron, but in fact hoping he wouldn't notice that her cheeks had turned bright red. For a woman who had always taken pride in her self-control, she was giving an excellent imitation of a giddy schoolgirl. At the sound of Lucas's deep voice, she jumped slightly, but managed to make it look as though she had merely been swatting off a mosquito.

"The saffron is harvested here," he was explaining. "Each fine yellow strand is the stamen of an autumn crocus. It takes about seventy-five thousand of them to make a single pound of the spice."

"No wonder it's so expensive at home," Emily said. "I usually end up substituting turmeric, which is cheaper and easier to come by."

Lucas cast her a startled look. "You really do know how to cook. Does this mean I'm in for more good meals?"

"Only if you let me pick out the provisions," she said lightly. "A good cook always does her own shopping."

He readily agreed, and they continued on their way, after buying a small quantity of the saffron that, not surprisingly, was much cheaper so close to its source of supply. Lucas was soon loaded down with bags of grapefruit, rice, tomatoes, bananalike plantains, West Indian pumpkins, and christophines—the pear-shaped vegetables whose spiny outside hid a soft and delectable interior. Emily was struck by his good-natured tolerance as he waited patiently at each stop while she picked out exactly what she wanted. Not until they had all they could carry did they head back to the boat.

By the time they had put away the last of their purchases, both were ravenous. Emily shelled the large prawns they had bought from a fisherman on the dock, split them and added a pinch of curry to each before sliding them under the broiler. They were ready in minutes and, with the salad she tossed together, made a welcome brunch.

"Where did you learn to cook?" Lucas asked after he had sampled the meal.

She shrugged and looked out at the water. "I picked it up somewhere along the line. And I had a couple of jobs cooking, so that helped."

"You were a professional chef?"

Despite herself she smiled. "That's a pretty fancy term for a short-order cook, which is what I was." His attentive silence prompted her to go on. "After I got out of high school, I needed a job to pay my way through college. About the only thing I could do decently was cook, so I went to work in a luncheonette on Chicago's South Side. After a while, I moved up to a slightly tonier establishment."

Lucas wasn't surprised by the story, but he was having trouble reconciling the beautiful, elegant woman before him with the image of a young girl slinging hash in a greasy spoon. There was a great deal more he wanted to learn about Miss Emily Nolan, but he sensed this wasn't the time. She was more than a little reticent about herself, and he didn't want to do anything to make her feel that he was prying, lest that cause her to raise her defenses even further.

The sun was at midpoint in the sky when they said good-bye to Saint George's and set sail on a northeast heading for Carriacou. With a fair wind, they would make anchorage by nightfall.

"This island is very different from Grenanda," Lucas explained as they approached the main harbor of Hillsborough. "It's much quieter and less developed. Provisions are scarce, so it's just as well we loaded up."

"Will we have much trouble finding your friend?"

Lucas shook his head. "Harry's usually at the Seafarer Tavern; it's pretty much the center of local social life." He grinned as he said that: Emily soon saw why.

Hillsborough was literally a one-street town boasting a handful of shops and bars. Most of the former were already shuttered for the night when they arrived. The latter were doing only a desultory business, except for the Seafarer. Visitors off several yachts were gathered there along with an assortment of the locals. Reggae music played softly in the background. Lucas ordered a couple of beers, then looked around.

"There's Harry," he said, pointing toward a table at the back where a young blond-haired man was seated alone. "I radioed ahead this morning; he's expecting us."

As he spoke, Harry looked up and saw them. He beckoned them over. The two men exchanged greetings, then Lucas introduced Emily. He put an arm around her waist, drew her close to him and smiled as he said, "Here's the sweet young thing I was telling you about. Isn't she everything I said?"

Harry grinned pleasantly. "And then some. Pleased to meet you."

Emily registered the fact that Lucas apparently didn't quite trust this cheerful young man he called his friend. At least that was the impression she got by his sticking to the cover story. Wary of jumping to unfounded conclusions again, she sat back, sipped her beer and listened to the two men talk.

In a much quieter tone, Lucas said, "Were you able to get what I wanted?"

Harry nodded. "Six tanks, plus the spare parts for the compressor. I'll drop them off in the morning. Pick up anything in Saint George's?"

"A few whiffs. Somebody's interested, but I don't know who. Do me a favor and keep your ears open?"

"Sure thing, pal. You carrying the usual?"

"Wouldn't be without it." Raising his voice, he said, "So how come you're still on the loose, Harry? I figured they'd have wised up to you by now."

"Sheer luck, ol' buddy. Plus my charming personality, of course."

Lucas laughed at that, and they went on to talk of ordinary things—where the fishing was good, what was new on the island, who had stopped by recently and who was expected soon. At length, Lucas stood up, held out a hand to Emily and said, "Good to catch up on old times, Harry. We'll be in touch."

"Yeah," his friend said, "you do that, but in the meantime, fair sailing."

They said their goodbyes and left. Not until they were back out on the street did Emily ask, "So Harry knows the truth?"

"He knows part of it," Lucas corrected. "And I trust him to keep his mouth shut."

After they arrived back on board, Emily went down to the galley to fix them both cups of cocoa spiced with cinnamon and nutmeg. She brought Lucas his on deck. He smiled his thanks, and they sipped in silence for a few minutes before she asked, "What's the 'usual?'"

He looked up swiftly. "The what?"

"What you usually carry. Harry asked you if you had it, and you said yes."

His mouth tightened in a grimace. Putting his cup down, he said, "I'm beginning to wonder if I can keep anything from you."

She met his eyes, noting their brilliance even in the faint starlight. "Should you want to?"

He laughed huskily. "A man has to be allowed some secrets."

"The 'usual'... is that a secret?"

"It has been until now, except from Harry and one or two others I really trust."

"Care to let a lady into the group?" She spoke as casually as she could manage, but the question was fraught with meaning. There was no telling what perils might lie ahead of them. If they were to survive, they had to trust each other.

"Sure," he said at length, "why not? Come below deck and I'll show you."

The 'usual' was hidden behind the bulkhead adjacent to Lucas's bunk in the stateroom. Cleverly concealed holes gave a grip for his fingers so that he could ease out three planks of wood that hid a cavity about a foot high, the same distance in depth, and five feet long. Inside were two plastic-wrapped bundles that looked for all the world like...

"Rifles?" Emily asked quietly. "Automatic, I presume?"

Lucas was not fooled by her apparent composure. Her face was pale, and her large blue eyes looked bigger than ever. Quickly, he said, "I keep these strictly for my own protection. If I had them out in the open, I'd have to be continually declaring them to customs and having them impounded every time I visited particular islands. So I just keep them stored away in here and hope I won't need them."

Emily hoped so, too. She didn't care to envision any scenarios in which the weapons would be required. But despite her best efforts, images of what might be intruded on her thoughts. She shivered and wrapped her arms around herself.

"Hey," Lucas said softly, "it's okay." Instinctively, he reached out to her, drawing her close against the warm breadth of his chest. She made a small sound deep in her throat, but did not resist. The sweet balm of comfort flowed over her. Comfort was such a rarity in her life, and so badly needed just then, that she shut off the clamoring doubts and warnings of her mind, and simply accepted it as it came.

Lucas was a wall of strength, a fortress of security, a shelter from the storm. But he was also a man. That did not escape Emily; on the contrary, awareness of his masculinity seeped through every pore of her skin, reaching to the very center of her being. Fear drained away, replaced by something far different.

She braced her hands against his chest, her fingers fanning out to explore the hard ridge of skin and muscle beneath his thin shirt. A tremor raced through him, inspiring her to be bolder. The clear delineation of his ribs gave way to a tapered waist and narrow hips. Shivering again, she reached around to caress his back, tracing the path of his spine upward to his broad shoulders.

"Emily," he murmured as he stirred against her, making her aware of the effect of her touch. Startled, and a bit abashed by her own boldness, she tried to move away, only to be stopped by his hands gently gripping her hips and holding her to him.

All thought of resistance fled as she settled back against him. Acting on impulse alone, she tilted her head and gazed up at him. His eyes—normally a light hazel—were dark with barely suppressed emotion. There was a faint flush on his lean cheeks, and his nostrils flared as he fought to draw breath.

The hard fingers that grasped her chin trembled slightly. She had an instant to marvel at what was happening between them before he lowered his head and touched his mouth to hers. The kiss was light and reassuring, a salute rather than a demand. As such, it made her yearn for more. Without hesitation, she parted her lips and let the tip of her tongue touch the sharp ridge of his teeth.

A low groan broke from him as his arms closed around her fiercely. She was so sweet to taste, so warm and responsive. His resolve to avoid any personal entanglement with her was consumed in the raging hunger she sparked. His tongue met hers and followed it back into her mouth, where he stroked the inner warmth lingeringly.

Emily arched against him, standing on tiptoe with her arms twined behind his neck. Mindless to anything except the exquisite sensations he provoked, she gave herself up to the demands of her body. Long moments passed as they remained clasped together, kissing and caressing with a growing sense of awe as both recognized the enormity of their response to each other.

For Emily, who had always privately thought of herself as too cool for real passion, it was a revelation into her true nature. For Lucas, it was confirmation of what he had suspected for some time, namely that a vital ingredient had been missing from all his prior relationships with women. Something that transformed the act of physical intimacy from a straightforward sharing of sex to the mysterious realm of lovemaking.

And that scared him. He felt as though the very fabric of his life was being torn asunder. Since reaching manhood, he had prided himself on his self-sufficiency. Now that was threatened, by a completely unexpected source. When all was said and done, he barely knew Emily. She was still very much an unknown quantity. How could he allow himself to be vulnerable to her?

Lucas was not alone in the reawakening of his doubts. Emily shared them. She was stunned by her behavior and deeply disturbed by it. The professionalism and objectivity she had always prided herself on suddenly seemed to have vanished. She was as susceptible—and vulnerable—to the attractions of a man as any other woman. Worse than that, she was even susceptible to the charms of a stranger.

They both drew back at the same time and gazed at each other warily. Lucas was the first to break the strained silence. "Uh . . . maybe we'd better cool it. We've got a tough job ahead and we don't need any distractions."

What an articulate way to put it, he thought grimly. He'd made it sound as though what had just happened between them was no more to him than a diversion he had just remembered he should do without; whereas in fact it was vastly more.

Emily stiffened abruptly as a wave of embarrassment flowed through her. She had been dangerously close to forgetting her professional responsibilities, something that had never happened before. That Lucas should have such an effect on her was nothing short of frightening.

"You're right," she said shakily, stepping away from him. "I don't know what came over me." In fact she did know, all too well, but not for the world would she admit it. If Lucas Hawkins happened to attract her more than any other man she had ever met, so be it. That didn't mean she had to give in to her susceptibility. Moving toward the door of his cabin, she added, "I'm sure it won't happen again."

Lucas looked after her darkly. On the one hand, he was glad she was being reasonable about the whole thing. On the other, he was more than a little put out by her apparent ability to brush aside what had been, for him at least, a shattering experience.

Long after she had left, he lay awake in his bunk, staring up at the ceiling. He was trying to puzzle out his contrary responses to a woman who had walked into his life scant days before, yet whom he already longed to know on the most fundamental level possible.

St. Vincent came as a relief to both Emily and Lucas. The long sail to reach the main island of the northern Grenadines had strained both their tempers. In such close quarters, it was impossible not to be acutely aware of each other's every moment. Though they were scrupulous in avoiding further physical contact, all too many times their eyes met in wordless contact that only served to heighten the tension between them.

At the first sight of the jagged green peaks of the island, both were able to relax a little. For a few hours at least they would be among other people. After clearing immigration in the port of Kingstown, they went their separate ways, Lucas to finish rounding up the provisions and Emily to buy some supplies of her own.

The day was brilliantly clear, yet despite that she felt an unexplained sense of apprehension. Though the scene before her was beautiful—filled with brightly dressed men and women, an abundance of flowering plants and the delectable scents of the tropics—it was also completely alien.

She was out of her element as thoroughly as a fish tossed up on the sand. For the first time, she faced the possibility that in sending her on this mission, Sentinal might be trusting her with more than she could handle.

She tried to shake off that grim thought as she shopped for a few extra clothes to augment her meager wardrobe. Since she had learned that even summer nights could be cool on the water, she bought a light sweater so that she would not have to borrow Lucas's again. Added to this were several pairs of white cotton pants and some T-shirts. Satisfied, she paid for her purchases and started back toward the wharf.

She was about halfway there when a vague feeling of anxiety suddenly made her stiffen. At first putting it down to no more than natural concern about the mission, she continued on her way, but the uneasiness continued. At length she paused and glanced behind her.

Nothing out of the ordinary caught her eye. Locals and visitors alike continued to amble along; cars squeezed by on the narrow road; the sun shone brightly. She shook her head wryly, thinking that she really had to get a grip on herself. Her imagination was beginning to run away with her.

Turning a corner, she cut through a lane that led toward the docks. No stores had their entrances on this road, so she was briefly alone. Or so she thought. The man came at her so suddenly that she had no time to think about what was happening. One moment she was walking along like any other tourist, and the next she was seized from behind, her bundles sent crashing to the ground, and her breath forced out of her by an iron-hard arm.

Panic washed over Emily. She struggled fiercely as she clawed at the hand covering her mouth. Her feet lashed out, kicking the man's shins, but without effect. He muttered something she could not catch and gripped her all the harder.

Blackness swirled in front of her eyes, pierced by whirling colored lights. Her lungs burned, and with a cold shock of horror, she realized she was suffocating. Her fingernails raked at the man's hand, and dimly she noted the warm stickiness of blood. Then consciousness faded, and she

knew nothing except a sense of falling endlessly into a bot-
tomless vortex of terror.

"Miss," a soft voice called urgently, "can you hear me,
miss? Are you all right?"

A faint thread of awareness lit the dark cocoon of obliv-
ion. Emily stirred hesitantly. She was lying in the cobble-
stone lane. Every inch of her body hurt, her breathing was
labored and she felt too weak to move. It took all her
strength to force her eyes open.

A young black man was bending over her, his face tight
with worry. He touched a gentle hand to her shoulder. "Can
you get up? I saw what happened, or at least the last of it.
What a terrible thing."

"The man..." she croaked weakly, "did he get away?"

"Yes, I'm sorry to say. He ran as soon as he saw my
brother and me." The young man gestured to his compan-
ion, who was also gazing at Emily with shock and concern.
"We came out of my father's store, through the back door,
and saw you struggling with him. When we shouted and ran
forward, he threw you to the ground and dashed off. I'm
afraid we were more concerned with you than with following him."

He looked so genuinely sorry that they had not been able
to catch her assailant that Emily managed a weak smile.
With the realization that she was safe, her strength was re-
turning, and she was able to get up. As one of the young
men supported her and the other helped her to her feet, she
said, "Don't worry about that. I'm so grateful for your in-
terference. If you hadn't arrived when you did..."

She broke off, abruptly aware that she really had no idea
of what her attacker had intended. Had he meant to rob her,
or was he bent on assault? Another possibility occurred to
her: that the attack had something to do with her mission
for Sentinal.

"You're very pale, miss," one of the young men said. "You'd better come inside the store and rest while we call the police."

She stumbled slightly as she took a step, but recovered her balance and straightened up. "N-no...I'd better get back to the boat." At their surprised looks, she explained, "I really don't want to get involved with the authorities. I'm sure they mean well, but I doubt there's any chance of them finding the man."

"You should still report it, miss. We don't like tourists being hurt here."

"It's all right, really. These things happen all over the world." She smiled again, a bit brittlely. "Thank you again for your help."

Before they could try further to convince her to let them call the police, Emily recovered her packages and hurried away. Her head swam dizzily and bruises were beginning to show on her arms and legs. But she did not slow her pace. The specter of violence drove her to flee even as she knew there could be no true escape.

Four

"Let's go over it again," Lucas said quietly. "The man came up behind you in the lane. He grabbed you and put a hand over your mouth. He was very strong and you think he was taller than you. What else?"

"Nothing. I didn't notice anything more. I was too busy trying to get away."

"You had to have seen more," he insisted. "You're just blocking it out. Relax for a few minutes and we'll try again."

They were seated in the lounge below deck. Emily had taken a shower and changed into a loose caftan that hid most of her bruises. Lucas had insisted she have a brandy. It had helped some. She hurt less and her fear was fading. But she was still not eager to relive her experience.

"I don't see what good it will do," she said. "It's over and done with. I'd rather just forget."

"That's understandable," Lucas told her patiently. He leaned forward, his elbows resting on his bare legs. When Emily had returned, he had been in the water beside the boat making a routine check of the hull. At the first sight of her, he had climbed swiftly up the ladder and demanded to know what had happened. She had told him, but only very briefly. Ever since, he had been trying to get more information.

"It's natural for you to want to put it out of your mind," he went on, silently reminding himself that she had been badly shaken and that he should be patient. "But we'd be better off knowing what we're dealing with."

"A man," she murmured. "Someone tall and strong and..." Her voice broke.

Lucas hesitated barely a moment before putting an arm around her shoulders and drawing her close. All his resolve about not touching her didn't seem to matter much under the circumstances. She was hurt and scared, and he was damned well ready to kill whoever was responsible.

Through gritted teeth, he asked, "When he put his hand over your mouth, did you see what color it was?"

"Wh-what...?"

"The color of his skin. Was he white or black?"

Emily thought for a moment, then said quietly, "Neither.... His skin was brown...but it looked more like the brown of a heavy tan rather than a natural color."

Lucas smiled broadly. "What did I tell you? You do remember more. It sounds as though he wasn't just some local thug trying to rip off a tourist. Whites are very much the minority in the islands, so we tend to stand out too much even to think about getting away with robbery, especially not in broad daylight."

"I see what you mean," she said slowly. "But the heavy tan would indicate he's from somewhere around here."

"Off a boat, maybe. Question is, if he wasn't out to rob you, what did he want?"

"I've been thinking about that myself," Emily admitted. "It doesn't make any sense to me. If somebody wanted to stop us from going on with the mission, you'd be a much more likely target. It's true that I know where the wreck is located—and might be forced to tell—but what you said about any would-be thieves waiting while we do the work and then moving in makes sense."

"There's something you're overlooking," Lucas said quietly. "Maybe someone was planning to hold you hostage for the diamonds."

She looked up at him incredulously. It was a possibility that had not occurred to her, but perhaps it should have. There were people who would do literally anything to acquire such wealth. "I'm not sure how Sentinal would react to a situation like that," she said slowly.

"You don't think they'd give up the diamonds to get you back?"

She hesitated, not wanting to be disloyal to her employer but not given to unrealistic expectations, either. "I think they feel that if they paid a ransom once they would be endangering their other employees who might also become victims of such attacks."

It was just as well she realized that, Lucas thought. The sooner she accepted that they were on their own without hope of backup, the better. "Whatever the reason for that man trying to grab you," he said at length, "we've got to take even more precautions. It's fortunate that we'll be at sea soon."

She agreed, though not simply for the reasons he meant. Nestled against him with her head on his shoulder and their bodies cradled closely together, she was vividly conscious of how strained her self-control was becoming. In the quiet solitude below deck, with the gentle roll of the waves rocking them, the temptation to yield to the strength and comfort he offered was all but irresistible. She thought of the kiss they had shared and knew that, in his arms, she would be able to forget everything except the sheer pleasure of being with him.

But afterward? It was the thought of how she would feel later that stopped her from turning to him. She had never been able to take physical intimacy lightly. Something in her nature—whether fastidiousness, reserve or just plain common sense—made her shy away from letting a man into her body without due regard for both him and herself.

Lucas felt her drawing away from him, and a pang of disappointment touched him. He loved the way she felt in his arms, all soft and warm and yielding. With very little encouragement, he would have carried her to his bunk and made love to her until all fear and pain were obliterated.

Yet he was also aware of the danger she represented. His relationships with women had always been honest, but casual. He had never made any secret of the fact that he was a loner intent on staying footloose and free. Except that freedom no longer looked quite so appealing.

Wryly, he told himself that he was simply going through a phase. He and Emily were no more than ships passing in the night. If she was right about the wreck and the safe, they would find the diamonds within a few days. Then he would need all his concentration to get them safely back to shore. The last thing he should want was a major-league distraction on the order of a beautiful, independent, spirited woman who seemed all too perfectly made for him.

"You'd better get some rest," he said quietly as he removed his arm from around her shoulders and sat up. "I want to move us to a quieter harbor for the night."

She nodded without comment. The removal of his arm made her feel curiously bereft, but she wasn't about to show him that. After he left, she tried to lie down for a few minutes, but visions of what had happened in the alley continued to haunt her. Giving up, she distracted herself by putting away the clothes she had bought, removed her caftan and donned a comfortable pair of shorts and a shirt. By the time she had finished, she could feel the low vibration of the engine beneath her feet as Lucas steered them away from the dock.

From a porthole, she watched the town fade into the distance. They were headed south, away from the capital along the western coast of the island. The sea was calm and the sky clear. Outside the harbor they caught a fair wind and were soon making good time.

She considered going up on deck to help, but decided against that. Her one earlier brush with the sails had shown her to be more of a hindrance. Besides, she had the feeling that he wanted to be alone for a while, a need she shared.

All too soon they would reach the wreck, and then she doubted that either of them would get much rest. In the meantime, she needed to go over in her own mind the steps she would have to take, after the packet was recovered, to get the diamonds safely back to New York.

They anchored that evening in the narrow channel between St. Vincent and Young Islands, within view of a popular resort. Sounds of music drifted toward them over the water. They could make out the shapes of couples strolling along the beach and heard an occasional hint of laughter.

"Looks like they're having fun over there," Lucas said quietly as he leaned back in his deck chair. His long legs were stretched out in front of him and his big body slouched comfortably. A lock of hair had fallen across his forehead. Shadows obscured his expression.

"I think I may come back here some day," Emily murmured, "when I can enjoy it properly."

He grinned whitely in the darkness. "You'd rather be playing tourist?"

"Wouldn't you? This job is beginning to get a little hairy."

"It goes with the territory. Besides, as I told you, this place is no paradise, no matter what the tourists think."

"I haven't forgotten that," she said, a little coolly. She was trying to keep her distance from him emotionally, but that wasn't working too well. Softly, she asked, "How did you get to be so cynical, anyway?"

He hesitated a moment, then shrugged. "Experience, how else? I was in the army in 'Nam, and when I came home, I had trouble finding a job so I bummed around for a while. I've seen too often what people will stoop to. If you're honest, you'll admit that human nature leaves a lot to be desired."

"I don't accept that. Most people are decent and honorable. It's only a few who make it tough on the rest of us."

"Believe that if you want, but you couldn't prove it by me. I think most people are out to get everything they can and don't care much how they do it."

"Does that include you?" Emily asked.

"I'm no better or worse than the rest of them." He peered at her narrowly. "Do you really think I'd be risking my hide if it weren't for the reward money?"

"No," she admitted hesitantly, "it wouldn't make any sense for you to do so. But why shouldn't you be well paid? That's only fair."

"And what about you?" he went on. "Why are you doing it?"

"Because it's my job."

He laughed skeptically. "You're just a loyal employee who does whatever her boss says, is that it? No way. If we can pull this off, Sentinal will reward you, too. Maybe not in cold cash, but unless I miss my guess, you'll be up for a big promotion."

"Perhaps," she acknowledged, "but that's also fair. It isn't as though anyone will be hurt by what we're doing. Whatever we gain, we'll deserve."

"And whatever we lose?"

She laughed a little shakily. "That's a different story. I'm counting on you to make sure we don't lose anything."

Lucas regarded her from beneath hooded lids. She had washed her hair earlier and pinned it up on top of her head. Stray wisps had come free and were blowing gently in the breeze. The shirt and shorts she wore did little to disguise the slender grace of her figure. He stirred restlessly in his seat.

"You may be trusting me with too much," he said at length. "I'm only human."

Emily was well aware of that. He was a vital, virile man who made her acutely conscious of being a woman. The irony of their situation did not escape her. In one of the most beautiful and romantic spots on earth, they were unwilling partners wary of each other and themselves.

That did not change as they approached the Barbados Ridge. Whatever doubts Emily harbored—and there were many—she at least saw no further reason to deny Lucas the real coordinates of the wreck. With those, he was able to plot a deliberately deceptive course that they hoped would confuse any pursuers and throw them off the trail.

The strategy seemed to be working—or perhaps it had not even been necessary—because there was no sign of other ships following them. Emily was reassured by that, until she mentioned it to Lucas.

"They wouldn't have to have us within sight," he said. "There are other ways to track a boat." At her puzzled look, he went on, "Remember that small plane that flew over us yesterday? That was only one of about half a dozen I've counted since we left St. Vincent. There's a busy airport on Barbados, so they may all be perfectly innocent. On the other hand, one or more of them may be keeping an eye on us."

"Oh," she murmured in a small voice, her confidence abruptly diminishing.

He caught the look in her eyes and gave her a dry smile. "Cheer up, it could be worse."

"How?"

"Any number of ways. We could get hit by bad weather, or have an engine break down. We might get to the site and find out the coordinates are wrong. Or we might dive and discover that something had happened to the safe."

"I can't tell you how much I appreciate your pointing all that out," Emily muttered.

Lucas laughed unrepentingly. "Just trying to keep you interested. I wouldn't want you to get bored."

"Fat chance of that," she said under her breath.

"But to be on the safe side," he went on, ignoring her, "this afternoon we start training."

She looked up hastily. "What for? I already know how to dive."

"That's fine. But there are one or two other things you should pick up. For example, I don't suppose you know how to use the 'usual?' "

Her eyes widened at the mere thought. "You mean fire an automatic rifle? No, of course not. A pistol's more my speed."

"That will have to change. And while we're at it, you're also going to learn how to handle *Banshee*."

This time Emily didn't ask why. She felt no urge to hear him spell out for her that if something happened to him, she would have no way of getting back to shore unless she knew how to handle the boat. The thought of Lucas being hurt, or worse, was even more painful than she wanted to admit. She couldn't imagine his life being snuffed out, any more than she could her own. But neither could she hide from the harsh reality they might well confront.

"Maybe we'd better get started," she said. "We don't have much time left."

"Look through the sight," Lucas ordered a short time later. They were riding at anchor near a reef. A row of empty tin cans had been set up along the railing. Emily was doing her best to shoot them down, without tremendous success. "Focus on the cross hairs," he went on. "No, don't move! You've got to stay steady."

"I'm trying! Yelling doesn't help."

Hands on his hips, he glared at her. "Then what the hell will? I thought you said you were a good shot."

"I am, but not with this thing," she gestured to the rifle she held in her other hand, "or on a rocking boat."

"You can compensate for that." Sarcastically, he added, "It would help if you wouldn't close your eyes before you shoot."

Emily flushed and looked away. The next round went better, perhaps because she was so angry at him that she kept her eyes open and fired steadily. Five of the ten cans landed in the water, and Lucas was grudgingly satisfied.

"That's not bad for the first day," he allowed. "We'll try it again tomorrow."

"Wonderful," she muttered, rubbing her shoulder. "More to look forward to."

"Now we'll run through a few sailing basics."

"I hope you're not going to yell at me about that, too."

"Only if you keep your eyes closed," he shot back.

She didn't, and slowly the confusion of sheets, canvas and winches began to make some sense. She had even learned to take a compass bearing and depth sounding, as well as how to use the radio, which was their only link with land. Understanding something of how the beautiful schooner worked made her feel oddly more at home on it. And made her understand something of why Lucas had chosen to live as he did. The boat was a world unto itself, where the only reality that mattered was the sea and the wind. She would deeply regret it when that changed.

The following day they reached the location of the wreck and prepared to make their first dive. "Sonar indicates a large mass fifty feet down," Lucas said, studying the instruments. "From the shape of it, *Venturer* looks intact."

"Not quite," Emily said quietly. "There's a large gap in the stern section that blew out the aft compartments and actually caused the sinking."

mily had no choice but to believe him. She only wished
she felt a little more confident about diving into a wreck
t might yet shelter hidden dangers.

With both the forward and aft anchors lowered and the
p as secure as they could make it, they prepared to sub-
erge. Lucas helped her on with her equipment as they
od on deck. He had stripped down to brief swimming
unks and his big, hard body glowed in the sun. Beside him,
mily felt unexpectedly small and fragile. She kept her eyes
verted from the broad sweep of his chest and was relieved
vhen he moved behind her to hoist her air tanks into place.

Beneath their weight, she sagged slightly and gripped the
straps tightly. "They're heavier than I remember."

"You probably weren't carrying as much air before," he
said as he slipped his own tanks into place. Their weight was
apparently negligible to him. "We've got more than an
hour's supply, which I don't think we'll need, but I'd rather
not take any chances."

Emily agreed with that readily enough; she knew they
were taking a risk simply by leaving *Banshee* unattended,
even for a short time. It wasn't impossible that any pursuer
lurking just over the horizon might get wind of what they
were doing and use their absence to move in. She could only
hope that they wouldn't surface to an extremely unpleasant
surprise.

After a final check of the equipment, they climbed down
the stern ladder and lowered themselves into the water.
"Ready?" Lucas asked. She nodded and put her mouthpiece in place. For several seconds she had to concentrate on
her breathing, remembering not to inhale through her nose.
But she caught the rhythm quickly enough. When he sub-
erged, she was right behind him.

They swam through a translucent veil of water so clear
at every detail of their surroundings stood out vividly.
der ordinary circumstances, Emily would have been en-
alled by the colorful beds of coral festooned with all

He turned away from the control panel, raised. "Anything else you've been keeping to

She hesitated a moment, then said, "We *Venturer* was sunk deliberately by a limpet mine her stern section while she was in port in Barba timed to explode at sea, which it did. Mr. Goodw idea who was responsible but I presume he's h matter investigated."

"I see...." Lucas said slowly. He was looking at unsettling intensity, as though trying to judge the t what she was saying. In this day and age, such attack by no means uncommon. Still, he wondered at its "Goodway has no idea?"

"That's right. As you know, he's a very successful nessman, so it isn't unreasonable to think that there ma people who resent him. Still, blowing up a yacht seems a extreme."

"At any rate," she went on, "the sooner we find the safe and recover the diamonds, the better." From her pocket, she withdrew a schematic drawing of *Venturer* and smoothed it out on the table between them. "The captain's cabin was located in the forward compartment, so it should be relatively undamaged. I'm hoping we can get in and out quickly."

"That may be a little overly optimistic," he cautioned "If I'm interpreting the sonar picture correctly, *Venturer* lying at a slight angle, positioned on her stern. That mea we may not be able to get in through the gap left by bomb."

"There are two gangways," she ventured, "one at ship and the other aft. We could go in through there.

He nodded thoughtfully. "We'll have to and hop isn't too much debris blocking the passages."

"Is that likely?"

"After what that ship's been through? Anyth sible. But don't worry. If that safe is there, we'll manner of marine plants and the vibrantly hued fish darting among them. But as it was, all her attention was focused on the ominous shape directly below them.

Venturer had been a beautiful oceangoing yacht—more than eighty feet from stem to stern—with private cabins for twelve and accommodations for at least as many crew. She had boasted a dining salon that rivaled some of the best restaurants in the United States and Europe. Other amenities had included a fully equipped gym, sauna, screening room and a communications center that put passengers in touch with any place on earth within minutes.

As Lucas had suspected, *Venturer* now lay on her stern propped up slightly with her prow pointing toward the surface, as though she were preparing to rise again out of the water and resume her rightful place. Her deck was intact, the railings undamaged and even the horseshoe-shaped life buoys still hanging over the sides at regular intervals every few yards. Only the dinghy that had carried most of the crew to safety was missing. Everything else looked just as it always must have.

At least at first glance. As Lucas swam toward the aft gangway, and Emily followed, she began to see the damage done by two months underwater. The brass fittings were turning green and the white paint was flaking. The wooden planks, once kept so meticulously varnished, were cracking and buckling. Barnacles were beginning to make themselves at home in various nooks and crannies. Some form of algae had overgrown all the windows and portholes, and various fish—everything from barracuda to minnows—had adopted the wreck as their own.

She had only scant moments to take note of all this before Lucas was flashing a powerful beam into the gangway and motioning her to follow him. They swam downward at a steep angle; the stairs were immediately below them and the central passage lay directly ahead. She knew where she was in theory, but the reality was so distorted as to make her doubt the evidence of her own senses.

In her death throes, *Venturer* had pitched onto her stern as millions of pounds of seawater flooded her inner compartments. Everything movable had been caught up in that relentless torrent and tossed about like bingo chips in a spinning basket. Bits and pieces of furniture littered the corridor. Emily recognized tables and chairs from the dining room, part of a couch that had been in the salon, fragments of the gilded frames that had held a nearly priceless collection of artwork, even sodden lumps that had once been books from the extensive library kept on board.

The sound of her own heartbeat was loud in her ears as an eerie sense of familiarity settled over her, as though she had somehow witnessed such a scene before. It took her a moment to realize where; the remains of *Venturer* had the same feeling of careless abandonment as pictures she had seen of ancient tombs looted by grave robbers who had roughly tossed aside anything they could not steal.

The only significant difference she could see was that the tombs had been completely dark, whereas here a green light filtered through the algae-covered portholes. It gave everything a ghostly appearance that made the soft hairs at the nape of her neck rise. Had she stumbled into such a place on her own, she would have wasted no time getting out. But as it was, she felt compelled to continue after Lucas as he cautiously explored their surroundings.

He had warned her ahead of time that no part of the vessel would be free of marine inhabitants, and she quickly saw what he meant. As they approached the gangway to the lower deck, an octopus eyed them warily. It wasn't particularly large as such things went, but Emily was glad to give it a wide berth.

In the part of the ship once inhabited by the crew, it was darker than ever. Here the worst effect of the explosion could be seen. Bunks had been ripped from the walls, steel struts lay twisted like taffy and remnants of the electrical wiring floated like writhing tentacles.

Emily swallowed hard and swam all the faster. She kept directly behind Lucas as they approached the captain's cabin. The door to it hung open, still connected to the wall by a single hinge. Inside they found the usual tumult. All the interior fittings—bunk, table, shelves, cabinets and so on—had been thrown against the far wall. Beneath them, positioned with its front down, was the safe.

While they hadn't expected to find the safe standing upright and waiting for them, neither had they bargained on it being quite so difficult to reach. Between the two of them, they managed to remove most of the debris covering it, but by then their air was running very low and they had no choice but to return to the surface.

Once back on deck, Lucas said, "It's worse than I thought. We're going to have a hell of a time turning the safe upright to open it." He had removed his equipment and stood slightly bent over, with his hands on his knees, breathing deeply. Water dripped off him in long rivulets flowing down his teak-hued chest and limbs. Exhausted as she was from the long swim and the tension of being inside the wreck, Emily could not help but be stirred by his virile beauty. Aesthetically he was a delight to behold, but her attraction to him went far deeper than that. He stirred her on an intrinsically sensual level she could not deny.

Fortunately there were other matters to distract her. "There must be some way to move the safe," she said as she dried herself off briskly with a towel. "With all the equipment you have here on board, surely we'll find something that will help."

Lucas didn't answer at once. He was briefly absorbed in watching the rapid rise and fall of her breasts in the thin maillot swimsuit that clung to her like a second skin. The dive had brought home to him the immense difficulty of the task they faced, and made him acutely conscious of how much he wished he had met Emily under different circumstances. It wasn't his way to regret what he could not change. Quietly, he said, "The best I can think of is the extra length of anchor chain I carry. It should be just long enough to attach one end to the safe and the other to the winch."

"Then we can actually bring it onto *Banshee*?" she asked eagerly.

He restrained a laugh and shook his head. "'Fraid not. The winch isn't powerful enough to lift a three hundred pound safe through fifty feet of water, but it can right it for us."

With both of them so tired and the light rapidly fading, further work had to be postponed until the following day. Lucas surprised Emily by announcing that they would begin standing watch that night. He took the first and she agreed to relieve him at midnight. Her eyes widened when she saw him take the automatic rifles from their hiding place and move them onto the deck, but she refrained from any comment. They both knew trouble could arise at any moment. There was no sense talking about it.

After brewing him a pot of strong coffee, she said goodnight and went below deck. Long after she closed her eyes, visions of the wreck floated on the inside of her lids, interspersed with images of Lucas. She lapsed into a half-waking dream in which she was swimming along beside him underwater—but without the restraint of the diving equipment. They were both nude, and as they swam through the blue-green light, they smiled at each other. So vivid was the dream that she could almost feel the warm water caress her skin and feel the gentle firmness of Lucas's hand holding hers.

Emily sighed in her sleep and turned over. The dream slipped away. She remembered nothing more until the insistent buzz of the alarm clock woke her.

Five

The following morning, about half-an-hour apart, two small planes flew over them. Lucas observed their passage narrowly. "Either the airport on Barbados is breaking traffic records," he said, "or someone is definitely keeping an eye on us."

"Could you make out any markings?" Emily asked.

He shook his head. "Wouldn't do us much good anyway. They're bound to be rented. It's easy enough to set up. You pay in advance and phone in randomly to get reports. That way you can't even be tapped. It could take weeks to track down the people who were actually behind it."

She nodded. She knew that most air-charter operators were scrupulous about the jobs they took on, but there were always exceptions, people who would take the money and ask no questions.

If they were indeed under surveillance, there was no time to waste. When the chain was attached to the on-deck winch, Lucas stripped off his shirt and began to get into his diving gear. Emily watched him for a moment before she said, "I still say I should go down with you. The most basic rule of safe diving is never to be alone."

"You don't have to tell me that," he protested quietly. "I don't like it any better than you. But the winch isn't automatic; someone has to stay here to operate it. Since it will be easier for me to maneuver the chain underwater, it makes sense for you to run things from here."

"You make it sound simple, but it isn't," she protested. "Anything could happen to you down there." She was glad he hadn't told her of his plan the night before or she would never have gotten any sleep. The mere thought of his entering the remains of *Venturer* alone made her stomach churn. If he became trapped...

"Just concentrate on letting the chain out slowly and steadily," he instructed as he sat down on the edge of the deck and prepared to enter the water. "And keep that guide rope coming along with it. When I reach the safe, I'll give two jerks to tell you to stop the chain. Then three more when it's ready to be reeled in. If anything strange happens, just give one strong tug and I'll head back right away." He didn't add what should have been obvious—that he was literally trusting her with his life. And he didn't let himself think about the possibility that such trust might be misplaced.

"You've made the instructions quite clear," she said tartly, "but I still think you're crazy."

He took his mouthpiece out long enough to ask, "Can you come up with a better plan?" Reluctantly she shook her head. He readjusted his equipment and, with a movement so swift and apparently so effortless that she almost missed it, backflipped into the water. Within seconds, barely a ripple remained to show where he had gone.

The chain fed out slowly. Emily kept her hand on the guide rope, waiting for the moment when Lucas would let her know that he had reached the safe. When the two jerks came at last, she breathed a long sigh of relief. Only then did she glance up and notice the large powerboat about a quarter mile off the starboard side. Without field glasses, she could not make out its flag, but there appeared to be several people on deck.

Any number of innocent explanations existed for the sudden appearance of the boat. It might be a party of deep-sea fishermen; the Ridge was very popular with them. Or it could be a group of sight-seers out for a pleasant day on the water. Or it might be whoever had been watching them, moving in for the kill.

Such a regrettably apt expression, Emily thought distantly as she kept her eyes glued to the boat. For several minutes she was able to cling to her hope that it had nothing to do with them. Not until she saw two men in diving gear slip into the water did she decide that coincidence was being stretched too far. Her hands gripped the rope tightly as she pulled back on it with all her strength.

In the captain's cabin, Lucas felt the tug and froze. It might just be a mistake, he reasoned. Emily had been understandably nervous when he left and might be giving the alarm without due cause. He wanted to believe that so he could ignore the warning and get on with the job, but he couldn't quite manage it. In the days that they had been together, he had come to appreciate her good sense and self-control, even if these qualities were responsible for his feeling more than a little frustrated. It was unlikely that she could come this far and suddenly panic. Turning, he began to swim swiftly back toward the surface. As he did so, Emily was already reeling in the chain.

He broke the water on the starboard side of the boat and climbed quickly onto the deck. The last of the chain clanked up after him. She dropped the handle of the winch and said quietly, "We've got visitors."

Turning, Lucas caught sight of the other boat. He studied it as she explained what had happened. "They looked like they meant business," she said of the other divers, "and

I didn't think it would be a good idea for you to be surprised down there."

"You thought right," he said gruffly. "I wouldn't have wanted to meet them as I was leaving with the diamonds."

"You think they would have...?" She broke off, not wanting to voice her fears yet driven to find out exactly how far he thought their pursuers would go.

Lucas laid a hand on her arm and said quietly, "Guys like that think it's untidy to leave witnesses. Remember that and don't get too far away from the rifles."

She gulped and nodded. With as much steadiness as she could muster, she asked, "What do we do now?"

He hesitated a moment before saying, "I dive again, after dark." Without giving her a chance to comment on the extreme danger of that, he went on. "Hopefully, they won't see what I'm doing. Then tomorrow morning we get on the radio and have a message relayed to Sentinal, reporting that we found the safe but that it had already been opened and the packet is missing."

"What do we do that for?"

"To throw our friends over there off the trail. I'll bet anything that they're monitoring our communication."

"All right...suppose they do pick up the transmission. What makes you think they'll believe us and let us go?"

"I don't," he said shortly, "but we'll face that when we come to it."

That was very unsatisfying to Emily. She thought it would be far wiser to try to anticipate the exact nature of the trouble ahead and come up with a plan for coping with it. But when she said as much to Lucas, he shook his head stubbornly.

"You're not in the corporate world now. No amount of planning will do you a damn bit of good in this kind of situation. Anything could happen in the next five minutes, let alone the next couple of days."

On that cheerful note, he went below and she shortly heard him whistling as he got into fresh clothes. He sounded as though he didn't have a care in the world.

Scowling, Emily finished securing the chain, then got a mop out and cleaned up the water where Lucas had been standing. She almost laughed as she did so, thinking how ironic it was to be doing such a mundane chore when their lives might be in imminent danger. At least it beat sitting around worrying about what was going to happen.

On impulse, she raised her head and looked at the other boat. It had come a little closer and she could see that the divers were back on board. Along with them, she made out three other men. Together all five were scrutinizing the *Banshee*. Emily watched them for a few minutes, then went below deck.

She found Lucas seated at the table toweling his hair dry. He had changed into shorts and a shirt, which did very little to conceal the lithe hardness of his body. Emily let her eyes wander over him for a moment before she said, "They're still watching us. Do you think they'll do anything else?"

"Not so long as we stay put," he told her, his voice muffled by the towel. He put it down and went on, "If we tried to leave, they'd be after us in a shot, figuring that we've got the diamonds. But as it is, they'll think we haven't finished the job yet and wait."

She nodded and, despite herself, smiled. He raised a quizzical eyebrow. "Why are you smiling?"

"Your hair," she admitted, "it's a little...unruly." Thick ebony curls were going in all directions, as though a miniature cyclone had struck them.

Lucas laughed wryly. "It's always like that when it gets too long." He hesitated a moment, then asked, "Do you think maybe you could help me out? I'm no good at cutting it myself."

"I guess so...if you'd trust me."

"Sure, why not? You can't make it any worse than it is."

Emily had her doubts about that, but didn't voice them. Lucas went to find the scissors, then took his seat again and draped the towel over his shoulders. "Ready when you are," he said cheerfully.

She touched a tentative hand to his hair, feeling its healthy springiness beneath her fingers. "I think I'd better comb it first." That took a while, since there were quite a few tangles. When she finished, she asked, "Is there any special way you'd like it?"

"Just shorter so it won't get in my eyes."

Emily sighed, thinking of the men back in New York with their "styled" hair. It went with everything else about them—neat, contrived, part of an image. Did Lucas have an image? Yes, she supposed he did, but it wasn't contrived. The image—tough, honorable, intelligent, and don't forget sexy—was the man. Somehow that made everything better.

"You have very nice hair," she murmured as she snipped at it.

"Thank you. I got it from my mother."

"Are they still alive, your parents?"

He nodded and she put two fingers on the back of his head to still it. "They live in Iowa near my brother and his family."

"What do they do there?"

"Farm," he said wryly. "What else is there?"

"So you grew up on a farm?"

"Barefoot boy and all that. Drove a tractor by the time I was six, could handle a combine by ten."

"Did you like it?" Snip, snip.

"I guess. It was the only place I knew."

"Why did you leave?"

"For the same reason. My brother Brad always claimed I was part Gypsy and maybe he's right. Anyway, if I'd stayed we'd have had to share the farm and it would have been tough for either of us to make a living. Besides, Brad's the one who really cared about it so it was only right that he take it over."

"Still, that was very generous of you. Was he grateful?"

"If he was, he had the sense not to show it. I only did what was best for both of us."

"How did your folks feel about it?"

"They worried about me when I was in the army, but since then they don't seem to mind. We stay in pretty close touch."

She remembered how she had thought he was rootless and regretted that. "It sounds as though you care a lot about them." Snip, snip.

"They're my family." He said that as though it was self-explanatory, but to Emily it was not. She had never known what it was to be part of a close family where the people both loved and respected one another.

Something of that must have come across to Lucas because he asked quietly, "What about you? Does your family like you working for Sentinal?"

"I have no idea.... The last I'd heard my parents had gotten divorced and moved to different parts of the country."

"You don't keep in touch?"

"Not since I was ten." She said it so wryly that for a moment he thought she was kidding. When he realized she wasn't, he turned around and looked at her.

Very gently, he asked, "What happened?"

Emily met his eyes hesitantly. She had known Lucas barely a few days, yet she found herself wanting to tell him everything. Quietly she said, "My parents were very young when I was born—seventeen and sixteen. They had to get married because of me and they just couldn't make a go of it. So they put me in foster homes. It wasn't a bad life. I was never abused or anything like that. It just left a lot...unsatisfied."

Lucas was silent for a moment, his gaze never leaving her. A small kernel of pain opened up in him. He hurt for the child she had been, and for all that she had missed. "Did you ever feel that you were part of the families you lived with?" he asked at length.

"That wasn't in the deal. I got a roof over my head, decent food and clothes and I went to school. Which is more than a lot of kids ever have."

"It's also less. Why won't you admit you had a tough time?" He was angry now and he didn't know why. Perhaps because she insisted on being so emotionless. He wanted her to admit that she was hurt so that he could help her. It was selfish, but he couldn't seem to do anything about it.

Emily put the scissors down and walked away from the table. She was finished anyway. His hair looked a lot better, she thought dispassionately. Maybe she should think about taking up haircutting professionally.

She shook her head slightly. After all these years, the automatic reflex to try to find something she could make her own, be good at, earn a living at, still remained. Just as though nothing of what she had achieved actually existed. Not her exciting career or her elegant apartment in New York or all the other trappings of success that were hers. What right did he have to overlook all that?

"Don't feel sorry for me," she said coldly. "I've come through fine and I'll continue doing so. I don't need anyone except myself."

"Are you sure about that?" he asked as he stood up and pulled the towel off. Strands of inky black hair fell onto the floor. He ignored them and concentrated on her instead. Beneath the light tan she had acquired, her face was pale. The dusting of freckles on her nose stood out in high relief. He was swept by the sudden temptation to kiss each and every one of them.

The smile that lifted the corners of his mouth was very gentle. As was the hand that gently stroked her cheek. Emily stiffened slightly at his touch, but only for an instant. This was what she wanted, had wanted from the first moment she saw him. Later she could ask why; now she wanted only to satisfy the remorseless hunger he triggered in her. There might not ever be another chance to do so.

"Lucas..." she breathed softly, "I'm not sure this is a good idea, but..."

He moved a step closer. "I want to make love with you, Emily. I could dress it up in a lot of fancy words and moves, but that's what it comes down to." His eyes met hers again. "I think you want the same thing."

He waited then, giving her the chance to say no. Whatever she decided, he would accept; there was no doubt about that. So far, all the risk was on his side. He had taken the first step, admitted what he wanted, given her the option of agreeing or refusing. The look in his eyes told her that he was vulnerable to rejection, even though he would accept it.

Somehow knowing that he cared enough to be hurt if she rejected him made the decision easier. Or perhaps she had already made up her mind and was simply seeking to soothe her innate sense of propriety.

Emily took a step closer to him, then another. She raised her arms and pulled him to her. Her body pressed against his as she said, "You're right, Lucas. I'd like very much to make love with you."

His big hands closed on her back, stroking gently as though he was afraid he might hurt her. His voice held a slight tremor as he said, "Did you ever notice how some people say 'make love to' and others say 'make love with'?"

She tilted her head back and smiled at him. "I prefer 'with.'"

"Me, too."

His mouth was light and cool on hers, barely touching as he savored her. She stood it as long as she could, then deepened the kiss. He tasted faintly of mint toothpaste mingling with a special personal flavor all his own; a good taste that she wanted more of. The surface of his tongue was slightly rough, like velvet rubbed the wrong way. She liked that, too.

Lucas moved his legs apart a little, cradling her beneath his thighs. She felt so damn good. So soft and delicately made, yet strong in a way that made his breath come hard and fast. He wanted to go very slowly with her, as much for his sake as hers, but he wasn't sure he could manage it.

"E-Emily...?"

"Hmmm?"

"Would you mind very much if I picked you up and carried you into my cabin?"

She met his eyes gravely. "That sounds very romantic."

"I hoped you'd think so."

He had no trouble at all lifting her, she noticed. There was no little catch in his breath or smothered grunt. One minute she had her feet on the floor and the next she didn't. Not that she minded. It was very nice to be in his arms. A soft giggle broke from her.

"What's so funny?" he asked bemusedly as he pushed open the door to the stateroom.

"I feel like one of those girls in a romance about pirates."

"Can't say I've ever read any of those."

"They're my secret vice."

"Oh, *that's* what it is."

She pushed against his chest playfully and he set her down, but kept his arms around her. "How do those stories go?" he asked as he nibbled her ear.

"Well...there's always a sweet young heroine who gets kidnapped by a dashing pirate captain who's usually an English lord in disguise. He's overwhelmed by her beauty and...oh, that feels good."

"It's pretty nice at this end, too. You were saying..."

"Oh, yes, he's overwhelmed and so is she, and one thing leads to another."

"It has a way of doing that."

They stopped for a moment and looked at each other. First seriously and then with smiles that grew wider until they were full-fledged grins. Emily laughed softly. "We look very pleased with ourselves."

"Why not? We seem to have stumbled onto something good."

Yes, something very good. But also very temporary. She couldn't lose sight of that. If she did, it would hurt too much when it was over. How ironic that she and Lucas should come from such completely different worlds, yet be so powerfully drawn to each other.

But then life was full of ironies. Little jokes pulled by a fey fate. This time the joke was on her. She couldn't stop it from being played out, but she could enjoy it along the way.

The muscles of his throat moved spasmodically as she kissed him there. She felt them beneath her lips, felt the pulse that surged forward raggedly and the flush of heat that warmed his skin. He was so vitally alive, so strong yet gentle, and he was hers, for some little time at least.

As she was his. Their bodies blended together as naturally as though they had made love together a hundred times before, instead of this being the first. Clothes fell away without clumsiness, or if there was clumsiness, neither noticed. They were too caught up in the fascination each held for the other.

"You're beautiful," Emily breathed when they stood naked beside the bed.

She could think of no other word to describe him. Every line and curve of him harmonized. The tanned column of his throat flowed naturally into the broad sweep of his shoulders and chest. His ribs were clearly delineated and there was a ridge of muscle at their base. His waist was narrow, as were his hips. His legs were long and corded, lightly covered in the same dark hair that dusted his chest, traced down his abdomen and burgeoned at his groin.

"You're not so bad yourself," Lucas murmured thickly. He couldn't remember ever having seen a lovelier woman. From the high, proud curve of her breasts down her slender waist and hips to the graceful flow of her thighs, she seemed perfectly made for him. Her skin where the bathing suit had been looked like cream. Her nipples were deep pink, like ripe berries. The hair between her legs was slightly darker than on her head. He touched her there lightly, feeling the softness. "Beautiful . . . especially . . ."

"Especially what?" she asked huskily, her hands gripping his shoulders to steady herself.

"Especially your belly button."

Her eyes opened wider. "My what?"

"Belly button. I guess I'd better tell you I'm something of a belly button man. Yours is about the best I've ever seen."

The twinkle in his eyes told her he was teasing, sort of. He really did like her belly button. "I've had it since I was a baby," she told him gravely.

"Really remarkable. Just the right size—" his finger traced it lightly "—and depth."

"It's a pusher-inner," she murmured as he probed gently.

"I noticed. So's mine."

"And very nice it is." Tentatively, she traced the feathering of hair around his navel.

"Don't be shy," he urged. "Turnabout is only fair play."

"All right. . . ." Her finger slipped inside his belly button to the depth of her nail. She scratched lightly. "Yours is deeper than mine."

"I'm bigger than you are."

"I noticed." In bare feet, she came just to his shoulders, which really wasn't a bad place to be. Her hands rested on his sides just above his hips. The skin beneath her palms was taut and warm. She moved a step closer to him and let her nipples brush against his chest.

"Notice anything else?" he murmured.

"As a matter of fact, I do." Everything about him was in proportion. A small shiver of anticipation ran down her spine.

"Cold?"

"Freezing."

"It'll be warmer in bed."

"I'm counting on it."

The mattress was firm beneath her back. As he joined her, she wiggled over a little to give him more room. The bunk was a double, but even so it was only suited for sharing by two very friendly people. Fortunately, they were.

"Is there anything special you like?" he asked as he stretched out beside her, his head propped up on one hand while the other lightly caressed her throat and breasts.

"What if I said something really weird?"

He wiggled his eyebrows suggestively. "Like what?"

"Nice, old-fashioned lovemaking?"

"Shocking."

"Depraved."

It was quiet then for quite a while, except for the soft sighs and moans of pleasure. As she had suspected, Lucas was a superb lover, controlled yet passionate, demanding yet giving. His hands and mouth roamed over her at will, tasting, caressing, igniting sparks of pleasure that spread quickly into an inferno of need.

The warm, moist lips that tugged gently at her nipples made her moan brokenly. She tangled her fingers in his thick black hair to hold him even closer. Looking down the length of their bodies, she saw the burnished power of his long back and taut buttocks rippling with strength and virility, contrasting sharply with her own paler, softer form. As he slid between her thighs, their legs entwined. Instinctively, she arched against him, feeling the hot demand of his manhood pressing against her belly.

"I wanted this to last so long," Lucas groaned hoarsely, "but I don't think I can manage it."

"Don't worry," she gasped. "I can't wait, either."

Lucas hesitated, his lean fingers stroking upward along the inside of her thighs, finding the molten center of her being. He touched lightly, carefully, yet with skill that made her cry out and grip him all the more fiercely.

"Please...now...come to me."

With a low groan of masculine triumph, he did as she asked. She gasped as his full power entered her, but accepted him quickly. Moving together, they soared toward a glittering peak of fulfillment. So complete was their union, so perfectly attuned was each to the other, that they might have been lovers for years instead of for the first time.

At the moment of her completion, Lucas's mouth closed on hers as he drank in her soft cries of joy. An instant later he followed, trembling in her arms as his life poured into her.

Afterward, she lay on her back with him still half on top of her, his head cradled against her breasts. Her fingers were twined in his hair, which was slightly damp. The air in the small cabin smelled of sweat and musk. It was warm, but not unpleasantly so.

The complete satiation of her body combined with the gentle rocking of the boat could easily have lulled her to sleep. She fought against that. The rapturous interlude would be over all too soon; she didn't want to miss the slightest part of it.

Time passed, she had no idea how much. Her body grew slightly stiff beneath his weight. Still she didn't move. Not until the light streaming through the porthole began to fade did she at last wake him.

Six

_____

There was a new moon that night, riding hidden above the clouds. A low wind blew out of the west. The water was all but still. So quiet was it that any sound, however faint, would travel for miles. It was three hours to dawn. They had chosen that time in hopes that the men in the other boat would be asleep with perhaps only a single guard left on watch. Fewer eyes and ears to avoid.

Lucas slipped a length of foam rubber over the deck where the chain would be let out. In a barely audible whisper, he said, "The same signals as before. Okay?"

Emily nodded. Her throat was too tight for her to speak. She knew this had to be done, but that didn't make it any easier to go through. They were standing on the port side of _Banshee_, behind the deckhouse, which they hoped would hide them from any prying eyes. Lucas had explained that the darkness would not help them escape detection if their pursuers had come equipped with infrared binoculars. He suspected they had.

The other boat was still anchored about a quarter-mile away. No lights were visible, but Emily thought she had caught a glimpse of movement when she came on deck. The rifles were out of their wrappings and propped against the deckhouse. If they were needed, they would be within easy reach.

"You've got the light?" she managed to murmur.

"Right here." He gestured to the large underwater flashlight he carried with him. It would be his sole illumination once he was submerged. The tanks on his back glinted darkly as he turned and slowly lowered himself down the ladder. Taking it step by step, he disappeared into the water without a splash. Emily's last sight of him was a reassuring grin and a thumbs-up signal. Then he was gone.

Despite the warm air, her hands felt cold as she began to feed out the chain. The winch had been carefully oiled and made no sound. Even so, she was tense with apprehension. The minutes dragged by, each weighing more heavily upon her. All too easily she could imagine what it must be like to be moving through impenetrable black water downward to the battered hulk of *Venturer*, with only a single ray of light to show his way.

Her stomach twisted painfully. It was all she could do to hold onto the chain and continue feeding it out, praying all the while that the dangerous gamble would succeed. Lucas's progress was much slower than it had been in daylight, but at length she felt the two tugs that meant he had reached the safe. Hardly breathing, she waited through a seemingly endless time until he tugged again, letting her know that it was time to begin reeling in the chain to right the three hundred pound steel box that contained the packet.

Would he open it down there? Not likely. He would have no way of knowing whether or not the diamonds were loose. If they were, they might easily float away on the current. No, he would wait until he was back on board to see what he had recovered.

The three tugs came finally and she began to reel the chain in, still going very slowly to avoid making any sound. She had barely finished before Lucas was lifting himself silently out of the water. "Got it," he whispered, the excitement evident in his voice. "Any trouble here?"

"No, not a thing. There's no sign that they have any idea what's going on."

"Good, let's hope it stays that way." He stripped off his equipment and headed below. Emily followed. Curtains were drawn over the portholes, but they were not heavy enough to block out light. The only place they could safely turn one on without being seen was in the windowless head. It wasn't built to take two people at a time, but they both managed to squeeze in nonetheless. Emily sat on the small counter next to the sink. Lucas stood in front of her. The packet was in his hands. It was small, about six inches long, and flat. The surface was shiny.

"Waterproof," he commented, looking at the rubberized wrapping. "Not really necessary for diamonds."

"No, I guess not."

He undid the fastenings. Inside was a slightly smaller package wrapped in plain brown paper and tied with string. "That's more like it," Lucas said. He quickly undid the wrappings and opened it.

Emily inhaled sharply. She had seen diamonds before, but never had she seen so many at one time of such size and clarity. They glittered in the pale light like shards torn out of the sun.

Lucas whistled softly. Under his breath, he said, "I can almost understand why people are willing to go to such lengths to possess these. They're magnificent."

"So is the wealth they represent," she murmured. "Two million dollars at current prices. It's hard to believe."

"I suppose Sentinal will be pleased," he said, rewrapping the package. "They'll recover their loss in full."

"Minus the two hundred thousand to you."

He cast her a quick glance. "I suppose that *is* a lot of money."

"Most people would feel that way."

"It's never meant that much to me, except for the freedom it buys."

Was freedom so precious to him then? It sounded like it. She pushed the thought aside and concentrated on more immediate matters. "We still have to get out of here."

"I haven't forgotten that. Let me get some shut-eye, and then we'll work on it."

She nodded and watched as he put the packet behind some wooden planks, then went down to his cabin to get some much deserved rest.

The remainder of the night passed slowly. Alone on deck, Emily had time to think over what had happened. No matter how she looked at it, there was nothing good about the situation. She still had to concentrate on getting the diamonds back to New York safely. Personal considerations had never been allowed to interfere with her professional responsibilities, and she wasn't about to let them start doing so now. However reluctant she was to face it, she had to accept the fact that what she had shared with Lucas might well be no more than a very brief interlude fated to be nothing more than a bittersweet memory.

Lying on the bunk where they had so recently made love, Lucas stared at the ceiling and tried not to think about Emily except in the most impersonal terms. He could not afford to be distracted from the overriding concern of how to get away from their pursuers, yet he found there were other dangers that concerned him.

Who was it who said love made idiots of men and survivors of women? Somebody must have, it was certainly true.

On that note, he fell asleep for a few hours, waking shortly after dawn when he went up on deck to join Emily.

After a breakfast eaten in silence, they got on the radio and patched through a call to Sentinal. Emily relayed the story they had agreed on.

"I'm afraid I have bad news," she began. "We reached the safe and found that it has already been opened."

The voice of her immediate superior at the firm, William Jeffers, sounded far away and slightly reedy. "That is a grave disappointment. Is Hawkins with you now?"

"I'm here," Lucas said.

"Do you have any idea who might have gotten in ahead of you?"

"'Fraid not. They didn't leave a calling card."

"And it was empty?"

"As Mother Hubbard's cupboard."

"May I suggest, sir," Emily broke in, "that you contact Mr. Goodway and let him know what we've discovered? He may have some idea of who's responsible." She hadn't planned to say that, but it made sense under the circumstances. Anyone listening in would expect her to be concerned about who had reached the safe first.

Jeffers certainly was. "I'll do that right away. Should I expect you back soon?"

"If you don't mind, I'd like to take a few days off and relax a bit."

"Certainly, you've more than earned it, even if everything hasn't worked out as I'd hoped. Enjoy yourself."

"He took it very well," Lucas said after they had signed off. "You'd never think Sentinal had just lost a fortune in diamonds."

"I hope they'll understand my reasons for misleading them. Do you think our watchdogs were listening in?"

"It's a fair bet. But that doesn't mean they'd buy the story. If we try to leave, they'll still make sure we don't get very far."

"I presume you don't intend to simply wait here?"

He glanced out the porthole and shook his head. "Not likely."

"Does that mean you have a plan?"

"Maybe."

"Good; the sooner I can get the diamonds to New York the better."

"You're going to try to fly them in yourself?" Lucas asked.

"I don't see that there's any alternative."

"Does Sentinal know about this?"

She nodded. "It's standard procedure in cases like this. The theory is that anyone wanting to steal something of great worth expects to find it surrounded by all sorts of security precautions. They'll be too busy looking for that to notice what's actually going on."

"Sounds very dangerous to me."

"It's worked many times before."

"Spare me the details." He didn't want to think about her undertaking such hazardous work. Once they got to shore he would have to figure out some alternative, but in the meantime he had his hands full eluding their pursuers.

"To get back to the matter at hand," Emily was saying, "do you have a plan for getting us out of here?"

"Yes, but you aren't going to like it."

"Why doesn't that surprise me?"

Despite himself, Lucas smiled. But only for an instant. The situation was too grim to find much humor in it. "There's only one way out of here for us," he said quietly. Then he explained what he had in mind.

Emily was pale long before he finished. She was thinking frantically, trying to come up with something, anything that would give them an alternative. She didn't have any luck.

"All right," she said at length. "If that's what you think we have to do."

"It is, so there's no point talking about it anymore." After a moment, he added, "How about some breakfast?"

She grimaced at the thought of food but then realized that she was hungry after all. Besides, cooking calmed her nerves. As Lucas went on deck to check the rigging—and keep an eye on the other boat—she made pancake batter, flavored it with a little nutmeg and ground lemon rind, and oiled the griddle. While maple syrup warmed in a saucepan, she ladled out the batter, waited until it began to bubble, then flipped each pancake once. In fifteen minutes she had a stack that she thought would satisfy even Lucas.

They ate in silence up on deck with the sunshade in place and a soft breeze blowing. Lucas helped himself to more syrup and took another bite. As he did so, he shot her a surreptitious look. It didn't seem fair somehow that a woman should be that good-looking, that much fun to be with, and a terrific cook. Whatever happened to sharing the wealth?

"These aren't bad," he said at length.

"Thanks."

"You made them like this when you were working in the diner?"

She looked up. Their eyes met. "Almost, but no spices. They didn't go in for fancy stuff."

"Must have been hard work."

She shrugged. "It was all right."

"Where did you live when you were working there?"

"I had a room."

Eighteen-years old, no family, a job slinging hash, and a room somewhere. Great life. "When did you join Sentinal?"

She took another sip of coffee and said, "When I got out of college."

"You must have climbed very fast."

"I got some breaks."

"And worked damn hard."

Emily shrugged. "So what? Hard work never hurt anyone."

"Your work is hard *and* risky. I don't even want to know how many times you must have put your neck on the line."

She smiled faintly. "Not as often as you may think. This is the biggest assignment I've ever had."

He'd already suspected that but was glad to have it confirmed; it gave him at least a little leverage with her. "Naturally you want to do it well."

"Of course."

"Has it occurred to you that you may be concentrating on that so much that you're overlooking your own safety?"

Emily met his eyes, seeing the worry in them. She felt oddly touched to know that he was so concerned about her, but she still felt compelled to straighten him out. "I can look after myself," she said firmly. "I've been doing it for a very long time now."

"But never in circumstances like this."

"I told you, I've never done a job exactly like this before. But I've always understood that if I continued to do well I'd eventually get a crack at it. That's what I've wanted."

"Why?" Lucas asked.

"Because...the better I do at Sentinal the more I get paid, and the more money I make, the more secure I feel. There's nothing strange about that."

"There is, when you have to take such big risks in order to get ahead. Where's the security in being tracked by a boatload of bad guys who would just as soon shoot you as look at you?"

"This is an exception," she insisted. "It will be over soon."

They continued to gaze at each other for a long moment, then Lucas nodded abruptly and stood up. He started to clear the table and Emily quickly helped him. "What do we do the rest of today?" she asked, no longer looking at him.

He shrugged. "Play tourist."

"They'll know we're faking," she said, tilting her head slightly toward the other boat.

"Yeah, but they won't be sure what it means."

That would have to do. For the next several hours they stayed on deck, reading and sunbathing. After lunch, Lucas got out a couple of fishing rods and they tried their luck. He caught a good-sized grouper, which she offered to fix for dinner. "It'll be good with the plantains," she said.

Lucas nodded absently. "I'm going for a swim." He dived in and swam around for a while, occasionally diving under the boat as though checking out the hull. In fact, he was getting warmed up for later that night, when he would carry out his plan.

"There's a new moon," he said a while later as they were watching the sun go down.

"You're still going through with it?"

"You thought of another way?"

She shook her head. In a very low voice, she said, "Be careful."

He took the rifles that still stood resting against the deckhouse and went below to oil them. After a while she came down and fixed dinner. Neither ate very much. Around ten o'clock they turned the lights off, hoping it would look as though they had gone to bed.

Some four hours later, Lucas lowered himself over the side and into the water. He was dressed in a black diving suit with a hood that covered his hair. His face was smeared with engine grease. Strapped to his waist was a ten-inch knife. In his hand was a spear gun.

"You're not James Bond, you know," Emily muttered as she crouched on the deck watching him.

"It's a piece of cake."

"Crazy macho lunatic."

He grinned whitely in the darkness. "You keep talking so sweet to me, I won't want to go."

Before she could comment, he was gone, vanishing into the black water with barely a ripple.

Emily stayed where she was, staring at the other boat. She could see nothing except the faintly white glint of its hull slowly rising and falling with the current. At least one man would be awake, standing watch. What if there were more?

"They'll be bored by now," Lucas had said. "Guys like that have a short attention span. They start to lose interest after being on guard twelve hours a day. Maybe they're drinking a little more than they should; maybe they aren't paying quite as close attention. It gives me an edge."

"Maybe you're wrong," she had countered.

"That's always a possibility."

Why couldn't he lie to her when she wanted him to?

Her eyes felt very dry. She realized that she was staring so hard she wasn't blinking. She closed her eyes for an instant, then opened them again. Nothing had changed. She had no idea where Lucas was, but reason told her he had to be very close to the other boat. Could he get out of the water and onto the deck without being heard?

He could and he had. His bare feet moved noiselessly toward the prow where he had spotted the guard. Reflexes trained long ago in a jungle thousands of miles away and sharpened up occasionally since then did not desert him now. The guard was tall, almost Lucas's height, and probably a few years younger. But he had no idea what hit him when a single, soundless chop to his throat drove the blood from his head and knocked him unconscious.

So far, so good. He figured he had about twenty minutes before the guard even thought of stirring. If he wasn't done in five, he didn't deserve to make it.

Below deck it was very quiet. He caught the faint sound of snoring from the direction of the staterooms, but bypassed them quickly and eased open the trap door that led to the engine. Beneath it was a crawl space barely large enough for a man to kneel in. He lowered himself into it and went to work. The quickest way to disable the engine was to remove the spark plugs, but there might be spares on board. He was willing to bet, though, that they weren't carrying an extra crankshaft. He removed that, and for good measure punched several holes in the fuel tanks, the main and auxiliary.

Nobody stirred as he climbed out of the crawl space and made his way back on deck. The guard was still out cold. He lowered himself into the water, let the crankshaft go and waited while it sank. Then he swam back to *Banshee*.

"You took your time," Emily said as he came back on board. Her voice shook, and despite her best efforts, she looked scared.

"When you're having fun, you don't like to rush it." His breezy tone faded away as he saw the fear in her eyes. He wanted to ignore it, but somehow he couldn't. A soft groan broke from her as he held out his arms.

She went into them unhesitatingly and nestled against him like a small animal seeking warmth. He wrapped his arms around her and held her tightly. Never mind that he was soaking wet and she was becoming the same. At that moment, nothing mattered except providing comfort to her.

He was angry at Sentinal for sending her on such a job. What the hell were they thinking of? She had about as much business being there as he, Lucas, did going to a fancy tea party. Not that he'd tell her that; she'd just be insulted. It was important to her to be tough, and she was in her own way. But not tough enough to deal with men who threw people away like used tissues.

"It's okay, honey," he murmured against her hair. "We're going to get out of here."

She nodded and murmured something he didn't quite catch but that sounded like his name. After a moment he released her and they stood apart, not looking directly at each other. "Come on," he said softly. "I'm going to need some help."

Generally he didn't sail at night, especially when there was no moon and clouds obscured the stars. Caribbean waters had almost no navigational markers. Compass headings had to be taken continually to avoid running up on one of the numerous reefs or sandbars. More than a few good ships had been lost that way. If he hadn't known the area around Barbados so well, he wouldn't have wanted even to risk it. But he would still have had to, considering the circumstances.

"I knocked the guard out," he told Emily, "but he ought to be back on his feet in a few minutes, and he'll give the alarm. It'll take them a little while longer to realize they're disabled, but in the meantime there's nothing to prevent them from starting to shoot."

He had barely spoken when a light suddenly shone on the other boat, followed quickly by another and another. Sounds of raised, angry voices reached them across the water.

"That's it then," Lucas said. "No sense worrying anymore about how much noise we make. Let's get the engine going and hightail it out of here."

The first shot ricocheted off the deckhouse even as the engine fired to life. *Banshee* normally ran under sail, but she still boasted an engine that would have done a medium-sized power yacht proud. Lucas pushed the throttle wide open even as the second shot rang out.

"Keep down," he yelled to Emily. "We can't count on those guys having as lousy an aim as yours."

She wasn't listening to him. One of the rifles was propped under her right arm, and she was sighting down the scope with her finger on the trigger.

"Get going," she said calmly. "They're putting out a rubber raft with two guys in it."

That was all Lucas needed to hear. As Emily gave cover fire, he got the anchor reeled in in record time, brought

Banshee up to full power and roared away from the reef, leaving an angry surge of white water behind them.

"Are they still trying to follow us?" he asked a few moments later, his eyes glued to the compass headings.

She answered from directly beside him. "Not hardly. I shot the raft."

He spared a quick glance in her direction. "You did what?"

"The raft. I shot it. It's sinking." A little smugly, she added, "I guess my aim got better."

"Depends."

"On what?"

"On whether or not you meant to hit the men."

Her eyes widened slightly. "No, I didn't."

He hadn't really thought so, but he figured he should take the opportunity to make a point. "It may come to that. Do you think you could do it if you had to?"

"Why worry about it?" she countered. "We got away."

"We bought a little time," he corrected. "They'll radio in and another boat will be after us fast, along with spotter planes. Our only chance is to hide out until the heat dies down a little and we can make for port."

So saying, he gunned the engine and headed *Banshee* swiftly through the night.

Seven

It was dawn when they reached the small, uninhabited island southwest of Barbados. The coastline was rocky with breakers pounding directly against the jutting sides of cliffs. There seemed to be no natural anchorage, until Lucas brought *Banshee* in past the breakers and guided her up between two spits of land to a hidden lagoon nestled between verdant hills.

"It'll be tough to spot us here," he said as he killed the engine and let the anchor down. "Especially since they won't have expected us to head in this direction."

"Where do you think they will be looking?" Emily asked. She was almost numb with the combined effects of fear and exhaustion, but she felt as though she might never sleep again.

"On Barbados. They'll have the boatyards and the airport covered."

"You think they know I'm supposed to take the diamonds to New York?"

He turned around and looked at her, taking in the pallor of her skin and the way her eyelids drooped. It wouldn't take much more than a stiff breeze to knock her over. Instead of answering directly, he said gently, "You'd better get some rest."

"I'm fine."

He started to say something, but thought better of it. She was a grown-up woman, not some little kid. If she didn't have the sense to know when she was done in, it wasn't his problem.

Except that he hated seeing her so worn-out and vulnerable. He wanted to pick her up and comfort her and keep her safe. Talk about crazy.

"Okay then," he said shortly. "Since you don't want to rest, you can take the first watch."

Emily nodded and looked away as he went below deck. She was so tired that she felt ready to cry, but she wouldn't admit it even to herself. After all, Lucas had done all the work and taken all the risks. It was only right that she do her part now.

It was very pretty in the little lagoon. Birds fluttered around, fish darted near the surface of the water and a gentle breeze blew. She could smell wild nutmeg and pepper. There was a narrow strip of golden beach on either side. Lapped by tiny waves and sheltered by the palm trees, it would be a perfect spot for lovers.

Emily's throat tightened. For the first time in her life, she had really come to understand what that word meant. Lovers. I love, you love, we love. What they had shared in bed had only been an expression of that.

She sighed and sat down on the deck. People liked to think that love was pure and untouchable, immune to the vagaries of fate. But that was wrong. Especially at the beginning, it was a terribly delicate thing, like a wisp of smoke rising from a smoldering fire. The fire could be fed and grow stronger, or it could be smothered and die.

She closed her eyes briefly in a quick spasm of pain. From the very beginning she had known that whatever she shared with Lucas would be temporary. She had never let herself forget that. So why wasn't she better prepared for what had happened?

The inside of her lids burned with tears she would not let herself shed. Sitting there in the midst of what was as close to paradise as any place on earth, only steps away from the man she loved, she felt more miserable than she ever had in her life. The frightened child had not suffered as much as the sorrowful woman. Perhaps because the child had understood the futility of love.

Somewhere along the line she had forgotten that. She had abandoned the first and most important rule of survival—self-sufficiency. She had let herself care—not about the big impersonal mass of humanity, but about one very special man.

She forced her eyes open and looked out over the water. How long could they stay there? A day? Two? Sooner or later their pursuers would close in on them. They would have to fight, or run again and keep on running until they either reached safety or were killed. Were the odds at least in their favor? She rather doubted it.

The thought that they might both die sometime in the immediate future snuffed out the last little bit of light left in her spirit. She recognized the deadening depression for what it was, a by-product of nervous exhaustion. But that didn't make it any easier to deal with.

She was still sitting there, fighting against the dark wave of despair, when a movement at her side brought her upright. Lucas had come on deck. He was dressed in shorts and an open shirt. His hair was mussed, as though he had been running his hands through it. At her quizzical look, he shrugged. "I couldn't sleep." Lowering himself beside her, he rested his arms on his bent knees and said, "Worrying won't do any good."

She sighed and leaned her head back against the deckhouse. "I know, but I can't seem to help it."

"Are you scared about what might happen?"

"There is that, but it's what *won't* happen now that hurts more." She was silent for a moment before going on. "Ever since the beginning of this, I've been wishing that we had met under different circumstances."

"It's the same for me," Lucas said at length. "I keep wondering whether the woman I'm so attracted to is real or a figment of my imagination."

She smiled faintly. "I can assure you that I'm real."

"That doesn't solve my problem."

"Which is?"

"How much I've come to care for you."

His stark honesty took her aback. She hadn't expected him to be so forthcoming about his feelings, especially not when she was trying so hard to deny her own.

Gathering her courage, she said softly, "I've come to care for you, too. That's really what scares me, far more than whoever is following us. You're so... different from everything else in my life."

He smiled faintly. "I can say the same about you."

"It's true. We're the proverbial ships that pass in the night." She was so tired now that her words were slightly slurred. "I can't see how it could be any different."

Gently, not denying what she had said, he murmured, "I'd be surprised if you could see anything, you're so tired."

This time she didn't contradict him. Instead, she said, "I read somewhere that fear is exhausting. It's true."

"There's no reason to be afraid, at least not right now." As he spoke, he put his arm around her shoulders and drew her against him. She went without hesitation, which he took to be a measure of her fatigue. "We both don't have to be awake," he murmured as he settled her more comfortably.

"Hmmm." Her eyelids fluttered shut. As he watched, her breathing slowed down and became deeper. The hand she had braced slightly against his chest relaxed and slid down a little, the fingers half-curled.

He held her like that for a while, then lifted her and carried her below deck. Beside the couch where she had been sleeping, he paused for a moment before going on to his cabin. After laying her on his bunk, he covered her with a thin sheet and stood looking down at her.

She seemed as innocent and defenseless as a child, but he knew she was a great deal more than that. No child could ever have made him ache as much as she did.

Emily woke up shortly after noon. She sat up stiffly and glanced around, not sure at first where she was. A fuzzy feeling of disorientation filled her. The last thing she remembered was being up on deck with Lucas. It took a moment to realize that she must have fallen asleep and he had carried her down to the stateroom.

Not wanting to ponder too closely the significance of his putting her in his bunk, she got up and went into the head to splash cold water on her face. Somewhat revived, she got out the coffeepot, put it on the stove to brew and went up on deck.

Another storm was approaching. Heavy gray clouds slipped across the sky. The tops of the hillsides were wreathed in mist. The wind had picked up and the water in the hidden lagoon was becoming a little choppy.

"How does it look to you?" she asked as she joined Lucas.

"Like the season's first tropical storm. I've been monitoring the weather frequency and it sounds as though we're in for a hard blow."

"Isn't it early for that?"

He nodded. "Yes, but remember what I told you about Mother Nature moving up her timetable? At any rate, we're well sheltered, and the storm will buy us more time. Anybody stupid enough to look for us in this weather won't last long."

Emily could see what he meant. A glance at the sky was enough to tell her that no pilot, however well paid, would choose to fly in such weather. And as for the sea, if the lagoon was anything to go by, the water outside was extremely turbulent. Even the most accomplished sailor would find it dangerous going. "So we just sit tight?" she asked.

"There's not much else we can do. We've got plenty of food, water and fuel, so we should be fine. Chances are the storm will have blown itself out by tomorrow."

The unexpected gift of a day free from the fear of imminent discovery buoyed Emily's spirits. She went below deck to start a fish stew simmering, then decided to bake several loaves of bread. While she was doing all that, the wind picked up further and heavy drops of rain began to lash the closed portholes.

Lucas came in after setting both the bow and stern anchors, as well as running a line onto shore and tying it to one of the large palm trees. Just in case they had to get away quickly, he could cut the line from deck. But he thought it highly unlikely that he would have to do so, and at any rate the line gave them that much extra stability.

He sat down by the small table where he kept his navigational charts and flipped on the radio. At first there was only static, but that soon cleared. Emily came to stand beside him, wiping her floury hands on a towel, as they listened.

"Winds of up to fifty knots," the commentator said, "with heavy seas and steady rain. The storm is on a northwest path, heading toward Barbados and adjoining islands where it is expected to hit later this afternoon. Stay tuned to this frequency for further reports."

"Well, that's it," Lucas said. "We won't be going anywhere for a while."

He didn't seem too concerned about that prospect. On the contrary, he gave every appearance of being perfectly content to sit back and watch Emily as she moved around in the galley. She kneaded the dough, then put it aside to rise while she seasoned the fish stew. His steady regard made her self-conscious and at length she said, "You're very quiet."

He shrugged lightly. "I don't get much chance to see domesticity in action. It's . . . enjoyable."

A faint blush warmed her cheeks. She told herself it was from the heat of the oven. "There's no big deal about making bread and fixing a stew."

"You don't think so? It looked very intricate and . . . graceful. Did you know that you have a great economy of movement, never a wasted motion? Almost like a dancer.''

Emily shot him a narrow glance, wondering if he was teasing her. But his expression was perfectly serious, and after a moment, she accepted that he meant what he said. "You're the same way, you know," she murmured. "I've seen you when you're putting up the sails or doing other things around the boat." Embarrassed by the admission that she had been watching him, she looked away.

Silence stretched out between them until at length Lucas said, "I guess we'd better find something to keep ourselves amused for a while."

"Yes . . . I guess so. . . ."

"Do you play cards?"

The tension that had been building in her over the past few minutes eased and she laughed. "Only poker."

He didn't hide his surprise. "Really? Not many women play that."

"Oh, I'm not very good at it." She widened her eyes and let the lashes flutter slightly.

He grinned broadly. "Why do I get the feeling I'm being hustled?"

"Would I do a thing like that?"

As he got out the cards and cleared the table, he nodded firmly. "In a second."

"You've had a little practice at this yourself," Emily said a short while later as she studied her cards. She had won the first hand but lost the second. Lucas played well and gave no clue as to his strategy.

"I've sat in on a game from time to time," he deadpanned. "Where did you learn to play?"

"At school, believe it or not. It was a favorite recess pastime."

He shook his head ruefully. "What ever happened to jacks and jump rope?"

"I think they went the way of the hoop skirt and the buggy whip."

"Straight."

She stared at the cards he had just laid down and grimaced. "That's another ten cents I owe you."

"I'm keeping track."

He dealt another hand. They played on largely in companionable silence. Emily took that round with a flush but lost the next to three of a kind. By the time the fish stew was ready there was all of a dollar in change lying on the table.

"I don't know," she said wryly. "This is getting a little rich for my blood."

He wiggled his eyebrows at her. "Want to play strip instead?"

She pretended to think about that for a moment, then shook her head. "It wouldn't be very sporting. We're hardly wearing any clothes as it is."

He'd noticed. The shorts she had on came barely to the top of her long, golden thighs and her thin T-shirt did little to hide the rounded swell of her breasts. It was all he could do to concentrate on the game.

Emily was having a similar problem. How did he manage to make frayed cutoffs and an old cotton shirt look seductive? There ought to be a law against that. She remembered all too clearly what it felt like to be nestled against his broad chest, enveloped in his hard arms and touched by the big hands with long, blunt-tipped fingers that . . .

Jerking her errant thoughts back to the game, she said, "I'll raise you a penny."

"That much?"

"I'm on a roll."

He shrugged and went along. It was getting darker outside. The wind had picked up and *Banshee* rolled with the chop. Rain lashed the deck and struck in heavy drops against the portholes. Lucas lost the hand and got up to catch the weather report. Nothing much had changed, except that the storm was now upon them. It was expected to last through the rest of that day and night before blowing off around morning.

Around six P.M., they called a halt to the game—with Emily ahead eleven cents—and had dinner. The fish stew, made with the grouper they had caught and some shrimp from the freezer, and seasoned with dill and cayenne, went well with the chilled bottle of Pouilly-Fuissé that Lucas opened. While the dough she had prepared earlier was still rising, she warmed the rolls from the day before in the microwave and served them with herbed butter.

It was very cozy in the cabin. Outside they could hear the wind whistling around the mast and thumping up against the hull, but inside everything was warm and dry. Music played softly over the radio. They talked little, but their eyes met often.

Taking a sip of her wine, Emily studied Lucas over the rim of her glass. The need to make love with him again was so strong that she could barely endure it. The darkness in his eyes suggested he felt the same way, yet he showed no inclination to take the initiative as he had before.

She would have to do something about that. But what? She'd never been much good at flirting, having an unfortunate tendency to giggle at the wrong times, and she didn't think she'd be much better at outright seduction. Vague visions of sultry vamps and pouting Lolitas darted through her mind. Neither role suited her.

Her front teeth worked the soft inner flesh of her lower lip as she contemplated her predicament. Was it like this for men? Did they go through these tortuous mazes of longing and indecision? How awful. No wonder Lucas had opted for the direct approach.

It had worked, too.

They finished dinner and he helped her clean up. Working together in the small galley, it was inevitable that they would keep bumping into each other. Arms brushed, legs touched, there were several mumbled "excuse me's" and awkward glances. Finally the dishes were done.

"Would you like a brandy?" Lucas suggested, knowing that he could certainly do with one himself. When she nodded, he poured generous measures into two snifters and carried them over to the couch. "That was a very nice dinner," he said as he sat down beside her.

"I'm glad you liked it."

Silence. He felt like a teenager on his first date. The sheer range and intensity of emotion she provoked in him left him bewildered and unsure how to react.

Did she have any idea how good she smelled? He had thought at first that it was some perfume she wore, but then he realized that the light, tantalizing scent was natural. He had found it all over her body, from the tips of her small pink toes to the top of her silken hair and in all the luscious places in between.

Why the hell did he have to think of that? It was bad enough just knowing how much pleasure she had given him without remembering all the erotic details. He stirred restlessly and took another sip of the brandy.

Emily was staring into her snifter as though it held the secrets of the universe. She couldn't recall when she had felt so tongue-tied, or so ridiculous. Surely a thirty-year-old woman should have some idea of how to let a man know she was interested.

"Lucas...?"

"Yes," he said quickly, relieved that she had broken the silence.

"I've...uh...been thinking."

"What about?"

"Us." Gathering her courage, she went on hastily, "I know what you're going to say: there is no us, only two people who happened to have been thrown together and will soon go their separate ways."

Actually, he hadn't been about to say anything of the kind, but he let her go on anyway.

"I realize neither one of us wants to get hurt...."

A deep sigh escaped him. He shut his eyes for a moment and opened them again to see her peering at him anxiously. Despite himself, the corners of his mouth quirked. Quietly, he said, "That may be unavoidable."

"I'm sorry," she murmured.

"So am I. For the first time in my life, I wish I was a different person. Someone very...stable, straight-arrow, with a regular life and security to offer you. But I'm not, and I think it's a little late in the day to try to change."

"I know...." She broke off, not looking at him. Regret welled up in her.

"The thing is," he said, "if we went on the way we were, it's only going to make parting harder."

There it was then. He was letting her know, not unkindly, that he didn't want to risk resuming their affair. Such a tacky word. She didn't like it at all and, besides, it didn't describe what they had shared. Perhaps no words could. "I understand," she murmured, staring into her brandy. "In your place, I'd probably feel the same way."

"Probably?"

She shrugged. "I don't know, it just seems so...wasteful."

He didn't have to ask what she meant. What had happened between them was special, something set apart from all prior experiences. It was meant to be savored, cherished, nurtured for whatever time it might be theirs—not turned away from because life offered no guarantees.

"Has it occurred to you," he asked softly, "that this isn't the best time to begin to care for someone else, with all that it entails?"

"You mean because of the danger we're in?"

He nodded.

"We can't always pick when things will happen to us." And we can't always control our emotions, either, she added silently.

"Are you sure you know what's happening to us, Emily?"

The question was asked so seriously that she could not dismiss it. They were from completely different worlds and would never have met but for a trick of fate. If the mission succeeded, they would part in the next few days and in all likelihood never see each other again. If it failed, everything else would be moot.

She knew all that, as surely as she knew her own name. Yet she didn't want to admit any of it. This tendency to evade the truth was completely unlike her; she hadn't gotten where she was by refusing to face up to reality, no matter how painful. Yet she shied away from it this time, sensing that there were some pains too great to bear.

Looking up, she met his eyes. "I know what I'd like to be happening."

This time the risk was hers; she was the one asking. He could always say no. He knew how important this job was to her career, and he'd resolved never to touch her again. So much for strength of will and all that.

His hand touched her cheek gently, tracing the satiny smoothness of her skin to the delicate line of her jaw and around to the curve of her chin. She arched slightly under his touch, like a cat wanting to be stroked. Memories of how she had been coursed through him. He remembered the sweet inner heat of her, the soft cries she made, and the fierce strength of her response. And he also remembered the light in her eyes afterward, happiness touched by wonder, as though she had never expected such a thing to happen to her and still couldn't quite believe that it had. He suspected that he had looked much the same.

A quiver ran through Emily, like deep water rippling beneath the wind. Her need for him was so great that she could barely contain it. It almost drowned out the little voice in the back of her mind that wondered why Lucas was doing this. Almost, but not quite. She knew him well enough now to understand that he was a man who, once set on a course, did not turn away from it easily. He had made up his mind to keep his distance from her, yet he was going back on that. Why? Because he was caught in the same maelstrom of desire that gripped her, or for some other reason she could not glimpse?

She should think about that, try to figure it out. But not just then. Not when his hand was slipping beneath her T-shirt to cup her breasts lightly, the calloused tip of his thumb rubbing in a slow circular motion over her engorged nipple.

Emily moaned deep in her throat. She was barely aware when Lucas drew her up on his lap, her slender legs stretched out on the couch and her back supported by his strong arm. Beneath the thin fabric of her shorts and panties she could feel the hard urgency of him pressing against her buttocks. Instinctively, she moved and was rewarded by a sound somewhere between a gasp and a growl.

Emboldened by his response, she undid the buttons of his shirt and slid her hands down his chest His skin was warm, almost hot. Soft, curling hairs tickled her palms. She lingered at his navel, and they shared a smile before she set to work on the zipper of his cut-offs.

He leaned forward and seized the lobe of her ear between his teeth, biting gently before he murmured, "It's your turn to carry me into the bedroom."

"So emancipated."

"Hey, I've had my consciousness raised."

"Well . . . *something's* been raised."

He laughed ruefully. "It's got a mind of its own."

"Not just a mind, a whole personality." Her fingers closed lightly around the object in question and were nuzzled appreciatively.

Long, sweet moments passed during which their breaths grew increasingly ragged. At length, Lucas murmured, "If you won't carry me, I'll walk."

"That might be better."

They rose a little unsteadily and, with their arms around each other's waists, their clothes hanging in disarray, managed to make their way to his stateroom. Emily distantly noticed that the storm was still lashing the boat. She gave it no further thought. The storm within her was far more enthralling.

Lucas smiled as he lifted the hem of her T-shirt and eased the garment over her head. Her bra quickly followed. He bent slightly at the knees and raked her nipple lightly with his teeth. Her fingers tangled in his thick hair, and her legs threatened to give way. His hands slid down her back until he was cupping the cheeks of her buttocks, urging her against him even as he held her upright for his ministrations.

Emily felt the cool wood of the floor beneath her toes as they curled under. She felt the rhythmic rocking of the boat that seemed to match the strong sucking at her breast. And she felt the aching emptiness inside her, demanding to be filled.

"Lucas...please..."

He went on a moment longer, heedless of her entreaty. Only when she thought she could not possibly bear it a moment longer did he finally look up. His hazel eyes were dark with thoughts and emotions she could not read, or perhaps did not want to. Beneath his tan, a flush darkened his cheeks. His mouth was drawn taut in a line somewhere between anger and resentment.

"L-Lucas...?"

He didn't want this, damn it. Not with all the emotion thrown in and the horrible feeling of vulnerability. He wanted to be able simply to take her and enjoy her and not think about what lay ahead. Or more important, what did not. No strings, no commitments, no hassles. That was how he had lived his life for years now and it worked fine. Except that he felt so damn empty inside.

His big hands stroked down the length of her back, relishing the touch of silk-smooth skin. She was so beautiful and so giving, how could he resist all that she offered? The lightly perfumed hollow between her collarbones was warm beneath his lips. With the tip of his tongue, he felt the drumbeat of her pulse and knew it was as urgent as his own. The thick ridge of muscles in his chest tightened spasmodically.

He stopped and raised his head, holding her a little away from him as he gazed at her. What made her different from all the other women he had known?

Why couldn't he simply enjoy her without thoughts of the future?

Sex should be simple and wholesome, like going for an invigorating run or eating a good meal. Some analogy, he thought grimly. Why didn't he just admit that he couldn't have sex with Emily? It was making love or nothing. What was that supposed to mean anyway? You couldn't *make* love; it was either there or it wasn't.

She was puzzled, he could see that in her eyes; maybe even a little scared. Regret washed over him. He couldn't stand the idea of her being afraid of him, not even a little bit.

"I'm sorry," he murmured thickly. Before she could respond, he lifted her and carried her to the bed. They fell across it holding each other; their arms and legs tangled together, their bodies pressing close.

He turned over on his back, drawing her with him. Her hair drifted across his chest. "Emily," he murmured hoarsely, "I need you so much."

She didn't stop to question why that admission seemed wrung from him. Instead, she concentrated on enjoying the freedom of being able to touch him as she wished. Her tongue played over his flat nipples, teasing them until they swiftly hardened.

His responsiveness emboldened her to go further. First with her hands, then with her mouth, she traced the line of hair stretching down his chest and across his flat abdomen to his groin. There it blossomed into a soft, thick nest for his manhood.

Gently, she took him in her hands, savoring the driving fullness of him. The musky fragrance of his arousal mingled with her own. She bent her head, stroking him first with her hair, then with her lips.

Lucas cried out her name. He bore the sweet torment of her caress as long as possible, then grasped her arms and drew her upright. Their eyes met as she settled over him and drew him within.

He was a wild horse, untouched by bridle or saddle. She was the wind, riding lightly on him. Together they raced across a field of golden sunlight rising higher and higher until all thought of everything except the single incandescent moment dissolved and there was nothing except the two of them.

And finally there wasn't even that. They were together, moving as one, feeling as one, bound up together in the ultimate dance set to cosmic music that was part prayer, part promise.

Please, don't let this end, Lucas thought just before he fell asleep with her still locked in his arms.

Please, let us have a chance, Emily thought as she tumbled after him into dreams rent by visions of inescapable danger.

Eight

————

Morning came too soon and brought with it an end to the storm. Emily and Lucas did not talk about what had happened between them. Words would shatter the tentative measure of trust attained in the night—a trust founded more on the need for each other than on any faith in what the future might hold.

Lucas hesitated to bring up what was on his mind but finally over breakfast, he said, "Like it or not, we have to plan for the worst. If something should happen to us, I'd just as soon the bad guys didn't get the diamonds."

"Of course," Emily agreed. "Perhaps we could hide them somewhere on board."

"That's the first place they'd think of. No, we have to think of another place."

"Somewhere in Barbados, if we can make it that far?"

"And if we can't? I think our best bet is to hide them right here on this island."

Emily looked at him in surprise. "But there's nothing here. It's just an empty island."

"All the better for our purposes. The old pirates picked places like this for hiding their valuables; there's no reason for us not to do the same."

"Buried treasure?" she murmured thoughtfully. "Basil mentioned that back at Devil's Reef, but I never really thought all those stories were true."

"Most weren't," Lucas admitted, "but there was some truth to the basic idea. There were pirate captains who amassed such large fortunes that from time to time they kept part of their wealth buried on remote islands to protect it. My guess is that almost all of it was long since dug up and spent, but there may still be a cache or two hidden in these parts. At any rate, it's the best way I can think of to thwart whoever's after us." He didn't mention that it was also the best way he could think of to protect Emily herself.

"All right," she agreed. "But we'll need something to put them in."

Lucas found a small steel box he had once used for storing screws and nails. He placed the diamonds, still in their original wrapping, inside and fastened it securely.

They left *Banshee* riding at anchor and took the dinghy the short distance to the beach. As she walked beside him along the stretch of golden sand, Emily was struck yet again by the incongruity of their circumstances. They should have been setting off to picnic beneath the spreading palm trees, snorkel in the crystal clear turquoise waters, make love in a secluded spot far from any prying eyes. Instead they were seeking to foil forces that might prove too strong for them personally and from whom they might have only the slimmest chance of wresting victory.

"This looks as good a place as any," Lucas said after they had walked for perhaps fifteen minutes toward the interior of the island. It was hotter here, away from the sea breeze. The drone of mosquitoes undercut the stillness. A macaw swooped out of a nearby tree, startling Emily. "Take it easy," he said gently. "This won't take long."

She nodded. "Shouldn't we make a map?"

"And have someone find it?" He gestured toward the small pond that lay over a slight rise to their left. "This is the northwest corner of the island. Look around and remember the landmarks—that pond, the gnarled tree over there, that large rock. Could you recognize the place again?"

"Yes, I think so."

"Then we don't need a map." He paced off ten feet from the far side of the rock and struck a shovel into the sand. It took less than five minutes to dig a hole deep and wide enough for the box. As Emily watched, he lowered it in and carefully refilled the hole. When that was done, he smoothed the surrounding sand so that it did not look as though anyone had dug there recently. "That should do it," he said when he was finished.

"Let's hope it doesn't have to stay there for long," she said.

"I've been thinking about that," he told her as they started back to the boat. "Basically, we've got two choices: we can try to make a run for it or we can stay where we are. Both have drawbacks. This island isn't very well known, but there's a chance we might be found. On the other hand, if we leave we have to cross open water again where it's much easier to be spotted."

"We can't just stay here," she protested. "Until I can get the diamonds to New York, we'll both be in danger."

Lucas hesitated before he said, "I'd hold off on trying to do that if I were you."

She turned and looked at him in surprise. "Why?"

"No reason, exactly. Just a feeling I've got."

"Intuition?" She smiled slightly. "That's supposed to be my line."

"Yours, mine, what difference does it make?" They were back on the beach where the dinghy waited when he said, "I

feel very strongly that we should stay put for a few days,
Emily, and I'd like you to agree to that."

She hesitated, not sure what to say to him. What he really
seemed to be asking was that she trust him. The more practical side of her mind was against that. They had known
each other only a few days, hardly enough to be sure that he
deserved her faith. And yet . . . in that short space of time,
she believed she had learned a great deal about him, on a
level where deception was all but impossible. Certainly she
would be taking a risk to go along with him, but she had to
think it was justified. That or turn her back on everything
she felt for him.

"All right," she said slowly, "I'll wait a few days. But not
longer than that. There's too much at stake."

"I agree," he said, obviously relieved that she wasn't
going to argue. He sat down, facing her in the dinghy, and
began to row them back to the boat, thinking that he had
bought himself some breathing room to try to decide how to
get them both out of the mess they were in. Now all he had
to do was come up with a plan. The situation reminded him
a little of a tight spot he'd gotten into in 'Nam when he was
on a patrol that . . .

"Lucas?"

He broke off his train of thought. She was staring straight
ahead at the rapidly approaching deck of *Banshee*. Her
voice was unnaturally tight and her eyes were suddenly huge.
He turned and followed the direction of her glance, staring
straight at the barrel of an automatic rifle.

"Nice to see you again, laddie," Captain Barnaby
Thatcher called across the short distance separating them.
"Put your back into those oars, and gie yourselves up here."

"What the hell . . . ?"

"Now, now, none of that. Especially not in front of the
lady. Nice to see you again, too, Miss Nolan." Barnaby
smiled through his thick red beard and, with his free hand,
tipped his captain's hat. He looked much as he had when

Emily last saw him, dressed in a frayed blue shirt that strained over his belly and khaki shorts that did little for his bowed legs. Ridiculous he might be, but there was no denying that the rifle lent him a certain authority.

Beside him, Basil grinned sheepishly. He was also armed, with the other rifle, but looked more embarrassed than threatening.

"I'm warning you, Barnaby," Lucas said the moment he set foot on the deck, "I'm in no mood for jokes. Put that damn thing down and tell me what you're doing here."

"You'd do better to speak more courteously, laddie. It's never a good idea to rile a man while he's holding a gun on you."

"Thanks for the advice," Lucas muttered. "Now you want to tell me what the hell's going on?"

"Right you are, laddie. I'll get directly to the point. I've come for those diamonds of yours."

"D-diamonds...?" Emily sputtered. "But how did you know...?"

"What she means to say," Lucas interrupted with a sharp glance at her, "is that you're welcome to stay for a beer and a meal, but anything more than that would be straining the limits of hospitality." In a softer voice that was somehow more dangerous, he added, "I might also point out that this little joke is getting old fast. You'd be wise to put that gun down now."

Barnaby shook his head. "You've got thirty years on me, laddie, not to mention a good eight inches and forty pounds. I figure I've got to have something to even that out."

"Maybe take more dan dat gun, Cap'tin," Basil said softly, exchanging a worried look with Emily. "Might be smart to do wha' Lucas says."

"Some pirate you make," Barnaby scoffed. "Should have left you back at the reef."

Behind him, Davey Jones fluttered his feathers and looked morose, while the ginger cat simply glared. Barnaby went nowhere without his parrot and cat.

"What did you get involved in this for anyway, Basil?" Lucas asked.

The large black man shrugged. "Figure somebody better keep an eye on de cap'tin so he don't get hurt none."

Lucas nodded thoughtfully and in the same moment, seemingly without pause or thought, launched himself across the deck straight at Barnaby. They went down in a crash, the rifle landing harmlessly some distance away. The scuffle lasted barely a moment. When it was over, Basil put the rifle he'd been holding back onto the deck with an audible sigh of relief.

"Glad dat's over. You all right, Cap'tin?"

Barnaby didn't answer. He was slumped over, holding his head in his hands. His bowed legs were stretched out in front of him and his chest heaved painfully. Lucas stood over him, not even breathing hard. Compassion softened his features as he held out a hand to the older man and said gently. "Come on."

After a moment, Barnaby accepted and, with Lucas's assistance, stood up. He sighed deeply. "Guess I'm not the man I used to be."

"I'll make some coffee," Emily offered. She didn't wait for a response before going below deck. The scene just now had upset her. She felt at once sorry for Barnaby and grateful to Lucas for handling him as gently as possible. But she was also vividly aware that if the red-bearded captain could find them, so could someone else.

By the time she returned, carrying a tray of cups and the coffee, the men were seated in the prow. The incident might never have occurred but for Barnaby's lingering look of embarrassment.

"So you heard rumors about the diamonds in Grenada," Lucas was saying. "Any idea who was spreading them?"

Barnaby shook his head. "It was just the usual barroom talk, nothing special. If I hadn't known about you taking off all the sudden with Miss Nolan," he inclined his head in Emily's direction, "it wouldn't have meant anything to me."

"How did you know where to look for us?" Lucas asked as he accepted a cup.

"I remembered you like to come here, but that not many other folks know the way in through the lagoon, so I figured you might turn up. Borrowed a fishing boat and came to have a look."

"We stayed around de other side of de island for a couple days," Basil explained. "Den waited back in de trees till you an' Miss Nolan went ashore, an' got over here quiet as could be."

"Not a good idea to leave a boat unattended, laddie," Barnaby pointed out. Whatever dismay he felt at the abrupt upsetting of his larcenous plans did not last long. He was quickly recovering his confidence.

"There wasn't any choice this time," Lucas said. He shot Emily a swift glance, then went on. "Not when there was treasure to be hidden."

"Eh...what's that?" Barnaby was sitting up straighter, his black eyes gleaming. He stroked a hand down his long beard and chuckled with satisfaction. "I knew it. There's treasure here. I can smell it."

"What you smell," Lucas corrected quietly, "is trouble, plain and simple, enough to put us all in Davey Jones's locker quicker than that mangy bird of yours can bum a cracker."

"I'll ignore the insults against Davey," the captain said grandly, "in return for a wee bit more information. Just how much are we talking about?"

"Two million dollars' worth," Lucas said succinctly.

Barnaby's mouth fell open as Basil whistled softly between his teeth. "You sure be right," the black man said, "dat be trouble."

Lucas nodded. "We were followed to the Ridge and just managed to get away. It can't be long before they're on our trail."

"Maybe dis be a good time to take a little trip somewhere, Lucas?" Basil suggested. "China, maybe. Dat pretty far away."

"Do you really think it would do any good to run?"

The black man sighed. "No, guess not. But you want to stay alive, you better think of somethin' quick."

"I'm trying. The best I've been able to come up with so far was to hide the treasure. At least that way, there's a chance it'll survive."

"Be nice if you two could do the same," Barnaby pointed out dryly.

Emily grimly stared out over the water. Listening to the men, the full hopelessness of their position had been brought home to her. No matter how she looked at it, they were trapped. Her stomach twisted at the thought of the measures their pursuers might take to discover where they had hidden the diamonds. The best they would be able to hope for was a swift death, and that would be highly unlikely.

She could not get around the fact that because of her, Lucas's life was in jeopardy. He certainly recognized that, yet instead of railing against her for what she had gotten him into, he was doing his best to salvage whatever they could from their dire situation. If she had needed any further convincing of the quality of the man she had come to love, she had it.

Feeling for him as she did, the thought that he might die because of her was unbearable. Any alternative, no matter how costly, was better than that. But only one occurred to her.

She waited until Barnaby and Basil were leaving in their fishing boat; they would take it to the far side of the island where they would be in a better position to leave early in the morning. Barnaby was sitting in the boat when she glanced over her shoulder to make sure Lucas was out of earshot, then said, "Captain, could I ask you for a favor?"

He shrugged. "Reckon I owe you one, lassie, after my foolishness."

"Forget about that; I have. But I need your help. I'd like to get to Barbados and Lucas won't take me there."

"Barbados? Now why would you want to do that?"

"There's no time to explain. Will you take me?"

"Well, now, as to that…if Lucas doesn't want you to go, I don't rightly see how I could manage it." He smiled ruefully. "As you may have noticed, I don't stand up too well against him."

"If I could get away and join you on the fishing boat, would you take me then?"

"If you . . . ? Now how are you going to manage that?"

"That's my problem. Will you wait until dawn? If I'm not on board by then, go without me."

He looked at her narrowly. "You really want to do this?"

Emily nodded firmly. "I'm sure of it. Will you help?"

"I've a feelin' I'm goin' to regret this…but if that's what you want…"

"Wonderful," she said swiftly. "I'll join you as soon as possible."

Barnaby nodded morosely. "And the good Lord help me if Lucas finds out."

"He won't, at least not until it's too late. Leave everything to me."

That advice didn't seem to fill the captain with confidence, but he went on his way without demurring further, leaving Emily to plan how she could leave *Banshee* unobserved.

That problem continued to preoccupy her as she and Lucas had dinner on deck. The sky was clear and the constellations stood out in brilliant relief. She found the three stars of Orion's belt and traced the shape of the hunter while mulling over how to assure that she could leave the boat without awakening Lucas.

"Would you like another beer?" she asked with an encouraging smile. She had never seen him drink to anything even remotely approaching excess, but perhaps tonight he could be persuaded to do so.

Lucas shot her a quizzical glance and shook his head. "No thanks, I've still got half of this one."

"Oh . . . would you rather have wine?"

"Beer's fine."

She stifled a sigh. Getting him drunk hadn't been much of an idea to start with. She'd have to come up with something else. Placing a hand to her mouth, she yawned and smiled apologetically. "Sorry, I seem to be so tired tonight." She yawned again and watched for any sign that he was responding to the power of suggestion.

He wasn't, but he did seem to take it on face value that she really was worn out. "Don't worry about cleaning up," he said gently. "I'll do it. Why don't you get ready for bed?"

"All right. . . ." She couldn't think of anything else to do and didn't want to make him suspicious by behaving oddly. Below deck, she took a shower, then put a thin cotton robe over her nightie. By the time she was done, Lucas had finished the dishes.

"Into bed with you," he ordered quietly after a quick glance at her pale, strained features. "And no nonsense about using the couch. We both know we're well past that."

"Are you going back on deck?" she asked.

"Yes, since the storm's over, we should be standing watch again."

"All right. I'll come up in four hours."

"There's no need," he insisted. "You should sleep more than that."

"You have to sleep, too," she reminded him gently as she headed for the cabin. Over her shoulder, she repeated, "Four hours."

In fact, she was up on deck in three-and-a-half, having been unable to sleep more than briefly. The knowledge that this was the last night she would spend with Lucas, and that she might well be walking into mortal danger, kept rest at bay. She got up finally with relief and dressed quickly. Before going up on deck, she took her purse from the storage compartment where she put it when she had come on board and hid it behind the gangway, where it would be out of sight but within easy reach.

The moon had risen; it floated regally in the dark sky. A few wisps of cloud could be seen but other than that the night was clear. Lucas sat in the prow, one of the rifles nearby. He looked up as she came toward him. "You're early."

"I thought you might be tired," she said quietly, trying not to look at him too much. Even wreathed in shadows as he was, she was vividly aware of him. The tips of her fingers tingled with the memory of how his body felt beneath her touch. She knew every inch of him now, from the way his thick hair curled in her hands like the pelt of a strong, healthy animal, to the tensile strength of his arms and the powerful hardness of his legs between her own. She knew where and how he was most sensitive to arousal, and how much of it he could bear before his self-control snapped. And she knew other things, too—where he was ticklish, how he liked to have his back scratched, even his favorite positions when he slept.

So much and yet she felt that if she were to know him for decades more, she would only begin to explore the many and varied facets of the man. Too bad she wouldn't get the chance.

He stretched and stood up, affording her a tantalizing view of his bare chest above the plain cotton shorts he wore. "I think I may be too wound up to sleep," he said.

"You should still try," she murmured, taking her place in the prow. Lucas stood above her, close enough for her to watch the steady rise and fall of his breathing. He put his hands behind his head with the elbows bent and stretched like a very large cat.

Emily averted her eyes. He'd go in a moment and she would be alone. Before first light she had to be on her way. Even though the note she planned to leave would tell Lucas that she was heading in the opposite direction from Barbados toward Grenada, she couldn't count on his being misled for long. "Go to sleep," she insisted gently. "It will be dawn soon."

"They won't come tonight," he said. "I'm sure of that."

"How do you know?"

"Because they won't have had time yet to figure out that we aren't making for Barbados. We've got a few more days." Grimly, he added, "and we'd better make the best use of them."

She intended to, if only he would go below and fall asleep. "You can't think when you're tired, Lucas. Get some rest."

He smiled a little crookedly. "So anxious to get rid of me?"

"Of course not," she said swiftly. "But I've slept and now it's your turn."

"I have something else in mind." Moving so lithely that she had barely an instant to realize what he intended, he sat down beside her and drew her into his arms. The immediate stiffening of her body did not deter him, any more than her faintly murmured protest. "Don't refuse me," he murmured huskily, "not when I need you so much."

Nothing he could have said would have had greater effect. The knowledge that this strong, proud man needed her overcame whatever hesitation Emily might have felt. Admittedly, that had not been very great to begin with. She desperately wanted this last night with him to be everything it could be.

Seemingly of their own accord, her hands slid along his shoulders, finding their way to the nape of his neck, where her fingers tangled in the crisp hairs. The scent of him filled her—salt and clean sea air mingling with the unperfumed soap he customarily used and the very subtle, very special aroma that was completely his own. She felt the warmth of his skin reaching out to caress her even before she knew its touch.

A sweet, poignant sense of homecoming filled her.

The arms that held her were rock hard, proof of long years of tough, physical work, yet they were also utterly gentle. She felt no sense of confinement, no pressure, however slight, to yield to him. On the contrary, within his arms she found the exhilarating freedom to be completely herself—a strong, sensual woman.

As he drew her closer, she went willingly, her breasts nestling against his chest. She had slipped her legs beneath herself and risen slightly on her knees so that the difference in their heights—even when they were seated—was eliminated and she could look directly into his eyes. What she saw there made her breath catch in her throat: passion and urgency, but also something more. Tenderness so great as to make her wonder at the as yet unplumbed depths of this man. There was so much more to him than she had yet experienced, or would experience. Only this night remained.

"Lucas..." she breathed, stroking down the long length of his back, "make me forget everything...please..."

His mouth was hot against the silken column of her throat, his kisses hard and urgent, the light raking of his teeth an exquisite pain. Her nipples were swollen to hard buds of urgency, and deep within her she throbbed achingly. The hand he slid beneath the waistband of her shorts was large and hard. His calloused palm covered her flat abdomen, the fingers rubbing gently against the slight mound hidden by soft curls.

Emily writhed in his embrace, unable to stay still. Molten heat flowed through her. If it did not find an outlet soon, she feared she would explode. Somehow they had slid to the deck, where a soft foam-rubber mattress lay. Normally used for sunbathing, it would serve a different purpose now. Lucas loomed above her, his face taut with the force of his need. Her eyes widened as he slid his hands down her slender legs to grasp her feet. A slight smile lifted the corners of his mouth as he saw her surprise.

"Relax," he murmured thickly, "this won't hurt a bit."

It didn't, unless pleasure so intense as to be unbearable counted as pain. The gentle kneading of the soles of her feet gave way to slow strokes with his tongue and tender nibbling at her toes. That tickled a little and she giggled, but amusement gave way swiftly to far stronger emotions.

From her feet he proceeded up her slim calves to the backs of her knees, lingering at each place until she could stand no more and tried to grasp at his hair. Eluding her, he laughed far back in his throat, a sound somewhere between a groan and a growl. "Patience, Emily," he advised huskily. "I want this to last."

So did she, but her body was on fire, and her need for him was growing more intense with each passing moment. When he moved between her legs, spreading them wide, she was struck by a piercing sense of helplessness and vulnerability that was startlingly erotic. Far in the back of her mind, she realized that with him she felt safe enough to indulge in such sensual play. She knew he would never hurt her.

He did not, but he did drive her almost mad and himself, too, in the process. The clothes between them were an intolerable barrier, yet Lucas would not remove them, at least not completely. He undid her thin blouse and the front clasp of her bra, filling his hands with her breasts. Gently he moved her back and forth against his chest, the crisp hairs against her swollen nipples providing a delicious torment. Her knees bent, her thighs tightening around him as she pleaded with him not to wait.

Reaching down between them, Lucas pulled off her shorts and the thin scrap of panties. He spread her legs farther as he unsnapped his pants and lowered the zipper. A moment later she felt him against her, hot and demanding, filled with need obviously as great as her own. Yet when she tried to bring him to her, he grasped her wrists in one hand and held them immobile as he continued to straddle her.

"Not yet," he growled, his breath coming hard and fast. The effort to keep from taking her immediately was almost beyond him, but sheer male instinct drove him to prolong the moment. He wanted her utterly mindless with desire as potent as his own.

Emily's head tossed back and forth helplessly. She opened her eyes wide, seeing past the dark shadow of his upper body to the glittering stars, mute witnesses of their passion. Time fell away. The rest of the world ceased to exist. There were only the sea and the stars, and Lucas.

The first touch of him entering her at last dissolved the remnants of her self-control like so many droplets of water striking a red-hot anvil. She cried out, the purely feminine sound captured by his mouth as he thrust his tongue into hers with the same rhythm of his manhood moving deeper and deeper within her.

The fury of their lovemaking might have stunned them if either had been capable of comprehending it. As it was, they could only be carried along by it toward a conclusion nearly shattering in its intensity. Some faint, lingering instinct for survival made Emily try to pull back at the last moment, but Lucas would not permit it. He grasped her buttocks tightly and lifted himself so that she felt him within her to a depth and power never before experienced.

Suddenly the very stars above seemed to explode in the heavens, and there was nothing for them but the blinding instant of completion. Then they lay, at last stunned and sated, on the deck, with the dark sea surrounding them.

Nine

Lucas was sleeping soundly when Emily slipped away. After the tumultuous episode of lovemaking on deck, they had gone below to his bunk. There, cradled against each other, they had murmured the sweet nothings that lovers do before exhaustion finally claimed him. She, too, could easily have given in to the need for sleep had she not been more set than ever on her plan. Whatever else happened, Lucas must not be made to suffer for what she had gotten him into.

Leaving him was the hardest thing she had ever done. Beyond the simple fact that she knew she was deliberately going into extreme danger, she would miss him terribly. He had become a part of her, without which she was not at all certain she could survive. Yet that didn't matter anywhere near as much as her determination to keep him safe.

Odd how that could be, she thought as she slipped from the bunk and allowed herself a last lingering look at him. He was sleeping on his side with an arm thrown out over the spot where she had been. Moments before that arm had rested across her waist directly beneath her breasts; she could still feel the weight of it there. The sheet had fallen back, revealing the broad expanse of his sun-bronzed chest. His lips were slightly parted, and as she watched, he sighed faintly.

Emily bit down hard on her lower lip to stifle the urge to make some sound that would wake him. That he would stop her from going she could not doubt. He would consider her plan the height of insanity, and there was nothing to prove him wrong. Still, she had no choice but to carry it out.

The note she left on the counter beside the coffeepot was short and to the point:

> I had no right to involve you in this and I can't stand your being in danger. I'm going to try to reach New York through Grenada. Please don't follow me.

She knew that he would ignore that last part and be after her the moment he read the note, but she was also confident that in doing so he would be heading away from danger. Meanwhile, she would be walking straight into it.

Picking up her clothes off the floor where they had eventually landed, she tiptoed out of the cabin and shut the door silently behind her, all the while determinedly keeping her thoughts at bay. If she once allowed the doubts and fears to be voiced in her mind, she would not be able to resist them. Instead she dressed swiftly, recovered her purse from behind the steps and went out on deck.

Getting into the dinghy was difficult; it rolled steeply from side to side as though trying to toss her out. She managed finally and, using an oar, pushed silently away from the boat. Careful to make as little noise as possible, she began to row. Lucas had made rowing look easy; she found it was anything but. The oars kept slipping in her damp palms, and she had trouble getting them both into the water together.

By the time she reached shore, she was panting and her arms ached. When the dinghy was securely tied to a palm tree, she started inland. The moon lit her way, but even so she found it rough going. Several times she stumbled and once she twisted her ankle. She was limping slightly long before she reached the place where they had buried the diamonds. Without a shovel, it took her some fifteen minutes to dig up the packet, then she went in search of the fishing boat.

Whoever had lent the boat to Barnaby had not done him any great favor. To call it dilapidated was to be overly gracious. If she hadn't known better, she would have sworn the peeling, sagging refugee from the junkyard could not possibly float. But it seemed to be doing exactly that, fortunately close enough to shore for her to wade out.

Basil was on deck when she climbed aboard. He smiled in the darkness and said softly, "Thought you might be by about now. Cap'tin still be asleep."

"Let's not wake him," Emily suggested. "I'll help you cast off."

He nodded and went to start the engines. They coughed and sputtered, but eventually turned over. She breathed a sigh of relief as the rusty hulk grudgingly edged away from shore and headed into the darkness.

"Can we get very far before light?" she asked when she joined Basil in the deckhouse. "I know there aren't any channel buoys."

"No reefs 'round here, either. Nothin' to get in our way."

That was good news. She had worried about how much distance they would be able to cover before Lucas found the note. It would have been ignominious to still be in sight when he started after them. "How soon do you think we'll make Barbados?" she asked as she peered out the cracked window.

"'By dis afternoon, with a little luck." Reassuringly, he added, "Don't worry, miss, we come out all right."

"I wish you'd call me Emily," she said with a soft smile.

Basil nodded graciously. "Dat fine, Emily."

They were silent as the boat slowly picked up speed. Emily glanced behind her, seeing the shadowy outline of the island vanishing into the darkness. She thought of Lucas and shut her eyes, willing the pain to go away. It didn't, but she was already learning to accept that.

"Mind if I ask you somethin'?" Basil said softly.

She shook her head, glad of the distraction. "No, of course not."

"You sure dis a good idea?"

A rueful smile tugged at her mouth. "Not at all, but I don't think I have any choice."

"'Cause of Lucas?"

"I . . . don't want him to get hurt."

"He a grown man. Know how to take care of hisself."

"That doesn't give me the right to endanger him."

Basil shrugged. "Speakin' of which, man got a right to protect his woman."

"I'm not . . ." She broke off, aware that her face was flushed. That was such a primitive term, "his woman." Yet she couldn't deny that it fit. "It's funny," she said at length. "I thought I was doing this for Lucas's sake, but I'm really doing it for my own. I simply can't stand the thought of his being hurt. Nothing that may happen to me could be as bad as that."

"He feel same way 'bout you?"

"Perhaps . . . but it doesn't make any difference. This is my problem, so I have to solve it."

Basil didn't look convinced, but he made no further comment. As the first rim of light began to show along the horizon, Emily went below. The galley was a grubby hole at midship outfitted with a hot plate, ice chest and an ancient metal sink. There was a coffeepot on the hot plate. She filled it and, while it perked, managed to locate three cups, chipped but usable.

The sonorous rumble of Barnaby's snores led her to him. He was sprawled in a hammock hung in the bow, an empty bottle of rum on the floor nearby. She shook her head ruefully as she set the coffeepot on an overturned barrel that smelled as though it had once held salted fish.

Back in the deckhouse, she handed Basil his cup. He took a sip and nodded appreciatively. "Sea be calm," he told her. "Makin' good time."

"Where will we come in on Barbados?"

"Bridgetown. Have to clear immigration there."

"Anyone coming in on a boat would have to do that?"

He nodded. "Less dey want big trouble."

Then anyone watching for her would know where to look. She swallowed some of the coffee and wished her stomach would stop hurting.

Barnaby stumbled up on deck a while later. He peered at her through bloodshot eyes and rasped. "So you decided to come along?"

"Obviously, or I wouldn't be here."

He shook his head and glared at Basil. "You should have woke me. Where the hell are we anyway?" Basil told him and he grunted in acknowledgment. "Engines holdin' up?"

"Seem to be. Clear sailin' so far."

"Let's hope it stays that way." He hitched up his pants and stared out suspiciously at the water. "Any sign of trouble?"

"There's no one following us that I can see," Emily said. "And even if we were spotted, there'd be no reason to think I was on board."

"We better damn well hope so," Barnaby groused. He slumped into a morose silence that neither Emily nor Basil tried to break.

Toward noon a rain squall passed overhead. The little fishing boat pitched wildly but, under Basil's steadying hand came through all right. Afterward, the sky cleared to an almost blindingly bright blue. A school of dolphins swam off to port, several lifting their heads to stare with enigmatic smiles at the humans.

"Ever have dolphin meat?" Barnaby asked as he watched Emily enjoying the sight.

"People don't really eat that?" she protested, dismayed at the notion.

"'Course they do. People'll eat most anything if they get hungry enough. Besides, dolphin's downright tasty."

"I'll take your word for it," she muttered. Until a moment ago, she'd been feeling hungry. Barnaby had neatly taken care of that. Which didn't mean that he intended to drop the subject.

"Long as you're on board," he said, "you might as well make yourself useful. There's fixings for lunch below."

"Should I take that as a hint?" she inquired tartly.

"Darn tootin', and bring up a couple of beers while you're at it." As an afterthought, he said, "Get something for yourself, too."

"Thanks so much," Emily muttered under her breath. If he and Basil hadn't been doing her such a favor by getting her to Barbados, she would have felt inclined to suggest what he could do with his fixings. But as it was, gratitude won out and she managed to put together a passably decent lunch from cold lobster meat, vegetables and sliced mango.

Basil had obviously packed the provisions. She doubted the captain's forethought extended to more than the half-dozen six packs of Venezuelan beer and a couple of extra bottles of rum similar to the empty she had found beside him that morning.

"I hope this will do," she said mildly as she set the tray down. Basil thanked her politely; Barnaby unbent enough to allow that she might have her uses after all. Remembering that she would have no chance whatsoever of succeeding at her dangerous plan if she didn't keep her strength up, Emily pushed aside thoughts of the dolphins and managed to eat her share.

The afternoon passed slowly. With nothing to do and nowhere to go, she was inevitably thrown back on her thoughts. Lucas had certainly found the note by now. He would be heading for Grenada, probably cursing her every inch of the way. She hated even to imagine how he would feel when he got there and realized that she had tricked him. If it hadn't been for his own good, she would have felt ashamed. As it was, she could only be grateful that he would be safe.

Basil called her name softly and she glanced up. He was pointing off the prow where a majestic sailing yacht was passing. "Startin' to get close to Barbados now," he explained. "Lots more boats."

There were everything from sleek schooners to dingy freighters. They also saw several planes. "I guess the airport is busy again," Emily commented doubtfully as she looked up, shading her eyes, to follow the course of a small prop plane that seemed to dip rather low over them.

"Even this time of year," Basil confirmed. "Lots of tourists still come."

Emily didn't blame them. Barbados was beautiful, a verdant paradise rising out of the turquoise sea, framed by golden beaches and washed by the balmy trade winds. From what she had seen on her way through, the people were friendly and outgoing. Though parts of the island were undeniably crowded, there was also an energetic, vibrant air she found particularly appealing. She wished she might have had a chance to experience it more and regretted that was not to be the case.

"Is it far from Bridgetown to the airport?" she asked Basil.

"Maybe twenty, twenty-five minutes by taxi."

The return ticket in her purse was for an open reservation on a flight that left for New York in early evening. Since they seemed to be making such good time, she wondered if there might be a chance of catching it.

They were close enough to the island now to see the buildings along the beach. Here and there, high-rise condominiums and hotels had sprouted, but mostly there were low stucco and stone structures that blended in with their surroundings. More boats passed, many heading toward the main harbor that was also their destination.

They found a berth between two small intra-island freighters. Emily went with Basil and Barnaby to the customs office to check in. She had her passport stamped and got directions to the airport. When they were back outside once again, she turned to the two men. "Thank you very much. I really appreciate your help."

Barnaby's glum expression softened somewhat. "I wish I felt better about this," he said gruffly. "Lucas would have my hide if he knew what I'd done."

"Don't worry about that. It's really for the best." She hesitated a moment, then added, "When you see him again, would you tell him that . . ." Her voice was suddenly unnaturally thick. She couldn't quite get the words out, which didn't much matter since she didn't really know what she was trying to say.

Barnaby sighed deeply. "It's all right, lassie. I know what you mean, and I'll make sure Lucas knows, too. Though to be blunt about it, I don't think it will make much difference to him. He's going to be madder than hell."

Emily nodded somberly, thanked them again and said goodbye. All her concentration was on getting to the airport. The street leading from the harbor was crowded. She was jostled as she hurried along but kept going, looking for a taxi. At the square north of the harbor, she paused for a moment and glanced around. No one seemed to be following her, at least so far as she could tell. Yet the fine hairs at the nape of her neck were standing up, and despite the warm air, she felt unaccountably chilled.

Nerves, she thought, nothing more. She couldn't afford to let her imagination run away with her. Yet despite her best efforts, the pretty, sun-washed street was taking on a decidedly sinister quality. She felt hemmed in by the old stone buildings and confused by the little alleys running off in all directions, each seeming to beckon her.

Fear of what would happen in the next minute, the next hour, the next day—if she made it that far—was growing within her. While she had been on the boat with Basil and Barnaby, she had not let herself think too much about what she would confront. Now there was nothing to distract her. She was face-to-face with the reality of being alone in a strange city, uncertain of who could be trusted, and aware that her life might be in jeopardy at that very instant.

A little boy rode by on a bicycle, ringing his bell gleefully. Emily jumped and only just managed to bite back a scream. A middle-aged woman passing nearby shot her a startled look, making her vividly aware of how odd she must look. It was as though she had become cut off from the ordinary world and cast adrift in a macabre place of lurking violence and merciless betrayal. Worse yet, she could still see the sane, safe world all around her; she just couldn't reach it.

At the customs office, she had briefly considered blurting out the true reason for her presence in Barbados. How would the meticulously polite men in sharply pressed uniforms have reacted if she had said she was carrying a fortune in diamonds and needed help? She might have done so except that it involved trusting people she didn't know. At the very least, the customs officials would have bustled her off to some bureaucrat's office where she would have been little more than a sitting duck. Better to at least be able to keep moving.

Two blocks farther into town she found a taxi stand. One car was waiting there, the driver—a tall, bullnecked man—leaning against it. She hurried up to him. "I need to get to the airport. Can you take me?"

He nodded gravely. "Glad to, miss. Hop in."

She kept her eyes glued to the road, except for several swift glances at her watch. The plane was due to leave in an hour. She still had time to make it. That hope began to fade somewhat when they became stuck behind a bus blocking the narrow road. Long, seemingly endless minutes passed before the driver was able to maneuver around it.

Fields of sugarcane sped by, interrupted by scatterings of one-story stucco houses, many with tethered goats munching out in front. They passed through several small villages, but generally there was little sign of life.

"Is this the main road?" Emily asked at length.

The driver shook his head without turning around. "No, miss, main road too busy. Get stuck like before behind bus. Better this way."

Was it? Her throat was suddenly very dry and she had trouble swallowing. The deserted fields whipping past offered no possibility of help. If she tried to jump out of the cab, she would at the very least be seriously injured. There was nothing she could do except wait to see what would happen.

By a supreme effort at self-control, she managed to ask, "Will we be at the airport soon?"

"Yes, miss. What plane are you catching?"

She told him, wondering if it mattered.

"Plenty of time," he assured her and stepped more firmly on the gas.

They drove for several more minutes and passed a few buildings. They seemed to be coming into a slightly more populated area but there was still no sign that they were going in the right direction.

"I hadn't realized it was so far," she murmured.

The man shrugged. "Has to be away from the main towns, miss. Nobody like to live near airport."

"No, of course not." She almost laughed, thinking of how neighborhood groups in New York had banded together to try to cut down on airplane noise. It seemed things really were the same everywhere. Desperately she tried to remember what she had seen of Barbados while her flight in was making its landing approach. Had the airport really been off by itself?

An intersection lay in front of them. The traffic light was red. As the cab came to a halt, Emily's hand fastened on the door handle. Should she jump out and try to make a run for it? There was no one else around who could help her and the driver looked in good shape. He might have an easy time catching her, and then what?

A sudden roar of sound made her head jerk up. A jet swooped low overhead, coming in for a landing. As she watched, it disappeared behind a line of palm trees off to the east. "Airport right there, miss," the driver said matter-of-factly.

So it was. Unable to recall when she had last been so glad to arrive somewhere, and ashamed of her suspicions, Emily tipped the man generously, assured a porter she needed no help, and hurried inside. There was a line at the check-in counter. She waited her turn, carefully surveying the people coming and going in the terminal or sitting patiently in the molded plastic chairs until their flights were called.

"First class to New York," the airline clerk said as she checked the ticket. "Yes, there's a seat available on the next flight, Miss Nolan. That's departing in forty minutes so boarding will be momentarily."

Emily took her boarding pass, cleared immigration and security, then found a seat in the transit lounge. It was crowded with Americans heading home and a smattering of West Indians going north on business. Duty-free shops temptingly displayed the usual assortment of perfume, liquor and china. She ignored those and instead found a bookstore where she absently selected a paperback thriller she'd been meaning to read. It wasn't likely that she would be able to concentrate on it during the flight, but she meant to try.

She was just beginning to relax a little and think that she might actually have a chance of making it back to New York by herself when the flight was called. As she joined the other passengers moving toward the gate, she felt something pressing into her back and glanced over her shoulder.

A tall man in a white linen suit stood directly behind her. She hadn't noticed him before and wondered where he had come from so suddenly. Unlike most of the other passengers, he wasn't tanned. He had a long white scar running, in a jagged line, from temple to chin. Only half his mouth lifted as he smiled faintly. "Sorry, miss."

She nodded and looked away hastily. Something about the man gave her the willies. Perhaps because the obvious expense and elegance of his clothing was out of keeping with the brutishness of his appearance. The thing—whatever it was—was still pressing into her back. Annoyed, she turned again. "Look, would you mind not . . ." Her eyes fell to the trench coat draped over the man's arm. He shifted it slightly, enough for her to make out the steel barrel of a gun pointing directly at her.

Her first reaction was one of simple bewilderment. How had he gotten the gun past the security checkpoint? Her next thought was that she should have expected this. Lucas had warned her that the airport would be watched. She had let down her guard a little too soon.

"We're going to leave quietly," the man said, his voice hard and flat. "We'll walk through the main entrance where a car is waiting for us. Don't be so foolish as to try to get away."

"If you shoot me here," she said bluntly, "you won't have a prayer of escaping."

Again that frozen half smile sent a shiver through her. "I got in here," he pointed out rather unnecessarily, "and I can get out. If you think otherwise, it will be your mistake."

"I'm no good dead," she insisted with a courage she was very far from feeling. The cold steel of the gun barrel pressed more firmly against her.

"True, and my instructions are to bring you in alive, if possible. Otherwise, to make sure you won't cause any further trouble." He spoke so matter-of-factly that a horrifying urge to laugh rose in her. They might have been discussing some routine work assignment. But then for him—they were.

Any thought of trying to bluff her way out vanished. She felt the stark implacability of the man and no longer doubted that if she did not do exactly what he said, he would kill her. The gun was undoubtedly equipped with a silencer. He could do it and be gone before anyone realized what had happened.

"All right," she murmured shakily. "I'll do as you say."

He nodded once and steered her toward a door at the far side of the lounge. It was closed and marked No Exit, but he opened it unhesitatingly and pushed her through. No one tried to stop them. Whoever the man was, whoever had sent him, he had powerful accomplices.

The terminal was less crowded than before, though there were still clusters of people scattered about waiting for flights to nearby islands. The schedule board showed that the next flight to the States wouldn't be for three hours, destination Miami. A porter walked by and Emily had to fight the urge to cry out for help.

"Don't even think about it," the man hissed, "unless you want some unlucky bastard to get it along with you."

She kept silent and continued walking, even though her legs felt almost unbearably weak and shaky. The sun was beginning to set as they left the terminal and approached a black Mercedes parked in front. The driver was also a young white man dressed in a business suit. He nodded at the man holding Emily as he opened the door and pushed her in.

Before the door had closed again, they were pulling away from the curb.

"Where are we going?" she said automatically.

The man with the gun shrugged. "You'll see."

"I don't have the diamonds. We weren't able to recover them."

He ignored her, his face an expressionless mask. Desperation rose in her. Was there nothing she could do to help herself? "I'll be missed, you know. People will be looking for me."

He raised an eyebrow skeptically. "Oh, yeah? Who?"

She wasn't about to mention Lucas, so instead she said, "My employer, Sentinal Insurance. It won't be long before they find out what has happened to me."

For some reason that seemed to amuse the man. He chuckled faintly—a sinister sound that did nothing for Emily's peace of mind—and said, "I don't like talky women. We'll be where we're going soon enough and then you can yap all you want. Meantime, shut up."

Grudgingly, she took his advice. There wasn't much choice. The door on her side had no handle and the window was rolled up all the way. The gun was still pointed directly at her. She toyed briefly with the possibility of trying to grab it, then forced that aside. There were easier ways to commit suicide.

The road they were taking wound upward toward the center of the island. The interior was much warmer than the coast and the air-conditioning was turned up full blast. Emily shivered in her thin shirt and shorts. She wanted to wrap her arms around herself but wouldn't give the man the satisfaction of seeing how uncomfortable she was.

They drove for about half an hour, getting farther and farther away from any sign of habitation. The thick canopy of tropical growth pressing in on them gave the sense of moving through a narrow green tunnel. Above, she could glimpse a sliver of sky but it seemed impossibly far away.

The car took a left turn and passed onto a narrow un-paved road. An iron fence blocked their way. They slowed to a halt as the driver took an electronic signaling device from the glove compartment and pressed the button on it. The gates swung open. When they had passed through, the driver used the device again to close them.

A high stone wall ran off in both directions as far as the eye could see. It was topped with barbed wire, which Emily suspected might be electrified. Just inside the wall she spot-ted a camera hidden in a tree. The camera whirred as they passed, rotating to follow their progress.

"Whoever lives here certainly likes his privacy," she said as lightly as she could manage.

"I told you to keep quiet," the gunman said.

She pressed her lips together and tried to ignore the bitter taste of bile at the back of her throat. There was a house in the distance, very large and ornate. Modeled on the style of a Spanish hacienda, its white stucco walls rose two stories to a red-tile roof. In front of the house was a large, perfectly manicured lawn dotted with bougainvillea and hibiscus bushes. A stone fountain stood in the middle of the lawn, spouting water into the air. The scene should have been lovely, but Emily was blind to its charms. She could think only of what awaited her inside.

The driver got out and opened the door on her side. He, too, was armed, Emily saw as she slid from the seat. The gunman came round and took her arm in a grip so tight it bruised. "Let's not keep your host waiting," he said sar-donically. They walked up the short flight of steps toward the carved double doors. As they approached, the doors opened to reveal a white-jacketed manservant.

Apparently, people being brought in at gunpoint were not an unusual sight here, for the servant betrayed no surprise. He remained utterly imperturbable as he said, "You are expected in the library."

The foyer was cool and shadowed after the bright heat outside. The tile floor was smooth beneath Emily's feet. She caught a glimpse of an inner courtyard at the far end of the hall before the gunman steered her toward a nearby door. He pushed it open with his shoulder, revealing a pleasant, book-lined room dominated by a large mahogany desk and overlooking a garden.

Emily shut her eyes for a moment, struggling to come to terms with her surroundings. Everything she had seen of the house indicated not simply wealth, but also refinement. The evidence of excellent taste was everywhere. She could not reconcile that with the circumstances that had brought her there.

A couch stood against one wall. She glanced at it and said, "Do you mind if I sit down?"

The gunman shrugged. "Doesn't make any difference to me." He released her arm and she sank onto the soft cushions, aware that her legs could not have held her much longer. A terrible suspicion was beginning to surface in her mind.

It was confirmed a moment later when the door opened and Winslow Goodway walked in.

Ten

"Good evening, my dear," the silver-haired man said. Dressed in gray slacks, a white turtleneck shirt and a navy-blue blazer, with his well-preserved features lightly tanned, he looked the very picture of a respected diplomat and businessman. At fifty-five, Winslow Goodway projected an aura of complete confidence and benign cordiality.

"I hope your trip wasn't too tiresome," he said not unkindly, as he opened an inlaid Chinese cabinet to reveal a well-stocked bar. Pouring himself a brandy, he went on, "That fishing boat couldn't have been too comfortable."

A terrible feeling of helplessness was growing in Emily. It compounded the sense of shock and unreality that had settled over her the moment her employer appeared on the scene. Huskily, she said, "How did you find out about that?"

He took a chair opposite the couch and regarded her chidingly. "You know I don't tolerate incompetency. The harbor was watched very carefully."

"Captain Barnaby...and Basil...what have you done with them?"

A slight frown marred Goodway's broad forehead. "They've temporarily eluded us, a condition I expect to hear at any moment has been corrected."

The brief surge of gladness that darted through her was dispelled quickly as he went on. "And now, my dear, to business. Where are the diamonds?"

Emily took a quick, steadying breath and said quietly. "I don't know. As I reported to Sentinal, we weren't able to recover them."

He took a sip of his brandy and set the crystal goblet down on the table beside him before he said, "Perhaps I should point out that I am not feeling particularly patient at the moment. You would be far wiser to simply tell me the truth."

"That is the truth...." She broke off, her face contorting with pain. At a gesture from Goodway, the gunman stepped forward and placed his hand on her throat, tightening until she could not breathe. He held her like that until, at a further signal from her employer, she was released.

"As you see, my dear, Carl is very adept at such measures. He's been quite gentle with you so far, but that will not necessarily continue."

Emily did not dare glance up at the man standing above her. She kept her eyes on Goodway. "I don't understand why you're doing this. You've been paid in full for the diamonds."

"My motives are of no concern to you." Goodway gestured with his hand, and the gunman stepped forward again. Instinctively, Emily pulled back, but was unable to stop him from grabbing her purse.

It took him barely a moment to find the packet. With a grin, he handed it over to Goodway. The older man quickly undid the wrappings. Emily closed her eyes for an instant, overwhelmed by her failure. When she opened them again, it was to find both Goodway and the other man staring dumbfounded at a small pile of smooth stones, such as might be picked up on any beach around the Caribbean.

"What...?" she began incredulously, only to break off as Goodway turned on her harshly.

"Enough of this. I congratulate you on your cleverness, but you can't possibly expect to get away with such a ridiculous ploy. For your own sake, I strongly advise you to end this ridiculous charade now."

Emily had no idea what to say. She was as shocked as he by the discovery of what was in the packet, but she had no hope that he would believe her. Moreover, she had to cope with the sudden, horrible thought that Lucas had betrayed her. No one else had had the opportunity to switch the diamonds. He must have done so, but why?

There were more immediate concerns to worry about. The threat implicit in Goodway's words was unmistakable. Emily's stomach twisted in fear, which she tried stubbornly to hide. "I told you we didn't find the diamonds. Now perhaps you'll believe me."

"You just happen to collect perfectly ordinary stones and carry them around in your handbag?" he demanded. "Don't try my patience with such absurdities. You found the diamonds and you will tell me where they are."

"There was nothing in the safe," she insisted.

Goodway sighed deeply. "You are placing me in a very awkward position, Emily. I have a great distaste for physical violence; that's why I employ men like Carl who are not hindered by such scruples. Do you really want me to turn you over to him?"

Her heart pounded painfully and a wave of coldness moved over her, but nonetheless she managed to say, "What you do is strictly your own responsibility. I've told you everything I can."

Goodway's mouth tightened. He flicked a finger in the direction of the door. "I have a fondness for lovely young women, Emily. Because of that I am going to give you a chance to reconsider. Just don't take too long. Carl, show Miss Nolan to her quarters.''

The gunman bared his teeth in a cold parody of a smile. He reached down and took her arm again, placing his hand exactly where he bruised her arm before when he had helped her from the car. She winced with the pain he inflicted. Only pride kept her from giving in to her fear. She held her head high and glared at Goodway. ''I wonder if you realize how pitiful you are? You have so much but you're overwhelmed by greed. You know you can only get a fraction of the diamonds' worth when you sell them on the black market.''

''Allow me to worry about that, my dear,'' he said with a faint smile. ''You concentrate on your own problems. If you decide to cooperate, it's not impossible that we might still be able to work out some sort of accommodation.''

Not for a moment did she believe him. As soon as she told him what he wanted to know—presuming that she could—he would have her killed. The only question was how long she would be able to hold out.

Carl seemed interested in that, too. As he hauled her down the steps to the basement, he said, ''I hope you're as stubborn as you seem. It's been a long time since I had a real challenge.''

''How unfortunate for you,'' she muttered, almost choking on her apprehension. The basement was dark and damp. Only a single overhead light shone but it was enough to illuminate the heavy metal door to which Carl led her. He opened it with a key from his pocket, revealing a small, bare cell.

''Let's see how you like it in here,'' he said as he shoved her inside. ''Nothing to distract you while you're trying to remember where those diamonds are.''

Indeed there was nothing. After he shut the door and locked it, she was in pitch-darkness. No light, no sound, nothing even to touch except the floor and the four walls.

They were as damp as the rest of the basement, slicked with a slime that made her skin crawl. She hated even the idea of sitting down, but eventually weariness drove her to do so. Her thin shirt and shorts were little protection from the dank chill. It seemed to seep into her very bones and eat away at her courage.

Emily had never been claustrophobic, but she was rapidly coming to understand what that condition must be like. The darkness pressed in on her from all sides. It almost seemed to be a living, breathing thing waiting to devour her. A choked sob rose in her throat. She pressed her head against her bent knees and struggled against the terror that threatened to overwhelm her.

Whatever happened, she couldn't give in. She had to think of Lucas, no matter how painful thoughts of him were. His life, too, hung in the balance. The more time she gained, the better chance he had.

She repeated that to herself over and over as the long moments dragged past and the darkness seemed to grow even thicker. She lost all sense of time except to know that it was passing very slowly. Her senses, devoid of stimulus, grew painfully acute. She strained for the faintest glimmer of light, the slightest sound. But when light and sound came to her, she did not welcome them.

Carl pushed the door open. He stood silhouetted against the light, his voice low and drawling as he said, "Changed your mind yet?"

Emily got slowly to her feet. Her legs cramped and she had difficulty standing, but she wasn't about to show him that. As steadily as she could manage, she said, "I could make up something, but I think Mr. Goodway would prefer the truth. I don't know where the diamonds are."

A pleased chuckle reached her in the darkness, sending a shiver down her spine. "I was hoping you'd say that. Goodway's going to be real disappointed."

"That's better than sending him on a wild goose chase," she insisted hurriedly. Carl was advancing into the cell. Despite herself, she moved backward.

"Real disappointed," he repeated. "And when that happens, he gets mean."

"I know you're only doing your job," she said hurriedly, trying not to gag on her fear and disgust. The man before her was a vicious predator, someone who enjoyed inflicting pain. She could see that in the anticipatory gleam of his eyes and the slow, almost lazy way he tracked her around the tiny room. He was enjoying her fear, feeding off it even as he looked forward to what would come next. "You'll be making a mistake," she went on despite the painful tightening of her throat. "There's nothing I can tell you. Mr. Goodway will realize that eventually, and be angry at you for what you've done."

"He won't care one way or the other," Carl told her bluntly. "You're mine now."

No words Emily had ever heard had struck such terror in her. She did not doubt for a moment that what he said was true. Since she refused to talk, Goodway had washed his hands of her. He would regard whatever happened to her now as strictly her own fault.

The cold stones of the wall were sharp against her back. She pressed against them nonetheless and put her hands out in front of her, even though she knew she had no hope of stopping him. The half of Carl's face that could move twitched in a chilling smile. "It's going to be a pleasure breaking you," he said softly. "I'm going to take my time about it and enjoy every moment."

"You're crazy," Emily gasped, no longer able to restrain her loathing. It was bad enough that he intended to hurt her, but looking into his cold black eyes, she knew how he intended doing it. The fear of being confronted with sexual assault burned like bile in her mouth. She thought of Lucas, of all they had shared, and bit back a sob of horror.

Quickly following came a pure, vitalizing flush of anger greater than any she had ever known.

How dare this obscene degenerate threaten her? How dare that disgusting creature upstairs let it happen? She was better than both of them and she was going to make sure they knew it. Lessons from her childhood welled up inside her. Maybe it hadn't been the perfect way to grow up, but at least she had learned that the worst thing anyone could do when confronted with a bully was to let him feel completely in control of the situation.

Her teeth gleamed whitely in the darkness as she bared them. A low growl rose from deep within her. Strength flowed like molten lava rushing on a river of rage as she launched herself forward. His hands grasped her shoulders roughly as he automatically tried to yank her away.

Somewhere Emily had heard that when confronted by a far larger and stronger opponent, it was wisest to fight in close. Without pausing to think of what she was doing, driven by instincts that were far greater at that moment than any squeamishness, she drove her knee up hard between his legs even as she thrust her thumbs toward his eyes.

Carl howled with pain and shock. He threw her from him so roughly that she bounced against the stone wall before crumbling to the ground. Before she could move, he was on her. "You bitch! I'll kill you for that. Slowly."

She twisted under him frantically, trying to regain her feet or at least maneuver into a position where she would have some chance, however slight, of protecting herself. But he was on to her now and alert to every trick she could pull. Her arms were twisted behind her back and pulled upward until, despite herself, she gave an exclamation of pain. Dragging her upright, he stared down at her with livid eyes, while he grasped her neck violently. "By the time I get through with you, your own mother won't recognize you."

A sick, agonizing laugh rose in Emily. She doubted her mother could have under any circumstances, but of course he had no way of knowing that.

"Don't laugh at me!" Carl shrieked, slapping her hard across the face. "Bitch! Laughing. I'll teach you. You'll beg me to..."

He broke off abruptly, his eyes opening wide. The hand, fastened so cruelly on her throat, loosened and fell away. Emily's hand went to her neck reflexively as she stared at him in bewilderment. Only when his eyes rolled back, exposing the whites, and he began to sink slowly to the slimy ground, did she shift her gaze.

A very large man stood behind him, his feet planted slightly apart. His broad chest rose and fell regularly as he flexed the hand he had chopped against the back of Carl's neck. The blow had not been strong enough to kill; he had been careful about that, wanting very much for him to live. But it had rendered him unconscious for several hours.

Now there was the woman to deal with.

"Sometimes," he said quietly, "I get a little annoyed at you, Emily."

"L-Lucas... Would it be too trite to ask what you're doing here?" Her voice broke even as he reached for her, cradling her gently in his arms.

His big hand shook slightly as he smoothed her hair. "Collecting something that belongs to me. And not a moment too soon by the look of it."

"I was in a bit of trouble," she admitted huskily, burrowing her face against his chest. All thought of her suspicions and doubts faded. It felt so good to be held like this, so safe and secure after the horror of the past few minutes, as though she had come home. She breathed deeply, drawing in his scent, that special mixture of salt, sun, and pure male that was uniquely his own.

Even in her exhausted state, she was aware that he held her so tightly she might have bruises from it later, but not for a moment did she object. A primitive sense of rightness moved in her. He had fought for her, saved her from another man, and was now leaving no doubt that he claimed her as his own. The modern woman in her was at least mildly shocked, or perhaps more correctly, bemused by such behavior. Yet another, far more ancient voice told her it was right.

Still there was no reason to let him get a swelled head about it. "A bit of trouble," she repeated. "He was stronger than I thought."

"He was a killer," Lucas said bluntly, glaring down at her. "Ordinarily, I won't attack a man behind his back, but in this case I gladly made an exception."

Bending swiftly, he pulled a yank of rope from his pocket and expertly tied Carl's hands and legs. When he was done, he looked down at the trussed and unconscious man with grim satisfaction. "That should hold him until the authorities can get here. Now where's Goodway...?"

"He was upstairs in the library," Emily told him as she followed him hastily out of the cell. Only then did she notice that one of the automatic rifles hung over his back and that on the belt of his waist was the leather scabbard of a hunting knife. Lucas had come prepared.

"Would you mind telling me how you found out where I had gone?" she asked, panting slightly. He was taking the stone steps two at a time and she was hard-pressed to keep up with him. "My note said I was heading for Grenada."

"You didn't really expect me to believe that, did you?" he demanded, glaring at her again. It was either that or shake the living daylights out of her. He had never been so scared as when he found her with that piece of scum.... "If I'd had my head on straight," he rasped, "I would have realized what you were planning. But I was a little...distracted." His mouth twisted ironically. That was putting it mildly. Their lovemaking had blown all thought of anything else right out of his mind—until he woke and found her gone and that stupid note left to taunt him. Then he had started to go quietly insane.

"At least Basil's got his wits about him," he snapped. "He followed you from the dock and saw what happened at the airport. By the time I reached port, he was able to tell me where you'd been taken. Damn good thing, too. If I'd had to waste time looking..." He broke off as they rounded a corner. The tall, black man was there waiting for them, the other rifle held ready.

"All quiet so far," he told Lucas in a whisper. "Cap'tin's keeping a lookout by de door."

"Good," Lucas said firmly. "Goodway's probably in the library. We'll take him there."

"What are you talking about?" Emily hissed. "He'll have guards all through the house, or at least servants. Let's get out of here and call the authorities."

"And tell them what?" Lucas demanded. "That he tried to steal his own diamonds back. Who the hell do you think will believe us?"

"But I was kidnapped.... I could have been killed!"

"You came to the home of one of your company's clients with a member of his staff," he went on relentlessly. "You've already radioed in to tell them we didn't find the diamonds, so Goodway will claim you argued and that you're just trying to cause trouble. He'll go scot-free. I'm not about to let that happen."

"So what are you going to do? You can't handle him alone."

He shot her a look that was half mocking, half defiant. Very softly, he said, "Want to bet?"

"Shh," Basil warned suddenly. "Somebody comin'."

The manservant who had opened the door when Emily arrived was coming down the corridor. He paused in front of the library, knocked and went in.

"Goodway's still there," Emily whispered. "I heard his voice."

Lucas nodded curtly. "We wait until the servant comes out. Then we go." Curtly, he added, "You stay here."

"No, you'll need all the help you can get and I . . ."

"You'll stay," he repeated flatly. "I don't want to have to worry about you while we're putting the bag on your firm's client."

"He's not a client any longer," she said matter-of-factly. "After what he's done, his policy is void."

Lucas chuckled deep in his throat. He could admire her spirit even as he was determined to keep her from further danger. "Emily," he said slowly and clearly, "I am only going to explain this one more time. You stay here. If you don't, I personally guarantee that you will not be able to sit down for a week. Got that?"

"Why you insufferably arrogant bullheaded bas . . ."

"Now, now," he chided with infuriating calm, "you can tell me how wonderful I am later."

She fully intended to give him a piece of her mind, but before she could do so, the library door opened again and the manservant came out. He disappeared back down the corridor from the direction he had appeared. Lucas waited several moments, then moved forward with Basil at his side.

Emily watched them, caught between chagrin at being told to stay behind and the reluctant, but undeniable, sense that Lucas had been right. Seeing the two men, their faces set in ruthless calm and their weapons at the ready, she had to acknowledge that she had no place with them. What was about to happen was vastly beyond both her experience and her ability, for which she could only be grateful.

Lucas did not waste time on niceties. As Basil guarded his back, he kicked in the door and surged into the library. An instant later a stream of grim, explicit curses told her what he had found.

Emily stuck her head in the room and looked around cautiously. "Where is he?"

"You tell me," Lucas grated. "He must have gone out the windows."

"No, laddie, he did not," came a voice from the French doors. Barnaby stood there, glowering fiercely. "Been right here the whole time and nothing went past me."

He spoke with such conviction that no one could doubt him. They were left to search the library in growing bewilderment. Goodway had clearly been there recently. The brandy snifter he had been drinking from still sat on the table beside his chair. Had he finished with it, the manservant would have taken it with him. Even more telling, a fine Cuban cigar still smoldered in a crystal ashtray.

"He must have realized the house had been broken into," Lucas said grimly, "and he couldn't have known how many of us there were. Probably figured it was safer to run and ask questions later."

"But how?" Emily asked, still staring at the room. "With Barnaby on watch, how did he get out?"

"Maybe he's just hiding," the captain suggested.

Meanwhile, Basil was looking closely at the floor-to-ceiling shelves of books. Softly, he called, "Lucas, better see dis." He pointed toward a section of shelf that looked oddly different from the others. It took Emily a moment to realize why.

"Those aren't real books. They're stuck together."

"I'm beginning to think," Lucas said quietly, "that Goodway has a flare for the dramatic." He reached out a hand and nudged the books toward him. Nothing happened at first, but he kept pulling the false books toward him until there was a sudden creak from behind the shelves and the entire section of wall slowly opened.

Barnaby shook his head in astonishment. "Would you look at that now! I'd heard there were old houses around here with hidden passages, but I never expected to see one."

Lucas didn't waste time admiring their discovery. Quickly, he said, "Emily, you'll stay here with Barnaby. Basil and I will check out the passage." He started forward only to be stopped by a soft, but firm, hand on his arm.

"I'm not sitting here worrying about you. We go together."

The glare he shot her would have shriveled a less-determined woman. "Out of the question."

"My mind is made up," she told him firmly. "Do you want to waste time arguing, or do you want to get on with the search?"

Behind them Basil chuckled softly. "Don' look like she's gonna change her mind."

"When we get out of this," Lucas muttered, "I swear I'm going to..." He left that thought unfinished as he plunged into the passage with the others behind him. The stone traverse was as dark and damp as the cell where Emily had been held. Lucas flashed a beam from the emergency light he had brought to show their way. He and Basil had to crouch beneath the low ceiling. Puddles of stagnant water dotted the molding floor and rustling off the side made Emily's skin crawl.

"How long do you think this has been here?" she asked Barnaby in an effort to distract herself.

"Two, maybe three hundred years. Probably an old smugglers' tunnel." He grinned in the darkness. "There were plenty of them on Barbados back then."

The passage was getting wetter as it sloped downward. A cool breeze touched her heated cheeks. "We're getting close to the outside," she whispered.

"Near water," Lucas agreed. "The tunnel must run clear from the house, through the hill, to the nearest cove. Makes sense if anyone wanted to get in and out without being seen."

A flicker of silvered light shone up above. Emily blinked, thinking she had imagined it. When she looked again, it was brighter. "The moon . . . I can see it reflecting on water."

Moments later they reached the tunnel exit and stepped out into the soft night air. They were standing on the edge of a small beach lapped by gentle waves. Shadows of palm trees surrounded them, blowing gently in the wind. The sky was crystalline clear, lit by a riot of stars dominated by the full moon pouring liquid silver into the dark sea.

"Look here," Barnaby called softly. They gathered around him at the edge of the beach as he went on. "See those marks? Been a boat dragged down here, not too long ago. Dinghy, probably."

"He can't get far in that," Emily said hopefully.

Lucas's hands tightened on the rifle. "Far enough. Goodway wouldn't have gone to all the trouble of using that tunnel unless he had a larger boat anchored here. Must have taken the dinghy to get out to it."

"He's gone," Emily murmured, almost to herself. It was so anticlimactic after all their efforts. Disappointment and frustration twisted through her.

Lucas turned to her. In the darkness, it was difficult to read his expression, but his voice was gentle as he asked, "Does he know where the diamonds are?"

"No," she said hastily. "How could I tell him what I don't know?"

He nodded but made no attempt to relieve her curiosity. "Then we've still got a chance. My guess is that Goodway will figure that with him gone, we have to recover the diamonds and take them to the authorities. So he'll be waiting out there," he gestured toward the Caribbean, "for us to show up."

"Sounds like we're in for a little game of cat and mouse," Barnaby said, not without relish. "Only question is, who's the cat and who's the mouse?"

"I'm sure Goodway has his ideas about that," Lucas said, his mouth lifting in a smile of anticipation. "But he's in for a surprise."

Eleven

The yellow-eyed cat stretched and blinked lazily at Emily. She had fed him a few minutes before and he was appreciative enough to butt his large head against her hand. Absently, she scratched his ears.

"You've been around some," she murmured. "You look a little worse for wear."

A deep purr rumbled from him. "I'll bet you've got stories to tell," she went on as much to distract herself as to amuse the cat. More softly, she added, "and I'm afraid you'll have another soon."

The cat and Davey Jones had accompanied Barnaby and Basil on board *Banshee* before they set sail from Bridgetown. Lucas had waited no longer than first light before slipping out to sea.

"The bastard will be suspicious if we make it too easy for him," he muttered, not hiding his contempt for Goodway. He was looking forward to his encounter with the millionaire with particularly sharp anticipation.

"Are you sure he's out there?" Emily had asked as she stood beside him in the deckhouse watching the movement of his strong hands on the wheel. He was so confident, so absolutely assured about what he was doing that she could not help but feel bemused. "Maybe he's just run for it."

"Not likely. He wants those diamonds, though I've got to admit I'm not sure why."

"You have them, I suppose?"

"Yes . . . I switched them because I wasn't absolutely certain you wouldn't try exactly what you did. I was hoping you'd think to open the packet, discover they were gone, and realize you had to stick with me."

"I wish I had," she'd admitted ruefully, trying to come to terms with how well Lucas had learned to know her. He had anticipated her actions almost precisely. That was unnerving, but also somehow reassuring.

"Think he's right about Goodway, too, cat?" she asked as a discreet swipe of a paw recalled her to the present. Mindful of his manners, the cat had kept his claws sheathed, but nonetheless succeeded in getting her attention. She rubbed his back as she gazed out the porthole.

The sun was almost directly overhead. It was warm inside the galley where she had gone to fix lunch. A faint smile—very faint—curved her mouth as she considered how she had fallen into the habit of preparing food during times of crisis. Things had better calm down soon or she would be in danger of getting fat.

Davey accepted a cracker from her grudgingly, not taking his small black eyes off the cat. He held the snack in one claw and pecked on it in between baleful squawks.

"Now don't you start," Emily warned him. "We've got enough problems without a scaredy parrot."

"I thought that was cat," Lucas said as he lowered himself down the gangway. For all he had been through in the past few hours, he looked remarkably fresh and at ease. Had it not been for the knife still strapped around his narrow waist and the rifle on his back, he might have been a tourist out for a pleasant sail. Except that no tourist was quite so at home in this environment—quite so at one with a ship, the sea and even the danger facing them.

"If I didn't know better," she murmured, "I'd think you were enjoying this."

He shrugged lightly. "Can you blame me for preferring to hunt rather than to be hunted?"

No, she couldn't. It wasn't in Lucas to sit by passively while others decided his fate. Yet the way he spoke of what lay ahead chilled her. It was a man he was hunting, a ruthless, cunning, infinitely deceptive man who would stop at nothing to protect himself. Under her breath, she murmured, "If only I had realized . . . maybe this all could have been prevented."

Lucas let out a long sigh. He put his hands on her shoulders and drew her to him. "I wondered how long it would take for you to get around to that. So you're blaming yourself for not seeing through Goodway?"

"I feel I should have. The way we were followed directly to the Ridge points to the fact that someone knew our exact movements. That could only have been William Jeffers— whom I've known for almost ten years and trust implicitly—or the only person he'd feel he had to keep up-to-date on the operation, namely Goodway himself."

"In hindsight that's clear," Lucas said, "but I didn't figure it out either, so I don't see why you should have. The idea of a multimillionaire stealing his own diamonds simply doesn't make sense."

"That's what I still think," she agreed. "The risk doesn't come close to equaling the return."

"Unless there's some additional element we haven't figured out yet. . . ."

"What could that be?"

"I don't know...." He drew her closer, his head resting on top of hers. "And frankly, I'm not interested in trying to work it out right now. There'll be time for that later."

Would there be? Right now there was only time to hunt and perhaps, if they were lucky, to survive.

"Headin' south by southeast," Basil said when Lucas and Emily came back on deck. "Should be dere in a few hours."

"Do you really think Goodway is going to Devil's Reef?" she asked Lucas as she sat down beside him.

He nodded, staring out over the water. "Nothing else makes sense. He's got to figure that you left the evidence with me and he knows I put in at the Reef frequently. At the very least, he'll hope to pick up a lead on where I've gone."

"He'll have men with him," she cautioned. "He won't be alone."

"That kind never is."

The implacable truth of that made her shiver. They were four against how many? Two strong men, an over-the-hill pirate and a woman going to do battle with vicious criminals who regarded murder and mayhem as no more than normal business practices. "Do you...uh...have a plan?" she asked hesitantly.

Basil chuckled at that and, before Lucas could answer said, "Fight like hell, Emily. Dat be de only plan."

"Couldn't have put it better myself," Lucas agreed with a grin. The smile faded as he glanced at her sternly. "Of course, you'll stay below."

"Like hell."

"Emily—"

"There's no point arguing," she told him loftily. "When the time comes, you'll need all the help you can get."

"And what makes you think you'll be a help? You'll just be in the way."

Ignoring the slur on her abilities, she said, "I shot that raft, didn't I?"

Barnaby's bushy red eyebrows rose, but before he could inquire as to what that was all about, Lucas said, "This will be...different. You don't realize how much. We won't be shooting at rafts."

She took a deep breath and nodded. "I know."

Did she, he wondered? Did she really have any comprehension of what they were soon to face? He'd been in more than a few tight spots in his time and knew that the response to danger and even death could be very different depending on circumstances. Shooting a man who stood so far away that you couldn't make out his face was not quite the same as digging a knife into his belly while he tried to do the same to you.

He would give anything he had to spare her the knowledge of what that was like, but it was not within his power to do so. Not if she insisted on involving herself. When Emily decided on something, he had long since realized, a speeding freight train couldn't knock her off her chosen path.

"We'll have to count on the element of surprise to even things out," he said gruffly. "Our best bet is to stay out of sight until after dark."

"And then sneak on board?" she asked.

"It's not likely we could manage that. Goodway is bound to have more than one guard posted."

"Then what?" she asked.

He hedged, not wanting to alarm her too much. "We'll manage to get on board, don't worry about that."

A wicked grin split Barnaby's face. "Aye, laddie, we'll manage all right. The ol' sod won't know what hit him."

"We hope," Lucas said quietly. "Anyway, we should all get some rest while we still can."

She tried to take his advice but found it very difficult. Lying below deck in the stateroom, she sought sleep unsuccessfully. Lucas was keeping watch above while Barnaby and Basil napped on the couches in the lounge. They had drifted off almost the instant they lay down, but she supposed they were more accustomed to such situations. At least Basil was. He had the same kind of steady strength and determination she sensed in Lucas. And Barnaby, however out of step he might be with the modern world, was also no stranger to danger. That left only herself, and the futile effort to keep her mind from graphic images of what was so shortly to be.

At length she gave up the struggle and went back on deck. Lucas frowned when he saw her. "You're supposed to be resting."

"I could take over for a while," she suggested.

To her surprise he agreed. "You might as well. The more practice you get handling *Banshee*, the better."

She didn't want to ask why, sensing that whatever the answer might be, she wouldn't like it. Taking the wheel from him, she was vividly aware of his nearness, the warmth of his body and the now familiar scent of salt, sun and pure virile male. A heady combination, she thought with a wan inward grin. Anyone who could bottle it would have his fortune made.

"What are you thinking about?" Lucas asked as he lowered himself onto the padded seat opposite the wheel and stretched out his long legs.

"Nothing in particular," she hedged, keeping her attention on the task of holding the boat steady on its course. *Banshee* bucked slightly, as though resisting the unfamiliar hands on the wheel, but then settled back down.

"You've got a knack for this," he said. "A few months at sea and you'd be a veteran."

"I doubt that," she said lightly. "There must always be something new out here to surprise you."

His hazel eyes ran over her as he nodded. "True, but then life itself is full of surprises."

She grimaced and cast him a rueful glance. "I think I've had my fill. A little boredom would be very welcome."

His brow furrowed beneath the stray locks of ebony hair that had tumbled across it. "You really think so?"

"Well...maybe not boredom. That's the wrong word. Peace, stability, security. Those I wouldn't mind."

"No...that might not be too bad."

They looked at each other awhile longer before she reluctantly turned her attention back to the boat. Above them the mainsail was pulled so taut by the wind that it seemed to hum. The great wooden hull creaked rhythmically as it plowed the trough between waves. Beneath her hands, *Banshee* felt like a living thing perfectly at home on the sea. Emily closed her eyes for a moment, savoring the sensation of being part of something vastly larger and more powerful than herself, something eternal and unchanging beyond the evil of men and the vulnerability of love.

When she opened them again, she could see the faint green smudge on the horizon that was Devil's Reef.

They had approached the island from the far side, opposite the pier where Emily had first sighted Lucas sailing *Banshee*. It seemed like a lifetime ago, but was in fact only a few days. Approached from this direction, the Reef looked virtually uninhabited and uninhabitable. Rocky cliffs rose a hundred feet from a boulder-strewn beach against which foam-crested waves pounded remorselessly. Gulls whirled overhead, their screeching a seeming protest against the intrusion of the humans.

"The anchorage here is poor," Lucas said, "but it will do until tonight."

"Have you considered going onto the island and trying to get help?" Emily asked when the anchors had been let down and dug as securely as possible into the sandy bottom.

"Fishermen all be gone right now," Basil explained. "Nobody left but de women and chil'ren. Not good to bring dem into dis."

"No, of course not," she agreed hastily. "I hope they aren't in any danger."

"Shouldn't be," Lucas assured her. "Goodway won't expect them to know anything about my whereabouts."

"The sods will probably search my place," Barnaby grumbled. "They better not try stealing any of my books or maps."

At his fierce expression, Emily caught herself grinning. "Don't take this the wrong way," she said, "but I can't help but feel sorry for anyone trying to search the Voyager's Rest."

"Why's that?" he asked innocently.

The other three exchanged glances before she cleared her throat diplomatically. "Uh...because it's so large, of course."

"Aye, it is that. A fine place."

Or at least it might be if some time and money were spent refurbishing it. Emily resisted the impulse to say so and instead asked how long Lucas thought they would wait.

"Long enough to let at least some of Goodway's gang get to sleep. We'll move at midnight."

This time there was no new moon to protect them. A waxing crescent sailed overhead. The ribbon of light it cast over the water stretched for miles. The wind was fair, out of the west as usual, and blowing steadily.

"All right," Lucas said when they had assembled on deck. "We'll tack round the island and come up on them from the leeward side. Basil, are the rifles ready?"

"Dey are, and the sheets."

"All set then. Let's go."

In the darkness, the looming cliffs looked even more ominous and the craggy beach more threatening. Without channel buoys, they had to rely strictly on their own knowledge of the waters surrounding the Reef to make their way through them safely.

"Sandbar to port," Basil called softly.

"Hold her steady," Barnaby instructed. "Coral ridge to starboard."

"See anything up ahead, Emily?" Lucas asked.

"Only dark water," she told him, looking back over her shoulder to where he stood at the wheel.

"That's the channel then. We'll cut straight through."

She barely breathed as he steered *Banshee* through the narrow opening between the sandbar on one side and the coral ridge on the other. Either was potentially treacherous to any boat. If they went aground, they would be helpless and it would be only a matter of time before Goodway discovered their whereabouts.

Lucas must have been aware of that, yet he gave no sign of the slightest nervousness as he guided *Banshee*. Not until they were safely through did he flash a grin in the darkness. "Glad that's over."

"Not bad, laddie," Barnaby allowed. "Make a sailor of you yet."

There were other obstacles to be overcome as they circled the island, hugging close to shore to avoid any possibility of being spotted. As they came around the leeward side, a faint scattering of lights in the tiny settlement by the harbor could be seen. A little farther on was the dark shape of a large power yacht.

"Goodway," Lucas muttered under his breath. "He must be confident, sitting there bold as brass."

"Probably figures he's got nothin' to worry about," Barnaby muttered. "What do you say we change his mind?"

The glint that shone in Lucas's hazel eyes would have frightened a lesser woman, but Emily took it in stride as she joined him at the wheel. "Time for you to take over," he said. "We're going to sail in as close as possible to the yacht."

"You mean to berth next to her?" she asked, puzzled.

He shook his head. "No, I mean to board her, from the sea side." Her bewildered look made him grin. "Don't worry about scraping *Banshee*'s hull, she can take it."

"That's not what I was worrying about," Emily muttered. The man was out of his mind, round the bend, cuckoo. How did he expect to get from one boat to the other...?

"Oh, no," she moaned raggedly as the answer to her question literally appeared in front of her eyes in the form of ropes suddenly loosened from the mast where they must have been placed earlier. The sheets Basil had mentioned...that's what he'd been doing. Rigging boarding ropes just like they used back in the bad old days.

Barnaby looked in seventh heaven. His hair and beard blew wildly in the wind as he stuck a pistol in his belt, grasped a knife between his teeth, and went up one of the ropes with an agility a younger man might have envied. Not that Basil or Lucas had any reason to do so. With the rifles slung over their backs and scabbards at their waists, they climbed hand-over-hand so speedily that she had barely time to blink before they were at the top of the ropes.

"Okay, Emily," Lucas yelled. "Bring her in."

"Bring her in," she repeated sourly even as she twisted the big wheel hard to port. "Just like that. The big galoot. Now he thinks he's Captain Blood!"

Cursing fiercely to herself, she gunned the motor. *Banshee* leaped in the water, dashing forward straight for the ghostly white hull of the power yacht. A man ran out on the deck saw them and shouted an alarm even as he cocked his rifle and began to fire. Two others quickly joined him as *Banshee* was showered with bullets.

Terrified that the men clinging to the ropes would be hit, Emily pressed down even harder on the throttle. All sense of caution was abandoned as she steered *Banshee* directly at the other boat. Their hulls were scant inches apart and the sound of gunfire was all but deafening when Lucas shouted, *"Now!"*

As one, the three men swung free on the ropes, flying out over the deck of Goodway's yacht where they let go and allowed themselves to fall directly onto the guards. Emily watched round-eyed, fascination mingled with dread as Lucas delivered a vicious uppercut to the chin of the burly, red-faced man trying to regain his wits. He followed it up quickly with swift hooks to the solar plexus, which had the desired effect.

On either side, Basil and Barnaby were doing much the same. The Captain might be undersized compared to the guards, and overaged, but he held his own with a combination of karate chops and just plain low blows delivered with the dizzying speed and unpredictability of a whirling dervish.

The scuffle was over quickly. However tough the guards might have been, they hadn't been prepared for an airborne assault by latter-day pirates. They went down with barely a struggle, rendered unconscious by the combined effects of having large, muscular men land on top of them and a judicious application of dirty fighting.

Emily did not fool herself into thinking that the danger was over. There were certainly others on board, if only Mr. Goodway himself. As Lucas and Basil quickly slung ropes across the deck to hold the two boats together, Emily scrambled over, the bird on her arm, the cat scampering behind.

"Dinna want to miss the fun, lassie?" Barnaby inquired. His usually bloodshot eyes were bright with excitement and his Scottish burr was becoming noticeably thicker. He looked as though ten years had dropped away from him, perhaps even twenty.

"Wouldn't dream of it," she muttered, thinking that men had a strange idea of fun. When this was all over, she was really going to give Lucas a piece of her mind. If he thought he could pull such crazy stunts and get away with it, he had another think coming.

"I told you to stay put," he said when he caught sight of her. For a moment he made a valiant effort to look stern, then gave up and laughed.

Emily supposed she deserved that. She must look a rare sight with Davey Jones perched on her shoulder and the yellow-eyed cat rubbing up against her legs. Even as Emily and Lucas continued to eye one another, the cat took matters into its own hands—or rather paws—and darted through an open doorway leading off the deck. Without pausing to think, Emily went after him. Davey Jones fluttered off to a more secure perch on Barnaby's shoulder as Lucas dashed after her. Together they caught a glimpse of a bent tail disappearing down a gangway.

"Damn cat," Lucas muttered, "never did have any sense."

"He could get hurt," Emily said, "and I'd feel responsible."

"Stop worrying about that animal. He's got at least two or three lives left. We're the ones who have to watch out."

"Oh, you're going to start being cautious now after that ridiculous bit with the ropes. Errol Flynn you're not."

"It worked, didn't it?"

That silenced her, at least for a moment. Which was just as well because the sound of footsteps approaching suddenly reached them.

"Get back," Lucas whispered, pushing her behind him as he readied the rifle. Over his shoulder, Emily caught sight of another guard just rounding the corner and drawing up short when he spotted them.

Lucas fired once, blasting the guard's weapon out of his hand and stunning the man sufficiently for him to be overcome by Basil and Barnaby, who were following right behind.

"Pretty fancy shooting," she said when she was able to breathe again.

He shrugged dismissively. "I'm just not crazy about killing people, even scum like this."

"That soft heart of yours will get you in trouble some day, lad," Barnaby said as he finished looping rope around the guard's wrists and ankles. With a gag stuffed into his mouth, the man was effectively immobilized.

"I think it already has," Lucas muttered. He stared at Emily for a moment before asking, "I don't suppose you've had enough excitement and will go back to *Banshee* now?"

Her only answer was a disparaging snort as she strode off in the general direction taken by the cat.

"This yacht is similar in design to *Venturer*," she whispered a short time later when Lucas had caught up with her. "Unless I miss my guess. Goodway's stateroom will be at the end of this corridor."

"All right, we'll try there. But Emily, this time you really have to listen to me. Goodway will have his strongest protection close around him. It could get very hairy."

"I'll be all right, Lucas," she told him quietly. "I can look after myself."

"I know that, damn it! But just this once couldn't you let someone do it for you? I don't want to have you on my mind when we go in there."

She hadn't thought of that. What he was saying made sense. If he was worried about her, he wouldn't be able to fully concentrate on what he had to do, and that might make the difference between success and failure.

"I'll stay back," she promised huskily.

Lucas nodded, realizing he had to be satisfied with that. Further efforts to get her to return to *Banshee* would only waste precious time. Basil and Barnaby were already on their way to the deckhouse where they would try to take command of the controls. If they succeeded, there would only be Goodway to finish off. That was the job—and the privilege—he reserved for himself.

As they neared the stateroom, Emily moved behind Lucas. She wanted to tell him to be careful, not to endanger himself, but she knew any such admonitions were senseless. He would do what he had to.

Yet even knowing that it was all she could do not to cry out when he thrust open the door and moved through it as swiftly and silently as a panther, with only the rifle between him and whatever might lie within.

The seconds ticked by as she waited outside in the corridor, hardly breathing. The cat suddenly darted out the open door and rubbed against her, purring throatily. She bent and picked it up, absently scratching behind its ears as she moved forward cautiously.

"L-Lucas...? Are you all right."

"Don't come in," he called, too late to prevent her from doing just that. He was standing in the center of the stateroom facing a large chair. For a moment his body blocked whatever there was in view. Then she moved closer and saw what he had tried to spare her.

Goodway looked almost as usual, sitting erectly with one arm resting on the arm of the chair as though he were about to reach for the brandy snifter on the adjacent table. There was no evidence of his flight from the house or the sail to the Reef. Every silver hair was in place and his perfectly tailored clothes were in pristine condition—except for the thin trail of drying blood that stained his white turtleneck.

Staring at his sightless eyes, she murmured, "H-he's dead...?" Her tone was questioning even though she had no doubt of the answer.

"Shot," Lucas said succinctly. "In the back of the head, one bullet from a small caliber weapon."

"But how...why?" Her face was pale and her voice trembled slightly. Though she could not feel much sympathy for Goodway himself, the shock of seeing anyone in such a violated state dismayed her greatly.

"I don't know," Lucas said quietly. "But my guess is it has something to do with his real reason for wanting the diamonds."

"Someone on board must have done it."

He nodded. "But I don't expect we'll ever know exactly who. Anyway, that can be left to the authorities to try to straighten out."

"I can still hardly believe it," she murmured as they left the stateroom, Lucas's hand firm and steadying on her arm. "It never occurred to me that he might die."

"I'm sure it didn't occur to Goodway, either, or he would have taken more stringent precautions. Nothing mattered with him except himself."

"It's a shame in a way. He's escaped justice."

"Do you really believe that?" Lucas asked, glancing down at her.

"I don't know," she admitted. "What do you think?"

"I think Goodway has gone to face the greatest justice there is, with no plea bargaining, no fancy lawyers, and no parole. I doubt very much that he'll be happy about the outcome."

"We're not finished yet," she reminded him quietly. "There's still whoever else may be aboard."

But in fact Barnaby and Basil had already seen to that. When Emily and Lucas reached the deckhouse, they found three more guards trussed up like chickens with Barnaby glaring at them over the barrel of his pistol while Basil serenely checked out the instruments.

"Looks like dat's 'bout it," he said when he caught sight of them. "What you want to do with dis bunch?"

"Take them to the police on St. Vincent." Lucas suggested. "They've got jurisdiction."

"Sounds good to me," Basil agreed. "You want to take the wheel?"

"No..." Lucas said slowly, casting a glance at Emily. "We'll follow you on *Banshee*."

The black man grinned. "No rush gettin' dere, right?"

Lucas matched his smile. "You know what they say about the islands. Best to stay loose."

"*Davey Jones'll get you,*" the parrot squawked.

"Be quiet, bird," Barnaby ordered, glancing indulgently at the ebony-haired man and the woman by his side. "You dinna know anythin' about it."

"You planning on holding onto that cat all night, Emily?" Lucas inquired mildly.

"Uh...no...I don't think so." She lowered the feline to the floor and watched it go off in a dignified huff. After a moment, she said, "I suppose we should get back to *Banshee*."

"I'm sure she'd appreciate it," Lucas said, once again taking her arm. As he steered her out the door toward deck, he added meaningfully, "And then there are one or two other things we are also going to do."

Twelve

So that's it," Emily said softly as she stared down at the pile of glittering diamonds lying on the counter in the small kitchen below deck. "Who would ever have imagined it?"

"Not me," Lucas acknowledged. He held up one of the stones, turning it slowly between his fingers. Beside him lay the high-powered magnifying glass that had at last solved the puzzle.

"I've got to give Goodway credit," he went on. "This was a very imaginative solution to what must have been a very disturbing problem. He used something valuable to hide something even more valuable."

"All that intelligence," Emily murmured, "and he used it for evil." She took the stone Lucas was holding and stared into it. "A glass diamond tossed in among dozens of the real thing, and in the glass what looks like an ordinary carbon spot but isn't. The mind that could come up with that ploy could have been put to so much better use."

She took the magnifying glass again and peered through it at the fake stone. "It's microfilm all right, though it's impossible to read."

"I can take a guess about what's on it. According to a couple of sources I checked with in the States, Goodway was fabulously wealthy all right, but his money was relatively recent and no one really knows where it came from. There have been rumors that he was involved with drugs, which is certainly consistent with his yacht having been blown up."

"And the microfilm?" Emily asked.

"Maybe a list of suppliers or other dealers. Whatever it is, given the lengths Goodway went to protect it, we can bet it's literally worth its weight in diamonds. The authorities will make the best use of it."

"Speaking of whom, I thought we were going to St. Vincent," Emily said. Lucas had dropped anchor a short time after they had left Devil's Reef. Goodway's yacht had gone on ahead, disappearing into the darkness. "Basil and Barnaby will need us there."

"They'll manage fine on their own until we arrive," he insisted.

"When will that be?"

"I'm not sure."

Hardly very reassuring. "Now look," she began sternly, "I know what you think about staying loose, but that isn't always possible. There are some things that have to be taken seriously."

"I know," he said a bit glumly. "I just hope you do, too."

"You're being very enigmatic."

His eyebrows rose fractionally. "Am I? That's not how I feel." He looked at her for a moment, his hazel eyes revealing nothing, then said, "Let's go below."

"Are you hungry?" she asked, following him down the gangway. "I can fix something."

In the golden light of the lounge, she saw him smile. "You're always doing that," he said gently. "Fixing food for people, trying to look after them. You're a nurturer at heart, Emily.''

She glanced away, suddenly self-conscious. "What's wrong with that?"

"Nothing, except that you seem embarrassed by it."

"I suppose I am...a little. In the world I grew up in, people looked out for themselves."

"It doesn't have to be that way forever." Slowly, he added, "I've been thinking."

She looked up at him with a gentle smile. "Don't hurt yourself."

His eyes widened slightly before he grinned. "There's that tart tongue of yours. I'd wondered where it had gone to."

"It's a defense measure, I suppose," she murmured. "I got in the habit of talking like that when I was a kid and I just never got out of it."

"That's all right," he assured her, stroking her hair lightly. She felt so good in his arms, strong yet soft, needing him, yet also everything that he needed. "I like the way you talk, and I like..." He bent and dropped a soft kiss on her mouth. "I like this...and this..." His lips moved on along the curve of her cheek down the slender line of her throat. Where they touched, there was fire. Where they lingered, something more than mere heat and light sprang into being—pleasure so powerful and tangible that she felt she should be able to grab hold of it and keep it forever.

"You said you'd been thinking," she breathed raggedly, afraid of the wildfire emotions rushing through her, of where they were leading and where they would leave her.

His eyes had darkened, she realized when he broke off reluctantly and raised his head. They were no longer hazel, but a dark, swirling green, like a primeval forest lit by shards of sunlight. "What...?"

"Thinking."

"Oh, that." He inhaled sharply, struggling to clear his mind. He really hadn't meant for this to happen, at least not yet. It had been his intention to go slowly and calmly, explaining what was on his mind in so logical a manner that she would not be able to resist. But logic had gone out the window as soon as he touched her. Still, he felt he had to try.

"About us," he murmured into her hair, as though saying what was on his mind was easier so long as he was holding on to her. "You'll admit we've shared a lot since we met."

Adventure, danger, love. Yes, a great deal. The thought of it was a gnawing pain eating at her. "It's meant so much to me," she murmured. "I can hardly tell you."

Try, he wanted to say. Tell me what you feel. Give me some reason to believe there's a chance for us. He loved this woman; he wanted her with him forever. Somehow, there had to be a way.

"Is there anything important for you back in New York?" he asked, hating the euphemism but unable to bring himself to ask if there was another man. He didn't think so, but he had to be sure.

Emily did not mistake him. She let her hands trace the firm line of his jaw, darkened by a day's growth of beard, as she said, "No, nothing, and no one. It's funny but that place doesn't even feel like home anymore." If it ever had. Where had she really ever felt at home except in Lucas's arms?

"Then you wouldn't mind . . . not going back?"

What was he saying? That he wanted her to stay? She would, too, but not without a clear understanding between them. "Lucas," she said quietly, "if I stayed here so that we could continue being together, it might be wonderful. But it would also be impermanent, without any real security or stability. I had enough of that when I was growing up."

The words almost choked her, so afraid was she that they would spell the end to her barely admitted dreams. He wasn't a man to be pinned down, pushed into anything, controlled in any way. He was and always would be in charge of his own fate. Was he willing to share that with her?

"I never want you to feel as you did when you were a child," he said huskily. His voice shook slightly as he thought of how much he hurt from what she had endured, and how determined he was that this valiant, admirable woman would never experience anything similar again.

He cleared his throat before he asked, "Did you know that I own Devil's Reef?"

"What?"

He smiled slightly, pleased that he had been able to surprise her. "I own it. Have for several years. Took every penny I had at the time to buy it, but I figured it was worthwhile." She watched the curve of his mouth as he added, "I guess there's a need in me to own land, even though I'll never be a farmer."

The same need, in a way, that was in her. To belong someplace, to have roots, to be part of something. "Does that mean you also own Voyager's Rest?" she asked wryly.

He had the grace to look abashed. "I'm afraid so. Pretty disreputable, isn't it?"

"That's putting it mildly. What does Barnaby do there?"

"Do? I guess you could say he's the caretaker. I hired him after the *Aberdeen* ran aground. He was at loose ends, had nowhere to go, so..."

He didn't have to explain any further. She understood what he had done and why. "You're a softie," she said gently.

He grimaced. "Don't tell anyone. I have a reputation to uphold."

"Your secret is safe with me."

"Hmmm...I wonder. Maybe I should assure your silence."

"Oh, really? And just how do you intend to do that?"

Very effectively, it seemed, with a kiss that was long and sweet and left her holding on to him, lest the knees that had turned to water gave way under her.

"You're a good kisser," she told him gravely when she could speak again.

"You're not bad yourself." His cheeks were slightly flushed, and his broad chest rose and fell rapidly against her breasts.

"As I was saying," he went on solemnly, "it occurred to me the place could be turned into a really nice hotel. I know it would take a lot of money to fix up, but I've..."

"I've got plenty of that," she said quickly. "Thanks to some very sensible investments. My apartment alone has more than doubled in value since I bought it."

His smile was so little-boy endearing that she had to blink hard against the sudden fogging of her vision. "That's great, but I haven't done too badly myself, even without the two hundred thousand from Sentinal. Staying loose is fine, but the plain fact of the matter is that I like to work."

"I'd suspected as much. Could you be content just staying on the island?"

"It would depend on...circumstances."

"For instance?"

"Well...just as an example, if we were married, then..."

"Married?" Remarkable how easily the word tripped from her lips, as though she hadn't been mentally stumbling over it for quite some time now.

"People do get married," he said, a little defensively. "It's not like we were a couple of kids."

"No...we aren't that."

"We're adults, old enough to know ourselves and what we want. And we're lovers, in the best sense of the word. Given all that, marriage really wouldn't be such a big step."

It sounded as though he was bent on talking her into it, which she didn't seem to mind. Still, she hedged just a bit. "We've only known each other a few days."

"Don't tell me you want a long engagement," he pleaded, the urgency of his body making her vividly aware of how little inclined he was to wait. "It's a lot to ask," he added huskily, "but if you'll only trust me, Emily, I swear I'll make you happy."

Trust. She had always had a problem with that, and she might easily go on having one. If she let herself.

Lucas had not failed in trust when he found her missing. How easily he could have concluded that she was in league with Goodway. But instead he had come after her, placing his life at risk in order to save hers.

"You know," she murmured, "there's an old Chinese saying that when you save someone's life, you're responsible for it ever after."

"That's interesting," he said gravely. "I've always suspected that you saved my life when you warned me about the other divers and got me out of the wreck in time."

"It sounds," she whispered against his mouth, "as though we are mutually responsible for each other."

"Might as well get married then," he said, his arms tightening around her, holding her safe from all the world.

"Might as well," she agreed.

Banshee rode at anchor beneath the waxing moon. The trade winds blew gently over the tranquil water. The Caribbean—ancient, mysterious, beautiful—was at peace that night, as were the man and woman joined for eternity.

⚡ Silhouette Desire

COMING NEXT MONTH

IN EVERY STRANGER'S FACE—Ann Major
Jordan Jacks had made his way into Gini's heart years before, but their different life-styles forced her away from him. Whether she wanted it or not, he was back in her life, and this time their desire couldn't be denied.

STAR LIGHT, STAR BRIGHT—Naomi Horton
The only heavenly bodies astronomer Rowan Claiburn was interested in were of the celestial variety. But Dallas McQuaid made an impressive display, and she found this man who radiated sex appeal impossible to ignore.

DAWN'S GIFT—Robin Elliott
Creed Parker fled from his dangerous, fast-paced world for the country life, but his peace of mind was shattered when he saw beautiful Dawn Gilbert emerging from her morning swim. Could Creed's past allow him to accept Dawn's gift of a future?

MISTY SPLENDOR—Laurie Paige
Neither a broken engagement nor time could quell the passion between Misty and Cam. She had left because they hadn't been ready for marriage—but now as man and woman they were ready for love.

NO PLAN FOR LOVE—Ariel Berk
Brian Hollander's "Casanova" style was cramped when he had to play surrogate daddy to his newborn nephew. Valerie knew even less about babies than Uncle Brian, but her labor of necessity turned into a labor of love.

RAWHIDE AND LACE—Diana Palmer
After Erin left Ty her life fell to pieces; then an automobile accident ruined her career. Now Ty wanted her back, for Erin held the key to his happiness. Could she give her heart again to the man who had once turned her away?

AVAILABLE THIS MONTH:

TREASURE HUNT
Maura Seger

THE MYTH AND THE MAGIC
Christine Flynn

LOVE UNDERCOVER
Sandra Kleinschmit

DESTINY'S DAUGHTER
Elaine Camp

MOMENT OF TRUTH
Suzanne Simms

SERENDIPITY SAMANTHA
Jo Ann Algermissen

Silhouette Desire

**Available
October 1986**

California Copper

The second in an exciting new
Desire Trilogy by Joan Hohl.

If you fell in love with Thackery—the
laconic charmer of *Texas Gold*—you're
sure to feel the same about his twin
brother, Zackery.

In *California Copper*, Zackery meets the
beautiful Aubrey Mason on the windswept
Pacific coast. Tormented by memories,
Aubrey has only to trust . . . to embrace
Zack's flame . . . and he can ignite the fire in
her heart.

The trilogy continues when you
meet Kit Aimsley, the twins' half
sister, in *Nevada Silver*. Look for
Nevada Silver—coming soon from
Silhouette Books.

DT-B-1

Silhouette Special Edition

**Sophisticated and moving,
these expanded romances delight
and capture your imagination
book after book.
A rich mix of complex plots,
realism and adventure.**

SIL-SE-1RR

Where passion and destiny meet...
there is love

Jesse's Lady

Veronica Sattler

Brianna Deveraux had a feisty spirit matched by that of only one man, Jesse Randall. In North Carolina, 1792, they dared to forge a love as vibrant and alive as life in their bold new land.

IT TAKES TWO TO LOVE . . . BUT ONLY ONE TO END THE RELATIONSHIP.

ARE YOU—

☞ **THE REJECTOR: WILLING OR UNWILLING**

Like Sharon, who ended her twenty-four-year marriage to Jeff, the most difficult aspect of the loveshock experience for the rejector is a feeling of guilt if the other person refuses to accept that the relationship is over.

☞ **THE UNWILLING REJECTOR: VICTIM AND VILLAIN**

Matt left Vicki because of her alcoholism. He still loves her deeply, but is alternating between his rage at her behavior and his self-blame. Matt, the unwilling rejector, is caught in the common loveshock symptom called zigzagging.

☞ **THE REJECTEE: THE REAL VICTIM**

Like unsuspecting Seth, whose wife, Alison, announced during dinner that she was ending their thirty-year marriage, the rejectee is the classic victim of loveshock—life has been made unbearable by a devastating loss of love.

IF YOUR LIFE HAS BEEN PULLED OUT FROM UNDER YOU,
IF YOU'RE IN DESPAIR AND PAIN,
IF YOU ARE LOOKING FOR SOMETHING THAT WILL REALLY HELP,
IT'S TIME FOR—

LOVESHOCK
How to Recover from a Broken Heart and Love Again

LOVESHOCK

*How to Recover
from a Broken Heart
and Love Again*

Stephen Gullo, Ph.D.,
and Connie Church

BANTAM BOOKS
New York • Toronto • London
Sydney • Auckland

LOVESHOCK: HOW TO RECOVER FROM A BROKEN HEART
AND LOVE AGAIN

*A Bantam Book / published by arrangement with
Simon & Schuster*

PRINTING HISTORY

Simon & Schuster edition published 1988

Bantam edition / September 1990

ISBN 0-553-28598-X

Published simultaneously in the United States and Canada

Bantam Books are published by Bantam Books, a division of Bantam Doubleday
Dell Publishing Group, Inc. Its trademark, consisting of the words "Bantam Books"
and the portrayal of a rooster, is Registered in U.S. Patent and Trademark Office
and in other countries. Marca Registrada. Bantam Books, 666 Fifth Avenue,
New York, New York 10103.

PRINTED IN THE UNITED STATES OF AMERICA

OPM   0 9 8 7 6 5 4 3 2 1

Contents

And the Lord is close to the brokenhearted . . .

ISAIAH

Preface

Oh, the tragic moments in history when love has gone wrong . . . Imagine Cleopatra with the asp clutched to her breast, Romeo and his Juliet dying so that they could in a sense live again, Henry VIII and his many unfortunate wives. And let us not forget how Van Gogh sliced off his ear and sent it to his true love. Songs have been written, great masterpieces painted, operas composed, ballets performed, novels written—all inspired by and depicting the agonies of a love loss. Artists have been moved to greatness as they tried to make sense of the many complexities of love—and especially, why love has to end. Is there anything more compelling, more painful in life than a broken heart? .

I'll never forget the night I received a hysterical phone call from one of my dearest friends. It was eleven o'clock, and when I answered the phone Genevieve was barely audible as she sobbed, "Connie, this is Genevieve—it's awful! Can you come? I don't know what to do . . . I'm at the Beverly Hills Hotel, the Polo Lounge. Please hurry."

Before I could find out what had happened, she hung up the phone. As I drove to the hotel, all I could imagine was that someone very near and dear to her had died. What else could have possibly put her in such a state?

When I found her in the Polo Lounge I was shocked by what I saw. There sat one of Europe's favorite starlets, slumped over a large vodka, a pack of cigarettes, and a mass of papers, looking anything but glamorous.

Her silk jacket lay in a heap at her feet under the table; one strap of her dress was sliding off her shoulder. The beautiful blond curls were in a wild disarray and her big brown eyes, which had become her trademark, were full of such sadness and grief that I anticipated the worst. As I sat down beside her she crumpled in my lap.

"Genevieve, what's happened? Has somebody died—your mother? Is Claude all right?" I looked around, worried about the scene she was creating. Fortunately, when you're famous you can get away with almost anything.

Genevieve suddenly sat up again and reached for her vodka. After a healthy gulp she said, "It's love. Love has died and my heart is breaking. Ryan is ending our marriage."

I couldn't believe it. "But I thought you two had such a great, exotic life. The travel, the glamour—you're both so successful. And you have your wonderful son."

As she made an effort to gather the papers, she told me, "He says he no longer feels the electricity, the excitement. And can you believe that he actually served me with all these papers two weeks ago, before he even called me?" She bit her lip, trying to fight back the tears. She began to laugh uncontrollably, and then she cried as she looked at me through her haze of pain and said, "Oh, Connie, what am I going to do?"

I didn't know what to say. For me, the solution to any emotional crisis was to throw myself into my work. And so I asked her my obvious "What about your work?"

As the waiter placed another vodka before her, she gulped it down before the ice had a chance to melt and then uttered, "They want me in Rome . . . Italian miniseries. And believe it or not, I'm to play one of the most sought-after women in the world—the woman that everybody wants but nobody can have . . ."

By the time I left Genevieve, tucked in, with her baubles and jewels on the nightstand beside her bed, it was 6:00 A.M. The vodka had done the job—she was out cold, her emotional pain on hold. As I closed the door to her suite, all I could think of was how typically Hollywood this drama was—and before she knows it, I thought, there'll be another husband or boyfriend, this one forgotten in time. Something straight out of the tabloids.

As I drove home to my husband and two children, little did I know that I myself was about to suffer the anguish and emotional pain that comes with a broken heart. What I thought was just typical Hollywood drama had hit home. I too was about to experience the profound emptiness and sense of loss that fills one up when love changes course and splits the heart in half.

Four months after my evening with Genevieve, my husband, Jim, and I had separated and I was on my way back to New York City with my two children in tow. While I kept myself together and plastered a smile on my face for the sake of my children, my insides were churning and I felt like I was dying. I could barely eat or sleep and was filled with anxiety. During that long plane ride I flashed back to my night with Genevieve, and for the first time I truly connected with her pain. Now I understood. No wonder she had drunk herself into a stupor. Had it not been for my children, I might have done the same. Like Genevieve, I was suffering from a broken heart. The symptoms were so intense that it was hard for me to believe that the pain would ever end.

Fortunately, when I arrived in Manhattan, a concerned friend referred me to a wonderful psychotherapist, Dr. Stephen Gullo, who has developed a special therapy for mending broken hearts. Dr. Gullo took me under his wing and guided me through a course of therapy for what he calls *loveshock*—what each of us experiences in varying degrees when we have loved intensely and lost that love. Since his therapy is really a program of personal coaching, not a psychological therapy, Dr. Gullo had me consult a psychiatric colleague before we began. This was to make sure that there were no significant pathologies involved.

During the process of my own therapy I realized that the insights and survival skills Dr. Gullo had to offer to those of us struck by loveshock should be shared. So we decided to develop his remarkable loveshock therapy into a book—and who better to write it than someone who was experiencing the phenomenon herself?

People need to know that they are not alone in their suffering when a love relationship ends. In fact, it is a rare human being who, during the course of a lifetime, will not experience some degree of loveshock at least once, whether it is through death, divorce, or the breakup of a love relationship. The only uncertainty is at what point or under what conditions it will occur in your life.

What Dr. Gullo and I offer are guidelines to help you get through your loveshock crisis, as we explain to you why you feel the way you do (no, you are not going crazy!), what you can expect to feel as you go through each stage, how to get through it, and ultimately, how to get beyond it so that you can rebuild your life and love again. As you read this book, think of Dr. Gullo as your personal coach, easing you through your pain so that you can resume a happy, productive life. This is what Dr. Gullo's loveshock therapy did for me and what I believe this book can do for you.

CONNIE CHURCH

LOVESHOCK

Introduction

When choosing a topic for my doctoral dissertation as a Ph.D. candidate in psychology at Columbia University, I was drawn to the meaning of love and loss, especially the emotional conflict they create for all of us when love leads to loss. This was the beginning of a personal journey that led to the discovery and definition of the loveshock phenomenon—a phenomenon that I have documented and researched for over a decade.

In collaboration with my distinguished colleague, psychiatrist Dr. Ivan Goldberg, I started my research by observing the lives of sixteen very special women who were unwilling psychological travelers on the road from life to death. Their husbands were terminally ill. I entered each woman's life when she was told that her husband had a terminal diagnosis and I stayed with her until he actually died. The emotional pain that I observed in these women was overwhelming, as they permitted me to accompany them on this journey to death.

In studying their trauma of a profound love loss, I found in this most tragic human condition a window back to life, the perfect setting in which to understand how people let go of love relationships. I realized that what I learned in working with the bereaved could be practically applied to those who had been unlucky or unwise in love, that there were coping skills that they could develop to rebuild their emotional lives and ultimately find the courage and ability to love again.

My loveshock work actually began when one of the women from the group of sixteen called me about her daughter who was going through the trauma of breaking off with her lover. When she asked for my help I hesitated, telling her, "Well, I haven't had any experience practicing that type of therapy."

She quickly snapped back at me, "But you've had plenty of experience, Dr. Gullo. You've been studying all of us letting go of our love relationships as our husbands have died. This is just another form of letting go of a love relationship." Her insight helped me realize that what I had learned in working with the dying could help the living. Freud once observed that a good doctor learns from his patients, and she taught me; her comment gave me the confidence to take that step. I was successful with her daughter, my first loveshock patient.

I came up with the term *loveshock* because of the research I had done on Viet Nam soldiers who were suffering from shell shock. As I read about their psychological disorientation, their numbness, their fear of love, and their inability to enter intimate love relationships, I realized that in that intense moment of facing death they had prepared themselves to let go not only of their lives but of all their love relationships as well.

I recognized some notable parallels between the symptoms of soldiers going through shell shock and the symptoms of people letting go of love relationships. Like soldiers being shelled, the first thing that happened to people when a serious love relationship ended was that they went into a form of shock. And in this state of shock, they were in many ways similar to soldiers in shell shock: they were unable to sleep, unable to concentrate, unable to feel deep emotion for others. The more I thought about shell shock and the letting go of love, the clearer the connection became between love loss and shock. I also realized that the soldier suffering shell shock experienced, simultaneously, loveshock as well. For during those brief moments, confronting the possibility of imminent death, he would have to let go of everyone and everything that he loved.

However, it wasn't until I presented my loveshock theory at an international symposium on "Women and Loss" sponsored by the Foundation of Thanatology at the Columbia Presbyterian Medical Center in New York City in 1978 that I realized how universal this phenomenon is. National news tabloids and magazines took notice. I began to be invited on television talk shows and radio shows to discuss loveshock. My phone was ringing off the hook from people who declared that they were suffering from loveshock. They wanted to know how to get through it, to know if there was a cure.

As I began to observe my loveshock patients closely, I recognized recurring symptoms and stages that are determined by the degree of loveshock one experiences. While I had no cure to offer my patients, I could help them make sense of what they were experiencing—make them realize that they could endure what they initially found to be unbearable.

There were guidelines they could follow that would help them to influence their personal outcome in a way that would lessen their emotional pain. I could teach them emotional survival skills, by helping them to understand the predictable course their loveshock would take and the possible stumbling blocks they might encounter along the way. When practiced, these emotional survival skills could get them through the most difficult periods of their loveshock, as they allowed their love-wounds to heal. However, I didn't want to downplay the motivation it would take on their part to get them through this time of emotional chaos.

Finally, I found that I could provide them with the necessary tools for rebuilding their lives as they prepared not just to love again, but to love well. With my personal coaching, as well as the skills and tools I had to offer, my patients could in a sense create their own cure depending on their personal needs.

Although I refer to the people I have treated for loveshock as my patients, it would be more accurate to describe them as students learning life skills that are vital to their emotional growth and development. Truly, loveshock therapy is a system of personal coaching, *not* a psychotherapy. I make this point because while you may feel as if you are going insane at different times during loveshock, it is not a form of mental illness: loveshock is an inevitable *process* for very nearly all of us.

As you read this book and take yourself through your loveshock experience, know that what I offer comes from years of research and intense sharing with my "students." There is no instant remedy, nor should there be! Love is one of the most profound human experiences, and severing a lovebond is one of life's most painful tasks. We cannot anesthetize ourselves to the pain of life without also anesthetizing ourselves to the joy of life— much of which encompasses loving. To feel deep emotional pain because of a love loss is an indication of your great capacity to love.

When you become deeply involved in a love relationship, you expose a part of yourself that very few people will ever know. This is what psychoanalyst Dr. Rollo May calls "the courage of love." And this is why you feel so much pain when a love relationship ends.

Yes, it takes courage to love. As you, open and vulnerable, share your innermost feelings and emotions with another person, there is an element of risk involved. And ultimately, whether through death or through breakup, loveshock is almost unavoidable.

While each stage of the loveshock experience can contain many painful moments for you, you can emerge stronger and wiser for all that you have endured. For in life, not only is there destructive pain but there is growth pain as well, which enables us to become stronger and more competent human beings. Loveshock is part of the growth pain of life, and by learning to manage and master it you will develop a coping skill that is central to living: the capacity to accept a loss and recover from it, realizing that you are still whole as you continue to live a full life, and I hope, love again.

CHAPTER ONE

Understanding
Loveshock

The Queen sobbed hysterically, pacing the palace floors. As she wailed into the silence of the night, the chambermaids looked at one another in fear. Special doctors had been called to her side, but nothing could be done to ease her grief. Mediums had been summoned, but it was impossible to raise Prince Albert from the dead. He was gone and she was powerless over his death—a fact she found unbearable.

As the weeks passed, the palace slowly became Queen Victoria's prison. For within those walls there was no escape from the memory of Albert or the realization that she would never hold his hands again, hear his voice, or know the pleasure of his embrace. Finally, overwhelmed by her memories and her inconsolable grief, she fled Buckingham Palace and ruled for the next thirty years from her self-imposed exile. She became known as the Widow of Windsor, clad in widow's weeds, drifting among the royal homes of Windsor, Osborne, and Balmoral.

So great was her loss that she put the entire British Empire into loveshock. The somber clothing, the austerity, the rigidity—the Victorian age was in truth an age of mourning, a reflection of Queen Victoria's grief, of her own loveshock.

Throughout their marriage, Jennifer lived with her husband's infidelities, his unfulfilled promises, and the hope that he would change. Rick was a promising young film director when they met, and she had stuck with him through thick and thin as he made his way to the top. Two children and twenty years later, as she sat in the library of her Malibu mansion, she realized that this was the last time she would ever wait for him to come home. She knew that there was another woman in his life—the call girl who was always on hand for the production company that he owned—but she wanted to believe that she came first. As the minutes passed painfully into hours, the grandfather clock loudly declared each one that passed.

When the phone finally rang, she picked it up breathlessly. She was sure that it was Rick. Instead it was the gardener, inquiring whether she wanted to plant perennials or annuals in the south bed. Jennifer barely got through the conversation when she dropped to the floor in a sobbing heap. It was at that moment that she realized she was married to a hope, not a reality, and went into loveshock.

The following morning, as her housekeeper packed her bags and helped her move into the Bel-Air Hotel, Jennifer was in a state of shock. Fortunately, her children were away at boarding school. Numb with emotional pain, she placed the Do Not Disturb sign on the door and withdrew into seclusion. Phone calls went unanswered, and she could not remember what happened from one day to the next. She kept the shades drawn, so that she never knew if it was day or night. As grief overwhelmed Jennifer, everything in her life seemed fuzzy and vague. For weeks she could barely eat or sleep.

Although Jennifer chose to leave Rick, she felt as if she had lost a part of herself. But to stay would have meant losing everything, because as each day passed she felt that she was being emotionally unraveled and diminished as a human being.

Immersed in her shock and grief, she knew that she had to bury her dream. And still, when she spoke of her love for Rick, she would say passionately, "If I had only one breath of life left, I would give it to him." It took Jennifer two years to recover from her loveshock experience.

It was Valentine's Day in New York. Standing by the open window, David gazed blankly down at the busy streets. The cold air stung his tear-streaked face. He wasn't sure if he had the nerve to jump, and yet the thought of living without Vanessa was more than he could bear. A promising young lawyer, who had proudly worked two jobs to pay his way through law school, David had everything to live for—except love.

Having never experienced open affection or love from his parents, as they were too busy struggling to clothe and feed their five children, David was sure that he had finally found emotional fulfillment in his relationship with Vanessa. This certainly had made it all the more painful when she had called him out of the blue four weeks earlier and broken off their engagement. Since that time he had felt totally abandoned and had not been able to function. Even the simplest of tasks seemed difficult to complete. Often he sat dazed and crying, forgetting what he had done the moment before. Unable to concentrate on his work, David had lost a routine case, which escalated his sense of worthlessness.

He had tried to block his pain with liquor, had flirted with cocaine, and had engaged in several one-night stands, hoping to remove Vanessa from his heart forever. But all he had achieved were bad hangovers, a lot of empty sex, and more loneliness. It seemed that the harder he tried to forget about her, the more she invaded his thoughts.

As his emotional pain gnawed at his insides, David listlessly walked across the room and flipped on his television. Slowly turning from one station to the next, he finally settled on a midday talk show. He hoped that the voices would give him some comfort and if not, that he would at least be able to gather enough courage to jump. Deeply in loveshock, David was sure that he was the only person in the world who felt the way that he did. He was convinced that he was alone in the intensity of his pain, that his broken heart separated him from the rest of the world. His loveshock had pushed him to the edge.

THE LOVESHOCK PHENOMENON

As dramatic as these stories sound, they are all true. Queen Victoria's case is an extreme example of the most obvious kind of loveshock—suffering a love loss through death. However, in our day and age, when divorce is almost as common as marriage and people have the opportunity for several love relationships in the course of their lives, loveshock occurs most frequently through the breakup of a relationship.

Those of you who are experiencing or have experienced loveshock can probably relate to some or several parts of these stories—especially Jennifer's and David's. I want to emphasize that as devastating as it can be to go through, *loveshock is a normal phenomenon with a predictable course of symptoms, stages, and events, for which there is typically a beginning and an end.*

Specifically, loveshock is that state of psychological numbness, disorientation, and emptiness that you experience following the breakup of a serious love relationship. No two individuals experience loveshock in exactly the same way, however, because human behavior varies so much from one individual to another. Usually the first loveshock crisis you experience is the most severe because you haven't developed the coping skills to manage it. I have also found that the degree of loveshock you experience is directly proportional to the intensity of your involvement in a love relationship. You can experience many breakups in the course of a lifetime, but if you are not deeply involved you will not go through an intense loveshock experience: you may feel some sadness, but you will not experience the degree of emotional pain that is characteristic of deep loveshock.

While I have found that it takes most people about one year to complete their loveshock experience, it is not unusual for recovery to take longer. Usually the time required, what I refer to as your *traveling time,* is determined by the amount of time you have spent with the other person and the depth of your commitment. For instance, couples who have been living together or seeing each other for just a year will have a shorter loveshock experience than couples who have been together for a few years. And couples divorcing after twenty or more years, with children, are likely to have the longest loveshock experience of all.

Whether or not it is normal for you to spend one, two, even three years in loveshock depends on how well you are functioning. If you are able to maintain your emotional center, act and react to situations reasonably, and motivate yourself through your daily routines, it is still not abnormal for your sadness and emotional pain to go on for a couple of years. What's important is that you continue to function—following the initial shock—while your lovewounds heal.

Many of my loveshock patients come to me at the onset of their loveshock because they are unable to function and feel as if they are emotionally unraveling. They are unable to concentrate and unable to sleep, and they have a sense of hopelessness. This initial inability to function is a normal result of their shock and grief. In fact, they are surprised when I tell them that their emotional state is appropriate, that the reason they are in so much pain is that they are in touch with their loss—and that this is healthy! But, I tell them, they must begin to confront their pain and move themselves through it. For them to bear the "unbearable," to face the loveshock experience head-on, by working their way through it and by understanding it—this forcing themselves to function is the beginning of their healing process.

Loveshock does not become pathological unless you try to repress it or inhibit it through denial or different forms of excess, such as drug and alcohol abuse. Failure to recognize and express your emotional pain can severely impair your psychological health and your ability to form new love relationships in the future. You may fear that the very same sequence of events will be repeated in your next relationship, or worse, you may doubt your ability to love. However, confronting your loveshock experience and learning from what went wrong in the relationship can turn the pain into a growth experience and provide you with insights and coping skills that can enhance your next relationship.

The repercussions of unresolved loveshock can damage more than your emotional health. When your life is filled with emotional pain and you don't deal with the accompanying feelings, the signal is put out to your body that you don't want to recover. Recent medical studies show that the stress created by unresolved grief, depression, and despair can depress the body's immune system, making you more susceptible to illness.

So loveshock, although painful, is a sign of health, and the *only* way to recover from loss of love. Not to feel loveshock after suffering from a significant love loss is to be disconnected from your emotions; to feel it is to be in touch with a very painful reality—but one that is vital to your emotional well-being.

WHAT TO EXPECT DURING A LOVESHOCK CRISIS

Jennifer and David both sought psychiatric help but were struggling to get beyond their loveshock until they came to me for therapy. In fact, what helped to prevent David from taking that fatal jump on Valentine's Day was that, by coincidence, I was on the talk show that he was watching, discussing the symptoms and stages of loveshock. He later told me that as he sat and listened to my description of loveshock, what he heard was exactly what he was experiencing at that moment and had been experiencing ever since the awful call from Vanessa. For the first time he was able to make sense of his experience and took comfort in knowing that there was a label for what he felt. He was dumbfounded to discover that what he was feeling was not unique, that millions of others had already suffered from the same symptoms and that many of them had gone on to love again. That day, learning what would happen next and that the pain he was feeling would not last forever kept him from jumping.

When I tell my patients, "This is what you are going through, and this is what you can expect next," it is as though a tremendous burden has been lifted from them. As they begin to understand the dynamics of their loveshock experience, their knowledge gives them an insight that helps them manage their fears as they constructively work their way through the experience. They also take a great deal of comfort in knowing that they are not alone, that I have treated many other people for loveshock, and yes, that these other people have lived through the experience. And perhaps most reassuring of all for them is to learn that the intensity of pain they are feeling at the moment will eventually decrease and even come to an end, that there will be a predictable course of events, a series of stages that they will go through that will enable them to reach that end.

Symptomatically, there are a wide range of symptoms that can be experienced at any given time by people suffering from loveshock. You may find yourself bingeing on food or alcohol and popping pills or taking drugs. As you react compulsively, what you are really seeking is a medicine to dull your pain, a balm to soothe your lovewounds. Unfortunately, there is no magic cure!

There can be waves of nausea and a loss of appetite.

You may become depressed and experience uncontrollable crying jags. Although extremely fatigued, you may be unable to sleep. You may find that it is difficult for you to concentrate, that you suffer from memory loss; you may feel as if you have little or no energy. If you drive, exercise great caution, as you may drive less attentively and at times even recklessly.

When you are suffering from loveshock you often wander through your daily routine unable to remember what you have done. The only thing you seem able to focus on is the other person and the relationship that once was. In your obsessional thinking, every aspect of your life can be invaded by thoughts of the other person. As your thoughts become locked on the other person and your pain, you just can't seem to break through and get beyond them. You'll try anything to get that other person out of your thoughts.

You may become totally reclusive, like Jennifer, retreating into seclusion and terrified of any involvement with the opposite sex. Or conversely, like David, you may plunge into an orgy of promiscuity. When you're in loveshock, your life can become uncontrollable.

The most acute symptom you can expect to experience, the one that all the other symptoms feed off, is that inner emptiness deep inside of you. You feel as if you've lost a part of yourself, that something has been wrenched from you. All of your feelings are intensified as you are embraced by the loneliness of your life without the other person. And you are overcome by your fear, fear that you will spend the rest of your life void of any tenderness and affection, cut off from love—the love that you want to give, the love that you need to have.

TRAVELING THROUGH THE SIX STAGES OF LOVESHOCK

The symptoms of loveshock progress in a predictable pattern that can be broken down into six stages: *shock, grief, setting blame, resignation* (the "goodbye" stage), *rebuilding,* and *resolution.*

The rate at which you move from one stage to the next is what I call your *psychological traveling time.* Some of you will travel through these stages quickly, while others of you will travel through them slowly. Regardless of your traveling time, as you travel through each stage the intensity of the symptoms will begin to lessen. During shock, grief, and setting blame you suffer the most; by the time you have reached the final stage of resolution, your pain has faded into the past like a bad dream. But you *must* go through all the stages to resolution. One of the goals of loveshock therapy is to help you effectively manage your emotional pain so that you don't lock in to any of the stages that precede resolution.

It is also important to keep in mind that although there are common patterns, human behavior is not linear. There are many different ways that you can travel through the stages. For instance, as you move from one stage to the next, it is not unusual for vestiges of the previous stage to remain with you. Or you may spend a considerable amount of time traveling back and forth between two stages—what I call *the zigzag effect.* You may experience certain stages more intensely than others, or you may have a relatively brief experience with one stage and a prolonged experience with another. While it is important that you complete each stage and travel on to the next, allow yourself to flow with the process.

Don't be surprised if you zigzag several times through-out your loveshock experience.

There are no "right" or "wrong" ways to travel through the stages, but you should be alert to any self-destructive behaviors and attitudes that may develop because of the pain, regret, or guilt that you feel associated with your loss. I call these the *love pitfalls*. They include various compulsive behaviors such as food bingeing, excessive drinking, and promiscuity. I will discuss them in further detail in Chapter Five. These love pitfalls are setbacks that can occur along the way and will only delay, not prevent, your arrival at the final stage of resolution. There's nothing to feel guilty about if you have setbacks, nor does it matter how often they occur. What's im-portant is that you recover as quickly as possible, get back on your feet, and continue to move forward. As you push yourself foward and as time passes, the set-backs will occur less frequently. Always keep in mind that you are going to come through this experience and that setbacks are normal.

The following description of the six stages of love-shock will give you a good idea of what you *may* ex-perience with each stage.

Shock

At the onset of loveshock you feel an immediate sense of numbness, disorientation, and disbelief. Your life seems to stand still as you focus on your loss. You may be unable to eat, unable to sleep; it's as though you have become a zombie. The intensity of your feelings and the sense of acute loss block out all other concerns and ac-tivities. Later, when you look back on this period of your loveshock experience, you may have little recollection of what went on. Jennifer doesn't remember her housekeeper packing her bags or the drive to the Bel-Air Hotel. The weeks she spent locked away in the hotel are a distant blur in her memory. A protective stage, shock actually insulates you from the full impact of the emotional trauma you are experiencing.

Your shock can last for a day or it can last for a month—but rarely longer. It is eventually pushed out of the way by the breaking through of your emotions: your overwhelming sense of loss and grief.

Grief

When grief sets in you are not just mourning for the loss of the person. You're also mourning for all the time you shared, for the dreams that you mutually held in your hearts, and for the unfulfilled promise of a life together. You may also mourn for your own failure, realizing that no matter how hard you try or wish it to be, you alone cannot make a love relationship: it takes two willing partners.

As you deal with your loss, and the pain it generates in your life, you may feel irritable and short-tempered, snapping at friends and coworkers. You usually find yourself unresponsive to offers from friends to "fix you up" with dates because you need to complete your grief first. You may even be angry that your friends don't understand your need to grieve. This is not the right time for you to try to involve yourself in a new relationship.

As you grieve, you may have the compulsion to telephone the other person just so that you can hear his or her voice. You are desperate to maintain some sort of connection, no matter how unrealistic it is. But after you hear the initial hello you hang up, unable to speak a word to the person with whom you could at one time speak forever. David confessed to me, with great embarrassment, that he used to call Vanessa at 1:00 A.M. because she was half asleep and would say hello several times before hanging up. But he also felt hurt that she could sleep while he was suffering and wide awake. Magnifying his own pain, he was convinced that because she was sleeping, she was adjusting well and going on with her life.

Depression often develops at this time, as you are overwhelmed with a sense of hopelessness. It is not unusual to become locked in this stage. When this happens you lose more than the person you have loved— you lose yourself. If Queen Victoria hadn't spent thirty years locked in her grief, she probably could have married again. While she might never have been able to find another Prince Albert, she might have found someone else to share her life with.

When locked in grief, people often need and seek help. It is at this point that Jennifer began her loveshock therapy. We discovered, together, that one of the reasons she was unable to get beyond her grief was that she was afraid that no one would want her. After twenty years of marriage she felt used up: as painful as it was, grief was the "safest" place for her to be.

Setting Blame

When the hysteria of your grief subsides you have a psychological need to make sense of what has happened. It is at this time that you start analyzing what went wrong and you progress into the third stage of setting blame. You begin to confront the different problems as you struggle to understand what precipitated the breakup. You start to ask yourself, "What happened? Where did I go wrong? Where did he (or she) go wrong? Where did we go wrong?" You may blame yourself, the other person, or others in general for the breakup. You may look to your general life circumstances as well—stress on the job, an ill-timed move, financial problems, health problems—to place the blame.

Along with your hurt, the strongest emotion you will feel at this time is usually anger, and it may be acted out with various compulsive behaviors—bingeing, alcohol abuse, drug abuse, and promiscuity.

Your anger may be directed at the other person for the hurt that he or she has caused you, or at yourself, as you consider yourself a failure. David's sudden, atypical behavior of one-night stands, debauchery, and near suicide was his way of dealing with his anger. He blamed himself, so his anger was self-destructive. He was convinced that the breakup was his fault because he wasn't worthy of love. After all, although his parents had done their best, they had never shown him any real affection, so why would a beautiful woman life Vanessa want to marry him? Because he was placing all the blame on himself, David's self-esteem was at its lowest point when he consulted with me.

Out of anger, you may also enter into another relationship where subconsciously you take out on the other person the hurt and pain you feel within. You may be verbally abusive, physically aloof or just disrespectful of the other person's needs. I call this *revenge loving,* as you act out on the other person whatever you feel has been done to you.

It is not uncommon to travel back and forth between setting blame and grief before you are ready to move on to the fourth stage of resignation. Jennifer found herself doing this. One day she would be mourning all that she had lost, and then a few days later she would come to me in a rage, saying, "If only he had bothered to call all those times that he said he would! I could have continued, if there had been phone calls. How little I must have mattered to him that I didn't even merit a phone call!" I saw her anger as healthy and was able to use it as a means to take her out of her grief. As she expressed her anger, she realized that she deserved a lot more than she had gotten from her marriage. Using her anger constructively, she was slowly on her way to rebuilding her self-esteem.

Resignation—The Goodbye Stage

Traveling from setting blame to resignation may be the hardest transition of your loveshock experience. I like to call this stage *the goodbye stage* because it is the point at which you are able to say, "This person is no longer in my life. I can spend my life mourning or being angry, or I can push myself to go forward." Not only must you accept that the relationship is over, you must release it completely, detaching yourself from the other person and withdrawing the energy that you invested in the relationship. This is a bittersweet time during your loveshock experience, as you say goodbye to the relationship and all the feelings that have been involved in maintaining it. You may have mixed emotions—at once relieved that you are ready to let go and sad that you have to let go.

While it may sound as if the worst is over once you've reached resignation, it is not uncommon to get stuck in this stage. Perhaps you have little or no life motivation left because you are so drained. You may really have to push yourself to move on to rebuilding.

Although David was finally able to detach from Vanessa, in some ways he felt more fatigued and drained than he had during any other part of his loveshock experience. As he so aptly put it, "I feel as if a vampire, no, vampiress, has sucked all the blood out of me—discarding me to go on to the next victim!" Because of the emptiness he still felt, it was impossible for him to move on to rebuilding enthusiastically.

While the senior partners at David's law firm had already lessened his caseload, they eventually suggested that he take a vacation. Perhaps a trip would renew his usual vigor and the fighting spirit they all admired. David followed their advice, and although he couldn't afford anything lavish, found that just getting away from it all and going camping for a week was beneficial. When he returned he felt more energetic and was finally ready to make a fresh start, as he began to rebuild his life.

Rebuilding

Once you have begun to actively rebuild your life, the worst of your loveshock experience begins to recede. At this point you realize that you have more happy days than sad days. Your concentration is back and you're working on correcting any compulsive habits that you've developed during your loveshock experience. Your life is yours again and your focus is on re-creating its equilibrium. You're ready to date; you want to get out and really start to live. And some of you are focusing on your own needs for the first time in your life, selective about whom you'll spend your time with so that you can love in a healthy, balanced way.

At this point of her loveshock experience, Jennifer suddenly realized that she was laughing a lot, going out with her friends, and just enjoying her life. She was even open to the possibility of a new relationship. She had come a long way since her initial weeks of seclusion at the Bel-Air Hotel.

When she accepted a date for the first time in twenty years, she felt very strange. She never thought she'd be interested in dating again or, for that matter, that anyone would want to date her. But it got easier, and she actually started to enjoy her life as a single person. At first she found herself comparing every man she went out with to Rick, in personality as well as physically. I call this *comparison shopping*. I reminded her that while people may share certain similarities, each person is essentially unique. Whenever she started to compare, I had her shift her focus to what was different about the man she was dating and what needs she had that this person could or could not fulfill. We discussed things that they did that made their time together special. The more confident she became, the less comparing she did. When she met Tony, who became her second husband, she was able to know him in his own right, not in terms of how he related to Rick.

For many, rebuilding is like learning to walk again after having broken a leg. You've mended, but you need to build your strength by developing your self-esteem and confidence. Often your social and dating skills have to be polished. You can expect to make a few mistakes along the way.

While you are still aware of all the pain that you have been through, you begin to understand what you have gained and what you have lost because of the breakup. For many of you, what you have gained is greater than what you have lost. And for the rest, you will have the opportunity to create a happier, richer life as you continue to develop a greater awareness of yourself and your self-worth.

Resolution

This is the beginning of a new life cycle. You have resolved the conflict and the turmoil that have been with you since your loveshock experience first began. In a sense, you've made peace with your emotional pain. Your life is back on course again, but it's a different course because of the personal growth that occurred as you traveled through all of the stages of loveshock. At this time you may choose to begin a new love relationship. If not, you have more confidence in your ability to create your own happiness and take care of yourself.

For Jennifer, the resolution stage did include a new love relationship. When she came to me for what turned out to be her last session, she told me the following story. "Tony and I were having dinner in Malibu, and who should I see sitting across the room? None other than Rick and his call girl girlfriend—Laura!"

At this point in the story, Jennifer had a pensive look on her face. I was afraid she was going to tell me that she created a scene. She continued, "You're not going to believe what I did, Dr. Gullo. I actually got up, walked across the room, and said hello to my ex-husband and introduced myself to his girlfriend. Can you believe it? I politely stuck out my hand and said, 'Hi, I'm Jennifer Wexler. You must be Laura.' After some chitchat, I held my head high and walked back to my table. And do you know that I overheard Laura say, 'The lady is a real class act'? I could hardly believe my ears, but I felt a sense of pride and wholeness. And Tony was amazed by my courage to confront pleasantly two people who had caused me so much pain."

Jennifer was beaming as she finished telling me what happened and how happy Tony made her. I too was amazed that she could put her loveshock experience and all of its pain in the past and take such a courageous step. Now it was my turn to comment, "Your loveshock experience is over; there is no need for you to continue therapy."

PASSIVE-ACTIVE RESPONSE PATTERNS

One of the intial challenges you must overcome during the early stages of loveshock is to realize that while the relationship has ended, your life hasn't. At this time it is important that you evaluate your response pattern to your loveshock crisis. I have found that most people respond in extremes, either passively or actively. Your goal at this time should be to monitor your behavior so that you can manage your pain and maintain balance in your life.

When your response is passive, you withdraw into yourself and become reclusive. Your seclusion becomes your safety net as you keep yourself locked in the second stage of grief. A victim of your fear, you may be overwhelmed by dread of what the future will bring. Filled with self-doubt, your mind spins anxiously: "What will happen next? Who will ever want to love me again? Will I ever be loved again? How will I go on?" Queen Victoria's self-imposed exile for thirty years is an extreme example of a passive response pattern. Fleeing to the Bel-Air Hotel, Jennifer felt that grief was the safest place for her to be. She had been able to take the initial step to end her painful relationship with Rick, but she could go no further because she was paralyzed by her fear.

Conversely, when your response to your loveshock experience is active, you literally act out your pain on yourself and others. Instead of becoming reclusive and withdrawn, you are more likely to act compulsively and erratically. Food bingeing, alcohol abuse, drug abuse, and promiscuity are typical compulsive behaviors. So great is your pain, so low your sense of self-worth that you may take your active response pattern to the extreme and embark on a journey of self-destruction. Remember David—his heavy drinking and drug abuse combined with his numerous one-night stands—eventually standing by his window as he contemplated jumping?

While it's normal to spend some time both passively and actively responding in extremes to your loveshock experience, it is very important to evaluate the degree and frequency of these behaviors on a daily basis. An effective way to do this is what I call *self-monitoring*.

Self-monitoring can be done by recording your feelings on tape, keeping a journal, or making a list of the day's activities and how you felt while doing them. Or you can just take ten minutes twice a day to have an internal dialogue with yourself about what you are doing, how you feel, and how you think you are doing.

Think of self-monitoring as an opportunity to step outside of yourself and watch what's going on. The self-awareness and self-knowledge you gain from it can enhance your personal growth during loveshock. And if you are totally honest with yourself, self-monitoring will alert you to any destructive patterns or habits that are forming. This exercise is not intended to make you feel bad about yourself. It is intended to help you grow from your mistakes and move you through loveshock with a minimal amount of pain.

Since Jennifer, reacting passively, was stuck in the second stage of grief, I suggested that she keep a journal and actually monitor her grief. This proved to be very constructive and helped her move on to the next stage of setting blame. She found in her journal an effective catharsis as she purged her feelings, writing pages and pages about all the hurt and humiliation she felt she had endured, especially during the last five years of her marriage to Rick. Keeping a journal also helped her pinpoint her fears of what the future would bring, specifically, of never being loved again. Once she acknowledged her fears they became less frightening and she began to work on overcoming them. Jennifer was functioning again as she began to manage her loveshock.

This exercise and the other exercises and therapies I offer in this book should effectively move you through your loveshock experience and help you remain emotionally, mentally, and physically intact. However, if you spend more than a couple of weeks in extreme passive or active response patterns, you should seek additional help from your physician, therapist, or family counselor.

CHAPTER TWO

Confronting Your Fears

In working with people going through loveshock, I have developed a great awe for the power of the human psyche, its determination to survive and heal itself, especially when properly directed through self-help or with the guidance of a counselor or therapist. While your emotional pain may at times seem unbearable, there is a natural resilience within you to go on and work your way through it. It is this ability to endure emotional trauma that helps all of us to survive.

When you first go into loveshock, the numbness of shock protects you from the full impact of the emotional blow you've just received. It is as though your psyche has put itself on hold to prepare itself to deal with an overwhelming and often tragic reality. This pause allows your psyche to marshal its resources and defenses before actually confronting the emotional pain at hand—a kind of psychological retreat before the advance.

However, as your shock begins to subside and you move into the second stage of grief, your fears begin to

emerge and may even overwhelm you. You start to deal
with the reality of your situation: an important love
relationship is no longer a part of your life. It is important that you accept your fears as a natural and normal dynamic of loveshock; know that everyone who
experiences loveshock is going to have to confront certain fears. And any anxiety, panic, or despair connected
with your fears is predictable. You are not alone and
you are not going crazy!

While loveshock can trigger a wide variety of fears
during any of its stages, including fears from your childhood that you thought you had resolved, there are some
common ones that I see in many of my loveshock patients. You may find that you experience just one or
two of these fears or all of them. Know that in your
own loveshock, some or all of these fears will probably
occur. In this way you can prepare yourself and find it
easier to cope. This knowledge will not diminish the
pain, but it will provide you with greater control because
you will understand what's happening. Keeping your
fears under control will help you manage your pain more
effectively. Use your knowledge to conduct a mental
"fire drill" in which you rehearse what to do, reflect on
what's working and what's not working, and anticipate
what might happen next.

THE GREATEST FEAR OF ALL

The first and greatest fear you confront occurs in the
second stage of grief. You may well be terrified that
you'll always feel the way you do at the moment—that
the intense emotional pain you are experiencing will
never go away and that the terrible empty pit of lone-

liness you feel will engulf you forever. You fear that because of it, you will never be able to move forward to really live and love again. As you are filled with self-doubt, thoughts of "I'll never find someone else" or "I don't have the ability to make a love relationship work" eat away at you.

What you must do during these intense periods of fear is to live moment to moment, easing yourself through your daily routines, and trust that with time your emotional pain will become less intense. Fortunately, as a protective mechanism, the human psyche naturally diminishes painful memories with the passage of time; otherwise you would be unable to function. To constantly relive acute, vivid memories of every negative experience would eventually drive you to real insanity, as you would be in a perpetual state of fear. (I will discuss this in greater detail in Chapter Four: Your Loveshock Traveling Time.)

Most of my patients find these intense periods of fear to be some of the most difficult moments of their loveshock experience, moments during which they feel that they are losing their minds, that they are out of control, that they just can't go on. In rare instances the temporary insanity brought on by this fear can push a person over the edge.

This was true for Earlene, a massage therapist originally from Barbados. She was so afraid that her emotional pain would never go away that she tried to take her own life. Because she was not responding to traditional therapy, her internist, a colleague who once worked with me at the medical center where I trained, asked me to consult on her case. As I sat beside her hospital bed, she began to tell me her story.

Her first marriage had been nothing more than a business arrangement so that she could get her green card to live and work in the United States. This marriage had ended by mutual agreement, and she had never experienced loveshock. Twenty-five years later at forty-five years old, Earlene met Ed. She knew that she had finally found the love of her life. A good-looking police sergeant, he became the center of her world.

She scheduled her days off to coincide with his and made herself available to fulfill his every need. Being a police sergeant, he was often on call, so their time together was infrequent and unpredictable. But the moments they did share were romantic and unforgettable.

"We'd have a little sherry and dance by candlelight to our favorite records before dinner. All Ed had to do was look into my eyes and I could just feel myself filling up with love. I've never felt this way about anyone or anything in my whole life. When we made love it was so incredible that I swear the earth stopped. He always made me feel so beautiful and special. It didn't bother him that I was middle-aged and a little overweight, because as he always said, 'Our souls connect.' While everything seemed perfect between us, the one thing I never understood was why we would never spend any time at his place. I guess deep down inside I suspected that he was married, but I couldn't understand how someone so perfect for me could belong to anyone else. So I just looked the other way. Finally, a little more than a year after we had first met, the truth came out. Not only was he married, but he had three sons."

"And you felt that you had to end it, even though having him in your life made you so happy?"

"Oh, Dr. Gullo, I just couldn't go on. Although I married so I could live in the United States, I was raised to believe that adultery is wrong no matter what the circumstances. And while I was married, even though I wasn't in love, I was never with another man. I guess I'm old-fashioned, but this is a value that sticks to me like glue. I can't go against it—but I'm miserable without him . . ."

"Then I would think that you would be proud of yourself for staying true to your values. It's a wonderful quality, Earlene—to have the courage of your convictions. Some people spend a lifetime trying to develop this quality and never even come close. You've also realized that shared values are necessary if you are to have a happy love relationship."

As she looked away, toward the white hospital wall, she said, "A lot of good the courage of my convictions does me. I can't bear the pain of not having him in my life anymore, and that's why I took all those pills. The emptiness was killing me, so I thought why not just finish the job instead of prolonging my grief."

"How do you feel now, Earlene?"

"Empty. Lost. I'm so afraid. I gave him a piece of my heart—and now it's gone."

While Earlene's story was as unique and as special as Earlene herself, I had heard her final analysis of her feelings many times before. Like so many other love-shock patients, locked in the second stage of grief, she was convinced that her pain would never end. What she needed now was something to hold on to, something that could help move her loveshock. Fortunately she had a career that meant a lot to her.

"Tell me about your work as a massage therapist."

"Oh, I just love helping people and making them feel good. You know, Dr. Gullo, massage therapy is a wonderful thing. It can help you relax when life gets tough. And it can even strengthen your immune system."

"Sounds like massage therapy might help you right now."

"Why yes, I guess I've been pretty tough on myself. And what I must have done to my body with all those pills! And you know, I've really neglected my clients over the last couple of months. Some of them are long-standing clients who have really counted on me for years. I've been a massage therapist for twenty-one years . . ."

Earlene still had a lot of grief and sadness to work through, but her pain became manageable as she poured all the extra energy she had expended on Ed back into her work. By helping others she was helping herself. The emptiness that had devastated her at the beginning of her loveshock slowly diminished. Six months later she called me to report, "You were right, Dr. Gullo, the pain has faded. I still miss Ed—I got rid of all of our favorite records—but things don't seem so bad anymore. I've also managed to take off ten pounds and feel pretty good about myself . . ."

LOSING YOUR EMOTIONAL CENTER

In the early stages of loveshock, the second stage of grief and the third stage of setting blame, emotional outbursts and even hysteria can be expected. Because you are so emotionally vulnerable at this time, you may even find yourself suddenly crying for no apparent reason. Or it may happen that a song on the radio, a favorite television show that you once shared, and even certain times of the day can trigger these outbursts. The intensity of these outbursts may really frighten you: your emotional reactions are running to extremes.

Many of my loveshock patients start therapy with me

at this time because they feel that they are losing the very center of their being. They are afraid that they will emotionally unravel into nothingness because they are unable to maintain their self-control.

During the first month of her loveshock, Marjorie remembers bursting into tears when a cab driver simply asked her, "Where to, lady?" She got out of the cab and ran down the street back to her apartment. Terrified of losing her emotional control in public, she didn't leave her apartment for a week. A secretary, she called in sick with "a bad case of the flu"—afraid that she would have one of these breakdowns at work.

For Ron, grocery shopping was extremely painful. "I'd hit the frozen food section, take one look at the double chocolate chip ice cream—Jan's nightly craving when she was pregnant—and suddenly feel my whole body shake. My throat would tighten and my lips would start to quiver. I knew that if I didn't get out of the store as quickly as possible, I might start to break down. The first time I went shopping after we split up, I panicked and fled the store, leaving a full cart of groceries behind. Until I felt more in control, which really didn't happen until I was in the fourth stage of resignation, I hired a housekeeper who did my shopping once a week. It was tough on my budget, but the expense was well worth it. I needed someone who could handle the domestic details of my life."

Leslie found that she needed another suitcase to pack her things, after making the decision to leave Jack because of his cocaine habit. "Here we were, a nice suburban couple, with two kids in college, living ordinary lives, and he gets hooked on cocaine. When I came home from work and found him free-basing at the kitchen table, in a state of shock, I made the decision to leave.

I went upstairs and started throwing my clothes into suitcases, but I realized I needed one more. In my zombielike state I drove to the local discount store. I must have stood there for an hour, staring at all those suitcases, totally confused about which one would be best. Finally a salesperson approached me and when he said, 'May I help you?' I stuttered and couldn't remember what I came for. As I left the store, I was too disoriented even to be embarrassed and ended up driving to my girlfriend's house. I stayed with her for two weeks until I felt more focused and able to manage my emotions. I was terrified that at any given moment I might lose control. For the next couple of weeks I was able to get through work, and that was about it. As I began to feel more in control I started to do more things. But boy, in the beginning it was tough to get through.''

While you're feeling emotionally overwrought, distraught, and out of control, it is wise not to add any extra stress to your life. Hire extra help, if affordable, to remove some of the burden. This is the time to call on family and friends for support. Take them up on lunch and dinner invitations. Let them help you out with your children or run an errand for you, if they offer. And ask them if you can call them when you are feeling lonely, afraid, or when you just need to talk, if they mind occasionally being your "911," or emergency number.

It may be difficult, especially while you are in grief, but make an effort to maintain any positive lifestyle habits you have already developed, such as an exercise program, meditation, or any relaxing hobbies that you enjoy. You'll find that exercise will help you release the feelings of frustration and anger that are prevalent during the third stage, setting blame. And if positive lifestyle

habits aren't a part of your daily routine, try to incorporate them into your life now. Or if your routine has
changed because of the breakup, make it your priority
to form a new one that suits your present needs. A
positive routine will provide structure where there is
emotional chaos and help you move back into the mainstream of life.

Ron was very wise to hire a housekeeper to do the
shopping and take over the chores that Jan always did.
Leslie's girlfriend was a real lifesaver, giving her the
moral support she needed as she tried to make sense of
what had happened and how she could best get on with
her life.

If you don't think that you can get through this period
with just your personal support system, don't feel ashamed
or become reclusive because you can't cope. Reach out
and find the help you need from a qualified and ethical
professional. If you find that you are suddenly suffering
from headaches, stomach pains, or heart palpitations,
see a physician for the appropriate guidance. Accept that
during this period you may have occasionally to rely on
antacids for your heartburn and tranquilizers for your
"nerves"—but only under your physician's supervision.

For Marjorie, initially unable to function because of
her grief, a "time out" week was the only way she could
cope. Her physician also prescribed an anti-anxiety drug
for her, which she used for a month, and sent her to
me. While she was fortunate to be able to take a week
off from work without being concerned that she might
lose her job, this isn't always possible. You must be
extremely self-protective against other losses at this time.
To lose a job after losing love will only compound your
fears and anxieties, so force yourself to function at work
and maintain your regular routine to the best of your

ability. You'll be surprised how losing yourself in your work or in a sport, activity, or hobby you enjoy will divert your attention, making you less fearful.

THE IMPORTANCE OF DIVERTERS

Before I discuss more of the common fears shared by most of my loveshock patients, I want to point out how useful *diverters* can be, during all stages of loveshock, in helping your to manage your fears. Basically a diverter is any constructive object or activity that you can focus your energy on—the very same energy that up until now you've invested in your love relationship. Just as an automobile needs shock absorbers to allow for a smoother ride over bumpy roads, when in loveshock you need a reserve of diverters to help absorb some of the emotional pain. And the more compelling the diverters are, the better they are, as they will command your attention in such a way that you will find yourself obsessing less and less on your loss and pain.

When Chuck and Darlene ended their fourteen-year marriage, they both wanted to stay in the house that they equally loved. Rather than going through a bitter legal battle, Darlene took the money from her settlement and decided to build her own house. While she couldn't afford anything too exotic, with the money she did have she was determined to design a house exactly as she wanted it. She became totally immersed in the project.

Building her house was such a compelling diverter that although Darlene was the rejectee, she traveled through her loveshock with less emotional pain than Chuck. She told me, "Every time I think I'm going to lose my mind, I remind myself that it is healthy that

I'm so in touch with my feelings. I also remind myself that my loveshock will end, and then I lose myself in planning another part of my house—whether it's the tiles for the bathroom floor or the kitchen wallpaper."

Douglas had always been what he called "a closet poet"—a traveling salesman with a love for lyrics. While he often submitted his work to agents and publishers, he had never had the satisfaction of being published. And his girlfriend, Brooke, did little to encourage him. In fact, she resented the time and energy he spent trying to get published. She constantly nagged him about using his time more realistically, and blamed his lack of promotion on his poetic obsession.

When Douglas and Brooke split up, he made getting published his top priority and it became his diverter. On the weekends, when he felt the pain of his loveshock the most, he concentrated on writing submission letters and investigating numerous magazines' guidelines for publishing. Nine months later a humor piece he wrote appeared in a local newspaper. This gave him the confidence he needed to continue. The last time we talked he was about to be published by *Reader's Digest*.

Unfortunately, many people don't realize the need for diverters in their lives until loveshock occurs. I have seen a tremendous amount of suffering in my older female patients, who have been living the traditional housewife role in which the husband and his needs come first. When divorce occurs these women are at a loss as to what to do with the rest of their lives. Those who have children, do charity work, and have created some outside interests cope better than those who have done nothing but focus on their mates. Their diverters give them something to hold on to as they work toward rebuilding their lives. Those women who have few or no diverters tend to be extremely slow travelers through loveshock, often becoming locked into the stages of grief and setting blame, and are prone to severe depression. To inspire them to take any sort of action to help themselves is difficult because they are often convinced that their lives no longer have any meaning.

When Greta came to see me, she had been stuck in the second stage of grief for a good six months. Her physician had referred her to me after he discovered that her chest pains were a symptom of her grief. After thirty years of marriage her husband had left her "to see the world" and had taken a blond ski instructor with him. Greta, who had come from Sweden with her husband when they were first married, had devoted her entire life to him. She had never been able to have children, which had always caused her great sadness, and now that Sven had left her she told me that she was ready to die. Greta was only fifty-five years old. She was pleasantly plump with a very sweet face. Her long gray hair was tightly braided and wrapped around her head.

As I asked her about herself she had very little to say. "Do you like to read?"

"No."

"Do you like to go to school?"

"No."

"Have you ever thought about getting a pet?"

"Well, I always wanted a bird, but Sven said no because he found them dirty."

"Yes, I understand. But Sven is no longer a part of your life, so why not treat yourself to a bird? It's time for you to focus on your wants and needs." As I watched her mull it over, a flicker of interest flashed across her face.

Two weeks later she had acquired a tame African

parrot whom she named Woody. He could talk a little bit, which enthralled her, and she began to teach him more. All the sweetness and love she had devoted to Sven she now gave to Woody. I was amazed not only at how intelligent Woody was, but at how quickly Greta was coming back to life.

Occasionally she would mention in our session, after Woody had mastered a new word or phrase, how clever her Woody was. Once when I called her she asked if I would like to speak to Woody. After we *all* had the following conversation I knew that she would be all right: "Here's what Woody has to say the next time Sven calls, Dr. Gullo." Suddenly I heard Woody's high, shrill voice squawk out, "Get lost, you jerk!" Greta's gusty laugh could be heard in the background.

FACING THE SILENCE OF ONENESS

While you are traveling through the stages of grief, setting blame, and resignation, you can expect a certain amount of fear and panic to overwhelm you as you confront living alone. For some of you, this may be the first time that you have ever lived alone. You went from living with your parents to living with your partner, so it's all the more challenging for you to adjust. Also, the longer you have lived with your mate, the more difficult you may find it to shift your lifestyle from togetherness to oneness. This readjusting and shifting, as you learn to live on your own, is what I call facing the silence of oneness.

Different patients interpret it in different ways, depending on how they are most affected. Marjorie called it "the screaming four walls" until she adjusted and decided that she liked the peace and quiet of her apartment after a long day at the office. However, it wasn't until she had reached the fifth stage of rebuilding that she made this adjustment. To Leslie it was "the empty bed syndrome," but after a few weeks she decided she'd rather sleep alone than with Jack, who was a restless sleeper because of his cocaine habit. Ron called it "TV dinners and boob tube time" until he began to motivate himself to cook some of the fresh food his housekeeper bought for him week after week.

When you first begin to live alone, it's natural to feel lonely and even to hate it. Your loneliness will probably be more profound on the weekends, late at night in bed, and during the holidays. Be patient with yourself. Adjusting to a new life experience always takes time and there are always setbacks.

So how do you cope; what can you do to counteract loneliness? Initially, during grief, when your loneliness and emotional pain are the most acute, do *anything* that makes you feel better—as long as it is not destructive to your well-being. Guard against excessive drinking, taking medications (except as prescribed by your physician), and any other negative lifestyle habits. When in doubt, it's best to abstain. Accept that the first few weeks, and maybe even months, will be difficult. Believe in yourself and know that you do have the strength to see yourself through.

If bedtime is particularly difficult, try taking a hot bath to relax. Sleep with the TV on or the radio playing, if the sound of voices comforts you. Ron chose to jog late every night, so that he would be too physically exhausted to care whether or not he was alone.

Concerned that there was something really psychologically wrong with her, Leslie admitted to me she was sleeping with her old childhood teddy bear. I reassured her that there was nothing wrong with her; in fact I congratulated her on being so resourceful.

Whatever constructive remedy works for you, use it. Don't worry about whether it's silly or not, getting hung up on the concept of what's normal and not normal. It takes enough self-control just to move yourself through the early stages of loveshock, remaining emotionally intact, without worrying about how normal you are.

Marjorie went through a period of insomnia, when she would sleep for a few hours and then find herself wide awake at 3:00 A.M., filled with fear of what tomorrow would bring. Rather than toss and turn in bed, she started to needlepoint. She kept the canvas and yarn by her bed and, when her insomnia hit, would turn on the light and immediately start working. Within half an hour she relaxed and found it easy to go back to sleep.

Coping with weekends will take some planning and real motivation on your part when your loveshock first begins. Do some traveling if you can afford it, go to the movies, or take a course. Try taking up a sport that you never thought you'd be good at and challenge yourself to do it. Do whatever it takes to divert yourself so that you do not start feeling sorry for yourself. Get involved!

Fill your free time with something meaningful. Greta became a volunteer at her local hospital, spending time with the sick children. She told them Swedish nursery rhymes, sang them songs, and even brought Woody to visit when the doctors would allow it.

In fact, one of the best ways to forget about your own suffering is to help someone else. And as you do, you will begin to realize your own strength, strength that will give you a renewed sense of confidence and self-esteem. Regardless of how weak and afraid you may feel, in helping others you are reminded that you are emotionally strong. This is why Earlene's work as a massage therapist was so effective in moving her through her loveshock. Although she was devastated to the point of suicide, her fears lessened each day as she gained confidence by realizing that she still had the ability to help others.

Holidays or once-shared events may be your toughest time—especially during the first year, and even if you are in rebuilding. It's difficult to feel happy and festive when you feel that you're all alone. Look to family and friends for support. Or treat yourself to a special trip.

While Jack eventually ended up in a rehab center, Leslie took her two children to Vermont during their Christmas break for a ski trip and had one of the best Christmases that she could remember. "I was amazed at how good and independent I felt. I realized that I didn't need Jack to have a meaningful Christmas. This trip also helped prepare me for resignation, for finally releasing my relationship with Jack. And the extra time and energy I gave the boys really brought us closer together. This has been a rough couple of months on them too."

YOUR POWERLESSNESS

Many people whom I have treated for loveshock have a hard time accepting that they are powerless over their situation and dealing with the fear that they have no control over the changes occurring in their lives. This is because they have spent the greater portion of their lives structuring situations so that they are in control. I encounter this problem most frequently in high-powered professionals and accomplished and attractive men and women. It's incomprehensible to them that they somehow can't buy, attract, or charm the relationship back into their lives.

No matter how much you have achieved, how successful you have become, or how attractive you are, you are powerless to hold on to a love relationship when it has ended. You can fantasize that it still exists, but the reality remains the same. And to continue with this fantasy, rather than dealing with the reality of your situation, only delays your progress through loveshock and may make it particularly difficult for you to get beyond the pivotal stage of resignation.

When Todd, scion of one of the greatest publishing families in the United States, came to see me, he was at once determined and confused. A man in his early forties, he was attractive, self-confident, and impeccably dressed. He had planned everything in his life, including the type of woman he would marry. When he met Barbara, an editor in chief of a popular's woman's magazine, he knew that she was perfect; he felt that their publishing careers beautifully complemented each other.

Initially he consulted with me not because he needed help with his feelings of despair or grief, but because he wanted to know what he should do to win her back. Barbara had left him three months earlier for a young writer who could barely pay the rent. Not only had she bought her own apartment, but she had moved the young writer in with her as well.

Todd refused to accept this, unable to imagine what in the world she could see in this struggling young would-be. Only fueling his frustration, he continued to send her flowers daily, had expensive gifts messengered to her office on a weekly basis, and arranged for a chauffeured limousine to pick her up every evening after work.

The gifts were sent back, the flowers refused, and the limousine left empty night after night. Barbara simply wasn't interested anymore; all the power and the money in the world couldn't get her back. Successful and self-sufficient in her own right, her needs were far more profound than what Todd had to offer.

As Todd talked, I felt as if I were taking part in a boardroom meeting, deciding the fate of some merger or big stock deal. Sitting back in the chair, with his arms folded across his chest and legs crossed, one of the most powerful men in publishing was looking to me for the answers.

"You tell me, Dr. Gullo. You're the love expert. What do I have to do to get her back? I'll do anything."

"You do nothing, Todd, except get on with your life and release the fantasy. Accept the fact that your relationship is over and have faith that eventually someone else will become a part of your life."

He looked at me with disbelief. "You're wrong. If there is one thing that I have learned, it's that there is a solution to every problem, that everything is resolvable."

But I replied, "Barbara is not a business transaction. She's a woman with needs that are now being met by someone else. The sooner that you accept that you are powerless over her decision, the easier it will get. You can't make another person love you."

Todd left my office in a huff, totally dissatisfied with my answer. I didn't hear from him for a month, until one day he called me.

"Okay, Dr. Gullo, I've had it. Now what? I'm so afraid to let go of the fantasy, but I'm such an emotional wreck that I can't make sense out of anything anymore . . . This is so hard. I always win . . . I don't know what to do . . ."

I proceeded to explain to him the stages and symptoms of loveshock and that he was in the second stage of grief. I reassured him that just as there is a beginning, there would be, in time, an end. As he was finally able to acknowledge that he was powerless over his situation, his fear began to diminish and he began to move constructively through the stages of loveshock.

THE THERAPEUTIC ASPECTS OF YOUR FEAR

When you openly confront your fears, it's like taking a long, hard look at yourself in the mirror. The flaws become apparent. The fears that surface during the different stages of loveshock often indicate general vulnerabilities and weaknesses—your personal demons—that you can correct.

As Marjorie worked through the anxiety of her loveshock, she realized that anxiety permeated all aspects of her life. If she was unable to finish a report at work, she'd stay awake that night worrying about getting to work early the next day so that she could finish it. Two weeks before her yearly physical she would become overly anxious and convince herself that her doctor would probably discover that she had some rare, incurable disease. She worried about everything. Her life was filled with a series of *what ifs:* What if I lose my job? What if I run out of money? What if I get in a car accident? What if no one will ever love me again?

Regardless of what kind of love relationship she would have in the future, she realized she needed to learn how to control her anxiety; she understood how important it was that she focus on herself first and foremost. Everything else would eventually fall into place.

Marjorie learned how to meditate and began experimenting with different forms of relaxation therapies. She volunteered to work overtime at the office and used her additional income to join a health club and learn how to swim. But most important, she began to concentrate on focusing on the present—on enjoying and appreciating what was happening in the moment, not worrying about what the future would bring. As her fears decreased, her *what ifs* began to disappear.

It is painful to confront your personal demons. But when you do it, you become aware of how your loveshock experience can make it possible for you to grow and develop a stronger sense of yourself. A wonderful sense of self-mastery pervades you as you begin to take control over your life and manage the pain of your loveshock, instead of being consumed by your fears.

CHAPTER THREE

Rejector or Rejectee?

It is rare for two people mutually and simultaneously to decide to end a relationship. Usually, in a loveshock crisis, there are two roles to be played: rejector and rejectee.

While you might automatically assume that the typical loveshock victim is the rejectee, as I have worked with more and more loveshock patients I have seen that the rejector can suffer as intensely and experience just as many fears as the rejectee. In fact, the person who suffers more during the breakup is the person who is more significantly involved in the love relationship. That's because the one who is more involved has invested more time and energy in the relationship and ultimately loses a greater part of him- or herself.

THE REJECTOR: WILLING OR UNWILLING

I suppose if there is a "good" position to be in as a love relationship ends, it is that of *willing rejector*. When you are the willing rejector you have already divorced yourself emotionally and intellectually from the relationship, although you are still living with the other person. Perhaps this has been a slow process for you; perhaps you have gradually grown out of love with your mate as other aspects of your life have become more important and the love relationship has become a less important part of your life. You may even never have felt a profound love for the other person. When you finally choose to physically leave the relationship, you are acting out in your behavior what you have already resolved in your thoughts.

As a willing rejector you may feel an initial sadness that the relationship is not for you and will not last, but your traveling time through the stages of loveshock may be very fast. In fact, you may barely experience loveshock. By the time you actually end the relationship, you have already eased yourself through loveshock, weaning yourself bit by bit from the relationship until you feel comfortable in finally ending it.

Usually the most difficult aspect of the loveshock experience for the wiling rejector is a feeling of guilt if the other person refuses to accept that the relationship is over. Regardless of your emotional detachment from the relationship, it's difficult to watch your rejected mate suffer. Your greatest fear may be for his or her well-being.

This is what happened to Sharon when she decided to end her twenty-four-year marriage to Jeff. They had married when Sharon was eighteen and Jeff was twenty-five. She had just graduated from high school and Jeff managed a popular restaurant. While she couldn't afford to go to college, Sharon was eager to break away from her conservative, religious family. So when Jeff proposed, it was easy for Sharon to accept. After having three children in a six-year period, once the youngest was in school Sharon attended college part-time to get her degree. Juggling motherhood, wifehood, and scholastic demands wasn't easy, but she did it and in six years received her bachelor's degree. Jeff was in constant awe of Sharon's determination and ability to do it all. She went on to graduate school, received her master's degree in psychology, and became so wrapped up in the academic world that she decided to go for her Ph.D. By the time her youngest child was a freshman in college, Sharon was only forty-two, had become an assistant professor at the city college, and wanted out of her marriage. While she still loved Jeff, she was no longer in love with him and realized that the more she had grown as an individual, the farther she had grown away from him. They had little in common except for their children, who were now on their own. Unfortunately, Jeff loved and respected Sharon now more than ever. In fact, the more she accomplished, the more attractive he found her.

When Sharon consulted with me, she really came for Jeff, not for herself. Probably the strongest emotion she felt was guilt for causing him so much emotional pain. But the guilt she felt was not self-destructive, nor was it preventing her from getting on with her life. She had already found an apartment and was preparing to move out. The only thing stopping her was her fear of how Jeff would react when she finally left.

"Dr. Gullo, I can't live a lie. Even with my studies, I've always been a good wife and mother, but now that the kids are gone it just doesn't work anymore. I feel like I'm living with a stranger. I guess over the years I've just fallen out of love with him. But I don't know what to do. Jeff refuses to accept this split. He cries constantly and literally throws his arms around me and begs me not to go."

As she shared her story with me, she was calm and almost clinical. While she was genuinely concerned for Jeff's well-being, it was also clear to me that she was emotionally free of Jeff and that she was anxious to get on with her life. When she asked me, "What should I do?" I told her that there was nothing she could do. She was functioning well. She had faced a difficult decision and resolved it in her own mind. The problems and emotional pain were Jeff's, and only Jeff could work through them. The only constructive advice I could offer her was she suggest to Jeff that he see me so that I could help him get a grip on his emotions and understand what he was experiencing. But I stressed that it was a process that he would have to go through alone.

When you end the relationship as a willing rejector, you are already emotionally distant and probably somewhere in the final two stages of loveshock: rebuilding and resolution. At some point in the relationship you have already severed your emotional ties to the other person, probably as the final stage of a subtle, slow process that you may not have even been aware of. Then one day you chose to physically leave the relationship. Sharon was in the final stage of resolution when she told Jeff she was leaving: she was definitely ready to begin a new life cycle.

THE UNWILLING REJECTOR: VICTIM AND VILLAIN

Whereas the willing rejector suffers the least during the breakup and retains the most control, the *unwilling rejector* can experience as much emotional pain and trauma as the rejectee. Maybe even more, as you are at once victim and villain. Victim because you still love your partner, villain in that you must end the relationship—because the emotional pain it causes you is greater than any pleasure it may bring. This is a difficult dichotomy of feelings that you must work through.

The pain that causes you to push the other person away may stem from something as simple as your no longer feeling that you are appreciated or noticed—you're not getting the attention you need. In a sense you feel as though you have already been rejected, and you act out what you feel has already been done to you.

This was Denise's dilemma when she came to see me after leaving Cliff. A successful dermatologist, Cliff commuted back and forth between his Manhattan practice and his house in Connecticut. "I love him so much, Dr. Gullo, and I understand the strain of his busy practice combined with commuting, but he never seems to have an extra moment to spare. It seems that I spend my whole life waiting to be with him."

"What about the weekends? Do you take trips or maybe share a sport?"

"Sports—ugh! I'm so sick of baseball, football, and basketball that I could scream. Is there such a thing as a 'sportaholic'? If he's not glued to the TV he's in a stadium somewhere. Sometimes I'll go along just to be with him, but it's hard to feel close to someone when there are thousands of screaming people around you."

"Have you told him how you feel, made suggestions of things you'd like to do?"

"Dr. Gullo, I've tried everything to get his attention. One night, as he watched a Giants game, I sat down next to him on the couch in a black garter belt and black lace stockings.''

"And?"

"And nothing else. Nothing happened! He merely patted my thigh while he continued to watch the game.''

Denise was a good-looking redhead in her mid-thirties. I found it hard to believe that the combination of her long red hair and exotic lingerie couldn't entice Cliff. But from the look on her face as she bit her fingernails, I knew that her story was true.

"Every time I tell him that I need some attention, his stock answer is. 'What more do you want, Denise? You've got a beautiful home and clothes; you get to do whatever you want. But nothing is ever enough for you. I work hard to pay for all of this and I have to have my time to unwind. Sports help me unwind. Why can't you understand this?' "

"Do you think he's interested in another woman? I know it's not pleasant to think about, but could it be possible?"

"No! I don't mean to snap at you, Dr. Gullo—but I'm sure I'd know. I'm sure I'd sense *that*!"

"What about marriage counseling?" I asked.

"He refused. He told me it was my problem. So I moved out two months ago." Leaning on my desk, her head in her hands, Denise looked at me glumly. "What do I do? I love him and miss him so much."

"Have you thought about going back?"

"Go back to what? Even when he's *there,* he's not there. As much as I love him, I'm not happy—and I can never be happy!"

Whether it's something as basic as needing more attention, as it was for Denise, or something far more dramatic, like physical abuse, each situation is unique.

The degree of the problem that forces you to take this final action depends on your sensitivity and basic life principles.

What one person can deal with in a relationship may be unbearable for someone else. For example, one woman may not mind her husband engaging in extramarital affairs, if he is discreet. As long as she has a beautiful home, car, clothes, and the freedom to do as she pleases, she doesn't really care. She may even choose to engage in her own extramarital affairs—a fling with the tennis pro, the pool man, or even her husband's best friend. However, another woman may be tortured by her husband's infidelity, regardless of the material assets of the relationship.

This was the case with Julie and Brett. They shared three homes, two children, horses, and the country club life—a flurry of excitement and social activity. However, Julie found Brett's constant flirting at parties humiliating and demeaning. Rather than enjoying the luxury of her life, she lived in a perpetual state of mistrust and paranoia as she wondered if Brett was actually sleeping with any of the women he flirted with. They discussed his behavior and how it made her feel, but nothing changed. Finally, Julie refused to go to any social functions or parties with Brett. They argued constantly and Brett accused her of being crazy. Thinking that he might be right, Julie sought counseling. But when the therapist asked to see Brett too, he flatly refused.

While Julie, like Denise, had many material assets, emotionally she felt that she had very little. She told me that the happiest days of their relationship were when Brett was struggling to make it as a stockbroker on Wall Street. She didn't mind that a big night out consisted of pizza and cheap red wine by candlelight, because they shared time together, bonded their mutual desires and dreams. Now she merely felt like another one of his possessions. So, tortured by her mistrust, she decided to file for divorce.

Ironically, as the unwilling rejector, often you are not just fleeing a painful relationship but may be trying to save it as well. In fact, your rejection may be a cry for help. While you are saying, "You are causing me so much pain that I must end it," what you really mean is, "I want you to stop causing me so much pain so that I don't have to end it."

This was Matt's intention when he left Vicki because of her alcoholism. He loved her deeply, but he could not bear to watch her destroy herself. Forgotten appointments, embarrassing moments at restaurants, and disastrous dinner parties didn't help. But it was the evening he came home to find her passed out on the couch while dinner was burning on the stove that finally made him end their relationship.

As he later told me, "It was like one last slap in the face. All the past humiliation I had felt welled up inside of me and I thought I would explode. As I looked at her, disheveled and snoring on the couch while the potatoes burned on the stove, I felt a loathing for her that scared me. I wondered how I could at once loathe and love a woman so much. I had to get out."

Typical for the unwilling rejector, Matt was alternating between the stages of grief and setting blame when he came to see me. There was no doubt that he still loved Vicki, but he was angry that she had allowed alcohol to destroy their life together. One day he would rant and rave about her lack of self-discipline and unwillingness to deal with her problem, and a week later he would weep in my office because he missed her so much. Then he would blame himself for her drinking. The classic "If only I had done this or if only I had done that" was a constant refrain in his dialogue. And, as often is the case for an unwilling rejector, he began to think that he had overreacted to her problem. Eventually he convinced himself that he had made the wrong decision. His guilt and grief got the better of him, and a month after he had left Vicki he moved back in. But because nothing had changed and leaving her was the right decision, two months later he moved back out.

During this entire period he continued to see me, and there was no doubt that this man was going through his own personal hell. If ever there was an unwilling rejector, it was Matt.

The extreme zigzagging of actually reentering the relationship only to have to leave it again is often characteristic of the unwilling rejector. The emotional pain becomes torturous, the victim and villain within the unwilling rejector unreconciled and splitting the person in two. I constantly remind the unwilling rejector that behavior speaks louder than words: before you zigzag back into the relationship, make sure that there is real evidence of change.

Matt's loveshock took not only an emotional toll, but a physical one as well. He began to suffer from migraines, and his handsome, thirty-six-year-old face mirrored his internal pain as he broke out with patches of acne. It wasn't until he left Vicki the second time that he was finally able to move on to the goodbye stage, releasing her from his life as each day he was able to gain more emotional distance from her. As he became stronger, her pleas for him to return, with the promise of her change, became less effective. But it took him a year before he felt comfortable being on his own and was able to begin dating again.

During the rebuilding stage of your loveshock experience, you might reunite with your partner *if* he or she has changed the behavior that pushed you away. In fact, if there is a drastic change in the behavior, and both of you are willing to work on the relationship, you may be able to end loveshock at any stage. When behavior is corrected and the problems that split the relationship apart begin to disappear, you may be able to begin again because the dynamics of the relationship will have changed.

If both of you are willing, family counseling can be beneficial and can provide a strong foundation for what is really a new relationship. Had Vicki sincerely sought help and actually made the changes she continuously promised, I think that she and Matt might have had a chance to reconcile their relationship. This is how much he loved her.

However, I want to stress that family counseling and therapy are not magical cures. They will be beneficial only if both partners really want to work at the relationship. Truly, it takes two to make love work.

Often one person will go to therapy to assuage the other person's pain, hoping that it will help him or her accept that the relationship is over, or to ease guilt. And out of the couples that go to therapy, a large number still split up instead of staying together because therapy only clarifies whatever the reality of the relationship is. So when you go into therapy or marriage counseling in hope of repairing the relationship, realize that there are no guarantees. If, after all your efforts, the relationship still ends, you will at least have the satisfaction of knowing that you did your best to make it work.

THE REJECTEE: THE REAL VICTIM

As emotionally tumultuous as it is to be the unwilling rejector, the classic victim in the breakup of a love relationship is the rejectee. As the unwilling rejector you, too, may suffer, and you may have the added burden of guilt for ending the relationship, but you also have the advantage of being in control. Since you're initiating the breakup, you've had time to prepare yourself mentally, emotionally, and even financially for what you are about to do. But as the rejectee, you have no control over what is happening as your life is pulled out from under you. You are helpless as the impact of rejection throws you into a state of deep despair.

If there have been few or no indications of problems in the relationship, you will be shocked when you hear that the relationship may end. You will be in a state of numbness and disbelief. Regardless of the sensitivity and compassion the rejector may show in ending the relationship, you will still experience loveshock.

Alison broke the news to Seth that their marriage was over while they were dining with one of Seth's good friends. As they ate she turned to Seth and said, "I'm glad you brought Bert along because there's something I want to say tonight and I'm glad that he is here to give you some support." She continued, "Forgive the timing and the occasion, but I want a divorce."

Bert nearly choked, while Seth dropped his fork and turned white. This was the first inkling he had that anything was wrong in the marriage. He and Alison were both in their early fifties and they had settled into what he thought was a very comfortable, happy life. They traveled, played golf together on the weekends, and still made love at least once a week. Seth was in a state of shock for a good two weeks before he could even begin to comprehend emotionally what was happening.

When I took part in a panel discussion about men who had been left by their wives, a successful electrician, a member of the panel, was still in a state of disbelief that his wife had left him the month before. As far as he was concerned, he had done everything right to make their marriage work. He had always made an effort to be considerate of his wife's needs and had even willingly shared the household responsibilities, since both of them worked. He had even remembered the little things, often surprising her with little gifts or flowers for no special reason.

"One day, out of the blue, she came home from the hospital, where she is a lab technician, and announced that she wanted a divorce, because she felt that we had grown apart; she felt that she was no longer in love with me." The pain and perplexity etched in his face were so great that I thought he was going to break down in front of the audience. There was no response that I could give him, no conclusion I could draw except that at times it seems that for no apparent reason people fall out of love.

While your shock is the greatest when the rejection comes unexpectedly, as it did for Seth, even if you know that it is coming, the moment of rejection is still greater than anything you could have anticipated. It can still put you into a deep shock. To suddenly learn that you will no longer be able to see, talk to, or experience this person on the same intimate level is always psychologically overwhelming. Regardless of your awareness of the problems that have piled up, the differences and difficulties that have already pulled you apart, you can never be totally prepared for the emotional turmoil that follows rejection. This is why the initial onset of loveshock, especially the first two stages of shock and grief, are so devastating. Any intellectual ruminations and preparations you have made for this moment are like fire drills: they pale in comparison to the real thing.

FACING FAILURE

An additional problem you usually have to deal with when you are rejected, beyond your love loss, is the loss of a sense of self-worth. You experience a profound sense of failure and inadequacy. Rejection in any form is never easy, but when it is love that you have shared with another person and wish to continue to give that is being rejected, you are usually hit the hardest.

Your depression and hopelessness, most intense when you are in the second stage of grief, can diminish you so completely that you may find it difficult to function in any aspect of your life. When you are rejected you believe that you are unlovable and inadequate to everyone. Your feelings of inadequacy can permeate other areas of your life, and if they are not managed properly, your career may take a nosedive and your friends may disappear. Your loveshock will begin to snuff out your life.

As Seth told me, two months after Alison had moved out, "As to my feelings, Dr. Gullo, I truly feel as if my life is over. I don't know how to go on . . ." At this point he began to weep—a once sales executive crumbling in his grief. This second stage would take him several months to get through, and during it he lost many accounts and more than one friend.

It is not unusual for rejectors, especially unwilling

rejectors, also to feel as if they have failed. Their sense of failure and inadequacy stems from their inability to make the relationship work. Matt was convinced that he was a terrible failure because he couldn't get Vicki to stop drinking; for a while he shouldered the burden of her alcoholism. Denise was worried that she was incapable of sustaining a love relationship, since Cliff was her second husband. Julie felt that if she had been more exciting, maybe Brett's eyes wouldn't have wandered so much and she wouldn't have been forced to leave.

It's important, when this sense of failure and inadequacy engulfs you, to remember that you are responsible only for *your behavior* in a relationship and that you can't make the other person change his or her behavior unless he or she wants to. Your only concern should be the changes you need to make. This is why I constantly remind my loveshock patients that to sustain a love relationship requires a mutual commitment.

CHAPTER FOUR

Your Loveshock
Traveling Time

When Carolyn entered my office for her fifth session, I could see the rage churning inside her. Although she was impeccably dressed in a black silk dress, her eyes were full of fire. I had been seeing her every two weeks since her husband Bill had left her for another woman— a fact I found somewhat surprising, given Carolyn's good looks and wise, steady approach to life. However, I have learned in working with my loveshock patients that every story is unique and that there are always reasons for the breakup, regardless of how obscure they may be. However, in the earliest stages of loveshock, especially grief and setting blame, rather than delve into all the variables of the breakup, what's most important is to help people deal with their pain and move them through it at a rate that is at once healthy and respectful of their personal needs. A part of this is to recognize that people heal at different rates just as they grow at different rates.

"I'm furious, Dr. Gullo! Why won't they all just leave

me alone instead of constantly meddling and trying to fix me up? If I have one more strange man call me up and say, I know your good friend, such and such, and she suggested that I call you, I think I'll just hang up on him!"

"But Carolyn, doesn't it make you feel better to know that your friends care so much and want you to be happy?"

"If they cared so much they'd respect my need for privacy and leave me alone until I'm ready, or until I ask. My God, it's only been six months since Bill left me. I need this time to sort through it all."

"But would it be so terrible to have a dinner date or see a movie?" I was purposely playing devil's advocate to make sure that she was in touch with her true feelings."

"Not you too! Why can't anyone understand that I need this time to be on my own and become a whole person? After fifteen years of marriage, I don't want to risk even getting involved until I'm sure I'm ready. I can't stand the thought of ever having to go through this again. And I don't want to become one of those desperate middle-aged women who focuses her whole life on who will be the next date."

Carolyn's anger was healthy; she was reacting because her traveling time through loveshock was being violated. While her friends couldn't understand it, she simply wasn't ready to date.

Psychologists have long recognized the concept of *psychological readiness*. For instance, you may try to get a friend to stop smoking, a friend with a drinking problem to go to AA, or an obese friend or relative to go on a diet, begin an exercise program, or seek some sort of nutritional guidance. But until friends or relatives are ready to take the initial step on their own, all of your encouragement and support will amount to nothing. In fact, it may only alienate you from them as you make them angry by reminding them of something in their life that they're not yet prepared to confront.

Psychological readiness also applies to loveshock. If friends and relatives are urging you to leave one stage and travel to the next before you are ready, you may become resentful of their good intentions. But you should frequently evaluate where you are in your loveshock, referring to the description of the six stages in Chapter One, making sure that you are not stuck in a certain stage and locked in its accompanying behavior patterns. If you find that you are and are unable to motivate yourself out of it, then seek professional help.

Had Carolyn still been in deep grief, numb on Valium as when we first started working together, or even blaming herself for not being good enough to keep Bill faithful, I might have been concerned. But I was pleased with her progress: she was on the brink of taking that precarious step from setting blame to resignation. Soon she would finally be able to say goodbye, as she released a relationship that had been the focus of her life for fifteen years.

While Carolyn traveled through the stages of her loveshock, in many ways she was what I consider to be the *moderate traveler.* She did not get stuck in either passive or active response patterns. She wasn't spending evenings at home in bed with the covers pulled over her head, lost in seclusion. Carolyn wasn't locked in a state of grief, cut off from the world. Nor did she go out every night or find herself overindulging in food, drink, or men. In fact, she had begun working part-time for a suburban newspaper, honing journalism skills that had been her strength in college, and she continued her volunteer work at the local hospital two evenings a week that she had begun five years before.

As a moderate traveler, Carolyn recognized and accepted her pain as an inevitable part of the process of loss. She made every effort to deal with her feelings effectively and was not afraid to indulge in a good cry, from time to time, to release them. While she was anxious for the pain to end, she was able to accept that it would not end overnight. After all, her relationship had been fifteen years in the making, and it would take time to sever the bonds. While she was patient with her psychological healing process, she did her part too, actively seeking to diminish her pain through therapy and by keeping herself involved with new interests.

In touch with the reality of her pain, she dealt with it as positively as possible. Carolyn knew that holidays and certain events would be painful, so she planned ways in which to distract herself during these times. For instance, Christmas was a tough one for her, so she went to the Mideast with her college alumni group, and as she later told me, "lost myself in the wonders of Egypt."

Carolyn sought constructive support, not sympathy from her friends. This is why she was so offended when someone tried to fix her up with other men. It made her feel that she had no control over her life, that she was a helpless victim, when all she wanted to do was get through this painful period and take charge of what was left of her life. She had a need for emotional completion before moving on to another relationship, and for her a part of this process was her privacy. It was a little over a year before she went out on that first date, but when she did she was happy with the direction her new life had taken.

ARE YOU TRAVELING TOO FAST
   OR TOO SLOWLY?

While Carolyn was moderate in her traveling time and traveled pretty smoothly through each stage, I don't want to play down the periods of deep emotional pain she experienced. However, she was able to manage her pain more effectively than would have been possible if she had traveled through the stages too fast or too slow. What was important for Carolyn and is important for anyone going through loveshock is to resolve emotional problems and personal issues that surface during a particular stage before proceeding to the next one.

However, I must warn you that this is not always a neat process. In fact, you can expect some problems that occurred in one stage to reappear in another. I actually had one patient who found herself still thinking about her first husband on the day that she was to marry someone else. While she loved her husband-to-be deeply, preparing for this wedding brought up tinges of sadness for the first marriage that had failed. I will discuss this zigzag effect in greater detail later in this chapter.

There is no ideal traveling time. But there is an ideal outcome of loveshock: to use the experience to grow emotionally and strengthen your capacity to relate and deal with loss in the future by overcoming personal vulnerabilities and major obstacles you meet while traveling through it. So the traveling time through loveshock varies in each individual, depending on the problems that emerge and the significance of the relationship that's ending.

One of the fortunate aspects of loveshock is that both your psyche and memory help you, gradually moving you through the stages. With time and effort on your part, your memory will block out your acute emotional pain, because if you had to live with the intensity and vivid memory of every hurt and loss that you have suffered in the course of your life, you would be unable to function. Your psyche has a natural tendency to move away from pain, seeking pleasure and equilibrium. When it is properly channeled through constructive activities, it will support your healing process. On many levels your emotional life is like your physical body. It too has a natural healing process that pushes you through your emotional pain if you don't resist it. Think of your emotional being as a psychological immune system, encouraging positive feelings as it attempts to block out what is negative and painful. Taking consolation in this, you should aim while traveling through the stages to flow with the pain while you allow your feelings to develop naturally, constantly reminding yourself that there is an end to loveshock.

Most of us deal with loss as we deal with life. If you typically run from stress situations in your life, you will be more apt to run from the pain of your love loss, traveling through the experience as quickly as possible and maybe even skipping stages. As a fast traveler you are so anxious to get beyond your pain that you learn little about the why of the breakup. You may continue to make mistakes in future relationships. Often your anxiety gets the better of you, causing you to become impulsively involved in behaviors and situations that may not be productive. You are also extremely prone to rebounding, throwing yourself into another relationship before you are ready. Eager to avoid the next wave of pain, you continuously jump from one thing to another at all levels of your life—ultimately accomplishing very little at all.

Palmer, a shrewd businessman, was good at juggling his numerous investments and loved manipulating his different financial interests. An upbeat man in his fifties, he preferred to avoid discussing anything unpleasant. Consequently, when problems began to surface in his marriage to Robin, who was twenty years younger, he kept a smile on his face and refused to acknowledge them. One day he came home to empty bureau drawers and closets: Robin had left him for another man, who, she explained in her note, "is kind, considerate, and always has time to listen."

Robin's abandonment hit Palmer hard. How could something like this happen to him? Instead of pausing, taking time to really look at the what and why of the failed relationship, he immersed himself in more business deals. As he later told me, "I decided it was time to diversify." His twelve-hour days became sixteen-hour days. His energy became frenetic and scattered. The only time he went home was to sleep. While his work in a sense became his compelling diverter, he took it to an extreme and consequently debilitated his health. He was terrified to relax because he was afraid of facing the fact that he was now alone. Six months later and nearly bankrupt, Palmer ended up in the hospital with what he thought was a heart attack. It turned out that his grabbing chest pains were manifestations of his anxiety and emotional turmoil: his loveshock was bound to surface somewhere. It wasn't until he was physically debilitated that he finally accepted that he would have to confront his emotional pain and go through his loveshock. And it would take patience and serious introspection on his part before it would go away. He would have to slow down and take a long, hard look at his life.

One of the most important things that the fast traveler needs to realize is that the pain of loveshock is an important part of the healing process. Do not be impatient with your psyche or try to ignore the pain. You can put it off by trying to race around it, like Palmer, but it cannot be avoided. Sooner or later you must confront and experience your love loss so that it can be released. Do not deny the pain of your love loss. It only delays the inevitable realization and, even worse, gives you a false sense of hope as you think you've reached rebuilding and even resolution, when in fact you haven't effectively completed resignation, emotional releasing of the relationship.

Whereas a fast traveler flees from pain, if you are a slow traveler, you tend to focus on your pain to the point of obsession. You may spend great periods of time reliving different aspects of the relationship and the pain of the breakup. While it's healthy for you to confront and play out your feelings, when taken to extremes the process may leave you stuck in the second and third stages of grief and setting blame. Passive in your response patterns, you may find yourself frozen with fear of what will come next. In a sense you are caught in your own personal time warp, as you move through each stage in agonizing steps. Getting to the point of resignation and actually moving through it, saying goodbye to what once was, can be overwhelming. It's as if you don't want to let go of the pain because to do so is to let go of a past that has meant so much to you.

Lindsey's loveshock overwhelmed her life to such an extreme that she was unable to hold a job. An attractive, bright, twenty-two-year-old secretary, she had fallen in love with her boss and was thrilled when he responded to her flirtation. While they were making wild, passionate love several nights a week, he was also making wild promises that he never intended to keep. Victor took her with him when he traveled, reassuring her that as soon as the time was right he would leave his wife. Whenever she expressed her doubts, he bought her a love gift to pacify her. Three years after the affair began, Victor sadly said farewell to Lindsey because his wife was suspicious.

But for Lindsey, saying farewell seemed impossible. Besides all the gifts, she had kept a postcard from every hotel they had ever stayed in and matches from every restaurant they had dined in. She also had ticket stubs from every movie they had ever seen together: Victor had become her whole life.

After ending their affair, he had found her a good job with another company, thinking that it would be inappropriate if she stayed on as his secretary. While the job was challenging and she should have been enjoying the tremendous salary increase, all she could think about was Victor: the candlelight baths they had shared, the intimate dinners, the cozy movies. With Victor, even a car ride was exciting. She relived the memories over and over again. Six months later she was still turning down dates and spending her evenings with her memorabilia. Eventually she lost her job and found herself drifting from one occupation to the next; her only motivation was to pay the rent.

Instead of constructively traveling through her loveshock, she was perpetuating her role as victim. Locked in the second stage of grief, she finally sought counseling when she ended up at the state unemployment bureau, standing in line for five hours, waiting to sign for a check.

You must guard against positioning yourself as victim, as Lindsey did. If you think you are a victim, you are more likely to respond to your loveshock crisis passively. Locked in the memory of what was and in the pain of what is, you often think that your life is no longer your own. In a sense it isn't, because your behavior defeats you as you resist your psyche's natural inclination to flow through the stages. You can't imagine how you'll go on with your life, so you purposely stop dead in your tracks. Your own resistance to traveling through the stages becomes a roadblock to your emotional well-being.

EVALUATING YOUR TRAVELING TIME

While the general profiles above can provide you with a good indication of whether you are a fast or slow traveler or a moderate traveler like Carolyn, you can probably identify in some way with all three. However, it is the predominance of any one pattern that will determine your traveling time through loveshock.

The following chart, which lists *general* characteristics of the fast, moderate, and slow traveler, is one way to further evaluate your traveling time. It will also make you aware of specific behaviors that may be operating in extremes and distorting your traveling time.

For each number, circle only one characteristic that best describes your behavior. Once you've completed the test, add up your total in each column. The column with the greatest total indicates your traveling time through loveshock.

Fast	Moderate	Slow
1. anxious during conflict	realistic during conflict	depressed during conflict
2. denies emotional pain, *avoids*	faces emotional pain, *confronts*	is overwhelmed by emotional pain, *retreats*
3. tries to do several things at once	finishes one task before going on to the next, methodical	lacks motivation or finds self-motivation difficult
4. makes hasty decisions	weighs decisions carefully	has difficulty making decisions
5. is uncomfortable with discussion or expression of feelings	deals with feelings openly and releases them	obsesses on feelings
6. blames others and situations	shares responsibility for blame when appropriate	feels confused about what went wrong, where to place blame
7. needs to control others, situations, feelings	focuses on self-growth first	needs to be nurtured by another, sees self as victim

8. extroverted	flexible, depending on the situation, adaptable	introverted, lacking confidence
9. has had more than one loveshock experience	has had at least one loveshock experience	has had little loveshock experience
10. overachiever, is never happy with what is	achieves realistic goals	underachiever, or is easily diverted from goals

Again, the speed at which you are traveling through loveshock is not the overriding issue. But certain characteristics of the fast and slow traveler can impair your recovery. If you were fast or slow for numbers 1 through 6, be aware that moderating these behaviors can help you move through your loveshock experience in a more complete and less painful way.

Remember that as a fast traveler your greatest obstacle to recovery is your avoidance and impatience with the pain, as well as the tendency to deny that your loveshock even exists. Remember Palmer? It wasn't until he ended up in a hospital that he acknowledged his loveshock. As a slow traveler your greatest obstacle to recovery is your dwelling too long in any or all of the stages. Look what happened to Lindsey because she couldn't move beyond her grief: she ended up unemployed and essentially nonfunctioning.

Whether you travel too slow or too fast, your goal should be to confront your emotional pain realistically and to allow your psyche to move you through each stage at a rate that is appropriate for you. It's how well you deal with the critical issues that come up at each stage that's important, not whether you are a fast or slow traveler. Ultimately, I discover what is best for my patients by observing what enhances or impedes their ability to function. In terms of your own loveshock, if you can say yes to the following questions—regardless of your pain—you are traveling at a rate that is right for you:

The Traveling Time Self-Test

· Are you accepting and dealing with your loveshock as you continue to function in your daily routines? (Are you getting to work on time, paying your bills, maintaining your personal appearance, taking care of your health, keeping appointments?)

· Are you learning from your loveshock things about yourself and your personal needs? (Perhaps you are discovering that you need to develop friendships and work on other family relationships. Also, your loveshock may make apparent personal needs that were not being fulfilled in your past relationship. Ideally, these needs will be fulfilled in a future relationship.)

· Are you gaining from your loveshock something that will ultimately enrich your life—not just the pain? (Maybe it is something as basic as a better understanding of yourself and your own strength or sensitivity. Or perhaps, as you've looked for ways to fill the void, you've developed a new skill or hobby, advanced in your career, or begun an exercise program.)

THE ZIGZAG EFFECT

Whether you are a fast, moderate, or slow traveler through loveshock, a critical dimension of your traveling time is what I call *the zigzag effect*. To zigzag is to spend a considerable amount of time traveling back and forth among the different stages.

In the early stages of loveshock, until you complete stage four, resignation, this is to be expected. One of the most common zigzags is to go back and forth between grief and setting blame. Remember Matt, the unwilling rejector of his alcoholic wife, Vicki? As he was working his way through loveshock, he would get beyond his grief, finally setting blame as he vented his anger that she had allowed alcohol to destroy their love. Instead of moving on to resignation, two weeks later he would zigzag back into grief, weeping in my office because he missed her so much. Zigzagging between grief and setting blame may go on continuously until you are ready to resign yourself to the reality that the relationship is over.

However, it is not uncommon, although it is painful, to complete resignation and actually be in rebuilding when suddenly you have an overwhelming desire to reconnect with the other person. While your intellect may know better, your heart pulls you back into the past. You may actually zigzag all the way back into grief. But if you really have completed resignation, this zigzag will be brief and the emotional pain will not be as intense as when you were actually traveling through the grief stage. The same is true if you zigzag back into setting blame: your anger will be of shorter duration and not as intense.

Remember the loveshock patient who found herself

thinking about her first husband on the day she was to marry someone else? She was actually in the final stage of resolution, starting a new life with another man, and up popped the memories of her previous marriage.

When Valerie called me after her honeymoon with Grant she said, "I know that my loveshock is over—in fact it has been for some time—but the strangest thing happened on my wedding day. I had just put on my peach silk wedding dress and was adjusting it, looking at myself in the mirror, when suddenly I started thinking about Hugh. And for a brief moment, as I looked in the mirror, I went back fifteen years in time and saw myself dressed all in white. My father was smiling at me: he took my hand and led me into the chapel . . ."

There was silence on the line and I waited for a moment. "Valerie?"

"Yes?"

I could tell by her voice that she was caught up in the memory again. "Are you all right?"

"Oh! I'm sorry, Dr. Gullo—I'm fine. I was just realizing that the brief sadness I felt then I don't feel at all as I tell you about it. I guess I just had a momentary zigzag. How silly of me!" She proceeded to tell me excitedly about her honeymoon in Acapulco.

Had Valerie not started talking about Acapulco, I would have told her that her brief zigzag was not at all silly but very normal. While your emotions during loveshock may follow a predictable course, at times they seem to have a mind of their own. It's not unusual for a piece of the past to suddenly haunt you when you least expect it.

As time passes and you continue to travel through your loveshock experience, the number of zigzags that you have will decrease. And each time you do zigzag you should find it to be a little less painful. As one patient put it, eight months into his loveshock experience after the end of a nine-year relationship, "Now if I zigzag, it's only a momentary twinge."

LOVESHOCK FLASHBACKS

Often a zigzag is set off by what one of my patients appropriately labeled a "loveshock flashback": a place, a person, an event, or a thing that reminds you of a special moment in the relationship or just brings up the memory of the other person. A song, passing by a restaurant that you once shared, or even a piece of clothing can trigger a loveshock flashback.

For Nancy, who had progressed to rebuilding, every time she opened her drawer and looked at the beautiful lingerie Gene had bought her when their affair first began, she had a loveshock flashback. Even though she knew that he was a married man, she fell deeply in love with Gene as the affair progressed. After two years, still in love but tired of being the other woman, she ended the relationship. The beautiful lingerie brought up such vivid memories that she had to throw it away. "I couldn't even give it away, because then it would still exist, somewhere, and so would the memory of him and all those exquisite moments we shared."

While it's fairly simple to get rid of things or avoid places that trigger loveshock flashbacks, holidays can present another problem. Also in rebuilding, Lloyd found it extremely difficult to deal with Mother's Day. When I answered his emergency call he was in a state of total despair, recalling how he and Liz had opened their house in Nantucket for the summer every Mother's Day during the previous five years. Suddenly he found himself yearning for her presence on all levels: the perfume she wore, the clam bakes they had shared, and her presence in bed. At that moment, even the thought of her weight problems didn't bother him. He couldn't believe his emotional tailspin, especially since he had started dating again and felt that he was finally over Liz. I reassured him that his feelings were perfectly normal and that during the first year following a breakup—regardless of where you are in your loveshock experience—holidays and special occasions could be emotionally draining. Because they have a special impact on your psyche, it takes more time to put emotional distance between yourself and these occasions.

CYCLES OF LOVESHOCK

There are also what I call the *cycles of loveshock,* which create a structure for zigzagging and loveshock flashbacks. I have found that most of my patients, even those who have had a minimal amount of emotional pain, have to travel through a full year following the breakup before they are free of zigzagging and loveshock flashbacks. I have also observed that as you approach the final season at the end of your year, you may once again focus on all that you have lost. And even though you have come so far, perhaps even to the final stage of resolution, the pain can be gut-wrenching.

James and Candace had ended their relationship the previous autumn. I hadn't had a session with Candace since July, when suddenly, at the end of October, she scheduled an appointment. As she stood by the window in my office, watching the leaves blow off the maple trees, tears began to stream down her face.

"I was doing so well—and now this. It's like I'm back there in it. I don't understand. I know that I was at the end of my loveshock, and now I feel like it's beginning all over again. I'm starting to think that loveshock is some horrible cancer that goes into remission for a while but never really goes away. When, Dr. Gullo, when? When will the pain really end?"

"Exactly what is going through your mind at this time? Where is your focus?"

"I keep thinking about the day he came to get his things. How I had to leave the house because I couldn't stand watching him put his life in boxes. And when I came home I felt so empty. His closets, his drawers— there was nothing in them. I can vividly remember going through the house, one room after another, and then suddenly realizing that we would never share any of it again."

"Do you remember what you did after you realized this?"

"Yes. I stood in front of the big picture window and wept as I watched the leaves blow and fall from the trees in the front yard. I was terrified, convinced that my life was over. I felt like I was withering up inside and dying . . . just like the leaves."

"Do you feel terrified now? Do you feel as if your life is over?"

Slowly she recouped, blowing her nose and blotting her eyes. "Why no. As a matter of fact, I'm busier than ever before. I just finished a course on astrology, something I've always been interested in, and a group of us from the class are going on a retreat to a holistic center in Vermont. However, I am convinced that there is a real man shortage; except there is this one guy from my class that I find rather intriguing . . ." She was laughing, her pain dissolving.

I explained to Candace that her sudden grief had simply been triggered by the season and that in reality she was at the end of her loveshock experience. I also reassured her that by the following autumn, while she might still have the memory, there would be little or no pain associated with it.

Time is your true friend when you are a loveshock victim. Each day that passes provides more emotional distance, the pain diminishing bit by bit, as you travel through the stages to an end that will arrive.

CHAPTER FIVE

Love Pitfalls: The Five Most Common Loveshock Mistakes

There are certain *love pitfalls* that you are vulnerable to during loveshock, usually during the stages of grief, setting blame, resignation, or rebuilding. These love pitfalls are destructive behavior patterns that you act out in reaction to your love loss. It is not unusual to experience more than one pitfall during your loveshock experience. You may go through different ones during different stages or experience two or three at the same time.

Recognize these pitfalls, rather than recoiling from them. Most of us fall into at least one pitfall during a loveshock experience. But there are strategies you can employ to work your way out of all of them.

The five pitfalls, which I describe in this chapter, are: *hanging on, rebounding, moth-to-flaming, escaping through excess,* and *comparison shopping.*

HANGING ON

When you're *hanging on*, you don't want to let go of the relationship mentally, emotionally, or physically. A slow traveler through loveshock, you are clinging to whatever you hope or think is left of the relationship. But in your refusal to let go, you are only prolonging the inevitable—confronting the fact that the relationship is over. Hanging on is acted out in three different ways, each of which hinders your traveling time through loveshock:

Obsessional Thinking

This can be torturous. You spend many hours thinking about your ex-mate, unable to focus on your own life. A prisoner of your obsessive thoughts, you cannot escape from the other person. He or she invades your dreams and can even alter your behavior.

You may find yourself arranging "accidental" meetings, constantly phoning the other person, or sending passionate letters of remorse. Night and day you are consumed by thoughts of what the other person is doing: Where is this person now? Who is this person dating? At what restaurant? Where is this person spending the weekend?

Samantha found herself reacting in all of these ways during the first two months of her loveshock. A former model and presently the owner of a little boutique, she was proud of how far she had come since her modeling days. "The fashion world thought that I was nothing more than a dumb blonde. What a surprise they had when I turned my love for fashion into a successful business."

When her ten-year marriage to Maurice ended because of his prolonged affair with a young model, obsessional thinking overwhelmed her. Instead of focusing on her lucrative business, Samantha spent numerous hours reliving her past with Maurice. In her thoughts, she remembered only the good times. As she lost herself in fantasy, her business began to suffer, and when Samantha went to bed at night she experienced sleep disturbances as well. As she told me during one of our first sessions, "Oh, Dr. Gullo, the torment of my Maurice, my lost love, haunts me and threads itself through all of my dreams. There is no escape."

If you're an obsessional thinker during loveshock, you too may toss and turn, sleeping restlessly, or wake up after eight hours and feel as if you have not slept at all. The anxiety that you are consciously experiencing invades your subconscious as well. Like Samantha, many of my patients complain about the persistent torment of their obsession.

Often you zigzag back and forth between the second and third stages of grief and setting blame. Songs, movies, particular places, and certain foods can trigger your emotions: first the longing to share a particular moment with the other person again, and then intense anger with yourself or the other person as you try to set blame. Even worse is the profound emptiness you feel, and the nagging doubt of "Will I ever find another?"

Regardless of the intensity of your obsessional thoughts, with time they will burn out. Until they do, try this *thought-blocking technique:* Every time you start thinking about your ex, adamantly say to yourself, *"STOP!"* Then begin thinking about another topic that's equally compelling, or engage in an activity that will divert your focus. Again, diverters are important; seek out new interests that really grip you. The key here is to block out thoughts of the other person by substitution. Don't expect immediate results. However, I promise that the more you practice this thought-blocking technique, the more effective it becomes.

Samantha found the thought-blocking technique difficult at first because a part of her was reluctant to let go of her obsession with Maurice. She diverted herself with the specific goal of discovering a new designer. I also had her make up note cards to place by her telephones, at home and at her boutique, that said in bold writing, *"STOP! DON'T CALL!"* As her obsession naturally faded, bit by bit, her self-respect also returned, because she knew that she had taken an active part in regaining emotional control of her life.

Revenge Loving

You are particularly prone to this pitfall if you are the rejectee. Hurt by the rejection you have experienced, not only do you involve yourself in another relationship before you are ready, but its dynamics evolve from your anger. You may act out your revenge loving in three different relationships styles:

First, you may involve yourself in another relationship (your new partner becomes the third party) strictly with the intention of making your former partner jealous. Desperate for attention, you arrange to meet up with your old love so that he/she can see how easy it is for you to find someone new. Often, the third party is hurt the most, aware too late, when already emotionally involved, that he or she is just being used.

Second, you may involve yourself in another relationship and then subconsciously act out on another person what you feel has been done to you. For example, if your ex abused you, you may find yourself abusive to your new partner. Or if your ex manipulated you, you may—determined never to be manipulated by another person again—become very manipulative of your new partner.

Or third, you may enter into a relationship where you feel that you can be totally in control, so that no one will ever have the power to hurt you again. Ultimately you become bored, restless, and angry with the other person who allows you to control him or her; in the end you find yourself unhappy and hurt.

After Lynn left him, Bruce immediately became involved with Louise, who was a waitress at the local restaurant where he and Lynn often dined. Because he knew Lynn's habits, Bruce usually entered the restaurant when she was there and made a point of showing not only Lynn, but everyone in the restaurant, just how friendly he and Louise were. So hurt by Lynn's rejection, Bruce was determined to hurt her and show her how desirable he still was. Fortunately Louise ended their relationship before she got hurt because she was aware of Bruce's true intentions: to get back at Lynn. Eventually, Bruce also realized that he had developed his relationship with Louise strictly out of vengeance. His was a classic case of revenge loving.

Gordon's wife, Yvonne, had also left him, but his revenge loving pattern was more complicated. When Gordon came to see me, I was in awe of the level his anger had reached. While he had been profoundly in love with her, she had only cared about him because of his wealth. Once she had taken all that she wanted, she simply packed up and left while he was away on a business trip. Within the six-month period since she had moved out, he had actually been with a different woman every weekend—and with each woman he subconsciously acted out the same style of abuse Yvonne had inflicted on him.

During the week, he would cruise the different Manhattan nightclubs until he found the "weekend woman" of his choice. Before the weekend he would send her flowers and a note promising a real relationship. What an enticement for any woman: good-looking, charming, independently wealthy, and only in his late thirties. It would be easy to believe that he was a real-life Prince Charming.

On Friday night he would pick his weekend woman up in his red Mercedes sports coupe and whisk her out to the Hamptons for the weekend, leading her to believe that she would be the next mistress of his house. Unfortunately for the woman involved, as the weekend unfolded, it was just one party after another and a lot of meaningless sex—but no true emotional contact with Gordon. Each Sunday night, after he had taken what he had wanted, he left the weekend woman at her front door with barely a civil goodbye.

When I asked him to tell me about some of the different weekend women he had been with in the last month, he could barely even remember their names, let alone what they did or any interests they might have shared with him. He was so lost in his anger and caught up in his revenge loving pattern that he had become completely disconnected from any emotional intimacy. His anger made it impossible for him to love.

In order to move yourself out of a revenge loving pattern, first realize that it is a natural reaction when you have been rejected. You need to recognize your anger and release it. The healthiest way to do this is to act it out within yourself, not with another person as Gordon repeatedly did.

Many of my patients have found that keeping a diary or journal of all their feelings (one method of self-monitoring) is extremely beneficial in working their way out of this pitfall. Gordon started doing this and found that he was able to write much of his anger out, experiencing a great sense of relief, as he became more in touch with how he felt and why he was feeling it. Just admitting that he was filled with anger was a big step for him. I knew that because his case was so extreme it would take a great deal of therapy before he could have a real relationship again.

Correspond with your feelings, through your journal, twice a day—even if it's only a few lines. In the morning describe what you're feeling in general, as you begin another day, and in the evening evaluate your reaction to different people and situations that you dealt with during the day. You may want to spend a considerable amount of time once a week writing out any hurt or anger you are still feeling. And if you have begun any other relationships, honestly evaluate your real feelings and the role these relationships are playing in your life. Many of my patients have found this form of self-monitoring invaluable in helping them understand and deal with their anger.

If you feel that you are unable to cope with your anger and find yourself going in and out of different revenge loving relationships, like Gordon, consult a therapist or counselor. You may need some additional guidance to get you back on track and to help you become more objective about your feelings. When you are able to objectify your feelings, the anger and the hurt begin to dissolve.

Magnifying

When you've been rejected, it's not unusual to magnify what you *think* your ex is doing. You are convinced that he/she must be having a great time living it up while you are brokenhearted. If magnification is your way of holding on to the lost relationship, you spend a great deal of time moping about in your grief. As your world seems to have grown smaller, you become convinced that his/hers has grown larger. At the core of your magnification is your own self-pity that here you are with nothing left while the other person has everything.

Teddy was convinced that Rosemary was going out every night, enjoying her new-found freedom, while he was struggling to put his new apartment together. He felt anything but motivated as he came home after work to "rooms of emptiness." Why hang a picture or a plant? Why paper the bathroom—what was the point? Surrounded by his self-created nothingness, night after night he collapsed into bed in a heap of despair. His life had no meaning. All he could focus on was what Rosemary was "probably" doing at any given moment. He would take long walks, filled with thoughts of Rosemary and the wonderful time she *must* be having. Rosemary had wanted the divorce, and for all he knew she was basking somewhere in the Mediterranean sun with a Greek lover.

Much to his surprise, a month after we started our sessions, he ran into her in a coffee shop where she was having dinner and reading the newspaper—totally alone. She was wearing no makeup and looked as if she had put on about ten pounds. Teddy seemed incredulous as he told me, "She's the one that wanted this, but she looks more miserable than me!" He began to realize how irrational his magnification was and how it was preventing him from progressing through his loveshock.

There is a natural tendency in some of us to enjoy our own sorrow. I've seen it in many of my loveshock patients. If you allow it, magnification can become a kind of martyrdom. You must be careful that you don't use it to avoid focusing on your own needs—things that you could be doing for yourself to move yourself away from your pain.

While you may be in loveshock because of the actions of another person, how you handle it is your responsibility. Again you must motivate yourself to do things, incorporate different diverters into your life that will take you out of yourself. Don't waste another day thinking about how miserable you are. As one of my patients so aptly put it, "Yes, I have to deal with the reality of my situation: I was dumped. But I can also tune out and stay in motion."

The thought-blocking technique used to redirect your obsessional thinking is also helpful in moving you through magnification. Every time you start magnifying the other person's life, adamantly say to yourself, *"STOP!"* (repeating several times if necessary) and engross yourself in a pleasurable activity. Terry would continuously repeat *"STOP!"* to herself the moment her magnification of Clint began, and would continue to do so as she took herself to a movie, play, art opening, or concert. Once there, she would lose herself in the performance. "I replaced Clint with the arts. After a while it became apparent to me what a waste of time it was to magnify his life, when I could be filling my life with so much culture."

Also sit down and make a list of every positive aspect of your life. This might include things like good health, a good job, good looks, good family relationships, close friends, a nice home, a nice car, or a healthy bank balance. Tape this list to your bathroom mirror and every time you start feeling sorry for yourself, stare at yourself in the mirror as you read your list out loud, beginning "I have . . . " and going down your list. You will find this form of positive programming very effective in moving yourself out of your self-pity.

Another aspect of magnification is idealization, constantly focusing on all the wonderful qualities of the person who has just rejected you. While your natural tendency to block out pain and to preserve what's positive and pleasurable in your life is vital in easing you through emotional trauma, it can also make it more difficult for you to separate yourself from the other person.

This happens most frequently during the setting blame stage. I recommend that whenever you find yourself only focusing on the positive aspects of the other person, sit down and make a list of every negative thing that you can think of. Do this often and you will find yourself becoming much more objective, as you begin to see the relationship for what it really was. Your idealization will lessen and you will be able to focus your attention on getting on with your life.

REBOUNDING

The opposite of hanging on, *rebounding* is a pitfall typical of fast travelers who fill their lives up with numerous activities to avoid their emotional pain. Whereas in hanging on, you need to motivate yourself through loveshock, when you're in rebounding, you need to slow yourself down so that you can effectively master each stage of your loveshock before moving on to the next one.

In rebounding, you find it difficult to stay in at night, just to read a good book or watch television. It is as though you just can't sit still. And spending a weekend alone can drive you right up the wall. So you escape loveshock through a whirlwind of one-night stands or by entering into a new relationahip prematurely, before you have reached the resolution of your loveshock. This premature relationship quickly burns itself out, only adding more trauma to your shaky emotional state. This was true for Gabrielle.

Gabrielle and Paul married because Gabrielle was pregnant. A year later, while he adored his young son, Paul unfortunately couldn't sustain the marriage because he just didn't love Gabrielle. After he moved out, Gabrielle was in such emotional pain that she was unable to properly care for her son. Her mother volunteered to look after him and suggested that she just get away from it all: perhaps a trip to the Caribbean or Mexico would do the trick, easing her heartache.

Choosing a secluded hideaway in Mexico, Gabrielle felt sure that the sun, sand, and sea were just what she needed. But she also hungered for something to fill the emotional void created by Paul's rejection. So rather than working through her pain alone, allowing herself just to relax in the beauty of Mexico and sort out her feelings, she quickly became involved with a man, also staying at the hotel, who showed her warmth and kindness.

She later told me that a few days after they met they went to bed and when they made love, she closed her eyes and fantasized that she was with Paul. When she awoke the following morning, finding this stranger beside her, she was filled with such anxiety and dread that she packed her bags and fled Mexico that afternoon.

Fortunately Gabrielle didn't continue this behavior, but often after one rebound you move on to another, regardless of your trauma. You continue to fill your life up with meaningless relationships because you can't bear to face your emotional pain or to be alone. Facing the silence of oneness, as discussed in Chapter Two, is one of your greatest fears. But as you run from one relationship to the next, your hurt and fear are still with you, unresolved.

Every time you think that you are "falling in love," you are really "falling in need." Rather than confronting your pain, you cloak it within the structure of another relationship. The dynamic is "I love you because I need you." What you're really looking for is a psychiatrist or baby-sitter, not an equal partner.

While Gordon's behavior was a form of revenge loving, as he abused his weekend women as his wife had abused him, he was also rebounding—going from woman to woman, weekend after weekend. Weekends meant playtime, and he couldn't bear to spend any time alone.

Continuous rebounding is particularly common among men because they have a greater difficulty than women in dealing openly with feelings and confronting emotional pain. In fact, some of the most severe cases of loveshock I have seen have been in men. As they go from one woman to the next, each conquest temporarily rebuilds their ego. But eventually even the thrill of the conquest becomes boring, providing less and less pleasure and making the man realize that he must meet his emotional pain, head on, once and for all.

In order to overcome this pitfall, you first need to

recognize what you're doing; acknowledge that your life has become frenetic and that your rebounding stems from your pain as well as your general inability to be alone. The next step is to gradually recondition your behavior so that you become comfortable with being alone.

Initially you may want to try alternating one night at home with one night out, working toward spending an even greater number of nights at home. For your evenings at home, plan some sort of activity that will make the evening pleasurable. At first, you may not be able to spend your evenings at home alone: this might be too radical a change and only intensify your pain. Invite someone over whom you enjoy being with. Or give a dinner party. This is a good time to cultivate new friends and call on old ones.

But eventually you are going to have to make yourself tough it out alone. Chances are you won't have a very good time, and you may feel a bit of panic at first. This is the time to have a new book on hand, to rent some new movies, or to work on a special project that you have been putting off. You may find yourself fidgety and on edge, pacing the rooms and unable to concentrate. Several of my patients have resolved this uneasy state by taking long, leisurely baths and listening to soothing music. Others report that some easy yoga exercises and some good deep breathing while saying to themselves, "I am calm," over and over again helps to ease the anxiety.

Whatever reactions you have, remember that pain is to be expected in the beginning, as you adjust to your aloneness. Know that every night you manage to stay home alone, you will become stronger and more self-assured and develop greater self-awareness. And in time, as you become at ease with yourself, the reasons for the breakup will become clearer to you.

One of the unique aspects of psychological growth is that when you force yourself to do something that makes you feel emotionally uncomfortable but that you know will ultimately benefit you, you start feeling better about yourself because you are taking control of your emotions, instead of allowing your emotions to control you. And as you gain more control over your emotions, your pain begins to diminish because you are mastering it. Remember that pain can be constructive; the challenge is to function to your best ability as you deal with it. Often the most self-destructive thing you can do is to continue to run away from your pain.

MOTH-TO-FLAMING

This is one of the most painful pitfalls of all, as you actually act out your obsessional thinking, and a form of zigzagging, as you are constantly drawn back into your old relationship only to be hurt over and over again. You are like a moth drawn to a flame. And just as the closer the moth gets to the flame, the more it's hurt, the more you subject yourself to the other person's continuous rejection, the more you suffer. It is your compulsion to constantly try to re-create the relationship, regardless of the humiliating rejection that makes this pitfall so devastating.

Although rejected, you continuously beg to be taken back and constantly look for ways to reintegrate yourself into the other person's life. You may find yourself constantly telephoning him/her, leaving presents, sending notes. All of your actions only reinforce your denial that the relationship is over.

Far from impressing the other person, this lavish attention is likely to be an annoyance. And as he/she reacts with continual rejection and indifference, you are subjected to further pain, feeling even more diminished as your self-esteem sinks lower. Just as the flame destroys the moth, repeated rejection destroys you.

In the grip of obsessional thinking over Maurice, Samantha was also moth-to-flaming in her attempts to entice Maurice back into her life. She would go out of her way to bump into him at his favorite nightclubs and restaurants—first spending hours making up and dressing up, hoping to seduce him back. She would leave impassioned messages on his answering machine and then sit up most of the night waiting for him to return her call, which he never did. She even sent him a rare orchid with a note: "Our love will never die, as it is as rare as this orchid."

The more Samantha obsessed and played it out, the more Maurice rejected her. But so blinded by the light of the flame, she continued in her attempts to get closer. However, Maurice became so annoyed by her obsessive and moth-to-flaming behavior that he got an unlisted telephone number and stopped going to his old hangouts.

While her impassioned telephone messages and the gift of the rare orchid helped her imagine that she was somehow once again a part of his life, in reality she was being ignored. It was her persistent compulsion to keep trying, regardless of his constant rejection, that made her realize she needed help. Samantha had reached her emotional bottom, for she had lost all sense of the reality that the relationship no longer existed. Later, as she regained her emotional control, she told me, "I thought I was worthless without him. I felt depleted and powerless. And the more he rejected me, the more I wanted him. It was as though he had become an addiction—he was my fix— and I didn't know how I could live without him."

In severe cases of moth-to-flaming, it is not until you've reached your lowest emotional level, like Samantha, that you finally realize that you cannot make someone else feel something that they don't feel. Not all the gifts, phone calls, or begging in the world is ever going to make the other person give what they cannot give.

If this is your pattern, what you must focus on is stopping any actions on your part that are going to subject you to further rejection. Again, as with obsessional thinking, this means taking action: leaving yourself a note on every phone not to call, applying the thought-blocking technique of saying *"STOP!"* every time you are tempted to reinvolve yourself with the other person, and filling your life with diverters to take your focus off the other person.

I've also had patients make a tape for themselves about the dynamics of the relationship: what was good about it, when and why it began to change, why it had to end, and in what ways it was beneficial to them that it did end. Making a tape helps you understand the difference between what once was and what now is. Whenever you are tempted to call or do anything that will draw you back into the relationship, listen to the tape. Hearing your own voice telling you the truth over and over again will make it easier for you to maintain your self-control. (I will give you more information about making a love-shock tape in Chapter Seven.)

Often we become self-deluded about the reality of our

relationships because we simply can't bear the pain that we associate with the final letting go. The denial can overwhelm us. We'd rather keep singeing our wings, fluttering closer to that flame, than fly away alone.

If the other person continues to act kindly toward you and even agrees to see you from time to time, you are going to have to do a reality check. Don't confuse kindness with love: the other person may initially respond favorably to your actions simply out of respect for you and your former relationship, without having any intention of ever coming back.

Time spent with someone you have broken up with may leave you with unrealistic expectations as you think, "Oh, gosh, this person really misses me, wants to come back to me." Now is the time for total self-honesty on your part, as you ask yourself these questions:

- Was your time together romantic, or are you creating something that wasn't really there?
- Did this person voluntarily make physical contact with you, or did you force it?
- Was there true tenderness and a real show of feelings, or are you seeing in the other person's behavior reactions that aren't really there?

If you are convinced that there is still some flicker of interest, a small chance that the relationship can be rekindled, ask the other person to think about your relationship for a week or two. Ask him/her to call you back. Nine out of ten times he/she never calls back; if anything, he/she is relieved to be let off the hook.

Taking this step, saying, "I'll leave it up to you, all right?" will take a lot of courage on your part. If he/she does not respond as you hope, your self-respect is still intact because you have allowed the other person to make the choice. Once again you are taking control over your life, moving yourself through loveshock, and ultimately doing what's good for you—instead of acting out of desperation for some momentary relief.

ESCAPING THROUGH EXCESS

Unfortunately, one of the most frequent responses to loss and rejection is compulsive behavior, or what I call *escaping through excess*. This is a pitfall that is easy to succumb to because without the other person you feel that your life is no longer balanced. As the scale is already tipped, it is easy to slide into excess.

The most serious form of excess is drug and alcohol abuse, using either or both to numb your pain and compensate you for your love loss. The problem with these substances is that since they only provide temporary, short-term relief, you may turn to them repeatedly to prolong your relief. In doing this, instead of regaining emotional control, you only lose more control. When full-blown, escaping through excess is the most dangerous love pitfall of all. That's why during loveshock it's important that you consider yourself in a high-risk period, and if anything be overly protective with yourself, avoiding all addictive substances. I have counseled many drug addicts who began their flight into addiction because a serious love relationship ended and alcoholics who began their heavy drinking as a way to numb the pain of divorce. You hear examples of this pitfall in the news every day, and you can probably think of cases among your own friends.

If this is your pitfall, you are denying a basic reality

of life: that what provides momentary pleasure and relief cannot provide you with any real happiness or solutions to your emotional problems. Seeking happiness through any of these excesses will only end up being destructive. I guarantee you that attempting to escape through excess while coping with loveshock is a no-win situation that can lead to permanent physical and psychological damage.

If you find yourself falling into this pitfall, do not tolerate it. Accept the fact that you need help. Be on your guard against your denial, which may lead you to think, "I can handle this. I've got it under control." This type of denial will only involve you more deeply, as you are literally digging your own grave.

Realize that the reason that you are escaping through excess is that you cannot handle your emotional pain; you really are out of control. Nobody engages in self-destructive behavior when they're in control of their lives.

I cannot stress enough how important it is that you take action immediately and seek professional help, whether it be through therapy, counseling, or one of the twelve-step self-help programs that are available. There is an anonymous self-help group available for almost every substance abuse problem that exists, including Alcoholics Anonymous, Narcotics Anonymous, and Cocaine Anonymous, to name just a few. If you have any confusion about how and where to get help, a community health professional (or, of course, your personal physician) will be able to point you in the right direction.

Perhaps not as destructive and dangerous, but also physically and psycologically damaging, is compulsive eating. While food may keep you company during those lonely loveshock nights, confronting the extra pounds when the worst of your loveshock is over will just be another psychological setback that you'll have to deal with as you rebuild your life. Beyond your appearance, sudden and excessive weight gain can contribute to health problems such as high blood pressure.

If you're prone to diving into a box of chocolates night after night rather than dealing with your feelings, I recommend that you carefully monitor your food intake. Know that for every unneccessary morsel you indulge in, ultimately there is a price to pay in pounds and inches, and maybe even with your health.

When Marlene started her therapy, she had gained five pounds in the two-week period since she and Bobby had split up. This was not difficult to do, since she worked in a delicatessen. A pretty woman in her twenties, with black hair and blue eyes, she told me that dieting had always been her demon. "It seems as though I've spent my whole life starving to remain a size ten. But I love food—cooking it, eating it and selling it. And since Bobby and I split up, I just don't care anymore. What the hell—why not eat the cheesecake? I can down a pint of ice cream and not even think twice about it!"

But the fact that she was in my office, seeking help, indicated that she really did care. The last thing she wanted was to come out of her loveshock a size fourteen. She also had a family history of diabetes. I advised her to keep a food diary. Before she ate anything she had to write down what it was she was about to eat and what her emotions were at that moment. The diary not only made her aware of all that she was eating, but provided her with some insight into how she was using food as a substitute for the love that was no longer a part of her life.

To control her snack attacks at home, I had her buy an exercise bicycle and place it in the kitchen. When she got the urge to snack, it was up to her to get on the bike and pedal for as long as it took for her to regain her self-control. When working at the delicatessen, I urged her to reach for raw vegetables instead of potato salad.

While I provided the therapy, it was up to Marlene to follow through with her own self-discipline. A month later, although still zigzagging between setting blame and resignation, Marlene had lost the five pounds and was ecstatic with her new thigh muscles.

COMPARISON SHOPPING

You feel that you are ready to date, but unfortunately no one meets up to your expectations because you are constantly comparing anyone that you meet to your ex. If comparison shopping is your pitfall, it usually takes one of two forms: either you are looking for someone who is just like your ex, or you refuse to consider anyone who has any similarities to your ex. You may fantasize what I call *the model of perfection,* as you create in your mind an unrealistic idealization of what a partner should be like. Anyone that you meet is bound to fall short of your expectations because there is no perfect person.

When you are looking for someone who is a clone of your ex, it may be because you still have not completely accepted your love loss and may be still experiencing some obsessional thinking. You're hoping to find an identical replacement. Conversely, if you dismiss anyone who reminds you in any way of your ex, it may be because you're afraid to experience the same emotional pain.

Either way, you're operating in extremes—but this is one pitfall that's fairly easy to correct. You have to get in touch with your needs and also to understand that regardless of how much you have been hurt, you stayed with your ex for perhaps several years because he/she did fulfill certain needs within you. The secret is to find someone who fulfills your needs without the hurt or incompatibilities involved in your previous relationship. So focus on your personal needs and how they can be met, and do not allow yourself to compare a new acquaintance to your ex. You must consider any new people that you meet as individuals.

I had one patient, a well-known actress, who had already been through three marriages when she came to see me. She had one of the most extreme cases of comparison shopping that I had ever counseled.

Each marriage had ended in similar unhappy circumstances, and as she contemplated taking the plunge for the fourth time, she became concerned. She didn't want to make another mistake. During the course of her therapy she realized that since her first marriage she had rebounded from one unhappy marriage to the next, never completing the stages of loveshock after any of the marriages had ended. And each time she rebounded, it was into the arms of another man who was similar to her first husband.

Brad had been the real love of her life—an exciting, sexy man who also had a bad gambling habit. So with the good things that made her happy, the bad came as well; she continued to attach herself to men who were slick. She thrived on the excitement. But unfortunately, with the excitement came the gambling. And whether it was because of risky business deals or the roulette wheel, ultimately each husband would rely on her for the money. In the end the business deal would fall through or Lady Luck would flee, and she was left with nothing but a smaller bank balance.

Concerned that her fourth marriage would disintegrate like the previous three, I had her make a list of her personal needs and what was important to her in a relationship. "Excitement" was at the top of the list, but so was "not to be used." What she needed to realize was that there were plenty of exciting men, exciting men who were independent and did not need to rely on her money or celebrity status to feed their excitement. Until she made this list, she had never stopped to think that by being selective, it was possible to have the excitement she craved without the risks.

As she analyzed her list and took a close look at the history and character of her current love, she made the decision to hold off on the marriage. A month later she called me, and I could hear a real sadness in her voice. "Jordan's gone. He left a week ago because I wouldn't back his latest venture. I think from now on, Dr. Gullo, I'm going to take it a lot slower. Comparison shopping is not for me, and I've got to stop rebounding. It's time that I face my emotional pain once and for all . . ."

When a love relationship ends, your emotional foundation—badly shaken—usually cracks where it is the weakest. Think of any love pitfalls you experience during loveshock as the cracks. Know that you can patch and smooth out these cracks strengthening your overall character.

Overcoming the love pitfalls is another of life's challenges, providing you with the opportunity to become emotionally stronger. As you work your way out of, over, and beyond the pitfalls, you will be left with an enhanced sense of self-worth and self-esteem. You will realize that *you* are capable of fortifying your emotional foundation, that *you* have the power to curb and maintain your emotional self-control.

CHAPTER SIX

Resignation: Saying Goodbye to Love

Lorna sat in my office with two rather large boxes next to her. The combination of her bright blue cashmere dress and medium-length white hair was stunning. In the six months that we had been working together, her physical transformation had been amazing. When she had first consulted with me she had been rather frumpy and nondescript-looking: the emotional pain had overwhelmed the person.

Initially Lorna had been in a passive response pattern, cutting herself off from everyone and everything in her grief—including the people who could divert the misery that had engulfed her since Andy had ended their thirty-year marriage. During our earliest sessions, when Andy had just moved out of their house and into his girlfriend's apartment, she would come to my office and for the first half hour of our hour session weep and claim that she must have failed miserably for this to happen to her. At times she would become hysterical, so full of rage that she secreamed at me, "What did I do to deserve this? I did everything I could to please him. Oh God, what are the kids going to think of me when they find out?"

Lorna dreaded telling her son and daughter about the breakup because she was convinced that they wouldn't understand and would blame her. Since her son was in the Navy and her daughter lived in Oregon, physical contact with either one of them was infrequent. But they were very close, keeping in touch through photos, tapes, and letters. Eventually they would realize that something had happened. I encouraged her to tell them before Andy did, stressing that while they might not understand at first, they would surely continue to love her as they always had.

Finally, a week later, she called her daughter from my office and explained to her as calmly as possible what had happened. As her daughter responded, Lorna began to cry. The conversation ended as Lorna quietly uttered into the receiver, tears running down her cheeks, "Nothing . . . Nothing . . . I'll call you soon."

As I handed her a tissue, I feared the worst. However, while she was still crying, her eyes were shining. "I can hardly believe it, Dr. Gullo. Do you know what she said? She said that I was terrific. She said that I was good and strong and the best mother anyone could ever have. She wanted to know if she could do anything for me. And the last thing she said was, 'Mom, I love you, no matter what.' "

She took the next step and wrote her son. He responded immediately, via radio from his ship, with concern and understanding.

From that point on, Lorna began to fight back and

actively deal with her loveshock. To fill the long hours of aloneness, she took a part-time job in a department store. Much to her surprise, she met other women at work, divorced and widowed, who had managed to rebuild their lives. They served as role models as Lorna realized that there was more to life than marriage. Her children's love was also an important incentive. Because her daughter's input had been so positive, I suggested that she call her on a biweekly basis for a boost of confidence to get her through the early stages of grief and setting blame.

It was hard work for Lorna to leave her self-pity and self-blame behind. And she struggled out of more than one pitfall: obsessive thinking, magnification, and compulsive eating were her personal demons. Ironically, her attractiveness and self-confidence blossomed as she worked her way through the pain. These qualities were, in a sense, the rewards of her loveshock.

But Lorna hadn't completed her loveshock yet. She was in resignation, what I also call the goodbye stage— the pivotal stage of every loveshock experience and for many, the worst part of loveshock.

Resignation is the most crucial stage of your loveshock experience; it is the time when you make the decision to release the relationship from your life once and for all. It is your time to say a final goodbye to what once was and will never be again, as you realize that you can no longer spend your life yearning for what might have been.

Lorna was at once desperate to let go and unable to let go. This is the major obstacle that all loveshock victims must get beyond in resignation before they can travel on to rebuilding, and why Lorna was sitting in my office with two large boxes full of everything that was portable that reminded her of her past with Andy. She found it too difficult to let go and get through her resignation on her own.

We were about to begin the *linking objects exercise,* in which she would get rid of any articles that evoked negative feelings, while keeping those that still affected her positively. And as much as she wanted to say goodbye and get on with her life, she was hesitant even to begin this exercise. This was not unusual; I had experienced this with other loveshock patients.

WHY YOU MUST LET GO

Long after love ends it may still linger in your thoughts, influencing your present and future behavior. While you are no longer in the relationship in reality, you are still married or emotionally attached in your mind. This is why completing resignation, the fourth stage of loveshock, is so important. Until you do, you are unable to continue traveling forward because you just can't let go, and you can't travel back to the past because your partner is no longer interested. Your life is on hold until you come to terms with your loss.

In fact, until you withdraw your emotional energy from the other person, you can date a hundred different people but none will ever please you because you are still married or committed elsewhere in your mind. It is imposible to get on with your life. If you are in loveshock and you want to know how long the pain will go on, I can tell you that it will last as long as you permit the relationship to exist in your thoughts. It will be difficult for you to let go and emotionally detach from the other person. But it is your responsibility to determine when you want to stop feeling the pain and take that final step of saying goodbye.

Choosing whether you should consider the other person as a friend or never even speak to him or her again may be hard. I have found that most of my patients who remain in contact during a divorce or breakup seem to have more emotional pain and often find it all the more difficult to let go. Sometimes, they find it necessary to have several *last meetings* before they can let go. The choice is yours, but I think that it is very important that you evaluate your feelings, and consider how you may feel afterwards, before you make contact with the other person.

There may, however, be practical considerations that make contact unavoidable, such as an amicable divorce settlement, shared business interests, or joint custody of the children. If these contacts with your ex-mate diminish you in any way or leave you feeling emotionally distraught, let your lawyer handle *everything*. You may have to sever your business connections. This is especially important if your partner has been cruel or abusive to you.

Unfortunately, many who should don't have the luxury of severing all ties because of joint custody of their children. If this is your situation, you may want to have a friend with you for support during those times when you must make contact with your spouse, for instance when he or she is picking up or dropping off your children. The discomfort you intially experience will begin to fade, once you have finally released the relationship.

WHY IT'S SO DIFFICULT TO SAY GOODBYE

While you know and remind yourself, "All I have to do is remove the other person from my thoughts," you still feel and have to deal with the realiity that you are losing a significant part of your life. And the longer the relationship lasted, the more difficult it is to accept that it is over. One of the most common statements I hear—in fact, I can't think of one loveshock patient who has come out of a long-term relationship who didn't bring it up—is, "I've invested so much time—all of those years. Where do I go from here? Is it worth it to start all over again?"

When a long-term relationship ends, you're not just losing the other person, you're losing an entire history. And you can expect to suffer multiple losses as well: your social network, your in-laws, and often your home, your lifestyle, your pet, and favorite possessions. Besides the love, you are losing a whole chunk of your life that existed within the context of the relationship. That is what makes it so hard to say that final, necessary goodbye.

What I tell my patients at this point is, "Yes, a part of your life is over. And you may feel, at this moment, that it was the best part that will ever be. But, in time, you will find that you will be able to build something in place of it that will be as rewarding and enriching as what you have lost."

Lorna compared traveling through resignation to walking through a long, dark tunnel filled with everything from the love relationship: "As you walk by it all, toward the light at the end of the tunnel, you must say goodbye as you keep walking. Your heart aches and you want to cry. And you want to stop and embrace each memory, each person and each thing one last time. But you realize the longer you linger and hold on, the longer you stay in the dark. So the trick is to keep walking, not to stop, because if you keep walking you will eventually have said goodbye to everything and be in the light. Once you are in the light, you can see clearly. You have regained your perspective of what is real and what is fantasy." The analogy is a good one; resignation isn't the destination, it's only a vital step to get you over your pain. Your life doesn't stop when you say goodbye in the darkness: it's about to begin again in the light.

I would add to Lorna's analogy that when you are walking through this unknown, dark tunnel, it's normal to stumble along the way. If you do, all that matters is that you get up and continue to move forward. Although you may be fearful, push yourself along. And take with you, from this journey, those things that give you comfort and will continue to enrich your life in the future—as you move on to rebuilding.

THE FINAL ACT OF SAYING GOODBYE

Because it is so difficult to say goodbye, to let go of an important love relationship, I have found an active therapy of actually acting out resignation to be very effective in getting my patients over this last major hurdle of loveshock. There are three parts to this therapy: the personal statement, confronting what went wrong in the relationship and why it ended, and the linking objects exercise.

First, it is important that you make a *personal statement* of what you saw in the other person, what attracted you to become involved with him or her, and what were the positive and negative aspects of the relationship. By doing this you acknowledge that you got involved with this person by *your own choice*. This process will also help remove any vestiges of magnification; you will cease to idealize the other person and the relationship.

You can either make a cassette of this personal statement or write it out. Do what you feel has the most impact on you. Some of my patients do both. Whichever method you choose, make sure that you begin and end your personal statement with "This relationship is over. X is no longer a part of my life. The sooner I let go, the happier I will be."

Lorna had been keeping a diary of her feelings since the beginning of her loveshock, so she chose to write her personal statement out: "This relationship is over. Andy is no longer a part of my life. The sooner I let go, the happier I will be. I was attracted to Andy the first time I watched him play football in college. He was a wonderful athlete—so strong and yet so graceful. And he did all the right things when we dated. He was the perfect beau. There were lots of flowers and he never pressed himself on me. He was a real gentleman. When he went to Korea and became a captain, I knew that I'd marry him if he came back alive.

"Andy was hardworking and always pushed himself a little more so that we could have more. We were one of the first couples in our apartment complex to have two cars, and I remember how proud he was when we moved into our first house. We took wonderful vacations because he liked adventures. But he was short-tempered and didn't have patience when it came to dealing with the kids. This is embarrassing to write, but he never really satisfied me sexually. In fact, I never really thought that he cared that much about sex: that's why I was so shocked that he left me for a girlfriend and still am. When he said, 'I do,' I thought he meant it. But now I know that he was with his girlfriend for two years before he left me. I married one man and ended up being married to someone else. This relationship is over. Andy is no longer a part of my life. The sooner I let go, the happier I will be."

The second important part of this therapy is to *clearly confront what went wrong in the relationship and why it ended*. Your personal statement will help you connect with this. After reading Lorna's, I asked her what her conclusion was.

Her response: "The man who left me for another woman was not the man I married. I don't feel that I have to blame myself for failing in this marriage. He changed, I changed—our changes took us in different directions."

And then I asked the key question, which would ultimately help her make peace with herself and release any guilt she was feeling: "What responsibility, if any, do you take for this relationship ending?"

Lorna looked away as she answered, "Well, I got pretty wrapped up in the kids and all of their activites. There were plenty of times when Andy needed to vent his frustrations or just talk about what was going on at work. I wasn't a very good listener: I was so involved answering the children's needs, I had no time to listen to Andy . . . I also let my physical appearance go. I know now how important it is to always look the best that you can. It shows the other person that you care not just about him, but about yourself as well."

Many of my male patients tell me that once the children came along, their wives stopped working on their relationships, and at times they felt extremely neglected.

This was where Lorna had been at fault, and felt she had to take partial responsibility for Andy's infidelity.

All of these realizations were bringing Lorna closer to letting go. She was finally able to step outside of the relationship and evaluate it objectively and even learn from her pain. Rather than thinking in terms of "failure," she had begun to think in terms of "different"— that Andy's needs were different and the dynamics of the relationship could not fulfill these needs. This is why he left.

If you have been in the role of rejectee, and the other person said, "I don't love you anymore," what he or she may really have meant was "My needs have changed and I no longer love what you have to offer me." Don't think of yourself as a failure or inadequate because of this. Realize that just as the other person needs to find someone else who is better suited to his or her needs, so do you. By the time you reach the final stage of resolution you will be in touch with your needs, aware of what it takes in a relationship to make you happy. Many of my loveshock patients have ended up finding someone better suited to them and are much happier today, in their present relationship, than they ever were in their previous relationship. Wisdom in love often follows loveshock.

Having taken responsibility for your part in the ending of the relationship, you must release yourself from the burden of being perfect. Lack of perfection, a characteristic we all share, is one of the major reasons we beat ourselves up psychologically. Instead, give yourself permission to make mistakes, and realize that working through them is what allows you to grow. Your objectivity in recognizing your needs and realizing your right to satisfy them, as well as acknowledging your responsibility for what has happened, will help you move on to the rebuilding stage of loveshock.

THE LINKING OBJECTS EXERCISE

Having made her personal statement and having clearly confronted what went wrong in the relationship and why it ended, it was the right time for Lorna to begin the *linking objects exercise*. As she began to take out snapshots, cards, jewelry, and a couple of pieces of clothing, she looked at me painfully and asked, "Why do I have to go through this?"

"I know that this is painful, but it is a necessary step in coming to terms with your love loss. All of these items were a part of a relationship that *was* an important part of your life; these are a part of your personal history. By remembering the positive and negative feelings associated with each article, you will be confronting your personal pain and will become less frightened of it. This exercise also allows you to release the energy of the other person once and for all, as you get rid of any articles that you feel still draw you back into thoughts of the relationship. And any articles that evoke negative feelings you should give away or throw away. It is also important that you identify any *unrealistic* romantic fantasies associated with each item. These fantasies could be preventing you from releasing the relationship."

Before Lorna began to go over each article that she had placed on my desk, I reminded her of the early days of her loveshock; I reminded her how far she had come. "Remember how you used to spy on Andy, watching him enter his girlfriend's apartment building from the pay phone across the street?"

She looked at me, shocked. "Oh lord! I was so obsessive! I really did some stupid things, didn't I? And what about my fake suicide attempt? I tried everything to get his attention. What a waste of time!"

"While this may be the worst experience you have ever been through in your life, Lorna, one look in the mirror will show you how well you have come through it all, how you have grown from your pain. You've progressed so far, it's time that you let the rest of it go. And as you do so, realize that you are also letting go of all the mistrust you once felt, the fear of not knowing where Andy was, and your feelings of betrayal."

"I know," she said. "You're right—let's get on with it. Okay. All the jewelry has to go. Andy always gave me a piece of jewelry for our anniversary. It's meaningless now."

"Perhaps your daughter might like it."

"That's a thought. And if she doesn't want it, I'll sell it—except for this . . ." Lorna held a gold charm bracelet with two tiny charms in her hand. I could see the tears in her eyes. She cleared her throat and continued, "Ah, he gave this to me when Tracy was born and added the second charm to it when Jimmy was born. This I'll keep and maybe even wear, because two wonderful kids did come out of that marriage."

As she went through the rest of her things, discussing what each one meant to her, there were more tears. But there was acceptance as well. She finally decided that except for a family portrait and the charm bracelet, everything she had brought with her had to go; these were the only things she felt strongly about in a positive way. The clothing would go to charity, the jewelry would go to her daughter or would be sold, and the photos, cards, and other bits of memorabilia she actually dumped in my wastebasket. "This way, I won't be tempted to retrieve them!"

While the linking objects exercise is extremely effective in moving you through resignation, helping you to resolve your feelings so that you can finally let go, it can also be painful. Your goal should be to integrate what you now see as the positive parts of your history into your new life while you remove the relationship itself from your thoughts. One patient said that when he did this exercise he felt the same grief and longing he had felt when he packed up his mother's possessions after she had died.

You may want to do this exercise with a friend, family member, minister, or therapist for support. And timing is also important: while it's natural to resist saying this final goodbye, don't force yourself to do it if you really don't feel that you are ready to handle it. If you have any doubt about what you are selling, giving away, or throwing away, ask a friend to store these items for you until you are sure. Or put them in a safety deposit box or vault. The point is to remove them from your daily contact. I had one patient who sold a valuable Oriental vase, only to learn a year later that it was worth far more than what she was paid for it.

If you decide to do the linking objects exercise alone, do it on a day when you are feeling good about yourself and the direction your life is taking. It's a lot easier to let go of the emotions that keep you locked in the past when you believe in your future. It's also helpful if you have an uplifting and positive activity planned for afterwards: a meal with good friends, a funny movie, a massage, or a shopping expedition. This will reinforce in your mind that your life is moving forward in a positive direction, that you have finally come to terms with the *what was* and *what is* of the relationship that has ended. As you complete this exercise, know that you have just taken a big step into your future.

Lorna had two wonderful children that would continue to be a part of her life no matter what. She also had a beautiful house that she loved and felt very secure in, regardless of whether or not Andy shared it with her.

Here is how some of the other people I've mentioned earlier in the book acted out the linking objects exercise:

Earlene got rid of all the records she and Ed used to dance to.

Nancy threw away the beautiful, sexy lingerie that Gene had given her and then replaced it with equally beautiful lingerie in a different color.

Lloyd sold the summer house in Nantucket that he and Liz had shared and bought himself a little fishing cabin in Maine, something he had always wanted.

While her closest girlfriend held her hand, Lindsey burned the postcards, matchbooks, and ticket stubs that she had collected during her romance with Victor.

Palmer gave the expensive designer bedding from his king-size bed to his maid. "Once I changed the bedding, I could read in bed at night without constantly being distracted by thoughts of Robin."

Remember Seth, whose wife, Alison, announced that she wanted a divorce while they were dining with their friend Bert? After he did the linking objects exercise, Seth decided to trade his car in for a new one because whenever he glanced at the passenger side, for a brief moment the image of Alison flashed through his mind. "It was as though I was seeing a ghost!"

The conclusion Seth came to, as he traveled through resignation and on to rebuilding, was, "This is my reality. I can go on being miserable or I can accept that this has come to an end. This means letting all thoughts of my ex-wife go. I am now free and ready to begin again. I'm on my own now. Whatever I'm going to have in my life is what I'm going to create for myself. If I allow myself to be miserable for one more day, then I have only added to my loss by giving up today."

CHAPTER SEVEN

Becoming Your Own Love Doctor

Much of the success of any therapy depends on the degree of trust between the doctor and the patient: the doctor's trust in the patient's commitment to move toward recovery as well as the patient's trust that his doctor will help him actually do this. So far in this book I have tried to help you gain a better understanding of what you feel and why you feel the way you do. Now it is time for you to call on your own capacity for self-therapy and self-healing.

The personal growth you've experienced up to this point—and will continue to experience—comes from the active part you have taken in your recovery. Think of yourself as your own therapist, your own love doctor, as you continue to move yourself through the final stages of loveshock. Ultimately, it is because you have taken control of your emotions, combined with your desire to get better and the passing of time, that you are recovering. When you take control of your emotions you have more control over your life.

In the difficult fourth stage of resignation or saying goodbye, you release the relationship from your psyche so that you can be free to begin to rebuild your life. Now, to continue that rebuilding process, you need to strengthen your courage and self-esteem.

YOUR EMOTIONAL SURVIVAL SKILLS

Throughout the book you have expanded your emotional survival skills with different exercises and therapies to get you through the early, critical stages of loveshock. These exercises and therapies are tools that you can continue to use any time you are going through a difficult emotional period, and you will want to use them whenever you feel yourself zigzagging or experiencing a loveshock flashback. (Even in the last two stages of rebuilding and resolution, you may still suffer setbacks.)

In summary, here are some of the most valuable exercises to help you through the final stages of loveshock recovery:

Self-Monitoring

As you evaluate your behavior and actions on a daily basis, self-monitoring provides you with the opportunity to step outside of yourself and watch what's going on. Self-awareness and self-knowledge enhance personal growth, especially during a loveshock experience. If you are totally honest with yourself, self-monitoring will alert you to any destructive habits or patterns that are forming—especially excessive smoking, eating, or drinking. This exercise is not intended to make you feel bad about yourself. It is intended to help you grow from your mistakes and move you through loveshock with a minimal amount of pain. Self-monitoring can be done by recording your feelings on tape, keeping a written journal, or making a simple list of the day's activities and how you felt while doing them. Or you can just take ten minutes, once or twice a day, to have an internal dialogue with yourself about what you are doing, how you feel, and how you think you are progressing. This provides you with perspective on how you are moving through your loveshock.

Thought-Blocking Technique

Every time you start thinking about your ex or feel yourself wallowing in self-pity, you instantly say to yourself, *"STOP!"* Then shift your thoughts to something equally compelling, or engross yourself in an activity that will divert your attention (see below), in spite of yourself. The more you practice this technique, the more effective it becomes.

Compelling Diverters

Any constructive activity or interest that you can focus your energy on—the very same energy that up until now you've invested in your love relationship—can be an effective diverter. Compelling diverters can be the shock absorbers of loveshock, with a bonus: at the end of loveshock you may have developed a new skill, learned a new sport, gotten a better job, or improved your appearance.

Relaxation Techniques

Develop safe, nonaddictive ways to get through high stress, panic, and anxiety periods. Some of my patients' favorites are exercising; long, hot baths with soothing music; massage; dancing; deep breathing; painting; going to the movies; playing a musical instrument; needlepoint and other crafts.

Power of Positive Suggestions

As you repeat different affirmations over and over again—such as, "My loveshock is ending, "I grow stronger every day," "I am in control"—they sink into your subconscious mind. Your subconscious will eventually begin to support the affirmation, turning your negative thoughts around. Every time you start to think, "I'm so miserable," replace it with, "I grow stronger every day."

Reminders

Affirmation notes, strategically placed, will also be very helpful. For instance, a *"STOP! DON'T CALL!"* placed by every phone will help you maintain self-control when you're tempted to pick up the phone and reconnect. Also, don't forget your list of the positive aspects of your life taped to your bathroom mirror, ready to be recited out loud as you stare at yourself and remind yourself how much you have going for you.

Let Someone Be Your 911

Create a personal support system of friends and family members who say it's okay to call them when you are tempted to call your ex or when you're just feeling down or lonely. Also, consider your church or temple or other organizations for additional emotional support.

When in Doubt, Reach Out

If you feel that you are completely out of control and you fear that you might do something self-destructive or desperate, reach out for help immediately. See a physician or have a trusted friend or physician refer you to a counselor or therapist for help. Or contact your community mental health association. Also, look to the many twelve-step self-help programs (Alcoholics Anonymous, Overeaters Anonymous, Narcotics Anonymous, etc.) that are available if you find yourself starting to escape through self-destructive means such as drugs, alcohol, or compulsive eating.

THE ROLE OF FAMILY AND FRIENDS

Your family and friends are a valuable emotional resource during loveshock. But be careful not to abuse their compassion and understanding. Make sure that it really is all right to call them at any hour, and be appreciative of the fact that they are there for you. As they have made themselves available to you, return the generosity. I remind you of this because it is not unusual during loveshock to get so wrapped up in your pesonal problems, so emotionally needy, that you forget about the importance of giving back. Treat your trusted friend or family member to a movie or dinner out. Make the effort to remove yourself from your problems by asking yourself, "Now what can I do for him or her?"

One of the hazards of loveshock is that you may become very tiresome as you discuss the same situations and events over and over again. Caught up in your pain, you may be unaware that every story you share you have already told many times before. In doing so, you may alienate and actually burn out the very people you are depending on for emotional support. They may even begin to dread your phone calls.

How do you know when enough is enough? Follow what I call the three strike principle. That is, if you've discussed the same topic or told the same story three times to the same person, either don't bring it up again or first ask whether your friend would mind discussing it with you once more. Ask for an honest answer, and don't be hurt if he or she suggests that you see a movie or go shopping together instead. And when you are out together, don't discuss your misery. It's always easier to talk about *your* pain, so make it a point to discuss your friend's concerns and interests. This will enhance your friendship and help divert, and maybe even end, your obsessional thinking.

If you need to continue discussing a particular feeling or problem, consult a counselor, therapist, or minister—someone whose job is to listen and counsel. Be aware that every friend and relative, however sympathetic, eventually grows tired of listening to your problems.

MAKING YOUR OWN LOVESHOCK TAPE

In my work as a psychotherapist I have been particularly impressed by the role of what psychologists call "the phenomenon of overlearning" in motivating and changing behavior. "Overlearning" means repeatedly hearing or otherwise being exposed to certain concepts or key phrases. When these concepts and key phrases are appropriate to the listener, they begin to influence conscious and subconscious thoughts.

This technique is used all the time by advertisers to motivate us to purchase different products. A classic example is a commercial for the American Express card: you may not remember the last time you saw the commercial, but you'll probably remember the slogan, "Don't leave home without it."

A kind of brainwashing, you can use this technique as a positive tool to ease you through your loveshock by simply making a tape that you can listen to as often as necessary.

I have all of my loveshock patients make a tape about the dynamics of the relationship that has ended: what was good about it, when and why it had to change, why it had to end, and in what ways it is beneficial that it has ended. Such a tape can help you understand the difference between what once was and what now is. If this relationship was self-destructive for you and you feel that you are moth-to-flaming, make sure that you listen frequently to the tape to remind yourself of all the reasons that this relationship was bad for you. When you find yourself getting bored, make a new tape with a variation of the same theme.

Whenever you are tempted to call your ex or do anything that will draw you back into the relationship, listen to the tape. Listen to it when you are filled with self-doubt. Slip it into your Walkman and listen to it while you are exercising. Auditory stimuli are extremely powerful. And hearing *your own voice* telling you the truth over and over again will create a greater impact, making it easier for you to maintain self-control.

We all have a "psyche tape" playing in our mind, composed of bits and pieces of all of our experiences up to the present time. Often the reason you get stuck in one of the stages of loveshock is that your psyche tape is playing a fantasy that you want to believe: "X still loves me. I'm still in love with X. The relationship will be reconciled and we will continue our life together . . ."

If you find that this sort of fantasy tape is playing in your psyche, constantly programming you with a message that is not productive, you should make yourself a truth tape to pitch the correct message. Begin by saying, "It's over. This is why it ended . . ."

I can't stress enough how valuable the loveshock tapes can be. I've had hundreds of loveshock patients make their own loveshock tapes, and all have felt that making the tape and constantly listening to it helped them at least maintain self-control when they were tempted to do something that ultimately might have caused them more pain. Others have reported that their tapes gave them a more profound sense of what happened and why their relationships ended, as hidden messages surfaced in the tapes after they had listened to them several times. Perhaps they were only reinterpreting their original statements; whatever the case, the tapes seem to be very beneficial.

ANXIETY CONTROL TECHNIQUES

Anxiety attacks can be frequent and quite severe during loveshock. They can take different forms and can trigger different compulsive behaviors. You may feel so unnerved that you would rather escape through excess than suffer another moment of anxiety. Suddenly you find yourself drinking excessively, taking drugs, eating compulsively, or maybe even gambling—anything to divert you from the anxiety that comes from your loneliness and your hurt.

I have two different relaxation techniques that you can use to manage anxiety attacks. The first one is a modification of one of the most powerful methods of relaxation that I know of; it is called the Jacobson Relaxation Technique. (Dr. Jacobson was a world-reknowned cardiologist who developed this technique to assist his cardiac patients and others to cope with severe stress.)

Take the phone off the hook so that you are not disturbed. Sit in a comfortable chair or lie on your bed. Close your eyes. Begin to listen to the gentle melody of your breathing—in and out. Now each time you breathe out, repeat to yourself, "Calm and relax."

After a minute or two of unwinding this way, keeping your eyes closed, take the deepest breath you can and hold it for around thirty seconds. When it begins to hurt, let go.

Take a second very deep breath. As you do so and hold it, feel all the pain, any loneliness or depression, any anger toward yourself or the other person. Really feel it and live it for that moment. And when you are ready, let it all go with a big deep breath.

Now focus on breathing slowly and deeply for a few moments, before you begin the second part of this exercise. In the second part you will make all of your muscles tense and firm. By tensing your muscles, you are actually forcing any accumulated tension to be released. When you tense your muscles and then suddenly release them, they react by actually relaxing and releasing the tension.

Continue breathing slowly and deeply, with your eyes closed, and gently begin to tense your muscles. Begin with your feet and work your way up your body. Tense your calves, your thighs, your abdomen, your chest, your neck, your face, the muscles around your eyes, your arms, your hands. And clench your fists. When your whole body is tense, think of it as one piece of wood. Hold the tension until it starts to hurt. If you feel any emotional pain, any depression, any sadness, or any anger—this is the time to let it go.

As you feel all of these emotions leaving your body, imagine your legs going limp, just like two pieces of rope. Feel the muscles in your abdomen and chest going limp like rope too. Feel your arms and hands going limp. Now feel the muscles of your jaw relaxing so that your teeth don't even touch. Feel the muscles around your eyes relaxing so that your eyelids seem heavy on your eyes. Breathe slowly and breathe deeply.

With every easy, deep breath you take, feel yourself becoming more relaxed. It feels so good to relax. And now, breathing slowly and deeply, see yourself happy and smiling. You are laughing again. You are at peace.

During this exercise you may feel as if your body is floating. Or you may feel that your body is melting into the bed or the chair. You are feeling calm and relaxed, as you listen to the gentle melody of your breathing.

Stay in this relaxed state for about five minutes. Think of it as your mini-vacation in the midst of a stressful day. Then, as you prepare to bring yourself out of it, see yourself resting on a beautiful beach—serene and in control of your life. As you continue to feel calm and relaxed, acknowledge that it's okay to worry at times and maybe even to be a little anxious. Now see yourself happy, managing, and taking control of your life.

And as you are feeling totally in control, slowly count from one to three. When you reach three, affirm to yourself, "I am in control of my life. After all that I've been through, I'm not going to let anxiety take over my life." Continue to breathe deeply and slowly as you bring yourself out of this state of deep relaxation.

You will be amazed at how refreshed you feel afterwards. This is the perfect way to release anxiety while you are at home. You may want to follow this technique with a warm bath.

If you are having an anxiety attack in a public place, you can release it with this simple technique that takes about sixty seconds: while sitting in a chair, first calm yourself with some deep breathing, slowly inhaling and exhaling. Now begin to tense all of the muscles in your body. Begin with your feet, as you did in the first technique, and work your way up your body. (You don't have to close your eyes or clench the muscles of your face if people are around.)

Once your whole body is tense and tight like a piece of wood, bring together your thumb and index finger so that they form an O. Clench the two of them together as hard as you can. You can do this with just one hand or with both hands.

As you clench, feel all the anxiety being drained into these two (or four) fingers. Repeat to yourself, "Drain, drain." When you are ready, let these fingers go. As they separate, imagine yourself flicking away all of that anxiety. Repeat this technique three or four times.

Also remember that one of the best ways to release stress, tension, and anxiety is through exercise. I often recommend more exercise therapy than psychotherapy for loveshock patients; sometimes this is the first time they have actively exercised in years. Besides all the gyms and health clubs available, there are numerous exercise videos that you can use at home. Invest in a stationary bike and some weights. Many people feel more comfortable exercising at home if they are out of shape; there is no need to add the additional anxiety of "How do I look?" What's important is that you find a means of exercise that you will do regularly. Exercise increases neurochemicals, called endorphins, which bio-chemically help to reduce anxiety. They are a natural mood elevator.

Not only will you feel better in general and have less anxiety when you exercise regularly—you'll start to look better too. Loveshock often makes you look pale and drawn; the emotional pain radiates from your face. Exercising will make you appear more serene because you are more serene after you exercise.

LEARNING FROM YOUR PERSONAL HISTORY: THE CAPITAL GAINS OF LOVE

When you make your personal statement as you travel through resignation, clearly confronting what went wrong in the relationship and why it ended, and taking responsibility for your role in the breakup, *you don't have to lose your personal history.* While you are releasing the last of the love relationship from your psyche, you should also try to preserve what was positive in the relationship and weave it into your new life. This is what I call the *capital gains of love.* Perhaps you had children, perhaps you traveled a lot or learned a new skill or expanded in

your career while you were in the relationship. Any of
these things can be very valuable in your future, because
they contribute to who you are as a person.

But often it is difficult to figure out exactly how to
integrate your past into the present and future. More
than one loveshock patient has asked me, "When it's all
over, where do you put the memories?"

One of the problems of loveshock is that while you
are trying to release yourself from the past, you tend to
negate everything—including any positive experiences
that you gained by being in the relationship. This was
Les's problem. He felt that the only thing that he got
out of his seven-year relationship with Sherry was a lot
of humiliation when she left him for a younger man.
Consequently, he thought that he had nothing to show
for all of the time and energy he had put into their
relationship. However, it only took one question from
me to make him aware of something he had gotten out
of the relationship, something that would come in handy
in future relationships.

"Les, I want you to look at your whole relationship
and tell me what you think the best part of it was. There
had to be something that kept you together for seven
years. What were the pleasurable moments in the relationship?"

He sat quietly for a few minutes and then suddenly
perked up. "The sex was fabulous. Sherry was absolutely incredible in bed: in fact, we did things together
that I thought you could only think about. On a daily
basis she was moody and difficult to live with, but once
you got her in bed she really turned on."

Regardless of all else, Les had developed sexual expertise during his seven years with Sherry because she
had been a very willing partner. And although she had

left him to be with a younger man, he knew that he was a good lover. This was one insecurity that he wouldn't have to deal with when he was ready to get involved again. In fact, he had gained a skill that would serve him well. "Even on that last horrible day, two hours before she moved out, we made exquisite love on the living-room floor. While I'm still not sure why she feels so drawn to this other guy, I do know that I more than satisifed her sexual appetite."

Occasionally I get a patient who has been emotionally battered to the point of mental cruelty. This is someone who justifiably feels that there is nothing to be salvaged from the relationship, except perhaps the knowledge of what he or she doesn't want in the next relationship (if there is to be one). Sometimes, the experience has been so horrible that afterwards the patient becomes love phobic—afraid to love at all. It may take additional therapy for the patient to overcome the love phobia, to be willing to take a chance on love.

This was true for Janis, an executive secretary who had given up her career to stay home and look after Brent's needs when she was twenty-seven. Brent was a charming Englishman who had entered the import-export firm where she worked and swept her off her feet. "God, he was so good-looking, with those steel blue eyes and black, wavy hair. I should have known he'd end up being trouble. I resisted at first, but he wore me down with the flowers, poems, and romantic dinners. I didn't think men like this really existed, except in romance novels."

Three months after they met they were living together. Brent maintained the charm, passion, and intensity for several months, and finally Janis agreed to marry him.

"After almost a year of wonderful, old-fashioned courtship, even after we were living together, I was convinced that I had finally found the perfect man for me. I even agreed to give up everything I had worked so hard to gain, because he said he wanted a real wife— not some career woman. Well, two months after I said, 'I do,' I wished that I had said, 'I don't.' Suddenly, he started coming home late, often drunk, and then would demand his dinner after I had put everything away. He would complain that the apartment wasn't clean enough or that the laundry wasn't done right. He began to belittle me and make me feel as if I were nothing. And one of the worst things that he did was put me down in front of our friends. I really started feeling like I was living in another century, when women were treated like slaves."

Janis looked away for a moment before she could continue. "When I miscarried, he never even came to the hospital. My girlfriend brought me home. And for days he wouldn't speak to me. It was as though I had committed some horrible sin . . . After five years of this, I think that I've finally had it. I mean, I'm only thirty-two, but I feel all used up. What were the good times? I don't remember anymore. Whatever they were, they got buried in the insanity of this relationship."

While I tried to reassure Janis that there was some good that had come out of all this in terms of self-knowledge, her knowledge of her own needs, all she could say was "What a fool I've been!"

Finally, I looked at her and said, "That's a very healthy statement. It shows that you are in touch with the reality of the situation. While what you are telling me is very negative, you are at the same time saying that you have learned from it." Janis would have been in trouble if she were thinking about going back into the relationship or idealizing it even though she had been so mentally abused.

"What amazes me more than anything, Dr. Gullo, was how he deceived me. I mean, we were together for almost a year and even lived together before I agreed to marry him. What could I have done differently?"

"Probably nothing. Unfortunately, we can't run a relationship check, like a credit check, on people before we agree to marry them. And there are some people that change in personality once they get what they want. Not until then do you see their real nature. You're not the first person this has happened to. Perhaps the only mistake you made was to give up your career and then center your life completely around his. We all need to maintain our own identities. You probably should have insisted on keeping your job, at least part-time, and to some degree maintained your independence. Brent is a taker. And the more you gave, the more he took. Now you know that this is not the type of person who will ever make you happy."

"But his change was so radical. How do I know who to trust?"

"Unfortunately, Janis, there are no guarantees; that's why it takes courage to love. Sometimes you can only operate by instinct. However, again I stress that your first concern when you get involved with anyone is for you to maintain your own identity—this means your career, your friends, and any interests you had before you met this person. While you may have to make some compromises, it is unwise to give your whole life over to another person."

I encouraged Janis to think of this relationship as a kind of dress rehearsal for the next one. While she had suffered terribly, she was now very aware of what her personal needs were and realized that she had the strength to endure. Perhaps she had gained some insights that would help her to have better future relationships. In this case, although it had caused her a tremendous amount of pain, what she had learned was her capital gain of love.

This was Janis's first loveshock experience. I reassured her that if or when she ever went through loveshock again, it would not be as painful.

"Well, that's a relief, Dr. Gullo, but why is the first loveshock experience often the most painful?"

"Because people who go through all the stages of loveshock always grow stronger as a result of it. Think of it as a strengthening of the emotional immune system. And after it's finally over, they realize, often amazed, that they have survived and grown stronger. When loveshock comes again, they've developed coping skills that they can utilize again. And because they know what to expect, what's happening to them is not so frightening. They also find it easier to be in control of their emotions, because they know their loveshock will end."

It was important to help Janis focus on what positive things had happened to her since the breakup. I reminded her that, in her case, just ending the relationship was positive.

"I find that I've cut back on my smoking, because I'm not so nervous anymore. My girlfriend is letting me share her apartment until I can find a new job. The lawyers are still arguing over a settlement, so money is tight. Also, I've stopped drinking. You know I never really drank at all until I met Brent, and then suddenly I was having wine every night. He was a real connoisseur and believed a meal incomplete without a couple of bottles of wine. It's strange; now that I'm alone again I seem more like my old self."

It actually wasn't strange at all. Many people are like chameleons—especially when they are in love. As their insecurities begin to surface, often they will alter their behavior to please the other person. In the process, they begin gradually to lose their own identity as they are, in a sense, absorbed by the other person. Ending the relationship, even as the rejectee, is essential to the recovery of their self-identity.

PROMOTING YOUR OWN PSYCHOLOGICAL GROWTH

Quite often the loveshock experience makes apparent a much larger issue: your need to promote your own psychological growth. Again, I remind you how important it is that you release yourself from the burden of being perfect. It's okay to make a mistake and make a fool of yourself. In fact, as I pointed out to Janis, to acknowledge that you've made a mistake is a sign of psychological growth. In accepting our humanity we must accept our imperfections; they're a part of life.

Accepting the end of a relationship and acknowledging it to have been a mistake is a growth step—although a painful one. That's why it's extremely important that you build up your self-esteem by involving yourself in positive activities and in positive relationships.

If, like Janis, you let your spouse become your whole life, you have realized that you can never rely on just one person to be your sole source of emotional support.

That's unrealistic, and it's too much of a burden to place on anyone.

Apply the same principle to your emotions that you do to your finances—diversify! Not only does a range of interests promote your psychological growth, but it makes your life full, and it makes you very interesting to other people. Now is your chance to become a part of the office group—people you may barely know socially because you always had to rush right home to be with your spouse. Join everyone after work for drinks, softball, or the bowling team. Become active with your church, community service group, or arts council. Get involved with a cause that you believe in. Become a part of the mainstream of life. This way, when you lose some part of your life or someone in your life, you won't be so devastated: these emotional shock absorbers will cushion the blow.

Also, take the time to spoil yourself regularly. Whether it's having a massage, exercising, having a manicure, or just a long bath—indulge. They may seem like little things, but they reinforce your sense of self-love, which may have been inadequate even before your loveshock began.

The more you help yourself, the better you become. As your self-confidnce grows, an inner contentment grows with it. Suddenly the future does not seem so hopeless, for you are reaching out to take an active part in life again.

CHAPTER EIGHT

How to Know When You Are Ready to Love Again

You wake up one morning, make your coffee, and sit down to read the paper. You feel satisfied and happy, just by yourself, as you get ready to begin your day. Business has been going well and perhaps you're up for a promotion. A long workweek is ahead of you, but it doesn't matter because you have a special ski weekend to look forward to. There's a promise dancing on the horizon, the promise of new friendships and maybe even a little romance.

Suddenly you realize that the pain is gone. Your first thoughts no longer focus on what your ex is doing; in fact, you really couldn't care one way or the other because you are too busy rebuilding your life. The bad memories of the breakup are fading away. You may still suffer from an occasional loveshock flashback, which quickly passes. But there is no doubt: your life is no longer centered on your love loss, and your energy is no longer focused on recovering from it. You have traveled beyond your personal pain and have overcome many of the problems that were a part of it. Maybe, for you, it was obsessional thinking, rebounding, and numerous fears that once overwhelmed your daily existence. Now you are very self-aware and self-protective, determined not to repeat any of your previous mistakes.

In the stage of rebuilding, you now feel as if your life is finally yours—that you are able to manage it and that you have your emotions back under control. And perhaps to your surprise, you find yourself wanting love to be a part of your life again.

Rather than avoiding socializing or just throwing yourself into your work, you're putting yourself in situations where you may have the opportunity to meet someone new. Or maybe you're encouraging your friends to set up blind dates or dinner partners for you. Ironically, the very same people whom you resented five or six months ago for trying to fix you up you now encourage.

However, as much as you desire to get on with your life, you may feel a certain apprehension about dating again. This is perfectly normal when you are coming out of loveshock, it is to be expected if you have ended a long- term relationship: your last date may have been twenty years ago. That's why most of my loveshock patients have found that easing back into life as a single is best done through transitional relationships.

MAKING TRANSITIONAL RELATIONSHIPS WORK FOR YOU

Whether it is sharing a movie, dinner out, a lot of telephone talk, or even a safe sexual encounter, don't underestimate the value of short-term relationships, or what I call *transitional relationships*. They can be especially valuable in helping you reconnect with your intimate feelings in a relaxed and nonthreatening environment without demands or pressures. Think of transitional relationships as a way to test the water, as a way to help you better understand your personal needs. And after all the emotional pain you have suffered during loveshock, transitional relationships can even make you feel lovable and desirable again as they fuel your self-esteem.

It's not unusual for a transitional relationship to go beyond a couple of dates and turn into a wonderful friendship, in which you can share some of life's burdens and some of life's joys. This was true for Bill and Joyce. I had counseled Bill during the darkest days of his loveshock and encouraged him to try transitional relationships when he felt that he was ready.

When Bill asked Joyce out, he knew that she was not the next woman he would marry. But she was nice. And she made him laugh and made him feel good about himself. Having been through so much emotional pain, he found it to be a tremendous relief to go out with a woman and just have a good time. They would hug and exchange quick kisses on the cheek—but that was it, and that was fine for both of them.

Eventually Joyce also started dating Sidney and they became romantically involved. But she and Bill still remained close friends and continued to look out for one another's well-being. When Bill got pneumonia, Joyce was there with the chicken soup before she spent the evening with Sidney. And when her car broke down, Bill gave Joyce rides to and from work until it was repaired.

When Joyce and Sidney married, Bill was thrilled for

his good friend—but sad because they would be moving to another state. "No matter where Joyce is, I'll always love her as my friend and be eternally grateful to her for making me feel like a part of the human race again. What started out as a transitional relationship was responsible for restoring a lot of my self-confidence—besides turning into a wonderful friendship."

In a transitional relationship you have nothing to lose and everything to gain because there are no promises, obligations, or strings attached. You only have to give what you want to give and you can take as much as you want of what the other person is offering. This may be the first chance you have had in years to be totally honest in a relationship.

However, keep in mind that in a transitional relationship you are still vulnerable to rejection, even though this is not a serious relationship. You may date someone a few times and wish to continue, while the other person may not want to go out with you again. There is no reason to take this rejection seriously or to allow it to lower your self-esteem. Or you may experience a partial rejection, as you desire more from the transitional relationship than the other person is prepared to give.

When Steve and Diane began dating, both were coming out of loveshock experiences and focusing on rebuilding their lives. Steve hated eating alone, so he and Diane became frequent dining partners. One night, after a lot of wine, Diane began to snuggle up to Steve, suggesting that they spend the rest of their evening together in bed. Steve hated sexual pressure, partially because his relationship with his ex-wife had been so performance-oriented.

"Suddenly, as I was about to say yes, I realized that

I didn't have to have sex with Diane if I didn't want to. This was something that I just wasn't ready for. What a relief to know that I could say no, that I didn't have to pretend, because my relationship with Diane was transitional. At that moment my attitude was that if my saying no meant that I would never see her again, so be it. Realizing this gave me the most wonderful sense of freedom and ease! Fortunately, Diane didn't push it and we continued seeing one another. Two months later I found myself ready for sex, and Diane and I began the sexual dimension of our relationship. But we always had the understanding that there were no strings attached. Right now we're close, but we also date other people. It's the only way because neither one of us is ready to take the next step."

Often, if all you have known is a long-term relationship, you may see a relationship as an all-or-nothing proposition. In other words, if it is not going to lead to marriage, then what is the point? Why waste the time? If this is your point of view, you are losing sight of the fact that all relationships provide you with the opportunity to enhance social skills, and maybe even love skills, that may have diminished during the course of your past relationship.

You should consider transitional relationships to be opportunities to learn about yourself as well as about the different types of people that exist. Think of them as your chance to grow emotionally as you meet new people, to get in touch with your specific needs, and to learn what is involved in a relationship before you commit yourself to one again.

INTIMATE AGAIN

After loveshock, being intimate again is never easy. For men, regardless of their age, there is often a period of impotency during and after their loveshock. And almost every woman I've counseled has reported going through a period of fleeing from any sexuality. As Emily, twenty-eight and very attractive told me, "It took me two months of dating before I'd let a guy kiss me good night. I even found a handshake awkward!"

Both lack of sexual ability and lack of interest are normal parts of the aftershock of loveshock. Often I'll hear from my patients, "Now on top of everything else I've been through, I've got to deal with this?"

As thirty-one-year-old Walt so vividly told me, "Here I was with this beautiful woman in my arms, and God, you know I was really scared because I couldn't get it up. But the scariest part of all was that I didn't have any desire to! I was totally deflated in all areas! It destroyed what little self-confidence I had, because all I could think of was what this woman must think of me. It was so embarrassing for both of us!"

To be intimate again is to expose yourself completely. It's not just taking off your clothes, but stripping yourself to the vulnerability that comes with sexuality. This is why it is so important that you don't push yourself to be intimate until you are really sure that you are ready. Steve had the right idea when he said no to Diane: otherwise he could have ended up in the same predicament that Walt did. And since sexuality had been an issue in his marriage, it would only have added to his anxiety.

Usually I advise my patients just to take it slow and let time in cooperation with the natural flow of their hormones be their therapist. However, if you find that you are obsessing on your lack of interest or sexual inability, seek professional help. Focusing too much on the problem, worrying that you'll never want to or be able to have sex again, could just make it worse.

Being intimate with someone new is usually more difficult for older people who are coming out of a twenty- or thirty-year marriage. For them even the idea of a simple date may be terrifying because it is so unfamiliar. They may also experience what I call a conflict of generations: confusion about how to act on a date because dating values and guidelines have changed so drastically over the years.

If this is your situation, you may feel frightened or even panicked the first time a person calls to ask you out. This is a normal reaction, and if you have any interest at all, try to say yes. You have to begin somewhere. The first few dates you have may be awkward because you are simply out of practice, so if they don't go well and you're uncomfortable, don't be hard on yourself. Accept these feelings as another part of your growth process—and don't give up!

Beatrice married Arthur when she was eighteen, had four children with him, and woke up one day at the age of fifty-four to an empty bed and a note. In the note he told her that his leaving had nothing to do with her— that he was confused about the meaning of his life, felt lost in the corporate world, and knew that it was time that he searched for the truth, whatever it was. At first Beatrice thought, "He'll get this out of his system and he'll be back."

A month later she was served with divorce papers and offered a more-than-fair settlement that amazed even her lawyer. Beatrice was in grief and a state of confusion for months as she tried to understand what had actually happened. It took her two years before she could even think about the possibility of dating because she always thought that Arthur would come back.

The first date she had ended after an hour and a half. She got nauseated and had to go home. "Not only was I afraid, Dr. Gullo, sitting next to someone I barely knew in a dark movie theater, but I felt as if I were betraying Arthur. I felt so guilty, being out with another man. And I feel so inadequate."

"In what way?"

"With my appearance. I mean, what if I did meet someone, and we really liked one another, and it led to sex? The only man who has seen me without clothes, besides Arthur, is my doctor."

Beatrice was voicing the fear and concern of many older people, most frequently women, whose bodies are no longer one of their primary assets. And any guilt or betrayal they feel is natural because they were in their previous relationship for such a long time. For many, the only person that they have ever had sex with is their ex. Unfortunately, the guilt feelings only fuel their negative self-image, making it all the more difficult for them to take those intitial steps as a single person.

I advised Beatrice to take it slow and to do what she could to make herself feel better about her appearance. Four months later, Beatrice had joined an exercise class to tone her body and had purchased a more chic, contemporary wardrobe. When we last talked, she was dating two different men regularly—but keeping them at arm's length.

Joan has just turned fifty and has been divorced for three years. She is quite wealthy and travels in a glittering social circle. Her hallmark is her extensive art collection: it became her compelling diverter during her loveshock. Two months ago she met a younger man, ten years to be exact, who keeps inviting her away for weekends. He's a very successful graphics designer and is crazy about her. They go to the ballet and the opera together. He escorts her to social events. In many ways they're perfect for one another—but she keeps making up excuses about why she can't go away with him for the weekend, because if she does go, she knows that they will probably end up in bed together. And she is convinced that once he sees her without clothes, she'll never see him again.

I've suggested to her that she go on a diet, hire a personal trainer (someone who will come to her home regularly and help her exercise), and even look into plastic surgery. If it's that important to her, and the only thing that's keeping her from realizing what could become her next love relationship, she should take action. Money is not an issue for her. In fact, she's lucky because she is one of the privileged who can afford to totally redesign herself, if she wants to.

But she resists. And things remain the same, as she and Vince play their cat-and-mouse game of "Will you go away with me?" She reasons that, as uncomfortable as the issue of intimacy makes her feel because of her body, she is content just the way she is. Joan is not psychologically ready for physical intimacy.

Whether it's from lack of sexual desire, the inability to perform, or being uncomfortable with their nudity, for men like Walt and Steve, and women like Emily, Beatrice, and Joan, intimacy brings with it a lot of psychological confusion. Sometimes the confusion is one of the last lingering reactions to your loveshock: you are afraid that any intimacy will ultimately lead to your getting hurt again. And for many, it is a terrible shock to go from having a complete sexual relationship with just one person all of your adult life to suddenly having to decide something as basic as "Do I kiss her (or him) or "Do I allow him (or her) to kiss me—and if I do, where will it lead?"

If you are having a difficult time reintegrating intimacy into your life, I recommend practicing what I call *phased intimacy.* That means making physical contact with another person *very slowly,* step by step. Until you feel comfortable with the step you've taken, you go no further. For instance, you may begin simply by holding hands. Not until you feel completely at ease with this would you progress to hugging and then kissing. And then you would ease into long embraces.

I think of phased intimacy as a kind of necessary sexual rehabilitation after a very painful emotional breakup. I compare it to the physical rehabilitation that is often necessary after you break an arm or leg. The limb must be strengthened before it can completely function again. The same is true in intimacy. You must be emotionally strong and comfortable with your sexuality before you can completely function again.

You should communicate to the other person exactly how you feel and how important it is that he or she lets you go slowly. Don't allow yourself to be talked into something that you are not ready for. If the time isn't right, don't be afraid to say no. Again, this is where transitional relationships are invaluable. If another person places demands on you that you feel you are not ready to fulfill, there is no reason that you have to continue the relationship. As one patient told me, "After having survived loveshock with my sanity intact, the last thing I'm going to tolerate is someone coming on to me, still persisting after I say no, before I'm ready."

While you may feel that you are ready to love again, seeking out new people and new relationships, allow yourself the time you need before you become intimate. Don't feel that you have to rush it. When you are really ready to physically reach out and touch, you will experience, in your comfort and ease, the beauty of truly connecting with another person once again.

CHAPTER NINE

Loving Again

Traveling through loveshock is a journey that you are unlikely ever to forget, nor should you, because what you have learned can prove invaluable in helping you to create your present and future happiness. While it may not be completely obvious yet, you have grown from the pain of your loveshock and are wiser for it. Loveshock forced you to confront yourself and different aspects of your life, as your personal flaws, your pitfalls, and your anxieties appeared. For many of you this was the first time in your life that you evaluated and dealt with your emotions so openly and honestly. Ultimately, your personal truth emerged as you became acutely aware of your needs. And as your fears and frustrations unfolded, you developed greater self-awareness.

After all that you have been through, having reached the final stage of resolution, you now know what gives you joy in a relationship, what situations you can tolerate and can compromise on, and what you find unbearable. Values and ideals that may have been dormant for many years have reemerged and become an important part of your life, along with any additional beliefs that have developed. And with all that you have learned and gained from your personal pain, not only are you able to love again, but you stand a better chance of developing a more satisfying love relationship because you have been through so much and you know yourself so well. You also realize that simply to love is not enough to sustain a love relationship.

PUTTING THE PAST INTO PERSPECTIVE

Before you can love again, completely and unimpaired, you must put your past pain into proper perspective. This means releasing any destructive feelings of anger or bitterness that can still linger even in the final stage of resolution. You may experience an occasional zigzag back to setting blame, set off by a love-shock flashback, that stirs up old feelings. Or perhaps you feel angry and bitter toward love in general, because you've been hurt. And you may even find yourself turning your anger inward, against yourself, which many psychotherapists believe to be the basis for depression.

While you may have a right to your anger, don't let it become the focus of your life—for your own sake, and for the sake of those around you. Life is too short for you to spend your time and thoughts consumed with rage. In the end it is just another form, and a destructive one at that, of hanging on to the past. Work on releasing yourself from the negative aspects of this rage. If you don't, you are likely to displace it onto others, especially your family, children, and friends—or even a new lover. Ultimately, all your relationships will begin to suffer, for you will be repelling love. Remember that no one is more unlovable or unattractive, regardless of physical appearance, than an angry, bitter person.

Philosopher Albert Schweitzer observed that "the tragedy of life is what dies inside a man while he lives." Don't let your loveshock experience make you afraid or unable to love again. For if you permit the failed relationship and your loveshock experience to make you afraid to love again, you will have lost more than the person and the relationship; you will have lost one of the most central of all human qualities—the ability to love, which is the essence of our humanity.

To continue to live happily in the face of the unhappiness you have endured in your life requires that you develop the capacity to distance yourself from the emotional pain of the past. This is an important part of your psychological growth. As I have frequently observed—and as you will have realized while traveling through loveshock—time and your psyche should move you away from this pain. However, it may take extra effort on your part to release its final vestiges. Remember that one of the joys of being in resolution is that it is your opportunity to make a fresh start, without the burdens of the past but with the added advantage of having grown from your personal pain.

If you find that you still obsess on anger or bitterness, employ the thought-blocking technique whenever these negative feelings surface. Again, this means telling yourself, "STOP!" and moving yourself away from these negative feelings as you engross yourself in one of your compelling diverters. Also, remind yourself of how much emotionally you have overcome and continue to focus on the new life cycle you are beginning in resolution.

Remember Beatrice, who woke up one morning to

an empty bed and a note from Arthur? One of the reasons it took her two years to even think about dating was that she had so much bitterness within her. But she realized that her bitterness would not change her situation. So every time it popped up while she was at home, she would go out and weed her garden. "With every weed that I pull comes a *'STOP!'* I don't stop weeding until my anger is gone; sometimes I end up weeding a whole flower bed! Sometimes I'll pick a beautiful bouquet afterwards and take it over to the hospital where I do volunteer work. It redirects my energy from the anger I feel to caring about the needs of others."

While you are releasing the last of these negative feelings, guard against discussing your past relationship in a derogatory way. It's unwise to bring into a potential new relationship bitter comments or remarks because you may be misunderstood. Only you know what you've suffered as you have gone through *your* loveshock, and discussing your past in this way only clouds what could and should be a clean slate. When questions do come up about your previous relationship, try to speak about it objectively and mention some of the good things that came out of it. However, if you presently feel incapable of doing this or uncomfortable in discussing it at all, say so and change the subject. This protects your privacy and keeps you from saying something that you may later regret. It also prevents you from dwelling on the pain of the past as you continue to move forward.

A positive way to utilize your anger is to analyze it and let it teach you something about your own emotional needs. For example, if your anger stems from betrayal, then know that loyalty is important for your happiness in your next relationship. Look for a person who embodies this quality, as well as the other essentials you value, to be your partner in developing and sustaining a meaningful relationship.

ATTRACTING THE BEST RELATIONSHIP FOR YOU

A leading divorce attorney once advised one of my loveshock patients that while he couldn't tell her what would guarantee her happiness in future relationships, he could tell her what would make for unhappiness in a relationship: marrying outside of her philosophy of life. His concept is brilliant because it applies to everyone and has proven true time and again. I call it *the shared philosophy of life*. I have used this concept when counseling my loveshock patients who desire to attract stable, lasting relationships into their lives.

As an example, if your idea of a satisfying relationship includes quiet evenings at home while your potential partner likes parties and traveling, you do not have a shared philosophy of life. While the two of you may be extremely attracted to one another initially and even marry, chances are that after that initial bloom of romance fades, your different life philosophies will begin to conflict. Unless a lot of concessions and compromises are made and your love is strong enough to overcome the differences, the relationship does not have a very good chance of lasting.

One of the positive aspects of the loveshock experience is that you do emerge from it with a much keener awareness of your philosophy of life. So consider your philosophy when you look at the direction a potential relationship may take; ask yourself, "If I love this person, can this person love me, in return, *in the way that*

I need to be loved?" I think that answering yes to this question is vital before seriously entering into a new relationship.

Having a shared philosophy of life doesn't mean you can't have different likes and dislikes. In fact one of the realizations that occur during loveshock is that it's important to maintain your individuality in a relationship. Many of you travelers through loveshock have only recently regained it. The essence of a shared philosophy of life is not that you're identical in outlook but that your relationship fundamentals and goals are basically the same; a shared philosophy means that most of your needs will be fulfilled just as you will be able to fulfill most of the needs of your partner. While there is no perfect relationship, a happy and satisfying one is certainly possible when your lifestyles harmoniously merge.

Most people, having gone through loveshock, prefer to avoid relationships that portend conflict—even if it means giving up some excitement as well. You may find yourself ending a relationship before it becomes serious, as you become aware of too many lifestyle differences. As Walt told me, when he began having transitional relationships, "I meet plenty of women that I could spend the night with—but never a lifetime. That takes someone special who not only understands my needs and shares my interests, but is also willing to meet me at least half way when she doesn't."

I make the general assumption that most people marry because they are in love; most marriages end, I believe, because the couple lack a shared philosophy of life and cannot meet each other's needs. While finding a partner with a shared philosophy of life does not guarantee happiness, it is certainly a positive start for a new relationship.

YOU CAN'T MARRY THE PROMISE

While many of my loveshock patients have learned this lesson from the direction their past relationship took, I still like to remind them that "they can't marry the promise." Or to be more blunt, when you involve yourself in a new relationship, remember that what you see is what you get.

Ideally we all continue to develop, improve, and grow in our relationships as well as in our professional lives. However, when you decide to commit to another relationship, realize that while the other person may have the best of intentions, *what he or she is at this very moment is the only guarantee you have*. Don't commit to a relationship because you are enticed by what he or she promises it will be. Or with the hope that you can change this person into what you think he or she should be. Approaching a new commitment this way is unfair to the other person and will only cause you tremendous frustration as he or she resists and perhaps even rebels against your attempts to play Pygmalion.

Before you make a commitment, wipe the stars out of your eyes and ask yourself these questions: "If he (or she) never becomes anything greater than what he (or she) is at the moment, is it acceptable? Can I love this person exactly as he (or she) is, including any bad habits—which may never change?" If you are unable to answer these questions with a strong yes, take time to evaluate the relationship before you proceed. This is your chance to make a clean break, with a minimal amount of pain to yourself or the other person. And realize that if there is pain now, in the initial phase of your relationship, you may experience much more pain in the future if you delay ending it. Sometimes deciding not to take action is, psychologically, the most costly decision of all.

When Matt met Vicki, he knew that she drank too much. But he idealized the relationship and really believed that he could change her. He thought that their love would cure all. Ultimately he ended up being the unwilling rejector, going in and out of the relationship until he realized that—because he was powerless over Vicki's alcoholism and could not live with her behavior—he had to end the relationship. He suffered terribly in putting an end to a relationship that should never have progressed to marriage.

WORKING TOWARD LOVE SYNERGY, OR HEALTHY LOVE

Many psychologists describe three basic types of love relationship that we can involve ourselves in: parasitic, symbiotic, and synergistic.

In a parasitic relationship, one person takes far more than he or she gives to the relationship. He or she feeds off the other person financially, emotionally, or both. Often this relationship ends when the parasite has taken all that he or she needs. A parasitic relationship can also end because the person who has done all the giving has nothing left—he or she is all used up—except what it takes to leave the relationship.

This is why Janis left Brent. She had done all the giving, while he had done all the taking. And when Janis finally left, she left out of fear—fear that somehow Brent would ultimately consume all of her.

However, Janis's role as the parasite's host, or giver, cannot be disregarded. Janis had never had a serious love relationship and was anxious to meet someone to share her life with. She had grown tired of the singles lifestyle and, as she approached her late twenties, became concerned that she was losing her physical appeal. When Brent appeared, although she resisted at first, she eventually succumbed to his charm because she was eager to have a permanent relationship. And once she was hooked she began her pattern of excessive giving because she was afraid that he would look elsewhere if she didn't; all of her girlfriends envied her, wishing that they could find a man like him.

Often a person is so desperate to be loved that he or she will give anything, including everything that he or she has, to hold on to the other person. Neither partner in this relationship is loving in a healthy, balanced way. Both are acting out of desperation and both need counseling or professional help to change the all-consuming dynamics of their relationship.

When a relationship is symbiotic, both partners feed one another. Alone they feel incomplete, as neither one of them is secure enough in his or her own identity. And even if they are miserable when they are together, as is frequently true, they are still happier together than they are apart. Sometimes this relationship is filled with mistrust and paranoia—one person becoming obsessed with what the other is doing when they are apart, even when the separation is necessary because of life's daily responsibilities.

Often the mutually possessive nature of this relationship allows for little growth within it. For many people this type of relationship works because they have limited expectations, not only of themselves but of love relationships in general. They are satisifed with what they have. Essentially, the dynamic of this relationship is "I love you because I need you," not, "I need you because I love you." Symbiotic relationships are very common and often endure until death—unless one of the partners feels the need to establish a stronger sense of self.

Joan, who is in resolution and still working toward intimacy with Vince, the young graphics designer, left her husband because their symbiotic relationship was starting to smother her. "We were both so insecure, constantly phoning one another and checking up on each other. But when we were together, we fought and disagreed over the stupidest things. One day I just realized that while I was terrified to be on my own, I had to leave the marriage and find out who I really was. In this marriage I had lost all sense of myself as an individual—and so had he."

In a synergistic relationship, both people become greater through their relationship than either one is capable of becoming alone. Separately both are reasonably strong, secure individuals who are content within themselves, but together their love creates a powerful, nurturing bond—providing each with more happiness than either one ever knew existed. While they have both mastered the skill of making themselves happy on their own, they realize that sharing their life with the right person can make them happier. This is a relationship based on a shared philosophy of life, mutual trust, and reciprocal giving and taking.

Remember Jennifer, who collapsed on the library floor of her Malibu mansion and then went into seclusion when she realized that she had to end her marriage to Rick? After all the pain that she endured, she emerged from her loveshock a stronger and more secure individual. When she met Tony she was finally content with herself and the new life she had created. He too is a secure individual with lots of interests and a very busy life. Since they have married, neither one of them has lost sight of their individuality. And when they're together, they enhance one another's happiness. Together they create love synergy.

Love synergy is a realistic ideal worth striving for. It is the type of relationship that I hope you will seek. You are certainly capable of attaining it because of the strength, competence, and self-awareness you have gained from your loveshock experience, and which you continue to develop as you travel through loveshock.

But even within the framework of a synergistic love relationship, you must maintain reasonable expectations: even the best relationships involve compromise and trade-offs. What's critical in creating a new relationship, working toward love synergy, is that neither of you compromise what's essential for your personal happiness and emotional well-being.

MAKING LOVE WORK

Often I am asked by loveshock patients who are in resolution and eager to love again, "How can I love again without experiencing loveshock again?" Unfortunately, there are no guarantees. And whenever you choose to love again, you are once again vulnerable to loveshock. This is not pessimism—just reality.

While the topic of making love work is vast and multidimensional, constantly being researched and explored by an increasing number of research scientists and psychologists, one of the best guidelines I have to offer is to approach love realistically. This means removing the *may be* and *could be* from love and dealing with the *what is.* Again, this means realizing that you can't marry the promise.

I'm the first to agree that the different love myths and romantic fantasies are wonderful ideals that can continue to ignite and fan the flames of passion that feed a relationship, but they have very little to do with the actual endurance of relationships. In fact, they may even hurt relationships by creating unrealistic expectations that few partners can live up to.

The reality of love is that it takes personal sacrifices from both partners if it is to be sustained. You must think, act, and react for two people rather than one to create harmony; you must consider your partner's feelings as well as your own. Your wants and needs only count for half of the whole, which is now composed of the two of you. There are endless compromises that must be made. And the moment either of you begins to take love for granted, it begins to end.

Many of you are already aware of the role neglect plays in the demise of a love relationship. Like so many of my loveshock patients, once your relationship was established you may not have continued to nurture it. Your energy was diverted elsewhere—perhaps into raising children or furthering your career. While these are also important, time-consuming parts of life, you cannot deny the demands of a love relationship. And because it usually creates the foundation for the other parts of your life, when it crumbles the rest of your life may begin to fall apart as well.

One of the toughest love lessons most of us have to learn is that lasting relationships don't just fall on us and then flourish on their own. They are created by mutual commitment and they only continue by mutual commitment—and often through very trying times. Without a doubt, the happiest and most enduring relationships are those that receive constant attention and true nurturing. Perhaps this is why the marriage vows, which celebrate and unite the love between two people, also remind us, "for better and for worse; in sickness and in health."

ROMANTIC LOVE AND OTHER TYPES OF LOVE

Resolution brings with it, besides a new life cycle, a serenity that will continue to develop as you grow emotionally stronger every day. Regardless of the direction your new life takes, you now realize that you are strong enough to live and live well on your own. You may wish that you didn't have to, but knowing that you can gives you a greater feeling of personal competence. After all, you have survived loveshock! You can take care of yourself and you are complete within yourself. While you may desire another relationship, it does not require another person to make you happy.

While many of my loveshock patients anticipate reinvesting their emotional energy in another romantic relationship, there are some who choose not to or can't. Elderly people who are widowed are not as likely to actively seek, or have the opportunity for, a romantic relationship. They usually seek companionship through community projects, family members, friends, or pets. Severe health problems also prevent some people from entering into new relationships, at least while they are focusing all of their energy on their recovery.

I've also had loveshock patients discover during the course of their loveshock that their work must and will always come first. Having reached this conclusion, they are convinced that there is no room in their life for a serious love relationship because they will never be able to put the relationship first. When I tell them that this does not have to be true, they are pleasantly shocked!

While it may not sound or seem very romantic, your love relationship does not have to be your first priority to be satisfying and enduring. Your career can come first as long as you and your partner are in agreement and emotionally comfortable with this arrangement.

I've seen many happy love relationships in which the career comes first for both partners or just for one. These relationships work because the balance of career and love was agreed upon at the outset; needs and expectations were clearly expressed as the relationship was established. Mutual agreement and continuing emotional comfort with this decision are crucial.

Since time shared is often minimal, that often-used expression, "It's the quality, not the quantity that counts," applies in this type of relationship. Because your primary energy is focused on your career, you may really have to stretch yourself to be loving and romantic after a long workday. However, I know several career-oriented couples who are convinced that because their time together is so limited, it is all the more exciting when it finally comes.

Whether you choose to invest your love in another person, in your work, in your children, or in a cause—what's important is that you now have the capacity to make this choice freely, unimpaired. Not out of anger, panic, fear, desperation, despair, revenge, or insecurity. To develop this capacity, to choose in strength the direction your life will take, is the essence of overcoming loveshock.

There is an expression in the Italian language that is translated as, "It's never darker than midnight, and after midnight comes a new day." You may know it as, "It's always darkest before the dawn." A part of growth and maturation is developing the courage to ride out the "midnights" of our lives without becoming self-destructive, without giving into bitterness and self-pity, without losing hope in ourselves, but continuing to believe in the promise of our own lives. Remember Albert Schweitzer's observation quoted earlier: "The tragedy of life is what dies inside a man while he lives!" There are certain qualities within us that belong to us alone . . . they are part of our inalienable rights. No one, no event, no lover must ever take them from us.

No matter how terrible you feel at this moment, no matter what stage of loveshock you are in, do not feel sorry for yourself. You must persevere with your courage and ride it out. Don't lose faith in yourself, your ability to overcome loveshock, and the promise of your future. You can be as happy as you make up your mind to be or as miserable as you let yourself become. If you are having problems moving forward and you cannot resolve these difficulties within yourself or with the support of family and friends, recognize you *can* do it, but you cannot do it alone. Seek the professional guidance and support you need.

And now the good news . . . almost all the people whose lives we shared through the pages of this book are happy again today! Indeed, many are much happier now than they could have ever been in the previous relationship. If that relationship had not ended, they would never have found the opportunity for the new happiness they enjoy. Almost all feel they would never want to go back to their former partner. They have grown too much through their loveshock experience. In a very real sense the pain of loveshock has become a positive force in their lives—it made them leave behind an unrewarding relation and move forward into a happier relationship or new commitments to family, careers or self-growth.

Although it took her many years, Queen Victoria had the courage to travel through her loveshock: she chose to return to Buckingham Palace after her self-imposed exile. At last, unimpaired, she was finally able to confront the palace walls that had once housed the love that she and Albert shared. Once again she presided over Parliament, not just ruling effectively, but leading the British Empire to its zenith.

Conclusion

It's been almost a year and a half since Genevieve's hysterical loveshock collapse in the Polo Lounge. She recently sent me a postcard from the Italian countryside that read, "Divorce settlement with Ryan in my favor. Baby Claude is happy and adores Franco. We met three months ago and are made for one another. I think I've finally found true love . . ." According to my calculations, it took her a little over a year to reach resolution, which for her means Franco. This seems pretty fast, but she has always been a fast traveler. Of course she was married to Ryan for only two years, so getting through resignation was probably not too traumatic.

Right now I have three close friends and several acquaintances who are in some stage of loveshock. Pamela was an unwilling rejector when she made her alcoholic husband leave their Vermont farm. But she's opened a gift shop filled with crystals and New Age books and finds that it's the perfect compelling diverter as she moves herself through her loveshock.

My friend Ross has just marked the one-year anniversary of his loveshock, which began when Alicia rejected him after ten years of marriage, and is still struggling through the final stages. He's definitely in rebuilding but suffers from loveshock flashbacks (he still can't eat Chinese food, which Alicia loved), and occasionally he zigzags and picks up the phone to reconnect with her. Actually, I think his biggest problem with loveshock has been integrating the ten-year history they once shared into his new life. I spent a lot of time with him while he was going through resignation and the only things he kept were the photo albums. For such a high-powered advertising executive, his traveling time through love-shock has been slower than I would have expected.

Then there's Jamie, whose girlfriend moved out three months ago. He actually met her when they were in the second grade, and they finally started living together four years ago. He's the first to admit that he's been obsessed with her since the first day they met. Refusing to accept that he has been rejected, Jamie is still locked in his grief and is up to his ears in obsessional thinking and moth-to-flaming. He's turning into an old man before my eyes—and he's only thirty-five! Fortunately, he's started therapy.

And there's Anne—poor Anne—who is about to go into loveshock but doesn't know it yet. I went to college with Anne and all she ever talked about was having a husband, babies, and a home. She ended up marrying Mark, who is ten years older and was one of our professors. He recently called me, confessing that he was having a mid-life crisis and was feeling smothered by everything, including Anne, their four children, and even the dog. Since Anne is one of my best friends, he wanted to know if I had any suggestions—specifically, "How do I break the news to her gently?" All I could answer was, "She'll be devastated." I can't even begin to imagine how long her loveshock will last.

As for me, as Thanksgiving approaches, it's been almost one year since my loveshock hit. Last Thanksgiving my husband and I barely spoke. Our misunderstandings, lack of communication, and personal problems had placed what seemed to be an indestructible wall between us. The only chinks were our two little girls.

We are both in the rebuilding stage of loveshock. *Together*. Given our history, I'm surprised too. But as Dr. Gullo explained in Chapter Three, it is possible to reunite with your partner during rebuilding if there have been drastic changes in behavior and both of you are willing to work at the relationship. Well, we've both made changes and we are working hard to repair the damage to our marital foundation. But the ground rules have been changed. We've become more tolerant of each other's personal needs and we have created an entirely different relationship from what we had. It is a relationship that many people don't understand, but for now it works for us.

Although we are rebuilding together, I still have loveshock flashbacks. Every time I drive by the hospital, I cringe and sometimes take a wrong turn, as I am reminded of the night my marriage finally fell apart. That night my husband, hurt and angry, went out and kicked a wall. He shattered his heel and ankle into too many pieces to count. As I watched him suffer in the emergency room, with my baby in my arms and my young daughter beside me, it made me sick to think that what had started out as love could end like this. Both of us were responsible for this unhappy ending.

While my story is unique. I know now that I'm not alone. Loveshock victims fill the world, as they have throughout history, and each has his or her tragic tale to tell. Without a doubt, going through loveshock is one of life's most traumatic experiences.

But I'm not afraid to love again. Love, no matter how brief, is a miracle to me. There are no guarantees that the cracks have been permanently sealed in my marriage and that my husband and I will spend the rest of our lives together. And even if we do, one of us will have to go through loveshock again because of death. But if or when it happens to me again, I will manage it and move through it better because now I understand it. Now I know that unless it takes a pathological twist, loveshock too has an end. Loveshock is not a mental illness; it is an inevitable process for anyone who suffers a love loss.

As difficult as it has been, my loveshock experience has made me a stronger person. Dr. Gullo's loveshock therapy gave me the courage to manage my pain, as I realized that I had the capacity to cope with the heartache and fear that comes with a profound love loss. While I had to push myself forward and at times had nothing to go on but my self-belief, the result has been an inner awareness of myself and a lot of personal growth that I'm grateful for.

There is no question that Dr. Gullo's loveshock theory and therapy are an invaluable contribution to the mental health field. He has named our pain and seen clearly how to mend a heart that has been broken by a love loss. He has given us loveshock victims hope and shown us that there is a light that shines at the end of that long, dark tunnel. Regardless of your pain, those loveshock days and nights won't last forever, and someday you will be able to love again.

Acknowledgments

Loveshock is not only an evolution of my professional work in the field of loss; it is deeply influenced by my own philosophy of life and loving. In this way it is a product of both my professional and personal life. There are many who have contributed enormously to these aspects of my growth. And so, in a very real way, they have contributed directly to *Loveshock*.

First and foremost, I would like to thank my agent, Al Lowman. This book would never have become a reality without his vision, guidance and deep belief in the value of loveshock therapy.

On a personal note, I owe much to my family: especially my father and my mother, Rose Pernice Gullo, who first taught me the meaning of unconditional love; my sisters, Angela, Marianne and Antoinette, whose sacrifices and commitment nurture me daily and were especially helpful during the many and often laborious years of my professional training; my nephews Christian Hanny and Matthew Touron and my niece Maureen Levine, who enrich my life and give me and my family the opportunity to pass the joys and the responsibilities of loving on to the next generation; my brothers-in-law, who have been so supportive of our family ties and who contribute so much to our family life, especially Joseph Barna and Bob Pahlck and Al Froehlich. Those who have a loving family are blessed.

I owe a special debt of gratitude to the physicians who

helped restore me to the fullness of life after a major illness: Dr. John Conley, one of the giants of American surgery, Dr. Robert De Bellis, Dr. Irwin Dannis, Dr. Irwin Lubowe, Dr. William Shaw and his devoted nurse Irena Ciccone.

Perhaps one of the most enriching aspects of my personal life has been the support and guidance of my dear friends. I owe a great deal to each of you: my life-long friends David and Marilyn Kahn, Richard Berger and Scott Yacker. Also: Ronni Janoff, Mark Lazar, Hal Parkerson, John Contini, Jason Capuano, David Sholtis, Dr. Daniel Cherico, Tony Danaro, Debbie Melendez, and Wilfredo Rivera, Al Galleau, Kurt Barnard, Mike Nelligan, Barry Schneider, Brian Snyder, Lee Ciardiello, Mike and Eric Francis, Howard Sussman, Millie Kenig, David Demattia, and of course my friend Peter Swersey for reminding me of the resilience of the human spirit and what honorable people can accomplish through commitment to growth.

Several other friends have enriched my life, not only through the joys of friendship, but through what they have contributed to my professional growth. As classmates at Columbia, and later as colleagues, they have been a major influence in my life. Dr. Daniel Carr, a brilliant researcher and physician, has been one of my great teachers. It was he who sensitized me and has taught me so much about the biological basis of human behavior. Our discussions continue to enhance my work and our friendship enriches my personal and professional growth. Psychiatrist Dr. Henry Berger helped me to understand much about the role of the rejectee in *Loveshock* and encouraged my *Loveshock* research through his insights and unfailing friendship. Dr. Marc Shatz has provided me with an intellectual form within which to refine my ideas. All of their insights, and most of all, their humanity as caregivers, in the highest tradition, have enriched this book and my capacity to help others.

Thank you to my dear friends: Michael Francis, Burt Primoff, Michael Kalnick, and Fran Brody, who guided and assisted me with their counsel during the formative years of my career. Their advice and friendship has improved the quality of my professional work and my life. And no expression of gratitude would be complete without acknowledging Florence Lazar and Lee Love, who came to my rescue during the first days of my work.

I'd also like to thank several colleagues who assisted me in my early research in the field of loss and generously shared their insights, including: Dr. Ivan Goldberg, Dr. Robert De Bellis, and the late Dr. Bernard Schoenberg. Also, the late Dr. Boyd McCandless.

I am grateful for the honors bestowed on me and my work by his Royal Imperial Highness, Prince Robert Khimchiavelli von Badische, Sir John Tewder-Reese, Ambassador Sir Victor Tewder-Reese, and the Honorable Ruggero Orlando.

A special thanks to my colleagues, with whom I work on a daily basis: Rosemarie Passaro, my wonderful administrative assistant and bookkeeper; my long-time colleague, Dr. Jerome Feldman; Dr. Robert Lipman and Dr. John Gross, for all that they contribute both to my life and to my work; Dr. Richard Corriere and Dr. Ruth Westheimer, whose counsel has enriched my work and enhanced my ability to use my talents to help others.

Also, my appreciation for two individuals who built the house that I designed in Southhampton, which has been my refuge and my haven wherein I found the serenity to formulate my ideas on *Loveshock*: Alex Dzieman, master builder, and Tim Suttmeier, whose dedication and resourcefulness made my house a reality.

A special thanks to my personal assistants, Lonnie Quinn and Norbert Bogner, who keep me organized and help my life run smoothly.

And finally, thank you to Jim, Eleanor, and Marisa Walker, for understanding and enduring all the long hours my coauthor, Connie Church, spent away from home.

—STEPHEN GULLO

In writing *Loveshock,* many professionals, loved ones, and close friends played an important part in its creation. I would like to thank all of you for opening up your hearts and sharing your loveshock experiences with me.

I would also like to thank my two dear friends, Marisa Berenson and Zoe Artemis, for sharing their homes with me and providing me with the solitude I needed. Also, thank you both for your constant love and support— especially during those dark days when my creative muse vanished.

A special thanks to Gerald Jackson, for his unconditional friendship which adds so much to my life and has guided me out of more than one pitfall.

And, finally, a special thanks to my family, for loving me—even when you didn't approve—and for just being there.

—CONNIE CHURCH

We would both like to deeply thank all those who played a vital role in the creation of this book:

Our wonderful editor, Bob Bender, for his guidance and patience. With the help of his editorial expertise, this book stayed on course and made its deadline—just in the nick of time.

Also to Brian Moore, Betsy Lerner, and Behrman Communications for your assistance during all stages of this book.

Murry Rogow, for his help and contribution in the initial stages of creating this book.

And, Patricia Soliman and Joni Evans, who helped bring *Loveshock* and Simon and Schuster together. And, to our Canadian publisher, Jan Whitford, at Collins, Canada.

DR. STEPHEN GULLO is an assistant clinical professor in Behavioral Sciences at Columbia University. He is one of the pioneering researchers in the field of loss and grief and has coauthored three books on the subject. He is the former codirector of the Family Bereavement Project of Columbia University Medical Center and current president of the Institute for Health and Weight Sciences. He maintains a private practice in New York City and Beverly Hills, California.

CONNIE CHURCH is a writer who lives in Los Angeles. She met Dr. Gullo while undergoing her own loveshock.

Bantam
On Psychology